ISBN 978-0-578-51903-6

A.S.GUINN

A.S.GUINN

ETERNAL KNIGHTS OF EDEN

GUARDIANS

A.S.GUINN

PROLOGUE

ABOUT THE WORLD OF EDEN

[To begin the story, skip to Chapter 1 on page 20]

In an alternate universe where the laws of nature are different than those we have come to know is a world known today as Eden. Before it was named Eden, however, it was a nameless world full of life nourished by the spiritual energy given off by the planet's unique living core. The planet has a single known inhabited supercontinent, but due to the planet's small diameter of only 3,700 miles, the various nations of the world have long been intertwined. Five nations once populated the land, though each has its own unique races and cultures.

The nation of the east is known as Erita, the land of the elven empire. Erita is ruled by the Elmeri, a species easily identified by their ears, which protrude straight out from the sides of their heads and end in pointed tips. The Elmeri are the longest-lived of the races of Eden, with the eldest being many thousands of years old. They possess strong spiritual cores, and they are the most magically inclined of all the races. Almost every Elmeri, regardless of their chosen profession, spends their life constantly advancing their knowledge. The Elmeri are a proud and elegant people, and this is reflected in their culture, especially their grand architecture. The architecture of their great cities is considered the most beautiful in the world.

Over the millennia, many Elmeri have had romantic involvements with their human neighbors to the west. This has resulted in a subspecies of their race known as the Drameri. Elmeri culture has not been kind to these mixed elves, easily identified by their pointed ears that lie along the sides of their heads rather than point outward. Elmeri nobles discriminate heavily against these "impure" Drameri, and almost none hold any position of power or significance.

The westernmost country is the jungle nation of Pandora. The mysterious catlike Nekomata rule this land, and they tend to have few dealings with the outside world. What little is known about the Nekomata is that they are unmatched in agility and their rangers are among the deadliest to be found in Eden. While they tend to be shorter than the average human or Elmeri, they make up for this in strength and tenacity. Their appearance is a curiosity among scholars, who debate whether they evolved from cats or a humanoid race. Their bodies are covered in a thin layer of fur that appears in many patterns, leaving only their chest, belly, and nether regions exposed. They appear to be very similar to humans and elves in their bipedal stance, and even their faces are remarkably similar. The main differences are the pointed ears atop their heads, their catlike eyes, and their tails. Their culture is a near total mystery, as even those who choose to leave their jungle homes never speak of their homeland in detail.

Pandora is also home to a modest population of Drameri who fled the persecution of their homeland and formed their own community. These Drameri are known as Junmeri, and they live alongside the Nekomata, following their reclusive ways.

On the northern stretch of the continent lie the nearly impassable Dorim Mountains, where the curious Termer make their homes. The Termer, also known derogatorily as the dwarves, are a short, stocky people with next to no magic capability but unmatched prowess as smiths and inventors. The Termer are tribal by nature, but all the tribes operate under a loose central government known as the Termer collective. The Termers' talent as inventors led to the creation of technology known as magicore. The Termer could not wield magic themselves, so they invented artificially manufactured magic, and now magicore technology can be found in all corners of Eden. In addition to their technological prowess, Termer-made armor and weapons are considered some of the best in the land, and all races consider owning true Termer equipment to be a status symbol.

In the heart of the continent of Eden is the human nation of Alastair. The humans have had a tumultuous history, having been involved in more wars than all the other races combined. Violent by nature, they spent millennia warring among themselves and the other races, with Alastair being the site of many grand conflicts. The humans are more diverse than the other races, with many showing magical prowess, talent for physical combat, and innovation not unlike the Termer. These combined traits nearly destroyed the land of Alastair many times.

The humans changed with the arrival of the celestial entity Eden. He used his great power to unify the people of Alastair, and eventually the world, before making his home in the human capital of Corallina. Now the humans are one people, mostly standing together for the sake of their nation.

ETERNAL KNIGHTS OF EDEN I

To the south is the final nation of Temenos, home of the great Mitera people. Temenos is a vast land of varying climates and terrains, but the land is not what makes Temenos so remarkable. The Mitera people, while nearly identical to humans in appearance, are far superior to their short-lived brethren. While humans may live for 150 years at best, the Mitera have a nearly infinite lifespan, like the elves. It is not uncommon for a Mitera to reach the age of three thousand years or more. They are also known as the world's best fighters, with superior technology, magic prowess, and experienced soldiers providing them with advantages no other race can boast. Because of their experience, many once considered themselves superior to their human brethren, and this has been the cause of much tension throughout history.

Ten thousand years ago, the world was on the brink of a massive world war. The Termer felt like they were being taken advantage of by the other races, and they were planning retaliation for what they perceived as the theft of their technology when the humans and elves began manufacturing their own magicore. The humans sought to expand their borders and continually encroached on Pandora, Erita, and Dorim lands, despite frequent warnings to remain in their own borders. The Elmeri, meanwhile, viewed themselves as superior to the humans and dwarves and were plotting to take over and rule their western and northern neighbors. Things looked very dire.

One day, a celestial entity fell from the sky and landed in Alastair. This was Eden. He was an alien being of immeasurable power, viewed by the humans, and eventually the world, as a god. Eden saw what was about to become of this beautiful land and decided to intervene.

Eden reached out to the races of the world, imploring them to cease their fighting. When they failed to listen, he made a show of overwhelming force, threatening to end them all if they continued their pointless wars. The people of the world listened, and Eden gathered the leaders of all factions on an isolated island, forcing them to make a resolution to work together for the future. This place is known today as the Isle of Heaven.

When the leaders of all warring factions came to an agreement, Eden rewarded the people of the world with his power of life and creation. He rejuvenated the planet's resources, ensuring that the people of the world would never need to go to war for survival again. This created a period of peace and prosperity that would continue uninterrupted for thousands of years. All nations agreed to hail Eden as their new guardian deity and created a temple for him to live in the capital city of Corallina. In time, the continent, and eventually the world itself, came to be named after him, labeling him as the world's god and protector.

Three thousand years ago, everything changed. A second celestial being fell from the sky, landing by the Temenos capital of Zion. This was Belial, the celestial of corruption.

When he first arrived, the people of Temenos rejoiced. They felt that they could learn so much from this new celestial, so they offered to make Zion his home. They were naïve.

In short order, Belial spread his corrupting miasma through the city. Everyone in the capital fell to the corruption, but they did not die. Instead, something far worse occurred. They became mutated, twisted shadows of their former selves, enthralled to Belial as his servants, all trace of who they once were gone forever. When the capital fell, all chance of Temenos's survival fell with it.

With the capital under Belial's control, he spread his miasma out from Zion and began the process of making the nation of Temenos his own. Not only did the people fall, but the animals and native beasts of Temenos fell to the corruption as well, becoming twisted and violent mockeries of their former selves.

The people of Temenos tried to launch a resistance against Belial's forces, but their efforts were in vain. Only those who were able to flee north escaped Belial's conquest. Those who were south of the capital were eventually backed into the mountains or ocean, and they were unable to escape.

The resistance cried out to Alastair and Erita for assistance, but for reasons unknown to this day, Eden would not allow them to intervene. Despite being forced to stand alone, the resistance in time organized into a formidable fighting force, and they managed to hold Belial's army and air fleet to the south for several years. They were absolutely determined not to let the corruption spread north even if their neighbors refused to help. Their numbers were limited, however, and they were fighting a losing battle. As time passed, Temenos's numbers steadily fell, while Belial's army grew. They could not survive alone.

Ten years after the invasion of Temenos began, the surviving Mitera forces were pushed back to the Alastair border. The humans finally realized they could not afford to ignore the threat any longer, and against Eden's advice, they mounted a massive counter-response. The entirety of the Alastair Royal Army and Royal Navy headed south, ready to hit Belial's forces with everything they had.

The humans quickly discovered that their decision to remain uninvolved was a tremendous and costly mistake. When they flew south, they found dozens of miles of land had already been lost inside the Alastair border, and the enemy forces had grown far more powerful than they could have ever fathomed. The humans were pushed back rapidly, unable to stem the tide of Belial's army.

When the fighting reached the border of Erita, the other nations decided they had had enough of Eden's inaction, and sent everything they had to aid their neighbors and push back the invading forces.

The elven fleet was the first to arrive. The entirety of the Erita Royal Military launched an overwhelming counterattack on the approaching army, joining with Alastair's scattered air fleet and drastically slowing Belial's advance.

Soon the Termer Collective sent in their combined fleets and soldiers, joining with the human and Elmeri forces. With the three great powers standing together, the advance of Belial's army was slowed to a crawl.

In the end, even the forces of Pandora arrived, and droves of Nekomata and Junmeri riding on sleipnir-back joined the battle on the ground, and Belial's forces could advance no further, bringing the battle to a stalemate. Belial's army was stopped scant miles from the capital of Corallina.

With all of the people of Eden unified and the war in a stalemate, Eden was able to remain neutral no longer. He decreed the formation of the Ceraph Order; an organization of warriors from all nations who leave their homeland in order to serve his will. Eden touched these warriors with his power, granting many of them enhanced abilities, and he awakened his children of the planet, the Angels, to fight alongside Ceraphs of their choosing.

With the Ceraph Order now leading the charge, Belial's army began to lose ground rapidly. The allied forces were relentless and drove the enemy back, recovering miles of land each day. Eventually, fifteen years after the war began, the allied forces drove Belial's army back to the border of Temenos.

Belial would not have this catastrophic failure and proved to be a sore loser. Rather than allowing the allied forces to reclaim Temenos, he launched a kamikaze, scorched-earth attack on the allied forces. With a chain of explosions far exceeding the power of the nuclear weapons of Earth, Belial destroyed everything along the border and poured his pure concentrated miasma into the land itself, corrupting Temenos beyond saving and killing the several million brave allied soldiers who were caught in the attack.

The corruption was absolute. The land itself began radiating the miasma, making it impassable to any mortal being. All who attempted to pass through would either die or fall under its corrupting influence. The corruption was so great that magicore engines would cease to function when crossing the border, making airborne reconnaissance of Temenos impossible.

ETERNAL KNIGHTS OF EDEN I

Temenos was declared the Deadlands by all other nations, and exploration was prohibited from then on.

Fifteen years after the war began, it was over.

Nevertheless, life went on. The surviving armies returned home to their daily lives. The Elmeri erected a monument in their capital to honor the fallen soldiers and the lost people of Temenos. The Termer began furiously rebuilding their lost ships and weapons, using work to distract themselves from their grief. The Nekomata returned to their forests and in time returned to their reclusive ways. The humans and surviving Mitera began to live alongside one another, eventually becoming one people in Alastair.

All four remaining nations pitched in and constructed the Citadel, a great fortress city that would serve as the home of the Ceraph Order from that day forward. Despite Belial being presumed to have perished in his final attack, vestiges of corruption remained across the land, and even without his influence, the world was a very dangerous place, with dragons, behemoths, and all manner of dangerous native beasts dotting the land. The Ceraph Order would become the symbol of hope for the world, their public purpose being the eradication of these corrupted beasts.

Corrupted beasts would stray north more often than one would expect, and the Ceraph Order would frequently go out and hunt these creatures to protect the local populations. It did not go unnoticed that as the years went on, the number of corrupted beasts and incursions seemed to slowly increase. Many expeditions were mounted, but no source could ever be determined. The Ceraph Order resolved to spend their days holding back the tide until a solution could be found.

Eden was different after the war. He seemed to be less powerful, as if the awakening of the Angels and the empowering of the Ceraphs had weakened him. He made one final prophecy before vanishing into the Temple of Eden in the capital of Alastair, never to venture out again. The Ceraphs have made it their life's secret mission to fulfill this prophecy.

When the three Archangels, named Archi, Telos, and Gaia, are awakened and have gathered at the temple of Eden's first son, the Eternal Knight shall awaken from his infinite slumber and purge all that opposes life from the world. When Bahamut awakens, the darkness shall fade, and peace shall reign eternal.

The Angels were not new to the Ceraphs. Many Ceraphs had found companionship with the children of the planet. When an appropriate person proved their worth, these lesser celestials would allow themselves to be summoned and would aid the worthy in their struggle against the darkness.

The Archangels are the exception. For three thousand years, the Ceraphs sought the Archangels but were unable to find any except for Archi. Even had they been able to gather them, the Temple of Eden's Son remained unreachable, lost in the great war. Soon, however, everything would change…

CHAPTER 1

THE PROMISE

An Elmeri mother watches out the window of her estate in Erita with a smile on her face as two children play in the garden below her. Her daughter has always had difficulty making friends, and it warms her heart to see her getting along so well with someone.

Her daughter is a pure-blooded Elmeri only ten years of age. She has long, silky hair that is a vivid pink, rare even among the Elmeri, and like all of her race, her long, pointed ears stick straight out from the sides of her head, poking through the curtain of pink hair. The irises of her eyes are also an unusual pink color, leading many of the children in her school to be cruel and to call her unpleasant names. Her prodigal talent with magic, her short temper, and her unusual appearance has earned her the nickname Daemon, and she spends most of her time alone because of it.

The child she is playing with is a human boy the family is watching as a favor for his parents. Their two families are close friends, and when his parents went away on a dangerous and lengthy mission, they asked Aria and her husband to look after him.

To be specific, this boy is not actually human. He is a Mitera. His father and Aria's husband served together many times on various small-scale missions to suppress incursions from the land to the south, and they wanted him to learn about Erita's culture firsthand while they were gone.

And so, Aria Tamiel watches over the children below with a smile. Despite him not being Elmeri, she is happy to see her daughter smiling with a friend.

Her daughter, Amari, is currently trying to find the boy as he hides from her. Aria can see where he is hiding without a problem, as she is two floors above them, but Amari is getting frustrated that she cannot find him.

Shaide, on the other hand, is peering through the bushes in a small cutaway behind the hedges, impressively capable of hiding himself even at their age. He has been with them for three weeks now, and Amari warmed up to him almost immediately. He obviously noticed her unusual appearance, but he did not judge her for it, and they became friends quickly.

Down in the courtyard below, Amari's eyes start to tear up as she is getting frustrated that she cannot find her friend. She is starting to fear he ran away on her, as nearly everyone else has done. She is right next to Shaide's hiding spot, but she keeps spinning in circles, her head turning frantically as she tries to find him.

Shaide watches her through the hedge and notices her getting upset. He feels a twinge of guilt at making her feel bad, and he intentionally rustles the hedge slightly to get her attention.

She turns around and looks at the bushes, and then she edges around the side. Her eyes widen and brighten as she squeezes into his hiding spot and smiles, saying, "I found you!"

Shaide makes a convincingly disappointed face, but above them, Aria knows different. She saw him intentionally give away his location to avoid making Amari feel bad. She smiles and walks away from the window, leaving the children to play as she goes to take care of some business around the house.

In the garden below, Amari sits down on the nearby bench, and Shaide does the same. He looks over at her and asks, "What do you want to play now?"

Amari looks shyly at Shaide. "Do you want to play house?"

Before Shaide can answer, Amari's Drameri maid opens the door nearby and calls out, "Amari! Shaide! It is time to come in and eat lunch!"

Amari pouts and replies, "Coming, Yania!" She and Shaide get to their feet as she mutters, "She'll come yell at us if we don't listen."

The two young children walk around the corner and enter the house through the door as it is held open by the maid.

Yania's appearance differs from that of the Elmeri in a variety of subtle ways. The ears are the most notable feature. Although pointed, Drameri ears run alongside the head rather than outward, just like a human's ear. Whenever an Elmeri has children with a human or a Termer, this trait of the ears changes, leading to the more human-like ears. Curiously, on the rare occasion a female Elmeri has children with a male Mitera, the children retain their Elmeri appearance.

The Drameri also have softer facial features, with their eyes losing the sharper angles of their Elmeri brethren. The perceived impurity of these changes has caused a great deal of discrimination among many of Erita's more aristocratic Elmeri.

Nevertheless, Yania has always been treated as a member of the Tamiel family, and she is quite content working for them.

She looks critically at Amari as she walks in. "Angels, child, you've gotten your clothes dirty again. Don't you know how hard it is to clean that outfit?"

Amari looks down, ashamed. "I'm sorry, Yania…"

Yania's expression softens. "Well, I suppose it cannot be helped. Run along and wash your hands now. Lunch will be on the table when you get done. You too, young master."

Shaide nods. "I will. Thanks, Yania."

Yania smiles softly at the two children. She is pleased to see the young mistress finally making a friend. Shaide is a mischievous boy, to be sure, but he is always perfectly polite and surprisingly proper. He has been a pleasant houseguest.

Shaide and Amari wash their hands in the nearby restroom before walking into the spacious dining room. Yania has laid out five plates on the dining table, and she is now waiting over near the wall. Amari notices and asks, "Yania? Is Father going to be home for lunch?"

Yania nods. "Yes, dear. Your mother told me he would be here very shortly, in fact."

Right on cue, Aria and a sharp-looking Elmeri man in a military uniform enter the dining room. Yania greets him with a bow and pulls out his chair for him. He looks up at her and says, "Thank you, Yania. That will be all for now. You may relax."

She nods. "Thank you, master Koraru." She bows and takes a seat by the children.

Koraru Tamiel is a battalion colonel with the Erita Royal Army and an old friend of Shaide's father. In addition, his wife, Aria, is the youngest daughter of the duchess of Erita, just below the royal family themselves. As such, they live a rather lavish lifestyle in a mansion with more land and space than they could ever need. He's wearing the standard officer's uniform, which consists of a long, elegant white coat reaching almost to the floor, with gold braided trim and buttons, and his chest is adorned with multiple awards and citations. On his shoulders is a black shoulder board with a silver crescent moon around a single four-point star, indicating his rank as colonel.

The family begins eating, enjoying roast river fowl and salads along with Yania's home-baked sweet bread, and the table remains silent for a few minutes. Finally, Koraru looks up at Shaide and asks, "How are you enjoying the accommodations since you've been staying here, Shaide? Are you comfortable?"

Shaide looks up and swallows before replying, "Yes, sir. Everyone has been very kind to me, and it has been very comfortable. Amari and I have been having lots of fun."

Koraru smiles slightly in spite of himself. "You two are getting along, then? That's good. I was worried that you might not, but I suppose my fears were unfounded."

Amari speaks up rather abruptly, slightly pink in the face. "Yes, Father. I've really enjoyed having him here to play with me!"

Koraru nods. "That's very good. I haven't been able to spend as much time with you all as I would like. It has been busy at the Bastion, and I have been having trouble finding time to come home at a reasonable hour."

They treat Shaide as if he is a part of the family, which is part of the reason his family chose to have him stay here while they were away. Being the son of a Ceraph and an Alastair Ranger has left Shaide with a hectic childhood, as it is rare for both of his parents to be around at the same time; in fact, it is rare for either of them to be around at times.

Aria turns to her husband. "Koraru, are you home for the day?"

He shakes his head. "I'm afraid not, Aria. I wanted to come home and have a proper meal with my family for once, but I must return to the Bastion when we are finished."

Amari pouts. "Aww, Daddy, why can't you stay home and play with us today?"

Koraru smiles sadly. "Because duty calls, I'm afraid. I help hold this kingdom together, after all."

Amari continues to pout and mumbles, "I don't see why the kingdom has to take my daddy away…"

Yania turns and gets onto her "Amari! Your father does very important work! You should be proud that he defends this kingdom! Don't be selfish!"

Koraru waves her down. "Easy, Yania. Amari is right. I do not spend as much time at home as I would like. She has the right to feel that way. Don't be so hard on her."

Yania nods and looks down. "As you say, master."

Once they all finish eating, Koraru stands up. Amari jumps out of her seat and runs over to him, grabbing him in a tight hug. "I'll miss you, Daddy…" she says in a muffled voice.

Koraru pats her on the head. "I'll be home tonight, sweetheart. See if Yania will take you shopping, and get yourself something for me, okay?"

Amari lets go and frowns, but then she nods. "Okay, I will. Be safe, Dad."

Koraru turns and hugs his wife, putting his forehead to hers before pecking her lightly on the lips. "I'll be home tonight, dear."

Aria nods. "I'll be waiting. Be safe."

Koraru walks out of the house and up to the gate, where his six-legged sleipnir waits for him. Despite the more advanced transportation available, sleipnir are still a popular form of private transport.

Inside, Yania says to the children. "Come on, you heard your father. Both of you go and get changed into something clean, and I will take you down to the marketplace to get out of the house for a while." She looks up at Aria "If that is okay, milady?"

Aria smiles. "That will be fine, Yania. I will catch up on some reading while you are gone."

Yania nods and turns back to the two children. "Go on, you two. Get changed."

Shaide and Amari simultaneously say, "Yes, Yania," and head upstairs to their respective bedrooms.

A short time later, the two children come back downstairs. They are wearing nicer outfits that are much better suited to going out. Amari wears a violet and gold dress, while Shaide wears a respectable-looking black doublet with silver trim.

Yania looks at Shaide and frowns slightly "Do you ever wear anything besides black?"

He shrugs. "Every outfit I own is black. I can't help it."

"I see," says Yania. "I had always assumed you just liked the color. Perhaps we can get you something nice as well while we are out. You are such a handsome young man. I am sure you would look good in something else as well."

Amari shakes her head. "I like it when he wears black. He looks cool!"

Aria chuckles in the background at her daughter's defense of Shaide. It makes her feel rather sad that he will be leaving when his parents return. She is certain her daughter will be sad when this happens. Nevertheless, she is grateful he has spent some time with them. Seeing her daughter smile this much and seeing her confidence improve has been a welcome change.

Yania walks to the door. "Come on, you two. It is time to go." Amari and Shaide obediently walk over to the garden door, where Yania stands waiting. She looks up at Aria. "We will return soon, mistress. Is there anything you would like while we are out?"

Aria tilts her head. "Perhaps some of those sweet rolls that Mrs. Reia makes, since you are asking."

Yania nods. "Very well, mistress. If she has any, I will bring some for you."

Yania and the two children walk outside through the garden to where one of the family helicars is parked. It is a sleek four-seater with a cargo compartment and four shrouded vertical turbines powered by a small but powerful electric engine that draws its power from a Termer-mined magicore stone. This particular stone contains synthesized lightning magic.

Shaide politely climbs into the back, offering the front seat to Amari. Like usual, though, she sits in the back with him, causing Yania to roll her eyes slightly as she sits in the pilot's seat.

Yania flips the switch to open the circuit and start the engines, and the car lifts off the ground, hovering smoothly just above the stone driveway. The turbines are remarkably quiet, as magicore technology produces next to no waste and the turbine shrouds are very effective at suppressing sound.

Yania lifts the helicar into the air and directs it toward the nearby market district. From up here, Erita's capital city, Sora, comes into full view.

Sora's architecture is highly reminiscent of gothic architecture except, rather than dark colors and shadows, the buildings are all pearl white with gold or silver accents. As they fly down to the nearby marketplace, Shaide looks in awe at the massive Bastion military complex beyond the estate, and the royal palace behind it. High spires and towers of the purest white reach into the sky, their golden accents gleaming in the sunlight.

ETERNAL KNIGHTS OF EDEN I

Docked with the Bastion are a number of airborne warships of grand design, bearing the same white and gold color palette of the city. These warships are massive weapon platform and troop transports, powered by technology similar to the helicar Yania and the others are riding in but with a different type of magicore that allows them to defy gravity in addition to their turbine propulsion.

Shaide is slightly disappointed when, a few minutes later, their helicar comes to land in the designated landing field of the marketplace, obscuring his view of the Bastion and palace.

Amari giggles when she sees his look of disappointment. "You really like those ships, don't you?"

He nods sadly. "Yeah, the Ceraph navy and Alastair naval fleet are just as big and grand, but they don't look as cool as your country's ships."

Yania looks back over her shoulder as the doors pop open. "You know, many of our people say the same thing about the ships of the west. They are far more intimidating and look more like mobile weapons. Everyone likes something they aren't used to seeing."

"Yeah," Shaide says with a shrug. "I guess that makes sense. Whenever I got to visit the Citadel, I always thought the

Nekomata looked really cool, but everyone there seems used to them."

Yania sighs. "Believe it or not, I've never actually seen a Nekomata in person. Only photographs."

"They look really cool," Shaide replies, nodding. "They kind of look like people, but they also look a lot like wildcats too. It's hard to describe."

Amari looks at him with wide eyes. "Really? That sounds cool! I'd like to see them someday!"

"I wonder if master Koraru would let you visit the citadel sometime," says Yania. "Thousands of miles notwithstanding, it would be a great learning experience."

"Do you think he would let me!" exclaims Amari. "I could come visit Shaide, and he could show me around!"

Yania chuckles. "Take it easy, child. Don't get ahead of yourself. We can ask him when we have time, if you would like. Don't get your hopes up, though. Travel over such a distance is very dangerous."

Amari is slightly disappointed, but to her credit, she chooses not to argue. The three of them climb out of the helicar and close the doors, looking down the street of the marketplace, where a number of stalls line the street, standing in front of the various shops occupying the buildings behind them.

Amari looks up at Yania. "Hey! Can we go look at the clothes! Dad said I should get myself something nice!"

"Yes," Yania replies with a smile. "Your father did indeed say that. Very well, let's go look at the clothes and see if we cannot find something new for the young master as well."

Amari grabs Shaide by the hands and hops excitedly. "I'll help you pick out something nice! Something that will make the other boys jealous!"

"Young mistress," Yania says, putting a hand on her shoulder, "please calm down. We are in public. You are expected to at least try and act properly." Despite her stern tone, she sounds more amused than angry.

Amari stops bouncing and looks disappointed. Shaide stares at her for a moment with an amused expression of his own, and she responds with a quizzical look. She looks down and sees she is still holding his hands and promptly lets go. Her cheeks flush as she says, "Oh, sorry," and turns away.

Yania smiles to herself. The children are much too young to understand, but it still warms her heart to see an Elmeri and a Mitera getting along without any concern for the fact that they are of two different races. After all of the discrimination she faced herself when growing up, it is nice to see that not everyone is that way.

Amari leads them to a nearby clothing store, one that carries her favorite style. Yania shakes her head at young Amari's energy. Shaide, on the other hand, just smirks as he saunters behind.

Amari enters store and smiles at the shopkeeper, an Elmeri who, despite looking no older than a woman in her thirties, is actually over twelve hundred years old.

Amari greets her enthusiastically. "Hi, Mrs. Rurolas!"

The Elmeri woman looks down and smiles. "Why, if it isn't Amari! I have not seen you in quite some time!"

"I'm sorry," Amari says with a smile. "We've had company, and we haven't gone shopping as often as we used to."

Shaide walks in behind Yania and looks around. Amari waves at him. "Shaide! Come meet Mrs. Rurolas! She makes most of my clothes!"

Shaide walks over and bows slightly. "It's a pleasure to meet you. I'm Shaide Darkmoon."

Mrs. Rurolas returns the bow. "My, you are a handsome little human, indeed. No, wait. Unless I am mistaken, you're Mitera, aren't you?"

Shaide looks up at her in surprise. "Yes, ma'am, I am. How did you know?"

Mrs. Rurolas chuckles. "Child, when you have been around as long as I have, you learn to recognize certain auras. Nothing against humans, but Mitera definitely have a distinct feel to them, and you have it."

"His mother and father are friends of my father," says Amari. "They are away on some kind of mission, so he is staying with us while they are gone."

Mrs. Rurolas slowly looks back at Shaide. "Is that so? Are your parents Ceraphs, by chance?"

"Mom is a Ceraph, and Dad is an Alastair Ranger."

Mrs. Rurolas nods. "I understand. That would explain your manners and posture. A fine young man you will become."

She looks up and notices Yania, and her demeanor stiffens slightly. "Yania. A…pleasure to see you again."

Yania nods, refusing to meet her gaze and looking at the ground. "Thank you for having me, Mistress Rurolas."

Shaide notices the tone shift when Mrs. Rurolas speaks to Yania. He'd heard that Drameri were sometimes looked down upon by the Elmeri for being impure, but this was the first time he had seen it in person.

Mrs. Rurolas smiles at Amari. "Well, let me know if you find anything you like, and I will take care of you."

"Thanks, Mrs. Rurolas!" Amari replies with a wave. She quickly grabs Shaide by the hand and pulls him along to look through the clothes on display.

The store has a number of mannequins showing off the various styles made by the shop owner. On the tables surrounding them, copies of the articles on display are folded and laid out, arranged by size. The shop owner frequently comes up with new styles, and this keeps her customers coming back regularly for her latest lineup.

Amari stops at a male outfit, and her eyes open wide. "Hey, Shaide! Look at this!"

He walks up to her and looks at the outfit she found. It is a high-collar long coat in midnight black, with gold buttons and black trim. It's intended to be nearly ankle length, but it is open on the front and back to allow free movement of the legs while providing full coverage of the sides. It has matching pants and boots that look remarkably comfortable.

"Shaide! I think this would look really good on you!"

Before he can say anything, she calls out, "Mrs. Rurolas? We would like for him to try this on, please."

Mrs. Rurolas walks over and looks at the outfit. "I believe I have this in just his size. It may be the smallest size I have, but I am sure I have it." She searches through her stock

 A.S.GUINN

and picks one up. "Aha! This should be just right. Just head on into the back there and try it on."

Shaide looks back and forth, but he decides not to argue. Amari watches excitedly as he heads into the changing rooms in the back to try on the new outfit. A few short minutes later, he walks out.

Mrs. Rurolas even looks surprised. The outfit fits him perfectly, and although he's only ten years old, he looks very handsome and mature.

He turns around. "Well?"

Amari nods her approval. "It looks really good! I'll get it for you!"

Shaide looks down. "It IS surprisingly comfortable. Elmeri fabric is VERY nice."

"I am glad that you like it," Mrs. Rurolas says with a smile. "I'll tell you what. As a present to the child of a Ceraph, and in thanks for you complimenting my work, I will give you this one for free."

Shaide opens his eyes wide. "For free? No, I couldn't!"

"I insist," replies Mrs. Rurolas, shaking her head. "Just remember to visit me next time you are in Sora. When you get older, I would like to set you up with my finest outfits. Please, accept it as my gift."

With a surprised look on his face, Shaide nods. "Very well. I will accept your gift, Mrs. Rurolas. Thank you."

She smiles. "So well mannered. It is my pleasure."

Amari works her way through the shop and finds herself a nice pair of boots that she likes. Before long, she and Yania pay for their purchases, and they head back out to the street.

Next, they head to a nearby toy store. Amari gets overexcited once again, as the store is full of all her favorite plush monsters and entertainment characters, as well as various electronic games. She gravitates to a particular toy: a high-quality replica of a mage staff wielded by the heroine of one of her favorite animated video shows. The rod is deep purple, with golden detail lines laid out in a curiously digital-looking pattern. At the head of the staff, a quartet of golden rings floats suspended around the center. She looks at the price and debates spending so much of her allowance on one thing.

Meanwhile, Shaide peruses the toy store with interest. Everything about Erita culture is jarringly different from Alastair, but on the surface, it appears that children here are little different than children at home.

The plush monsters here are different from the ones in the city of Eden. Their quality is much finer and more detailed, and the materials they are made from are a much higher quality.

ETERNAL KNIGHTS OF EDEN I

Elves are obsessed with quality and appearance, and it shows in nearly everything they make.

This isn't the only difference, however. The types of plush animals here are very different as well. Erita doesn't have the same indigenous wildlife as Alastair. Consequently, Shaide is looking at plush monsters and animals he has never seen before.

He is amused to find such highly detailed sleipnir plush dolls, and he notices they look slightly different than the sleipnir of Alastair. He caves into a guilty hobby of his and picks up a unique-looking sleipnir to add to his collection.

He walks over to find Amari debating furiously over the toy staff. He recognizes the design from the show they watch together about an Elmeri Ceraph. It is a VERY high-quality replica, downsized for a kid.

Shaide smiles and asks her, "Hey. Do you really want it?"

She looks at him and nods. "Yeah, but I don't have enough." She looks down, disappointed, and walks away.

He feels bad that she looks so sad about it. The price is pretty high, but when he checks his money pouch, he finds that he has more than enough. He picks one of the boxes from the shelf and heads to the counter, paying for both his sleipnir plush and the staff he picked up as a gift.

He goes to the front door and waits for Yania and Amari to come out. A few minutes later, he sees Yania track down Amari and urge her to the door. The young girl still looks put out and depressed as she follows her housekeeper.

When she reaches the door, Shaide holds out the box with a smile on his face. She looks at it for a moment, and her eyes dart back and forth between him and the box, a confused expression on her face as if she doesn't understand what he is doing.

Shaide smiles. "It's for you. I didn't like seeing you so sad, so I bought it for you."

Her eyes open wide, and she jumps on him, hugging him tightly around the neck. She has tears in her eyes as she says, "Oh! Thank you! I've had my eye on this for a long time, but I couldn't ever afford it, and Dad wouldn't buy it for me!"

Shaide can barely suppress his laughter; her gratitude is a bit excessive. Finally, he pats her on the head with the hand holding the plush and chuckles.

Yania coughs. "Umm, little miss? We are kind of causing a scene..."

Amari coughs and steps back, still pink in the face. "Oh, I'm sorry... Shaide, really, thank you!"

"Not a problem. Here." He hands the box to her, and she holds it tightly. Yania can't help but smile. It really is going to be sad when he has to leave. This boy has really done wonders to make the little mistress happy.

She notices the looks they are getting and reluctantly interrupts this adorable scene. "Come on, young masters. It's starting to get late. We need to get what your mother asked for and head home."

Amari has a broad smile on her face and doesn't even try to argue. They head up the street a little further and find the bakery that Amari's mother spoke of. Yania orders a box of Aria's favorite sweet rolls, and soon they are walking back up the street to the helicar field.

The whole way, Amari keeps a tight hold on her present as she walks right next to Shaide. He, on the other hand, can't stop smiling at how happy she is. He didn't realize his gift would be such a big deal. He's had plenty of friends, but never anyone like her before. Part of him misses his parents, but part of him is also really enjoying staying here with Amari and her family. He feels like if he had to leave home, this is where he would like to stay.

The sun is starting to set as Yania opens the helicar doors and allows Shaide and Amari to climb in the back. She sets Shaide's old clothes and their purchases in the front seat, all except for Amari's new staff, which the young girl refuses to part with. She fires up the magicore engine and prepares to leave.

Amari scoots over and sits right next to Shaide in the backseat. Shaide is confused by her behavior, but he doesn't shoo her away. Yania catches this interaction out of the corner of her eye and smiles. Amari has her first childhood crush, and it has to be the most absolutely adorable thing she has ever seen. She smiles to herself as they fly back to the estate.

Shaide leans forward slightly as the sun shines off of the white warships on the Bastion. The golden rays glinting off their pearly hulls entrances him for most of their trip, until they come in to land in the motor pool of the estate. Shaide catches sight of something strange in the motor pool, and Yania says what he is thinking.

"Why is a Ceraph helicar here? Your parents weren't supposed to be back yet."

Shaide has a slightly worried look on his face, and Amari's eyes are tight with anxiousness. While Shaide is worried about what's wrong, Amari is just afraid that he'll have to leave early.

They climb out of the car, and the first thing they see is Amari's mother standing by the door, waiting for them. She has a very serious look on her face, and Yania is overcome by an ominous feeling.

A.S.GUINN

The three of them carry their shopping in through the door as Aria holds it open for them. Yania whispers as they walk by, "What's going on, mistress?"

Aria just shakes her head and closes the door behind them.

As Shaide and Amari walk into the family lounge to set down their purchases, Shaide notices two men talking to Koraru Tamiel. They are not his parents…

He can sense from everyone's demeanor that something is wrong. He may only be ten years old, but he is exceptionally sharp. "Order Master Armstrong? Uncle Aton? What are you doing here?" he asks nervously.

Koraru lowers his head, walks over, and takes Amari by the arm.

She looks up, alarmed. "What's wrong? What's happening? Is he leaving already?"

Koraru just lowers his head. "They need some privacy, Amari. Let's go."

She looks over her shoulder with concern at Shaide as her father walks her out of the room. The door closes behind them, leaving Shaide alone with the two men.

The younger man is Atondier Norvus, a Ceraph specialist whom Shaide has spent a lot of time with. In fact, he is Shaide's godfather. He is in his thirties, but he has been through hell, and despite his Mitera heritage, he looks far older than he really is. He has a ragged scar running across one eye, and from the story he tells about it, it was a miracle he didn't lose the eye. Shaide thinks he is as cool as a man can be.

The other man Shaide does not personally know very well, but he knows who he is: Ceraph Order Master Orville Armstrong, the man who runs the Ceraph Order and supposedly works directly for Eden himself, if the rumors are true.

Armstrong looks up at Shaide with a solemn expression. "I believe it may be better to let Aton tell you…"

Atondier, or Aton for short, leans forward and puts his hands together. Shaide sees the shadow of grief and sadness on his face. He closes his eyes and takes a breath.

"There's no easy way to tell you this, kiddo, and I would give anything not to be bringing you this news."

Shaide feels a certain sense of foreboding. There is only one reason they would be here.

Aton sighs and hesitates, struggling to find the words. How do you break this news to a ten-year-old child?

"There was an unexpectedly large battle down by the ruins of Highwatch. The Ceraphs and their Ranger escorts were ambushed by a swarm of corrupted beasts and, we suspect, some rogue Formers as well."

He walks over and puts a hand on Shaide's head, and Shaide looks up at him with eyes that seem to have guessed the truth. "Nearly everyone was lost in the battle. Including your parents. I'm so sorry, Shaide."

Shaide just sits there, looking up at Aton with a blank expression on his face. He's a strong kid. His parents always made sure he knew this was a possibility, but you can never really prepare a young child for this. The two look at each other for some time in silence, and then Shaide's eyes finally tear up. He grabs Aton around the waist and buries his face in his midsection, sniffling. Aton is like family to him, always around when he was growing up. With a stabbing realization, it hits Shaide that Aton is basically the only family he has left.

Armstrong walks over and puts a hand on Shaide's head. "I'm very sorry, son. This was never supposed to happen. If there is anything I can do for you, just let me know."

Shaide just nods, his face still buried in Aton's midsection.

The door to the lounge opens, and the occupants of the Tamiel household slowly enter. Amari walks out from behind her father and watches Shaide as he cries into Aton's shirt. Koraru looks at Armstrong and shakes his head.

Aria walks over to Shaide, pulls him away from Aton, and wipes the tears from his face. Then she pulls him into a hug, calming him with a soothing voice.

"What will happen to him now?" asks Koraru. "His mother and father were good friends of ours. I would be happy to take him in and raise him here, if that will not be a problem. Some of the Elmeri may not like it, but they do not govern my household."

Armstrong shakes his head. "I am afraid that will not be possible. For our part, my Ceraph Order has no issue with Shaide remaining in your care, but as his father was an Alastair royal officer, no less a Ranger, Alastair law is clear that as a child of a commissioned officer, he must remain in the care of the nation of Alastair."

Amari feels the tears building when she hears that Shaide has to leave. She looks at him as her mother comforts him, not sure what to say or do.

Koraru's eyes darken. "So, rather than be cared for by a family that welcomes him, he must become a ward of the state?"

Aton shakes his head. "Do not worry, Colonel. Because of the nature of Alastair law, His parents long ago appointed me legal godfather to Shaide. He will come with me, and I will raise him myself. You should know, Koraru, his father wanted you to be his godfather, but our law simply wouldn't allow it."

Koraru nods in understanding. He looks over and sees his daughter's heartbroken face and asks, "Would it be too much to ask for him to come visit us when possible? Our daughter does not have many friends, and the two of them have grown close since he has stayed with us."

"If it can be done, I think that would not be a bad thing. Again, however, I need not remind you that our nation is very strict on minors traveling between nations. If you would like, though, I promise to do whatever I can."

Koraru looks at his daughter again. "Yes, I think we would appreciate that. He feels like a member of our family now, after all."

Aton looks down at Shaide as Aria hugs him for a moment. "Shaide, I know this is sudden, but I need you to gather your things. There is some business that we must handle back home, and unfortunately, we don't have the time to put it off."

Shaide nods and slowly walks out of the room. Amari begins to follow him, but Yania puts a hand on her shoulder and shakes her head.

Shaide walks up to his bedroom and begins packing his suitcase, a feeling of numbness washing over him. It doesn't really feel real yet. He takes a long last look around the bedroom, and a short time later, he returns to the lounge with his suitcase in hand, eyes glued to the floor.

Aton sighs. "Thank you all so much for looking after him. I know his parents would be very grateful for what you have done."

"No," says Aria, shaking her head, "he has really been very pleasant. It has been our pleasure."

Aton, Armstrong, and Shaide all walk out of the mansion and into the motor pool where their Ceraph Order helicar is waiting. As they put Shaide's belongings in the cargo compartment of the helicar, Aria kneels down and pulls him into a motherly hug.

"Take care of yourself, Shaide. You are always welcome here. Please, come back and visit us."

Shaide nods and says quietly, "Thank you, ma'am."

Koraru holds out a hand, and Shaide shakes it. Koraru says to him, "My wife is correct. Should you ever choose to visit, you will always be welcome here. Come back and see us soon."

Yania walks over and kneels down, pulling Shaide into a tight hug. "Take care of yourself, child. It has been very nice having you. I am happy to serve you anytime, young master.

Amari, still holding the box with the staff Shaide bought her, awkwardly rocks back and forth on her heels for a moment. Then she walks over and hugs him tightly around the neck. He awkwardly returns the gesture by patting her on the back.

"I don't want you to go…"

"I don't want to leave either, but I have to. I'm sorry."

"Please come back and visit me soon. Okay?"

"I will."

She looks him dead in the eyes, tears running out of her own. "Promise me."

Shaide nods and meets her gaze. "I promise I will come back and see you."

She lets go of him, and the two look at each other for a moment.

Armstrong glances down at an old antique pocket watch. "Come on, Shaide. It's time."

Shaide nods and says, "I know… Okay."

He climbs into the backseat of the helicar as Aton sits down in the driver's seat and Armstrong sits down beside him. Aton fires up the engine, and the helicar rises off the ground. Shaide looks out the window and sees Amari waving at him, and he waves back, not relaxing until she is out of sight.

He leans back in the seat, and asks quietly "Are we riding all the way back in this?"

Aton smiles sadly. "Don't worry. You'll only be back there for a few minutes. We came here in a light corvette. We'll be taking it home."

Shaide looks up and catches a surprise. There is a small warship in the front viewport. A corvette is the lightest capital ship, closer to a troop transport than a weapon, but it will be much more comfortable than riding in a helicar for thousands of miles.

Aton flies the helicar into a small cargo bay on the ship that serves as the hangar and sets the vehicle down on the deck. He looks over his shoulder. "Come on, I'll take you to our quarters. It's a long flight, so we may as well be comfortable."

CHAPTER 2

WEEKEND

[Four years later]

Shaide Darkmoon opens his eyes, slowly regaining consciousness after a long night's sleep. It's Saturday, so he has no reason to rush getting out of bed. He looks around his dorm room and notices his dormmate and best friend, Reno, is still fast asleep in his own bed. Shaide sighs and lies back on his pillow, thinking about a strange dream.

In the dream, he saw a massive spacious cavern near the peak of an unknown mountain. The ceiling of the cavern was nearly perfectly round, shaped almost like a dome, and in the center was a vast opening to the sky.

This wasn't the strange part of the dream.

An altar of sorts sat in the center of this cavern, with the relief of a woman carved in stone. On the altar, however, sat the woman herself. She was shrouded in shadow, and her eyes glowed a burning yellow, with vertical slits like the eyes of a snake or a cat. Her skin appeared to be a deep purple or blue, with ornate black tattoos in glyph-like patterns covering what was visible of her skin. She wore an elaborate but revealing set of black metal armor, ridged and patterned to look almost like stone or shells. Her flowing black hair seemed to defy gravity as it floated around her head, and curled black horns were visible through its curtain. She also had a strange reptilian or drake-like tail, black and scaly in appearance. Overall, she almost looked like a Daemon lord you would find in old storybooks.

The woman took no action regarding Shaide's presence. She simply sat on the altar, with one knee raised to her chest, watching him as he stood there. He felt the urge to approach her, but when he tried to step forward, he had no strength in his legs. He resigned himself to standing there and exchanging gazes with her, waiting.

Shaide sighs and rubs his eyes. He has been having this dream every few days for months now. He asked his spiritual priests at the academy, but they did not seem to have any ideas what the dreams meant, or even if they meant anything at all.

He pushes the dream from his mind and contemplates his plans for the weekend.

Four years have passed since his parents died defending a small town in the southern reaches of Alastair. Since then, he has been living with his godfather, Aton, in the Citadel of the Ceraphs. When he was old enough, he enrolled in the Alastair Royal Military Academy to complete his education in preparation for entering the service as an Exorcist. The Exorcists are a specialized branch of the Royal Army who are specially trained to wield magic against the corruption. He is now in his second semester at ARMA.

Traditionally, it is very difficult to gain entry into ARMA, but as Shaide's mother was a Ceraph and his father was a Ranger, Shaide was on the shortlist for the academy long before his parents passed away.

Shaide slowly swings his legs out of bed and begins getting dressed. Now fourteen years old, he is beginning to lose his childlike appearance and look like a young man. He has short, spikey black hair that he keeps buzzed on the sides and dark sapphire-blue eyes.

His personality has also changed. He used to be very outgoing and friendly, but after his parents' funerals, something changed inside him. The dangers of the world were no longer just some distant story told by his parents and uncle when they were home. For the first time in his life, he felt real loss, and the gravity of the dangers the world became all too real for him.

As a result, he became much quieter and more reserved. He was always wary of his surroundings, and he wasn't typically the one to start any kind of social interaction. In spite of his reserved nature, however, he is still a kind young man. He usually helps out whenever he sees trouble, and around the people he is comfortable with, he can be surprisingly friendly.

Shaide walks over to his mirror and looks at his black hair. He wets his hands and sweeps his hair back slightly, giving it the naturally spikey look that he favors. He opens his closet and pulls out a pair of black leather pants and coat and pulls them on over the white tunic that he slept in. He finishes the outfit with a pair of black boots and heads for the door. He pauses and turns around, picking up his money pouch and tying it around his belt.

He looks at Reno and smiles to himself; his friend is sleeping heavily, without a care in the world. Shaide turns and walks out the door.

The dorms at ARMA are a lot like small apartments, and a number of them are in blocks on each floor of the building, separated by class and gender. As Shaide walks down the hallway, he can hear movement behind some of the doors, indicating that at least some of his classmates are awake as well.

He reaches the spiral staircase at the end of the hallway and makes his way down to the first floor.

When he comes out to the atrium, a uniformed royal constable sits at a desk by the entryway. Shaide waves and walks up to him, and then he stands straight, waiting.

The constable looks up and asks, "Name and business, please?"

Shaide looks straight ahead. "Shaide Darkmoon, sir. I am departing the academy for the weekend on leave."

The constable checks for his name on a list of students allowed to leave the academy. He nods when he finds it. "Very well. Enjoy your weekend, Mr. Darkmoon."

Shaide nods and relaxes. "Thank you, sir." He turns and walks out of the dorm building and onto the academy grounds.

A number of students are outside enjoying themselves. Even though it is technically winter, the weather this weekend is remarkably pleasant. Shaide can see them loitering around the fountain and athletic yard, and he even spots an older teenaged couple under a nearby tree in the shadows.

The academy is shaped like a giant sleipnirshoe. There is a large U-shaped courtyard in the middle, with the athletic track, a large fountain, and several training yards arranged in an organized fashion.

On one side of the sleipnirshoe sits the main dorms, the campus apartment building, and the recreation center. On the opposite side are the two academic centers and the mess hall. At the head of the sleipnirshoe, directly opposite the entrance to the academy, is the campus's Temple of Eden, a tall, grand building built of white stone, with the campus bell atop the tower at the front of the building. The administration building and library bracket the temple on either side, looking substantially less impressive than their neighbor.

Shaide proceeds down the main walkway towards the checkpoint out of the academy. When he arrives, he finds a short line has already formed in front of him, so he waits patiently as the constables working the gate verify the students leaving the academy to go into town. Naturally, this early in the morning, no one is trying to come in through the entry checkpoint.

After a few minutes of waiting, it is Shaide's turn to hit the checkpoint.

"Name, please?"

"Shaide Darkmoon. Weekend leave."

The constable signs off on his departure on the checklist in front of him. "Alright, son. Have a good weekend."

Shaide nods in thanks and proceeds out of the gate and onto the street into town. Now outside of the walls of the academy, the city of Corallina comes into view.

The nation of Alastair is a large, broad land with a relatively small number of heavily guarded settlements spread throughout, as well as a handful of smaller villages that take their chances alone. On top of the animals you would expect to find in the wild, Alastair is home to many species of beasts that are far too dangerous for the average person to deal with. These greater beasts range from oversized venomous and carnivorous bugs all the way up to the rare behemoth or drake. A handful of dragons are even known to make their home in Alastair, although, thankfully, they choose to remain in their own territories and do not disturb the population unless provoked.

Corallina is the largest and grandest city in Alastair. It is protected by a huge circular wall over twenty miles in diameter. The entire city is built around a large hill, with the Sanctum of Eden in the center, overlooking the city from atop the royal palace.

The Royal Army base is built around the Sanctum, giving them a high central point with which to monitor the city and, if needed, respond quickly to any emergency. A tall spire serves as the dock for the air fleet, and many naval vessels of varying sizes are docked there. Around the city, a dozen smaller warships patrol the skies. If one looks south of the city, you will also find over two dozen warships hovering low over the plains.

The academy is adjacent to the south entrance of the military base, with emergency access to the base if needed.

The city below him is a beautiful sight. It is structured in a series of stair-stepping, concentric rings, alternating between residential, commercial, and industrial districts, providing everyone ease of access to their various jobs and services. The people of Corallina live a reasonably comfortable life on average. The transient population is at its lowest point in over a hundred years.

Shaide chooses to walk rather than catch a ride, and he proceeds down to the Mou commercial district, which is the highest civilian district in the city. The buildings here are almost all several floors high, with various shops and businesses at street level and helicar access to the upper floors.

He reaches the main street and turns left, looking for his favorite tailor. He placed an order a couple of weeks back, and the tailor said it should be ready about now. As he makes his way down the street, he sees quite a few of his fellow students are out and about. Being so close to the academy, this is the street where most of his classmates spend their weekends, just like he is doing.

He reaches a stone building with the name "Wellsley" on the front, and as he enters, the bell on the door rings.

The elderly human tailor looks up and smiles in greeting. "Shaide, my boy. It is good to see you again. What can I do for you today?"

"Good morning, Mr. Wellsley. I wanted to see if my order was finished yet."

Mr. Wellsley claps his hands together. "Yes, indeed it is. I still believe it is a rather strange choice of garment. I don't know why you would want the elven style, but I won't judge. I copied the design of the original you gave me, and I believe it turned out quite well, if I say so myself. I even managed to acquire some of the elven fabric for it."

He reaches under the counter and pulls out a box, pushing it across the counter to Shaide. "Go ahead and take a look. It's not perfect, but I believe you will be pleased with how it turned out."

Shaide opens the box and pulls out an ankle-length elven-style coat. It has a high collar and flared shoulders, and it is split in the front and back, allowing easy mobility of the legs. It is very similar in design to the coat Amari picked out for him the last time he saw her. He examines the buttons and trim and then looks questioningly up at Mr. Wellsley.

The old tailor smiles. "Yes. I was slightly worried you might be upset, but when you told me the original outfit was a memento of an old friend, I decided to take a chance and scrap the old outfit and use it in the creation of your new one. I salvaged the buttons and trim and even managed to use all of the original fabric in the making of this. I hope you are pleased."

Shaide runs his hands over the buttons and the original elven fabric, and he can't help but smile. The old tailor relaxes when he sees Shaide's approval.

Shaide looks up at him. "It's perfect. Thank you. You did better re-creating the design than I could have ever hoped."

Mr. Wellsley bows his head. "I aim to please, especially with such a loyal customer as yourself. The pants have been done in much the same fashion, maintaining as much of the original fabric and adornments as possible. I even planned ahead and left a significant amount of extra fabric in the hems so that as you grow, I can let out and alter the outfit so you can continue wearing it."

Shaide sets the agreed-upon fee on the counter. "Thank you very much, Mr. Wellsley. I really appreciate it."

The old man puts the money in the safe. "No, it is my pleasure, my boy. It is not very often that an old human like me can work with such elegant elven designs. I consider it a treat to have gotten the opportunity."

"Have a good day, Mr. Wellsley." Shaide bows and heads back out onto the street. He looks around, trying to decide what he wants to do today. He would like to visit his uncle Aton, but last he knew, he was still on a mission down south near the city of Broadspring. He decides that he is getting pretty hungry, so he decides to head to a nearby café for breakfast.

The café in question is run by a retired royal officer who always treats the academy students well. While he does not exactly offer discounts, he tends to give them extra food "to help them grow big and strong."

Shaide enters the café patio and has a seat, setting the box in his lap. A young waitress, who happens to be the café owner's granddaughter, walks over to Shaide and smiles. He feels himself grow slightly hot around the collar as he looks up at her. She is a very cute redhead with a friendly demeanor, just about three years older than him. He's had a slight crush on her since he started at the academy.

"Hey, you," she says. "What'll you have today?"

He coughs. "Yeah, Ashlie, let me have a hot chocolate and a small stack of flat cakes."

"Do you want your usual side of sausage?"

"Umm, yeah, sure. Thanks."

Ashlie winks. "Alright, I'll bring it out shortly."

Shaide waves as she turns and walks away. He leans back and looks around at the street behind him.

As he watches the people going about their daily business, Corallina's unusual diversity on the upper levels is showcased. While the vast majority of people walking the street are human or Mitera, there are a handful of Elmeri or Drameri as well. He notices a new food stall he has never seen before and sees a clean-shaven Termer selling meat.

In his peripheral vision, he sees a strange pattern, and he turns his head to find a young Nekomata girl, scarcely older than him, visiting with her human friends. She is wearing a fur top and skirt typical of a hunter, and her figure catches the fourteen-year-old boy's attention for a moment. She turns and sees him looking at her, and she winks at him. He rubs his neck awkwardly and turns to face the table again.

Just then, Ashlie returns to the table with his food and sets it down. "Is there anything else you need?"

He feels the heat around his neck again, as the cute girl surprised him. He is also embarrassed that the Nekomata girl caught him looking. He perseveres through it, however, and says "No thank you. That'll be all." He hands her the money and tip for his breakfast.

She takes the money and bows slightly. "As you wish. Enjoy." She turns and walks away to help the next customer as Shaide helps himself to his breakfast.

Once he finishes eating, he gets to his feet, picks up the box from the tailor, and heads back out onto the busy street. The Nekomata winks at him again as he walks by, and he responds with a shy half-wave. He gets only a short distance past her when he hears a gruff voice behind him.

"Hey there, kitty-girl. Are you feeling lonely? Maybe you come hang out with us for a while. We'll take real good care of you."

There is an unpleasant tone in the voice, and Shaide stops to look over his shoulder. A group of older teenage boys, looking rather arrogant and haughty, have the Nekomata and her two friends backed into a corner. Typical of Corallina's human culture, everyone just ignores the boys harassing the foreigner.

The Nekomata starts backing away, looking extremely uncomfortable as she says, "I'd rather not, guys. I'm sorry." Her friends shake their heads as well, scared to actually say anything.

Shaide closes his eyes for a moment and lets out a long sigh. He turns around towards the boys and decides he has heard enough.

The boy who spoke to her grabs her by the arm. "Come on, sweet pea. Don't make me insist. It might not be as fun for you if I do."

The girl squirms and tries to pull away, her ears flat against the top of her head. She makes a strange hissing noise at him.

The boy's eyes grow wide. "How dare you—"

Shaide walks up behind him and taps him on the shoulder. These boys are older and quite a bit bigger than him, but he's been trained by the best, so it's a fair fight. Besides, he can't stand bullies.

The boy looks down at him in surprise. "What do you want, small fry? Can't you see we're busy?"

Shaide rubs the hilt of a dagger concealed behind his back as he stares the boy dead in the face. "The girl said no, jackass. Walk away before this ends badly for you."

The boy turns to face him, and his friends gather around as well. "Do you really want to do this, pipsqueak?"

Shaide pulls the dagger from under his coat and channels lightning magic into the blade, causing electricity to arc along the silver metal. He hasn't perfected using it in combat, but a sparking blade is more than enough to make someone think twice.

The boy's eyes lock onto the blade, but it seems he doesn't want to lose face in front of his friends. He says in a fake-brave tone, "Come on, is that supposed to impress me? You gotta do better than that."

Someone says behind them, "How about both of us, then?"

The boys spin around to find Shaide's best friend, Reno, bumping his fists together. He's wearing a set of steel-knuckles, and they crackle with lightning magic as he knocks them together.

Shaide leans forward and puts the point of his dagger to the ringleader's back, and the boy promptly stands up straight. Shaide whispers, "We're with the Alastair Royal Army. I can kill you right here and now, and nothing will happen to me. Now, walk away."

The boy nods stiffly, the brave attitude gone. "Yeah, umm, okay. Boys? Let's go. We can do better than this cat."

The three boys very quickly power-walk away, up the street. Shaide quickly re-sheathes and conceals his dagger and turns to the girls. "Hey, are you three okay?"

The two human girls nod shyly, still in shock over the boys harassing them. The Nekomata, on the other hand, boldly steps forward. "Thank you for that. That was brave. Those boys were real jerks."

Shaide nods as Reno walks up behind him. "It was no problem. That was pretty brazen of them to do that out in the open like that."

"Yeah, people tend to turn a blind eye to anyone harassing us Nekomata. They think we're strange because we're different."

Shaide looks at her purple eyes with slits for pupils, the short black and tan striped fur around the outside of her face and all down her body and arms, the pointed ears atop her head, now perked up instead of flat, and her striped tail. He admits to himself that up close, the Nekomata ARE a bit different, but it doesn't bother him. In fact, the girl is kind of cute.

"Well, I grew up with elves and dwarves for friends. I even knew a Nekomata, though not very well. I don't judge people for being different."

The girl smiles. "Well, that's good to hear. You're an academy student?"

Shaide nods. Behind him, Reno is pouting because the girl is only paying attention to Shaide and ignoring him entirely.

The girl smiles broadly. "Well, I stay in the residential district down below with my friend's family." She indicates one of the girls behind her, who shyly waves. "We should meet up and hang out sometime if you're in this part of town again. I'm Nyu, by the way."

Shaide tilts his head. "Nyu?"

She nods. "It's actually Nyuralisiania, but it's tough for humans to pronounce, so I just go by Nyu."

Shaide chuckles. "Okay, Nyu it is. I'm Shaide Darkmoon. The silent dude behind me is Reno Coltide." He points over his shoulder.

Reno waves and quietly says, "Hey."

Nyu leans forward, "Well, I won't keep you for now. We need to be heading back, but those boys got in our way." She suddenly steps up close to Shaide and licks his cheek, and he twitches in surprise.

"Thanks again! I hope to see you again soon!" She and her friends walk up the street and turn south towards the residential district below.

With amusement, Shaide watches them go, reaching up to touch his cheek where she licked him. She winks at him before she turns the corner.

"Dude," says Reno, "what in the hell did I miss?"

Shaide shakes his head. He notices they are still drawing a lot of stares after that little incident. "No idea, bud. Those boys were harassing her, and now I think I have a new friend?"

Reno chuckles. "I think she likes you. Nekomata. You could have an exotic first girlfriend!"

"I dunno, dude," Shaide says with a sigh. "I'm awkward around girls."

Reno laughs and looks around. "Hey, uhh, let's move somewhere else. We're getting a lot of attention, and I don't want to get in trouble. We're technically not supposed to take our weapons off campus, after all."

Shaide rubs his neck and nods. "Yeah, let's go that way." He points towards the next district.

Reno and Shaide set off up the street as people begin returning their attention back to their own business. As they walk, Reno looks over at Shaide. "Why did you leave without me, anyway? I woke up, and you weren't there."

Shaide puts his hands on his belt and looks up at the sky. "You were sleeping. I didn't want to wake you if I didn't have to. You're grumpy when you don't want to wake up."

Reno opens and closes his mouth several times, acting like he wants to argue. After a moment, however, he shrugs and nods in defeat. "Yeah…you have a point."

"Yeah, I remember the clock you broke because you couldn't get the alarm to stop."

Reno bumps him with his shoulder. "Ahh, well, probably for the best, then. The cute girls would never pay attention to you with a dashing young man like me beside you, anyway."

Shaide raises an eyebrow. "And, which one of us just got ignored by the cute Nekomata girl and her two friends?"

Reno makes a twisted face like he has an unpleasant taste in his mouth.

Shaide laughs. "My friend, you make it WAY too easy sometimes."

Reno sighs and looks around the increasingly crowded street. "I'm hungry. I know you ate, but do you mind if we sit down and let me catch lunch?"

Shaide shrugs. "I could go for a cup of tea, if you want to eat."

"Yeah. Let's go to that little café with the elven waitresses."

Shaide raises an eyebrow.

Reno gets a defensive look on his face. "What? I think their little pointed ears are adorable. Don't judge me."

Shaide stares him dead in the face. "I am judging you."

"Didn't you have that little Elmeri friend out east?" Reno says with narrowed eyes.

Shaide sighs and looks down. "Yeah. I haven't seen her in a long time. I wonder if she even remembers me."

Reno pats him on the back as they walk into the café. "Dude, Shaide? You are a tough guy to forget. I'm sure she remembers you. Don't worry."

"I suppose it does no good to worry about it now."

This area of the commercial district has a different feel than the one they were at before. This little region of the capital has a higher population of foreigners than the eastern area, and although it is mostly humans running around, there are quite a few Eritan as well.

The café itself is in a distinct Erita style. The exterior still conforms to the designs of the top commercial tier, but the interior is definitely reminiscent of the owner's homeland. The walls are lined with white stone, and the accents are a highly polished golden color. The floor is laid with natural stone worn flat for walking, the tables all appear to be hand-carved from large tree trunks, and the chairs are made of a golden metal, with white cushions.

While not nearly as elegant as the Tamiel family's home, Shaide can tell the design is very much of Erita origin.

A little Drameri waitress only a couple of years older than them walks up. Her pointed ears are pierced on the top and bottom, a common trend among Drameri who reject their brethren's discrimination. She smiles. "What can I get you boys today?"

Reno says quickly and nervously, "I'll have a small bomoth steak and a side of eggs, scrambled. And…a coffee. Black."

She nods and turns to Shaide. "And you, sir?"

Shaide looks up and says simply "Hot tea, no sugar. I already ate."

She nods and bows. "As you wish. I'll have it out as soon as it's ready." She heads back into the kitchen, and the two boys relax a bit.

Reno looks at Shaide "What do you think about the upcoming visit to Broadspring on Monday?"

Shaide considers the question. "Honestly, I'm just looking forward to getting out of the capital for a bit. I Haven't left the city since first term started, and I'm feeling a bit…confined."

A look of understanding crosses Reno's face. "That's right. I forgot. Your uncle was away when first term ended, so you stayed here."

Shaide nods "Yeah. So I'm just ready to get out of the capital for a while."

The waitress comes back with their drinks and sets them down on the table. "Are you two doing well?"

Reno looks up "Yeah, we're alright. We're taking some time off from the academy to come into town for a while."

The girl's eyes widen. "Academy boys? We don't usually see many of you here. Your schoolmates tend to favor the human establishments."

Reno shakes his head. "I don't have any problems with the Drameri. Your girls can be just as pretty as humans."

The girl gives him a little curtsey "Do you think all Eritan girls are pretty?"

Reno speaks boldly "Well, you are."

She giggles and blushes slightly. She looks behind her "Well, I should go check on your food and my other customers. I'll visit with you again in a few minutes." She turns and walks away.

Reno looks slightly proud of himself.

"See dude?" says Shaide. "The girls notice you too."

Reno looks at the ceiling thoughtfully. "I wonder what my parents would say to me if I had a Drameri girlfriend."

Shaide raises an eyebrow in amusement. "Well, look at you. Getting a little ambitious, aren't you?"

"Why shouldn't I be? We're training to be royal officers and to go out into the frontiers to fight the monsters in the dark. We have to experience everything we can while we still can!"

Shaide raises his tea and takes a sip. "I suppose I can't argue with you there. Any day could be our last, right? Although, it's not like we're fighting yet."

Reno sips his coffee. "Yeah, I guess you're right." He licks his lips as he looks down. "That's the other reason I like this place. Eritan coffee is better than the stuff we have here. Supposedly, they ship it in from Erita."

Shaide shrugs "The tea is pretty good. I won't lie."

Reno smiles "Yeah, but you like Ashlie from Andall's place, so you'll keep going there."

Shaide sighs. "Dude. I've got things on my mind other than just girls, you know?"

Reno chuckles as he gives Shaide a mischievous look "Yeah, but you DO have girls on your mind, so it still makes a difference."

Shaide chokes on his tea as he laughs a little at Reno's comment.

After a few minutes, the waitress returns with Reno's food. "How does everything look?" she asks as she sets it down.

Reno looks up at her and asks playfully, "Are you asking how the food looks or you?"

She giggles. "Does that change the answer?"

Reno shrugs "No, I guess not. Everything looks good, thank you." He gives her the money for the bill, covering Shaide's tea as well.

She takes the money and winks. "Okay, you let me know if you need anything else." She turns and heads to another table to take their order. Unfortunately, she heads into the back afterward, and they don't see her again.

After finishing his food, Reno leans back happily. "That hits the spot."

Shaide looks around. "I wonder what happened to your little girlfriend? I haven't seen her in a while."

Reno looks around sadly. "Yeah, I know. I'm kind of wondering myself."

"Well, where do you want to go from here? I took care of all of my plans for the day." He indicates the box in his lap.

Reno frowns. "Well, we could go hang out at the spring pond up by the academy? Enjoy the weather and just relax a little."

Shaide stands up and stretches, putting the box under his arm. "Yeah, that sounds like a good idea."

Reno stands up with him and looks around the café, presumably searching for the Drameri waitress he was flirting with, but there is no sign of her. He sighs and heads for the door with Shaide. "Yeah, let's go."

The two of them walk out onto the street and turn back the way they had come. It is already nearly noon, and the sun is hitting the street, making it feel warmer than the winter breeze would indicate. They reach the main southern road and turn back towards the academy, climbing the path for a few minutes until they reach a branch in the road leading to the Corallina spring lake.

ETERNAL KNIGHTS OF EDEN I

The spring lake is in a large nature reserve near the top of the city. The land here is naturally level, and the lake is encompassed by a small area of woodlands. Many centuries ago, it was decided that this section of the city would remain untouched, serving as a sort of sanctuary where the military personnel, as well as the residents of upper Corallina, would have a place to go and relax without making the journey to the plains outside of the city.

Shaide and Reno head down the path through the trees until they reach the clearing around the pond. Reno looks at Shaide and shrugs, and the two walk over to a thick shade tree away from the water's edge and sit down at its base.

Around the pond, Shaide notices that they are not the only academy students who had this idea. Several of their classmates are hanging out under trees and near the water's edge. Here and there, they can see couples cuddling and kissing. Displays of affection such as this are not permitted on academy grounds, so weekend leave like this is a bigger deal to the various couples in the academy.

Shaide and Reno both lean back against the tree and start to drift off. The air is cool but soothing at the same time, and the two boys find it especially easy to nod off, especially with food in their bellies.

Shaide ends up falling into a nap as Reno chooses to pull out some notes that he brought with him and study ice magic theory to stay awake. Ice magic is actually a hybridization of wind and water magic, neither of which Reno has mastered yet, but he still finds it very interesting.

Shaide is having a rather pleasant dream when, suddenly, a pair of soft hands covers his eyes. He jumps as a slightly playful girl's voice says, "Guess who?"

The hands come off of his eyes, and a familiar teenage Nekomata is leaning in his face.

Shaide's eyes open in surprise. "Nyu! Where did you come from?"

She plops down against the tree and scoots next to him. "I didn't know you were coming here, or I would have said something!"

Reno smirks at the arrival of the Nekomata. He didn't see her coming until she greeted Shaide. He tilts his head and asks her, "Where are your friends at?"

She shakes her head "They're still at home. I just like coming up here to the spring. It's relaxing."

Shaide, feeling curious, asks tentatively, "Does it remind you of home?"

She nods sadly. "Yeah. I don't regret my decision to leave with my mom, but I still miss the jungle sometimes."

Reno asks, "Why DID you leave?"

Nyu shakes her head. "It's not something we talk about. I'm sorry. Even for those of us who have left our jungle homes, Pandora is a sacred place, and its secrets are not for outsiders to hear. You can only experience it for yourself."

Reno coughs. "I'm sorry, I didn't mean to be rude. I've just, well, never really spoken to a Nekomata before. Your ways are kind of unknown to me."

"No worries. Your ignorance does not offend. A person cannot be blamed for what they do not know unless they intentionally choose not to learn."

Reno raises an eyebrow, impressed. "That's kind of deep, actually."

Nyu turns her head to Shaide. "Thank you again for saving me from those boys earlier. I probably could have handled them, to be honest, but it would have been messy. Not many people would have done what you did, though."

Shaide chuckles. "That kind of cheapens the gratitude, you know."

Nyu giggles "I'm a hunter. I go out into the plains and harvest local fauna to sell the meat and furs and whatever else is valuable from them. I'm well accustomed to fighting. I'm also not known for my modesty."

Shaide shrugs "No offense taken, Nyu. Just making a comment."

Nyu does a kind of spinning roll and ends up sitting on Shaide's outstretched legs, her face very close to his. Before he can react in any way, she puts her hands on his cheeks, puts her face to his, and kisses him squarely on the lips. Her ears twitch happily when she sees his stunned face, and her tail curls up along her back.

"Does THAT show my gratitude better?"

Reno coughs and looks away, not sure how to react to what he's just witnessed.

Shaide nods and struggles with his words for a moment. He finally manages to say, "Yeah. Yeah, I can't argue with that."

Nyu narrows her eyes, and her ears point forward curiously. "Don't tell me that you've never kissed a girl before."

Shaide looks down and rubs his neck awkwardly.

Nyu's eyes open wide with surprise, revealing her beautiful violet irises in full. "Oh, my mother, you really never have kissed a girl before…"

Shaide coughs and says meekly, "No, no, I haven't."

Nyu's ears perk back up happily. "Yay. I got to be your first!" She turns around and sits on his lap, leaning back and resting her head on his chest. "I'm gonna take a nap here, if that's okay."

Shaide looks over at Reno with an amused look on his face. Reno shrugs and says, "I've got nowhere to be. Get comfortable."

Nyu smiles and closes her eyes. "Already am. You make a good chair. Or bed."

Shaide feels his face burning. He feels incredibly awkward, for he has never been this close to a girl before, but she is surprisingly light and soft, and he does not find her presence unpleasant.

Nyu says with her eyes closed, "Just don't go getting overexcited. If you do, I can't promise what I will or won't do to you."

Nyu seems to be a bit of a naughty teenager, teasing Shaide rather aggressively, although he doesn't seem to catch her meaning.

She picks up on his ignorance and sighs. "Wow. You humans really are sheltered."

The three sit under the tree in silence for a while. While uncertain what exactly to think, Shaide finds the Nekomata sitting on him to be rather comfortable. She's a nice girl, after all.

After some time passes, Nyu turns her head and looks at Shaide. "So, I really don't know anything about you. Tell me, how did you end up in the academy?"

Reno makes a worried hissing sound, as Nyu has touched on a dangerous subject.

The memory of how he ended up here is painful, but Shaide proceeds to answer the curious cat's question. "Well, a long time ago, my mother was a Ceraph, and my father was a Ranger with the Royal Army Reconnaissance and Expeditionary Force. Joining the army was pretty much decided for me long ago. My mother and father passed away in an operation a few years ago, and I had to live with my uncle in the Citadel for a while. When I was old enough, I found out that I had a spot waiting for me at the academy, set up by my parents a long time ago. So, I came here."

Nyu's eyes open wide. "Your mother was a Ceraph?"

Shaide nods. "She was strong. They both were."

Nyu eyes grow wide. "Wow. I would have never known." She suddenly frowns. "I'm sorry. I didn't mean to bring up any painful memories for you."

Shaide shakes his head. "No, it's fine. I made my peace with it. I knew from the time I was little what could happen."

They visit for a while longer, enjoying each other's company, until the sun begins setting below the tree line.

Nyu looks at the setting sun, and her ears flatten sadly against her head. She gets to her feet and says, "I'm having a really good time, but it's getting kind of late."

She pulls Shaide to his feet, and he says, "Not a problem. We should probably be getting back too."

As Reno gets up beside Shaide, Nyu asks, "Will you come back out again tomorrow?"

Shaide looks at Reno, who shrugs. He turns back to her and says, "I will try to."

Nyu perks up, and her ears pop up excitedly. The handful of Nekomata Shaide had met before were very subtle about their expressions, but Nyu is easy to read. "Okay, let's try and meet up again tomorrow if we have the chance!"

"You have a deal."

The trio walks along the bank of the pond and onto the small road leading back to the main city. When they reach the fork, Nyu jumps on Shaide and hugs him, sniffing him for some reason. "I'll see you tomorrow, I hope! Bye!"

Shaide rubs his neck awkwardly. "Yup, see you later."

Nyu skips off down the hill, back towards the commercial and residential districts.

Reno shakes his head. "Dude. Would it be in bad taste to make a pet joke?"

Shaide rolls his eyes. "That's very racist, you know?"

Reno sighs. "Yeah, I know…"

The two walk back up the winding road to the checkpoint. The constable seems very bored. He looks up as they approach and says, "Identification, please."

They present their holo-crystals, which contain their identification, and the constable scans them against his record.

"Okay, welcome back. Before you come in, what is in the box?"

Shaide opens it and shows him. "An outfit from the tailor."

The constable looks inside the box for a moment and then nods. "Alright. You may proceed. Welcome home."

Reno nods "Thank you, sir. Good to be back."

Shaide and Reno walk back up the sleipnirshoe path to their dorms. As they reach the front door, Reno says, "Hey, I'm kinda hungry again. We visited with your girl so long that I didn't notice the time."

Shaide nods "Yeah, me too. I just want to run this up to the dorm room first so that I don't have to carry it around all day."

"Alright. I'll wait for you here. Then we can head to the mess."

Shaide enters the dorm and presents his identification to the constable. Moments later, he is climbing the stairs to his floor and walking down the hallway.

He unlocks and enters their room and places the box on a shelf in his closet. He rests his hand on the box for a moment, thinking about his old friend Amari, before leaving to meet Reno.

CHAPTER 3

RIDING THE NORTH STAR

Shaide wakes up early Monday morning feeling especially groggy. Yesterday, Reno and he went back into town to enjoy the rest of the weekend and wound up meeting Nyu and one of her friends. Nyu stayed right by Shaide's side all day while her friend hung out with Reno most of the time. Shaide strongly suspected that she was only there to keep Reno distracted so Nyu could have Shaide all to herself.

Their day culminated in watching a fireworks show in honor of the anniversary of the alliance between Erita and Alastair. The festival went on well past midnight, and Nyu kept Shaide out until he finally had to insist on going to bed due to today's trip.

ETERNAL KNIGHTS OF EDEN I

Shaide wasn't complaining about Nyu's company, however. It was very pleasant, and she sure as heck made his weekend a lot more interesting than it would have been without her. She was particularly affectionate towards him, and Shaide strongly suspected she was hoping to be his first girlfriend. He would be lying if he said he wasn't seriously considering it.

Sadly, the fun of the weekend is over now, and it is back to the grindstone like usual. Today he and Reno are going on a training mission down to the gateway city of Broadspring to get some firsthand experience regarding their future careers in the military.

As Shaide swings his legs out of bed, he notices just how heavy his head feels. If seeing her does become a regular thing, he makes a mental note to make sure she doesn't keep him out that late on a school night again.

Their trip this week is an unusual one. It's being treated as a formal operation rather than a traditional school trip, and it is going to be several orders of magnitude more dangerous than their typical excursions. As such, they are going to be traveling in full field gear in order to be prepared for any situation that may arise.

Shaide digs around in his wardrobe and moves his daily clothes aside to find a crate containing the winter field uniform that was recently issued to him. This particular uniform consists of heavy blue canvas pants that have several pockets, an insulated cotton undershirt, and a heavy blue overcoat that, when fitted properly, reaches about to groin level. Although the outfit looks uncomfortable, it is actually remarkably flexible, allowing for a full range of motion in combat.

Shaide turns around and notices that Reno hasn't moved yet, so he picks up Reno's boot and throws it, hitting him in the face. "Hey, jelly roll. Wake up."

Reno groans and sits up, picking up his boot and looking at it in confusion before scowling at Shaide.

Shaide ignores the scowl and finishes getting ready. He tightens down the straps on his black leather boots and then puts on his combat harness. In his case, the harness is a belt of very heavy black leather with straps crossing his back and coming straight down his front. The harness also has a second portion with straps wrapping around his upper thighs. It has several pouches designed to hold various pieces of survival gear as well as a small detachable backpack. Shaide's harness in particular also contains a pair of scabbards on the back for the two large daggers he favors in combat.

Reno drags his feet while getting ready, struggling to wake up. He manages to slowly put on his uniform and then pulls out his own combat harness. Reno's gear is nearly identical to Shaide's aside from the weapons. Reno has a pair of pouches just behind his hips that contain a pair of heavy metal gauntlets that he favors as his primary weapons. They were a gift from his parents and contain a magicore band that moderately enhances physical strength.

Reno finishes strapping up and looks at Shaide with sleepy eyes. "Buddy…let's never stay out that late on a school night again. Okay?"

Shaide chuckles. "You're the one who goes on and on about wanting a girlfriend. Are you saying you didn't have a good time?"

Reno raises a finger and opens his mouth as if he wants to say something, but then he closes it in defeat. Shaide has a good point; he DID have a good time.

Shaide yawns and stretches, turning to his friend. "Come on, bro. Let's go eat breakfast before heading to the motor pool."

Reno perks up at Shaide's suggestion. "Food? I'm in! Let's go!"

The two boys walk out into the hall, noting the sound of their classmates getting ready in the neighboring rooms. Another boy their age, Bryon Atlas, sticks his head out and looks at them. "Hey, Darkmoon, Coltide! Where are you going?"

Shaide looks over his shoulder at their classmate. "We're going to get breakfast. Meet you there?"

Bryon nods "Yeah, I'll see you down there in a few minutes. Joslin is being slow."

Shaide nods and waves at Bryon, and then the two of them walk down the staircase and out of the dorms, stopping to check out with the constable on the way. Once they walk out onto the campus, they turn left towards the mess hall, which sits between the dorms and apartments. Shaide notices Reno seems to perk up again as the smell of food reaches their nostrils.

The pair enters the mess hall to find a number of students already eating breakfast. They catch a few looks since they're in their field uniforms, but no one's gaze lingers. It's unusual to see field uniforms at the academy, but everyone knows what it means.

Shaide and Reno get into the line for breakfast and load up on sausage, biscuits, gravy, and fruit before heading over to join their classmates' table.

One of their female classmates, Lania, looks up as they sit down. "Hey, Shaide. I'm kind of surprised to see you up this early. You were out kind of late last night."

Shaide coughs and rubs his neck awkwardly. "Yeah, I kind of lost track of time."

Lania leans forward. "I bet you did. Who was the Nekomata girl? I saw you two a couple of times, and that jungle cat couldn't have been more into you if she tried."

The other students smile in amusement. Shaide turns slightly red. "I saved her from some bullies on Saturday, and I haven't been able to shake her since."

"Well," mutters Reno, "you haven't exactly tried to get rid of her either, to be fair."

Shaide shoots him a glare. "Hey, don't judge me. She's really cute and sweet. And maybe slightly scary."

Lania sits back and resumes eating. "Aww, don't take it personal, Shaide. You've always been so quiet and shy around girls that it was just weird seeing you with one all over you."

Reno raises his fork. "She has a point."

Shaide laughs awkwardly and resumes eating.

A few minutes later, Bryon and his roommate, Joslin, take a seat at the table next to Reno and start eating. Bryon asks, "What ship do you think we're taking to Broadspring?"

Reno looks at Shaide. "You're the ship guy. What do you think?"

Shaide thinks for a moment. "Well, there's twenty of us going, plus the instructors. It's over a thousand-mile flight if we go over the mountains, so we're looking at a nine-to-twelve-hour flight. We'll probably be in a frigate. ARV *Chase the*

Horizon most likely. It's old and mostly used for transport rather than combat now."

Bryon nods. "You can always count on Shaide to know his ships."

"What?" Shaide replies with a shrug. "I like ships."

When everyone has finished eating, they look up at the oversized clock on the wall. One of the boys further down, Rayn Jarvis, stands up. "Come on, cadets. Let's head to the motor pool. Does everyone have everything they need? Once we hit the helicars, it'll be too late."

Rayn is their class captain. Like Shaide, he's from an extensive military family, but he is more outgoing and assertive in social situations, making him a suitable leader for the class. Shaide doesn't know him especially well, but they've always gotten along.

The class murmurs a series of halfhearted acknowledgments, and Rayn gives them a piercing look.

"Yes, Captain. All ready!"

Rayn nods. "That's better. Come on, let's move out."

Shaide chuckles. They were obviously not the only cadets who stayed out too late last night partying. Many of their classmates look rather tired today. The class walks out of the mess and onto the path leading to the entrance. They're moving informally today, so they are more of a gaggle than a formation.

ETERNAL KNIGHTS OF EDEN I

Several of them look up into the sky at the new object hovering over the academy.

Shaide follows their gaze and sees the airship hovering overhead. As he guessed, a light frigate is hovering in place about a hundred feet off the ground. What's surprising is the identity of the ship. Rather than an older vessel like the ARV *Chase the Horizon*, they are looking at the newly commissioned ARV *North Star*. The vessel is an elongated oval tapering to a point on both ends. From underneath, they can see the fourteen oversized turbines on their gimbals, used to propel and steer the frigate while the magicore keeps it aloft. The hull of the ship is more industrial looking than the elegant ships of Erita, more befitting a vessel of war in many soldiers' opinions.

Three navy dropships are waiting for them in the motor pool. The dropships are essentially a form of heavily armored helicar. The cockpit sits at the front of the dropship, with a large troop or cargo compartment behind it, depending on the configuration, and they can transport eight to ten fully equipped troops with room to spare. On top of the superstructure is a set of stubby delta-shaped wings, with a turbine on each tip, as well as a pair of turbines both behind the cockpit and at the rear or the fuselage. The power supply is a standard electrical magicore reactor housed inside of a compartment on top of the vehicle.

Beside the dropships stands the class's chief instructor, First Lieutenant Nikola. He surveys the arriving class and clears his throat before addressing them. "Good morning, company. Today we are departing on our field mission to the frontier village of Broadspring. As you are all aware, Broadspring is one of the two fortress cities guarding the mountain passes between north and south Alastair. It has a large civilian population as well as a battalion of rangers tasked with defending the region. Three thousand years ago, Broadspring was the site of one of the bloodiest and most drawn-out battles of the great war. The city stood its ground against the invading forces for weeks before falling to corrupted forces, and to this day, it holds a great historical significance. In addition to the city itself, there is a temple deep in the mountains devoted to our lord, Eden, which is traditional for first-year students to visit at least once."

Lt. Nikola gives the class a serious look before continuing. "Before we depart, I need to make something very clear. Where we are going is most definitely very dangerous. Stay with your squad at all times and follow all orders given by ARA personnel to the letter. They know what they are doing. Do as they say, and nothing bad will happen to you. Any questions?"

The class shouts out, "No, sir!"

He steps back. "Alright. Load onto the dropships, and we will board the *North Star*."

Shaide, Reno, Lania, Bryon, Joslin, and Rayn all board the same dropship, along with several of their classmates. On the outside, the dropships may look like oversized helicars, but inside they are different. Rather than the family-friendly rows of seats found in civilian vehicles, the dropship has a back hatch that drops open into a ramp to allow boarding, and the seats are arranged in benches along the walls.

Despite the utilitarian design of the troop bay, they have more than enough room to move around. No one bothers to sit down, as they are just going to the frigate overhead.

Once everyone gets loaded onto the transports, their engines flare and engage. Reno's and Bryon's knees buckle slightly from the unexpected vertical acceleration, and everyone hangs onto the ceiling loops to help maintain their footing. Less than a minute later, they feel their horizontal inertia shift, and then gravity seems to lessen slightly as the dropships descend a few feet and land on the deck of the hangar bay.

A moment later, the rear hatch opens, and the ramp extends, allowing the cadets to file out and stand in formation as they wait for further instructions.

An older man stands on the deck of the hangar bay with a commander's leaf on his collar. Lt. Nikola walks up to him and salutes across his chest. "Commander Winslow. Lieutenant Nikola of the Alastair Royal Military Academy, requesting permission to come aboard with ARMA Company Oscar."

Commander Winslow returns the salute. "Permission granted, Lieutenant. You can relax."

The entire class relaxes their stiff postures slightly. Being on a Navy frigate, around real active military personnel is intimidating to most of the class; they don't want to do anything to embarrass themselves around the very people they hope to serve with someday.

Shaide looks around the hangar with interest. On top of a half-dozen dropships, including the three they flew in on, it is also home to what appears to be eight gunships.

The gunships have an interesting design. From the top, they are shaped like a T, with the wide part in the rear. From the side, however, they are sloped downward from back to front, with mechanical landing struts built into the rear "wings." The gunships have two high-power turbines on the ends of the wings and a single turbine mounted directly behind the cockpit, which sits at the very front of the ship. The magicore engine for the turbines is presumably in the fuselage between the front and back engines. The gunship is armed with a single tri-barreled Gatling cannon mounted on a moving gimbal under the nose of the aircraft.

Cannons in Eden do not use gunpowder. Instead, they use fire-based magicores to create rapid thermal expansion, obtaining velocities far exceeding the powder weapons of the past. This also allows them to drastically increase their ammunition capacity as well as their firepower.

Shaide realizes he is spacing out on the gunships, so he shakes his head to refocuses on their instructor.

Lt. Nikola finishes talking with the commander, and the senior officer leaves them, presumably returning to the bridge.

The lieutenant turns back to face them. "Okay. We are going to be waiting in the ship barracks. Any of you that stayed out too late last night will be able to catch some additional sleep for two hours. After this break, we will proceed to the bridge so you can learn firsthand about the operation of Alastair warships, which some of you may serve on in the future."

The lieutenant leads them out the back of the hangar bay and into the rear section of the airship.

Frigates are not very large by warship standards, with the whole vessel being around four hundred feet long. The relatively small ship makes good use of its space, however, packing everything needed for its crew into its hull.

The interior of the ship is very industrial in appearance, just like the exterior. The walls are undecorated gray steel at the bulkheads and are actually made of heavy wood in some of the unarmored sections. When they emerge from a short hallway into one of the barracks, they realize how comfortable their dorms at the academy really are.

A recreation area sits open in the middle of the main aisle, scarcely larger than the hallway they were just in. On either side of the aisle are the bunks, which are double-stacked and appear to be just barely large enough for the beds.

The lieutenant looks around as their inertia shifts; the frigate, presumably, has begun moving. Smaller vessels like helicars are fairly quiet, but the turbines of the frigate seem to scream outside of the walls as the vessel slowly accelerates to somewhere around eighty miles per hour, and then the turbines back off.

As the vessel gets underway, many of Shaide's sleepy-eyed classmates take advantage of their instructor's suggestion to take naps. Reno is among the first to climb into a bunk and is out cold in seconds, and even Rayn and Lania sit against the walls to take light naps.

Shaide lets himself slide down the wall, and before he closes his eyes, he notices a white-haired girl with a halberd watching him with an unreadable expression on her face. She looks away when he notices her, so he shrugs and leans back, closing his eyes.

*   *   *

ETERNAL KNIGHTS OF EDEN I

Two hours later, Shaide's eyes open on their own. He feels much better after that nap, and he climbs to his feet. Just then, Lieutenant Adeline, the young female instructor, hollers out, "Okay, students, wake up! Get to your feet. We have an appointment with the commander to see the operation of the frigate. Come on, everyone up!"

The students who were asleep reluctantly get to their feet, but a few of them do seem to feel better than they did before.

Nikola sighs in mild exasperation, annoyed at his students' slow response. "Everyone on your feet! Form up!"

The sleepy students jump to their feet and form into a single-file line.

Twenty students and their instructor march out of the barracks and through the hallways of the ship. They proceed across the hangar bay to the bow section of the ship and then up a staircase to a modest room with various crew and control stations. The most striking feature of this room is the large domed viewport occupying nearly half the wall, giving an open view of the sky in front of them as well as the ground below.

The commander turns around. "No need to be shy, cadets. You are my guests. Come on up here and take a look."

The students exchange glances and file up to the panoramic viewports at the front of the bridge. For the students who have never traveled outside of the city, this is the experience of a lifetime. Even for those students such as Shaide, who are accustomed to travel, it is still a breathtaking view.

From the position of the sun, Shaide knows they were flying south-east. Looking down from the viewport, they seem to be close to nine thousand feet in the air. Ahead of them, the Heartland Mountains slowly approach, and he notices they are below the top of the ridge. Down below, endless plains, hills, valleys, and rivers stretch out as far as the eye can see, vast expanses of green, dotted here and there by blue and brown. It's truly a sight to behold.

One of the students raises a hand. "Excuse me, Commander. Is it just me, or are we flying into the mountains instead of over them?"

The commander points at her, an impressed look on his face. "Very good. Yes, this frigate is not airtight, so we cannot go above a certain altitude lest we risk suffocation. Instead, we are using the Broadspring Pass to fly straight through the mountains to our destination, which is significantly faster than flying around."

She nods. "I see, sir. Thank you."

Shaide's eyes watch a wyvern, a relative of the dragon family with its forearms attached to its wings, fly across their viewport like it is playing with them. The gunner sitting right behind Shaide whispers, "Don't worry. Wyverns almost never attack warships. They'll harass fighters and dropships, but they know the big ships like us are too dangerous."

Shaide nods, watching it dance in the sky in front of them.

The gunner on the opposite side calls out, "Commander, do you want me to shoot down that wyvern? Show the kids how the guns work?"

The commander shakes his head. "No, while that might be entertaining, that wyvern isn't a threat. Attacking it could just provoke any friends hanging around. No, leave him be for now."

The gunner turns back with a disappointed frown.

After a while, the class returns to the barracks to play cards and word games to pass the time. Lania quietly ribs Shaide about Nyu, but her banter is lighthearted as she and Shaide are actually friends.

Six hours after their initial launch, a crewmember walks into the barracks to speak with Lieutenant Nikola. "Excuse me, sir?"

Nikola looks at him in curiosity "Yes, Sergeant? What can I do for you??"

"Well, sir… The engineering crew has been talking, and we wanted to know if your students were interested in seeing the engineering section of the ship."

Nikola looks around. "Seems like a good idea. Cadets? Let's go and take a look at how these big hunks of metal and wood stay airborne."

All of the students, Shaide included, get to their feet with interest. None of them have ever seen the core room of a long-range airship before.

Reno stands next to Shaide as they start filing out of the barracks. "Have you ever seen the core of a warship before?"

Shaide shakes his head. "No. Even when I was a kid, they kept us away from engineering. It's a very delicate part of the ship. One mage can bring the whole ship down from there. Granted, it would be suicide, but they don't take chances."

The whole class follows the engineer up to near the top of the ship. If Shaide had to guess, they were just over halfway back from the front. The engineer turns a large crank on a heavy steel door and slowly pushes it open. The whole class is stunned by what they see.

The magicore units on this ship are massive and much different than the units on the smaller personal ships. The class files into the room, staying near the front wall, as a handful of engineers monitor the cores.

 A.S.GUINN

ETERNAL KNIGHTS OF EDEN I

The thunder magicore units providing electricity to the ship and its turbines each stand around twelve feet high and are stacked three high, accessible from the ground and two additional catwalks above ground level. Each of the generators consists of two violently rotating rings, one on its vertical axis and the other on its horizontal axis. They are moving at several thousand revolutions per minute. Mounted in the center of these rings are large glowing yellow stones, visibly arcing electricity into the spinning rings. There are dozens of these cores in the engineering bay, but they are not the most impressive part of this room.

In the middle aisle, spanning from the floor to the ceiling, are three spinning cores of a different design. Rather than paired rings, these cores each have three rotating pylons stretching from the base, bowing out halfway up, and then tapering back to the axis at the top of engineering. In the middle of these is an elongated black stone. The space inside the rings appears distorted, and as Shaide's eyes attempt to focus on it, he suspects the stone is the cause of the distortion. A deep subsonic thrumming noise seems to be emanating from these black cores.

The engineer turns to face the class. "Impressive, isn't it? The yellow spinning devices you see, as you have probably guessed, are the ship's electrical magicore generators. The magicore draws on the ambient magical energy present in the air of Eden, and the generators around them siphon that energy into the ship, powering everything from the lights to the engines pushing us forward."

One of the girls raises a hand. "Excuse me, sir? What are those, then?" She points at the giant black cores.

The engineer rubs his hands together. "Those, little miss, are the crowning achievement of Termer, Eritan, and human engineering. Those are gravity magicores. They are the heart of the continental airships. Have you ever wondered how these larger airships stay in the air even when the engines aren't running?"

The cadets look around and exchange nods. They have always just taken it for granted, but in truth, none of them understand how these ships fly.

The engineer continues. "Gravity magicores have a unique effect. The stones inherently distort the effect of gravity on an impressively large scale. Our generators allow us to control those distortions, channeling them through the ship's hull and keeping it aloft even when the turbines aren't running. Our researchers are currently working with dwarven engineers to design propulsion systems that operate via gravity magicore as well, eliminating the need for electrical turbines. We are, however, likely decades away from such a breakthrough because trying to harness gravity fields in multiple directions tends to be…disastrous."

A couple of the more technologically inclined students look in complete awe at the engineer's explanation of their airships, and even the less tech-oriented students show some degree of interest.

The engineer proceeds to walk them through the engineering bay, explaining various features and operational details of the engines, including why only around one-third of the electrical cores are running. As it turns out, the ship cycles through cores to prevent overheating, allowing the ship to fly almost indefinitely. The ship only goes one hundred percent if going into heavy combat.

Finally, the class finishes their lesson about aerial ship operations and makes their way back to the barracks. They are rapidly approaching their destination, so everyone gathers their belongings so they can disembark.

Lieutenant Adeline enters the barracks after being going for some time and calls out, "Does everyone have everything?"

A chorus of voices replies, "Yes, ma'am!"

She nods in satisfaction. "Alright, cadets. File out and head for the hangar bay and stand by. We'll be arriving shortly."

Class One-Echo files out into the corridor and heads to the hangar bay of the ARV *North Star*. As they walk back into the bay, they notice the heavy steel drop doors are currently closed. The spacious room is lit by overhead lights powered by the same system they learned about while in engineering. In truth, they now know that the electrical system of a warship is scarcely different than the power in their own homes.

They still have some time remaining, so the students pair up with their dormmates to begin practicing martial exercises. Shaide pairs up with Reno, and the two begin exchanging blows in sparring fashion, avoiding any actual direct hits. The instructor watches with interest as the class practices, assessing their various strengths and weaknesses.

When it comes to fighting, Shaide and Reno are essentially opposites. Reno is very strong physically. He is a husky young man with a lot of muscle on him, especially for his age. When he hits, he hits hard. His problem is his speed. He is physically slow due to an abundance of extra weight and is at a huge disadvantage against smaller and faster opponents. His biggest strength is his constitution, as he can take a substantial beating.

Shaide is at the other end of the spectrum. Hit for hit, he is scarcely stronger than the average fourteen-year-old, but his speed and precision are nearly inhuman. He is the fastest student in his class by an order of magnitude. His godfather insists that he has the fastest reflexes he has ever seen.

ETERNAL KNIGHTS OF EDEN I

Shaide also has a unique fighting style against human opponents. In sparring matches, he focuses on defending until he sees an opening, and then he tears his opponent apart with well-placed critical hits. Only especially durable opponents can really stand up to him.

Because of this, Shaide and Reno make ideal sparring partners. Neither of them seems able to take the other one down, so they can get in lots of practice.

After a little more than an hour of sparring, everyone is sitting on the hangar bay floor, exhausted. Suddenly they feel their inertia shift forward, and the turbines outside begin screaming as they fire up to full power and forcibly decelerate the ship.

Their instructors each put a hand on the nearby dropship to steady themselves. The hangar bay technician looks at the students with a grin, and he throws four switches. A tremendous metallic groaning and clanking noise fills the hangar bay, and twenty-two sets of eyes are drawn to the large steel drop doors as they rise into the ceiling, revealing a view outside that they could have never imagined.

The entire class climbs to their feet and walks over to the open bay doors, and Shaide gets his first ever view of South Alastair. The sun is setting to the west behind them, and a dim orange glow reaches across the plains in the distance. Endless trees, plains, and hills stretch out to the south, and the orange sun glints off of the surfaces of lakes and ponds there, giving a view that is nothing short of breathtaking.

Down below them, the city of Broadspring is nestled inside of a wide mountain pass, acting as a gateway into the mountains. The large town is well lit, and many villagers seem to be gathered in the town square around a bonfire, having some kind of celebration. The walled-in town seems to have two unique sections, one being the town proper and the other having a distinct military appearance. Out beyond the walls of the town, Shaide can just barely make out what looks like a handful of farms.

As the frigate slows to a stop and the engines dial back, Reno taps Shaide on the shoulder and says to him, "Hey, look over there."

Shaide turns and looks out the starboard hangar doors, and two large warships enter his field of vision. They are both several orders of magnitude larger than the frigate. The smaller of the two ships appears to be a heavy cruiser over six hundred feet long bow to stern. Cruisers are heavily armed and armored capital ships, bristling with magicore cannons and able to carry a respectable contingent of single-craft on board.

The second ship is a mammoth of an airship known as a carrier. It is mostly engine and hangar bays, and it sits at just under a thousand feet long. Its sole purpose is to transport troops and aircraft over large distances, functioning as a mobile base.

Lieutenant Nikola smiles and nods when he sees the awestruck looks on his students' faces. "There is also a heavy destroyer out in front of us, though you can't really see it right now. We keep a heavy presence at the Broadspring pass."

Destroyers are the enforcers of the Royal Navy. They are designed for a single purpose: destruction. Destroyers only carry a few dropships, and other than that, they are designed entirely around ship-to-ship and ship-to-ground combat. They are barely larger than a frigate, but they are superior in every way. They are faster, more heavily armored, and carry over ten times the firepower of their frigate counterparts. Their only disadvantage is cost. A single light destroyer costs as much as five or six heavy frigates, and they can't respond on such short notice as their lighter brethren.

The presence of a small heavy combat fleet here is a little unnerving. The students look around uneasily at the amount of military force concentrated out here, seemingly in the middle of nowhere.

The instructor picks up on their unease. "Broadspring is basically the gateway to the northern half of Alastair. The mountains stretch nearly all the way across the nation, and the pass we followed to get here is one of the few easily accessible passes through the mountains. We keep a sizable military force here to repel the corrupted and prevent as many of them as possible from crossing into the north."

"So," says Shaide, "since we are training as exorcists, you want us to see firsthand what our future will be like so we will be better prepared when the day comes?"

Nikola points at him. "Very good. As expected from a Ceraph's kid. Speaking of which, we may also meet with the Ceraph detachment currently stationed here. Ceraphs aren't part of the Alastair military, as you all know, but down here, we tend to work very closely with them."

Shaide frowns and thinks for a moment. Now that he considers it, he is pretty sure his uncle Aton is working in this region right now.

The commander walks back into the hangar bay, this time by himself. He holds out a hand to the Nikola, who shakes the commander's hand with a surprised look on his face. "No need to look so uptight, Lieutenant. You teach these kids as much as you can and worry about the formalities some other time."

Nikola nods. "Yes, sir." Behind them, the pilots have gotten back into their dropships and are warming up the engines. Nikola turns to the students. "Okay. Climb back on board your dropships and get ready to go down into the village. I'll see you down below."

Rayn looks around and hollers, "Alright, you heard him. Let's go!" He stands back as Shaide, Reno, Bryon, Joslin, and Lania all board their dropship and sit down, buckling in this time since they are descending. Rayn gets in last and sits by the door.

The turbines spin up, and a moment later, they fly out of the hangar bay. Shaide enjoys the feeling of vertigo for a moment as gravity shifts from liftoff to descent. Their drop down to the village seems like it will be the least eventful part of their day.

Suddenly the pilot yells, "Oh shit! EVERYONE HANG ON!" The dropship veers violently off to one side. "DAMN WYVERN! WHERE DID IT COME FROM!"

Something slams hard into the side of the dropship, crunching the metal. Everyone grabs onto each other, and loud screams echo in the troop bay as they feel the dropship lurch violently to one side. Then it starts violently spinning through the air.

"Mayday, ARV *North Star*, this is dropship *D346*. We've been hit by airborne bogey and are going down. I have lost all controls. Do you copy?"

The lights flicker and flash as the engines scream in full overload, and the dropship bucks around violently as the pilot struggles to maintain control. A loud warning siren blasts through the cockpit as the pilot screams expletives while struggling with the crippled vehicle.

Reno grabs onto Shaide and holds tightly onto a cargo loop, his eyes closed as he tries to brace for what he knows is coming.

The pilot yells back, "EVERYONE HOLD ON! I'M TRYING TO BRING HER IN A SOFT AS I CAN! HOLD ON! EVERYBODY JUST HOLD—"

The whole world explodes into debris and bodies flying across the compartment as the dropship suddenly slams into the ground at over one hundred miles per hour and snaps several of the students out of their harnesses. Somebody, Shaide doesn't know who, lands on his lap, and he grabs them tightly to stop them from flying around the troop bay.

The dropship seems to be skidding along the ground at high speed. Suddenly Shaide feels it buck as something sends it into the air again. This is followed by a jarring crash as it slams into the ground once more.

Shaide holds tightly onto whoever is on top of him, and he feels Reno's vice-like grip on his arm.

ETERNAL KNIGHTS OF EDEN I

The dropship hits something once more, and Shaide is ripped out of his harness and slammed into the wall of the ship. The world fades into darkness…

CHAPTER 4

SHIPWRECKED

An hour later, the dropship sits on the ground at the end of a long trail in the mud. Smoke rises from the crippled wreck as pieces lie all over the valley. The dropship seems to have crashed a great distance from its parent vessel.

Shaide wakes up, and the first thing he notices is a throbbing pain in the back of his head. He reaches up and gingerly feels the source of the pain, and then he pulls his hand away to see something red, wet, and sticky on his palm. He groans and tries to focus his eyes, and also to remember what happened.

He feels pressure on his lap, and he looks down. In the dark, he sees Lania unconscious and lying up against him, his arm tight around her. He blinks in confusion for a moment, still disoriented from the crash.

With a start, everything that happened comes flooding back to him. He tosses aside his shredded harness and struggles to his feet. He checks Lania's pulse and breathes a sigh of relief. She has a strong heartbeat, so she is just unconscious. He looks to the back of the ship and sees that the rear hatch has been ripped clean off. All he sees are trees.

He turns around and sees Reno lying on the opposite side of the dropship, slumped against one of the jump seats. He doesn't appear to be moving. Shaide hesitantly checks him for a pulse.

*Thump*Thump*Thump*

Shaide breathes a second sigh of relief; his friend is alive.

He carefully drags Reno out of the crashed ship and lays him on his back just outside. He repeats this with Lania, laying her on the ground next to Reno. Shaide looks around nervously, noting that they seem to be in some kind of valley surrounded by trees. The dropship evidently spun around when it crashed, because the long gouge in the ground stretches away from its front.

He limps back into the dropship and checks Bryon. He feels for a pulse but, unfortunately, finds none. He isn't breathing, and his skin is cool and clammy. He's dead. Shaide shakes his head, drags him out of the dropship, and lays him out of the way.

He re-enters the ship and finds Joslin lying at an awkward angle. He reaches to check for a pulse, but then he pauses, realizing Joslin's neck is broken. There's nothing he can do for him, and he takes him out and lays him next to Bryon.

He returns to check on Rayn, but as he reaches for a pulse, Rayn starts groaning and opens his eyes.

Shaide claps him on the shoulder. "Thank Eden you're alive. Can you hear me?"

Rayn nods groggily. "Yeah, I'm okay. Give me a minute."

Shaide gingerly checks on the pilot, but he soon sees this isn't necessary. The crash tore the pilot out of his straps and sent him through the windshield. The unsightly mess makes it pretty clear that the pilot did not survive the crash. Shaide closes his eyes, silently mourning the man who tried his best right up until the end.

He opens his eyes and turns around. Rayn is struggling with his harness, so Shaide cuts it off of him and leans down to let Rayn use him for support. The two limp outside of the dropship, and Shaide eases Rayn to the ground.

Rayn looks at everyone lying unconscious or dead on the ground, and then nervously asks Shaide, "Are we the only ones who made it?"

Shaide shakes his head. "No. Reno and Lania are alive but unconscious. Bryon, Joslin, and the pilot didn't make it."

Rayn looks at Bryon and Joslin's bodies and lowers his head. "Oh. I see…"

"What should we do?"

Rayn looks at the crashed ship, where their pilot's body lies. "Well…normally, I would say follow the pilot. They're trained for surviving after a crash. But given present circumstances…"

Shaide nods and looks around. On top of everything else, he feels like they are being watched for some reason. Nothing concrete, just a feeling.

Rayn looks up at the sky, dried blood visible on his face. "I say our best chance is to stay with the dropship and wait for search and rescue to arrive. What brought us down, anyway?"

Shaide kneels and lowers his voice. "The pilot yelled something about a wyvern right after we were hit. My guess is that we collided with something."

Rayn shudders. "I hope help comes fast. This area is really dangerous."

"Do we even know where 'this area' is?"

Rayn opens his mouth, but then he closes it again and just shakes his head.

Shaide looks around again. He can't quite shake the feeling that they are being watched. He peers into the trees, but in the darkness, he cannot see a thing. He pulls out his daggers and checks them over. Thankfully, they are still intact, so if anything does happen, he should be able to fight.

He reluctantly checks Bryon and Joslin's remains and relieves them of their survival supplies. After a second thought, he also takes Bryon's short sword and Joslin's mace. They won't be needing them anymore.

Shaide walks over to Rayn and sits down, putting his back against his class leader's so they can keep a better watch on their surroundings.

They sit there in silence for some time, still in shock from the crash and unable to gather their thoughts. *We're fourteen years old!* thinks Shaide. *We were never prepared for this type of situation. Then again, who would have ever expected this something like this to occur on a simple educational trip?*

Reno stirs, and then he slowly sits up, hand on his head. He says rather loudly, "Oh, hell… What ha—"

Shaide cuts him off with an urgent, "Shhhhhh…"

Reno lowers his voice, looking around as his eyes start to focus. "What happened, dude?"

Shaide whispers, "Dropship crashed. Bryon, Joslin, and our pilot are all dead. You, Rayn, and Lania survived."

Reno catches sight of the two bodies and lowers his head. "Damnit… Rest in peace, buddies."

Rayn whispers over his shoulder, "Reno, are you hurt?"

Reno rubs his head gingerly and slowly climbs to his feet, testing out his knees and shoulders. Satisfied, he responds quietly, "No, I'm sore, but I seem to be okay."

Rayn nods and gently elbows Shaide. "Good. You may be in better shape than we are, then."

Shaide freezes stiff, seeing movement behind Reno. His hands tighten on his daggers as he watches a pair of golden eyes fixated on Reno's back. He slowly eases his leg underneath him as he prepares to move.

Reno catches sight of him and asks curiously, "Shaide? What's wrong?"

Shaide just stares past him and mutters in a flat voice, "Don't move."

The shadow behind Reno suddenly darts forward, and Shaide launches forward at the same time. Reno's eyes open wide as Shaide and the beast collide in mid-jump. Shaide grunts with exertion, and the beast snarls and seems to bark as he sinks his daggers into its side. The beast survives the hit and seems to struggle, and Shaide pulls out one of the daggers, stabbing it rapidly several more times.

The beast howls loudly and whines, its breathing gurgling before coming to a stop.

Rayn is on one knee now, facing Shaide with his single-edged short sword in his hands. Reno had started to turn around, but now he is frozen in shock. All three of them turn their gaze upon the dead creature under Shaide.

At first glance, the creature appears to be some kind of wolf. Its structure looks distinctly dog-like, and it is covered in green and brown striped fur. Closer inspection reveals that's where the similarities end.

Its claws are long and blade-like, longer than the paws themselves. The tail is forked, and it has some kind of short spines all down its back. The eyes are bright yellow, with slits for pupils, and its teeth… The teeth are not that of a canine. It has a mouth full of pointed needle-sharp teeth, clearly suited for one thing.

The beast likely weighs seven hundred to eight hundred pounds….

Rayn limps over and looks down in astonishment. Reno looks at the two of them and asks, "Okay. What in the hell is that thing?"

Rayn mutters unpleasantly, "Mountain lobo. That's not good. These things are pack hunters. Keep your eyes open."

Rayn and Shaide move back to back again, staying on their feet this time. Reno puts his hands into his weapon pouches and slides his gauntlets on.

They stand in silence for a few minutes, subconsciously moving to surround their unconscious classmate and watch their surroundings carefully. The feeling of being watched is maddening, and they can all hear subtle sounds of movement in the trees around them.

Suddenly, all around them, creatures begin howling loudly. No fewer than six pairs of glowing yellow eyes appear in the darkness and race towards them.

Rayn yells, "Oh, I was not ready for THIS today. Protect Lania!" He sidesteps and slashes a deep cut in the side of the first lobo as it leaps at him, causing it to slide past Shaide, who promptly slams his daggers into its side. He stands up just in time to react to the second charging lobo. He lashes out with a straight kick to its nose and then aggressively slashes its face no less than eight times, causing it to step back in pain. Reno slams his gauntlet fists together and then punches the lobo in the head, knocking its head sideways and allowing Shaide to finish it off with a dual upward slash.

The other four lobos charge in now, and Reno is first on the menu. The lead lobo leaps through the air at him, but he immediately punches straight down, catching it on the snout and knocking it to the ground. With his metal gauntlets, he proceeds to lash out with several violent hits to the lobo's face, knocking it around and sending it backward and to the ground, where it lies unmoving.

The third and fourth of the six dash in an arcing circle, turning towards Rayn at the last minute. Rayn times his move carefully, and then thrusts his sword straight out in front of the front lobo, making it shish-kebob itself on the blade.

The second lobo of the two turns on Shaide and catches him by surprise. He tries to move out of the way, but a set of razor-sharp claws digs deep into his calf, making him yelp as a jolt of pain shoots up his leg.

The lobo itself sails past its intended target and hits the dropship hull head first. It shakes its head, whining, and turns around in time for Reno to punch it hard in the nose. He either knocks it unconscious or kills it instantly.

Behind Reno, the fifth of the six lobos leaps at him while he is distracted. Rayn sees it just in time and leaps at the lobo, missing his cut but tackling it hard enough to make it miss Reno. Shaide grits his teeth and turns around, sinking his daggers into its side repeatedly, more than was likely required.

The last lobo slides to a stop, looking far less certain now about their choice of prey. It backs away and begins to turn and run, but Shaide roars in anger and hurls his daggers at it. Apparently, either one or both of his daggers finds a vital spot, and the lobo hits the ground, dead.

Silence reaches their ears, and the three boys exchange glances, smiling slightly. This is the first true combat experience they've ever had, and they share some pride in their victory.

Suddenly the pain shoots through Shaide's leg again, and he yelps. He drops as his injured leg gives out beneath him.

Reno turns and catches him. "Whoa, Shaide, are you okay?" He eases Shaide onto the ground.

Shaide shakes his head. "That one got me pretty good. I don't think I can walk."

Rayn kneels down and takes a look at Shaide's injured leg. There are three deep slashes in his right calf, and it looks like the lobo's claws cut all the way into the muscle underneath. An alarming amount of blood flows from the wounds.

"Hey," Rayn says to Reno, "get the first aid kit from the dropship. It's in a heavy steel box. It should be okay,"

Reno nods, staring at the wound for a minute. Then he climbs back into the wrecked ship and digs around, looking for the little red box. He carefully averts his eyes from the pilot's body.

Rayn elevates Shaide's leg and sighs. "Damn, dude. You WERE the fastest one here. Lania's been studying healing magic, but she is still out cold. I don't know if she could even heal this or not. For sure, it would take some time."

Shaide groans as his wound throbs. "At least she is okay. Or at least, alive. Thank Eden for small miracles. It's amazing ANY of us survived that crash."

Reno exits the dropship with a badly dented medical kit and hands it to Rayn.

Rayn pries it open and frowns. "This is probably going to hurt like hell, but it's the best I can do for you."

Shaide closes his eyes and grits his teeth, nodding at Rayn.

Rayn dabs some herbal antiseptic ointment on Shaide's wounded leg. Shaide roars through his clenched teeth as the ointment burns and goes about sanitizing the wound. After around a minute, the ointment finishes burning and hardens into a gel-like substance, sealing the wound. Shaide's groaning eases, and he breathes heavily.

Rayn takes some sterile bandage out of the kit and tightly but carefully wraps Shaide's wounded leg, protecting it from infection and giving it some support. Once he finishes, he looks him in the face. "You okay?"

Shaide nods, his eyes watering from the pain. "Thank Eden you paid attention in that class. But still, I know that herbal ointment is essential, but mother of hell, it burns worse than the cuts themselves!"

Rayn gives him an exasperated look. "Do you want to keep your leg? Then don't complain."

Shaide manages a weak chuckle.

Reno, who spent the whole time cringing while Rayn treated Shaide, finally says in a lowered voice, "Hey, Shaide, can you walk?"

Shaide shrugs. "I'd rather not try just yet. Do me a favor and check on Lania."

Reno turns and checks her pulse and breathing. He looks over his shoulder at Rayn and Shaide. "She seems to be okay, just knocked out like I was. So, again, CAN you walk?"

Shaide looks at Reno with narrowed eyes, but Rayn seems to catch on. He says to Shaide, "He's right. I don't think we can stay here."

Shaide looks up at Rayn for a moment, but the confusion on his face gives way to understanding. "The bodies."

"Yeah," says Reno. "The smell of that fresh meat and blood is going to bring a lot of unwelcome attention. We need to move somewhere. Anywhere but here."

Shaide nods and slowly eases himself to his feet. His leg is in a great deal of pain, but it is somehow able to support his weight if he is careful not to lean on it. He tests it out a little, but he ends up shaking his head as he gasps in pain. "I won't be able to move very fast."

Reno frowns and spots a low-hanging tree branch nearby. He walks over to it and, with all his strength, snaps it from the tree with an unpleasantly loud sound.

"I get it," says Rayn. "Let me see that, Reno."

Reno hands it over, and Rayn uses his sword to cut it to an appropriate length and take the extra twigs off of it. He hands it to Shaide. "Here. This should help you walk a little."

Shaide sheathes his daggers and sets the top of the branch under his shoulder. He finds an offshoot partway down that is conveniently about where his hand sits. He leans on it like a crutch and limps in a circle for a moment. Once he decides it will work, he looks up at Reno and Rayn. "Thanks, guys. What do we do about Lania, though?"

Reno squats down and gently picks her up, cradling her in front of him. "I'll carry her. At least until she wakes up."

Rayn frowns. "Any idea which way we should go?"

Shaide looks around. "Hell, until sun up, we won't even know which direction we are headed."

"Damn," says Rayn, shaking his head. "Well, my best guess is that we need to move uphill. The higher we can get, the farther we can see. Maybe we'll be able to spot any attempted rescue and signal for help. Or at least find a cave to take shelter in."

Reno frowns and looks uphill, but he doesn't disagree. "This is gonna suck…"

Shaide looks at him in amusement. "Reno. This already sucks."

Reno laughs nervously.

"Okay," says Rayn, "do we have everything we can salvage from the dropship? Once we leave, there's no guarantee we can come back for anything."

Shaide and Reno nod in response.

"Alright, guys. Let's move out."

*   *   *

Immediately after launching the dropships, an unexpected wave of corrupted wyverns seemed to appear out of nowhere and attack Broadspring and the airships parked above it. The aerial fleet immediately launched a counterattack against the attackers, and in combination with the troops on the ground, they managed to eliminate or drive off all of the attackers.

Lieutenant Nikola, however, is pacing around on the ground in front of the two dropships that landed. In all of the confusion with the wyvern attack, one of the dropships full of trainees is missing, and he is feeling very concerned. They heard a very broken radio transmission just after the launch from the ARV *North Star*, but no one actually saw what happened to their third dropship.

It has now been over an hour since the dropship went missing, and all four capital vessels have since launched all operational gunships and dropships to conduct search and rescue operations, and they are now attempting to locate the missing ship. Unfortunately, they have no idea where to begin searching, so they are just running a slowly expanding grid.

The students were escorted to the inn by Nikola's junior instructor, so he is with the two pilots who are waiting for instructions at the moment. One of them walks out of his cockpit and looks at Nikola. "Sir? Commander Winslow is ordering us to join in the search and rescue operation. We have to go. I'm sorry."

"I'm coming with you," says Nikola. "These are my students. I'm not leaving them out there and doing nothing."

The pilot nods. "I won't decline the company, sir."

ETERNAL KNIGHTS OF EDEN I

Both men walk back on board the dropship and take their seats. A moment later, both dropships' turbines spin up, and the vessels launch into the air.

After a quick stop in the hangar bay of the *North Star* to pick up additional search personnel, the two dropships head north into the mountains to help with the more difficult search up there.

As they head towards the mountains, Nikola notes the fast-moving storms rolling over them from the north. Time isn't on their side.

*   *   *

Nearly four hours have passed since the dropship crashed. The four survivors are slowly trying to make their way to higher ground and hopefully find some shelter. Dark clouds are moving in and obscuring the stars, and the temperature is starting to drop. The boys are beginning to fear a storm may be moving in.

Shaide limps along with the help of his crutch, Reno carries their unconscious classmate Lania, and Rayn takes the point position with his weapon out in case of wildlife attack. Their progress is slow, but they are gradually making their way to higher ground. They're currently walking along a rocky path with a moderate incline.

They follow this winding trail for another two hours, slowly climbing higher and higher. Six hours after the initial crash, Shaide leans against the stone wall, panting heavily. He waves at Rayn. "Hey… I need… I need to rest. This isn't easy."

Rayn and Reno decide to rest with him. Reno gently sets Lania against the wall and sits down "Yeah, I'm with you. Lania isn't heavy, but I've been carrying her a while."

Rayn leans against the wall as well. "We need to find shelter soon. We've been up all night. It's got to be sunrise soon."

Just as he says this, lightning arcs across the sky, and a rumble echoes through the mountains.

Rayn immediately closes his eyes and looks down. "Damnit…"

Shaide gets back on his crutch. "So much for that. Come on, we have to move. We don't want to be caught out in the cold rain up here."

Reno pouts and looks at Lania, whom he has just set down. He narrows his eyes and looks at Shaide. "Hey, don't call Rayn cold."

Shaide gives him an "I'm not amused" look, and Reno looks down in shame. He picks up Lania again and turns up the path. "Come on, Rayn. We should go."

Rayn sighs, and just a moment later, the three boys are climbing the mountain once again. They walk for another twenty minutes, and then the lightning becomes more frequent, and raindrops start coming down. All three boys look up at the sky with sour expressions, but they continue to climb the increasingly steep path as the storm intensifies.

Finally, they round a corner and see a large crevice in the wall of the mountain. Rayn runs on ahead of the other two and looks inside. He is grateful to see that it is a mildly spacious cave, at least large enough for them to rest comfortably.

The rapidly intensifying rain and wind makes it difficult to hear, so he yells, "Hey! Hurry and come in here! We can take shelter!"

A soaked Shaide and Reno exchange glances and hurry along the path as fast as they can. Less than a minute later, they are limping into a small cavern that seems to wind into the mountain itself. Shaide breathes a sigh of relief as he gets out of the rain, and he walks over to sit down against the wall and catch his breath.

Reno gently sets a soaked Lania against the wall and sits down himself, exhausted from carrying her for the past several hours.

Rayn walks around, gathering the mess of dry leaves and twigs that litter the ground near the entrance, and then he places them in a pile in the center of the cave. He squats next to the pile and holds out his palm.

A glowing red circle envelops his hand for a split second, and then his fire magic ignites the kindling.

Reno looks at the small fire with a smile. "Yes… Heat…"

Just after Rayn lights the fire, Lania stirs. She rubs her head and looks around the cave in confusion. She spots Rayn, Reno, and then Shaide, and she blinks her eyes several times, trying to focus. The first thing she says is: "What happened? And why am I all wet?"

Rayn frowns. "Lania? First thing, I need you to stay calm. Our dropship crashed in the mountains, and we are stranded."

Lania looks around in confusion. "Where are Bryon and Joslin? And the pilot?"

"They didn't make it."

Lania looks down. "Oh…"

"We were attacked by mountain lobos at the crash site, and we were forced to leave it and find somewhere safer, so we proceeded up into the mountains to find shelter and a vantage point. Reno carried you the whole way. It started raining some time ago, and that's why we're all wet. Any questions?"

Lania just looks at him. blinking several times. "I, uhh… Not yet."

Rayn nods. "Okay. Everyone take off as much of your wet clothing as you can and lay them next to the fire. I don't know how long it will last, so try and dry them out while you can. We don't want anyone getting hypothermia."

Everyone rather uncomfortably strips down to their undergarments and lays their uniforms next to the fire before gathering around it themselves to warm up. Before long, Reno lies back on the ground and drifts off to sleep, exhausted from the night's events.

Rayn says to Shaide, "We'd better catch some sleep too while we can."

Shaide nods.

Lania sets her single dagger on her lap. "I'll keep watch. I've been out the whole time. It's the least I can do."

Rayn looks at her with concern. "You're not freaked out by all of this?"

"Of course I'm freaked out! I'm still trying to come to terms with 'stranded in a mountain cave.' But it won't do any good to panic. So, I'm fine."

Rayn recoils a little at her attitude. He wasn't expecting her to handle this so well. He coughs. "Umm…okay. I'll leave it to you."

She nods and turns her back to the fire, watching the cavern entrance.

Rayn and Shaide exchange glances and shake their heads a little before lying on their backs and drifting off to sleep.

Lania watches them in amusement for a moment, and then she frowns at the small campfire. The tinder won't last for very long, and then it will be cold again. She also makes note of the passageway that seems to take the cavern deeper into the mountain. She comes to a decision and stands up, heading out of the cave.

*   *   *

Shaide ends up sleeping for nearly four hours. He's awakened by a familiar nightmare he was having involving the altar and that strange cavern.

He keeps his eyes closed for a minute, still hearing the sound of rain echoing through the cave. He also notices it seems fairly warm. He opens his eyes and sees a surprising amount of light, so he sits up.

The first thing he notices is their campfire is bigger than before. It has a proper base of wood now, and their field uniforms are lying over some logs next to the fire. Shaide notices Lania sitting next to the fire, her undergarments still fairly wet.

He frowns and says in a low voice, "Hey, what happened to the fire?"

Lania replies quietly, "I knew it wouldn't last long, so I went out and gathered as much wood as I could. There are trees all along the mountain path and plenty of fallen branches and logs, so I brought some of them back."

Shaide frowns. "But they'd all be wet."

Lania shakes her head. "As long as the fire is going already, it dries them out. They also burn longer, although admittedly not as hot."

Shaide grins slightly. "Look at you, miss survivalist."

"My family used to go camping when I was younger. I learned all kinds of skills from that."

"Well, count me impressed."

"By the way," she says, "what happened to your leg? I didn't want to mess with it without knowing what happened."

Shaide sighs. "Well, when the lobos attacked, one of them got me in the leg. It was pretty deep. Rayn packed it off with that herbal ointment and bandaged it up."

Lania picks up the medical kit next to Rayn's clothes and crawls over to Shaide "That was hours ago. We need to check that wound."

Shaide groans. "Oh, this is gonna suck."

Lania slowly unwraps the bandages around Shaide's leg. The gelled-up ointment did a good job of sealing off the bleeding, but the bandages are still soaked with a fair amount of blood. Shaide draws a hissing breath in pain as she peels the last layer off and checks the wound.

She makes a face. "Well, Rayn knows what he's doing. It's sealed properly. Still, that's worse than I was expecting."

Shaide leans forward and shivers as he sees his wounded leg and the translucent green gel packed into the cuts. "That looks bad…"

Lania shakes her head. "I don't think I can heal it completely, but I might be able to make it a little better. I've been mostly studying healing magic."

Shaide nods, his leg throbbing substantially. "Do it."

Lania holds her palms out over Shaide's leg, and her hands glow with a green light. At the same time, Shaide's claw wounds start to glow with the same green light. He feels an intense tingling sensation in his leg as his wound starts to slowly knit itself back together. His leg twitches, and he watches in amazement as the flesh closes over the wound. The tingling sensation subsides, and the green light fades from his leg.

Lania focuses and tries to apply more magic, but his wound won't respond anymore. Finally, she gives up, breathing surprisingly hard. She frowns. "I couldn't heal your damaged muscle. I guess it's still beyond my skill to heal anything beyond surface wounds, but that should stop the bleeding and prevent infection, at least."

"Hey, don't look so down. You did your best. Thank you."

She nods and looks a little happier. "How does it feel?"

Shaide eases himself to his feet. His right leg still doesn't want to support his weight, and the muscle underneath still feels incredibly sore, but he can at least move it unsupported now. The flesh where she healed him is still red and raw looking, but it has closed over the wound, so he is out of the woods now.

She notes him flinching in pain. "Come on. Let's bandage it up to make sure it stays clean."

Shaide nods and sits down, allowing her to apply the antiseptic ointment over his leg and bandage it up again, tightly enough to support his injured calf muscle. She pats his leg. "Okay, you're good to go."

Shaide bends his leg a couple of times and nods "Thank you again."

"No problem. Really."

Rayn makes a sound and slowly sits up and looks around. He says groggily, "Hey, the fire is bigger."

Lania raises her hand. "You're welcome."

Rayn nods and rubs his eyes. "How long did I sleep?"

"I'd guess about four hours or so."

Rayn looks at the opening. It is still raining heavily, and only the slightest touch of sunlight shines through the storm clouds. "Well, crap. It's still storming. That's just dandy."

"What should we do now?" asks Shaide.

"We can't do much until the storm stops," Rayn replies, frowning.

Shaide sighs. "Yeah, you're probably right. We'll all get hypothermia and die in this weather."

"Yeah," says Lania, "our clothes are finally drying out. Defeats the purpose if we go outside, and even then...where would we go?"

They exchange glances and fall into silence. Lania pulls a deck of cards out of one of her pouches. "Anyone want to pass the time?"

Rayn frowns. "Aren't we a bit young to gamble?

"Spoilsport. No gambling. Just to pass time."

"I'm in," says Shaide.

The three play cards together in the cave for the next couple of hours. About the time they get bored and Lania puts her cards away, Reno stirs from his sleep and sits up, looking at the three of them in surprise.

Poking fun at him, Shaide says, "I was sure you would sleep for at least several more hours. Welcome back."

Reno waves halfheartedly.

Shaide looks at Rayn. "Well, now that everyone is awake, what do we do?"

Rayn stands, walks to the mouth of the cave, and looks out at the stormy sky. He turns back and sighs. "I don't think this storm is letting up anytime soon, but I also don't think we can just stay here. They'll never find us in a cave."

"Airships don't do well in inclement weather," says Shaide, "especially not single-ships. They won't even be able to look for us until the weather clears up."

"Yeah, you're right. We also need to get up somewhere high and flat so we can make a signal fire. We make a big enough signal fire at night, and they won't be able to miss us."

"So, you think we need to keep going up?"

Rayn nods, and without further explanation, he walks to the passageway at the back of the cave. He holds out his hand, and a glowing light emanates from his palm, lighting up the passageway ahead of him.

He nods with satisfaction and turns around. "The passageway seems to go up. Most mountain caves were formed by running water, I think, which means this passageway must come out somewhere. If we follow it, we might find higher ground."

Shaide and Lania exchange glances. "Is it a good idea for us to keep moving when we have no idea where we are going? It also seems like we would be taking a big chance, going through a cave when we have no idea where it leads."

Rayn crosses his arms and looks at them. "Do any of you have any better ideas?"

Two blank faces and one sleepy face just look at him.

"I didn't think so. Come on, we better get moving."

Reno pouts and points, saying, "But…fire…"

Rayn rolls his eyes. "We can make another fire. If we just sit here, we're dead."

Without any better plan, the four put their now dry and warm field uniforms and gear back on, and Shaide props himself up on his walking stick. His leg is in much better shape since Lania took her healing magic to him, but it is still injured, and he wants to keep the stress off of it.

Rayn tightens down his last strap. "Are we all ready?"

A series of unenthusiastic affirmations come back to him.

He nods. "Okay, let's go."

The party sets off down the passageway as Rayn casts illumination magic to light up the passageway in front of them.

ETERNAL KNIGHTS OF EDEN I

*　　　*　　　*

Sixteen hours after the initial crash, the thunderstorm finally moves out, allowing the search to resume. The Ceraph Order frigate COV *Light of Eden* has ceased its operations further south to join search and rescue attempts with the Alastair Navy.

A very annoyed quartet of Ceraphs is meeting with Lieutenant Nikola, Commander Winslow, and Captain Rockwell of the Alastair forces.

Atondier Norvus has one hand on the staff table onboard the Alastair cruiser and the other hand over his face. He says in a half-muffled voice, "You're telling me that you lost an entire dropship full of ARMA students and you have absolutely no idea what happened to it?"

Commander Winslow nods, slightly intimidated by the four Ceraphs in the room. "Yes. We were attacked by a flock of wyvern when we launched the dropships, and in the ensuing chaos, one of them went missing."

Aton looks at him in frustration. "How did you get to be a commander in the Alastair Navy if you can't even track a damn flock of... Never mind. Who was on board?"

Lieutenant Nikola answers nervously, "One pilot, Ensign Jenkins, and six students. Reno Coltide, Rayn Jarvis, Bryon Atlas, Shaide Darkmoon, Lania—"

Aton suddenly strides around the table, grabs Lieutenant Nikola by the collar, and picks him up, slamming him against the wall.

Everyone in the room takes a step back except one. The lone female Ceraph in their squad, a woman in her thirties named Lucy, steps forward. "Aton, take it easy."

Aton stares Lieutenant Nikola in the eyes, an angry look in his own. "Did you say Shaide Darkmoon was one of the missing students?"

The lieutenant nods frantically.

Aton lets go of his collar and turns around. "So, my godson is missing." He looks over his shoulder at Lieutenant Nikola and says in a dangerous voice, "You don't go home alive until Shaide does." He walks out of the staff room to cool off.

Captain Rockwell, who has been quiet up until now, finally speaks up. "So, that was interesting. Can someone fill me in on that little detail?" He looks expectantly at the remaining three Ceraphs.

Lucy looks up at him, mildly exasperated. "Shaide Darkmoon is the son of one of our Ceraphs who passed away a few years ago. She and Aton were very close, so much so that he was appointed Shaide's godfather. Aton was raising Shaide like he were his own son until a few months ago, when Shaide began attending the Alastair Royal Military Academy to become an Exorcist. So, basically, Aton is pissed that his godson is missing."

The captain nods. "I see. Now, that being said, do you personally believe the missing students are alive?"

Lucy shrugs. "It's hard to say without knowing where they crashed. This region is extremely dangerous, as you know. ARMA kids are tough. though, so as long as they survived the crash, they COULD be alive. Shaide especially."

Lieutenant Nikola coughs, rubbing his throat slightly. "The six students on board that dropship are some of my best. If anyone can survive out there, they can."

"Very well," replies the captain. "If you believe there is a chance they survived, then we will devote all of our resources to the search. Commander Winslow, give the order. We will send out all available craft once again to begin searching the region, starting from the village and working our way out.

Commander Winslow salutes across his chest. "Yes, sir."

*   *   *

Several hours later, the four teenagers are deep in the winding passageways inside the mountain. Rayn's assessment appears to have been correct: the slope of the passage has been constantly going up. Occasionally they would find an offshoot that went back down, but Rayn reasoned that as long as they went up, they would eventually find an exit because the water that formed these caves flows down, meaning it had to come from an opening somewhere upstream. Logically, that meant that it couldn't dead end.

Shaide limps along in front of Reno, who is staying at the back to make sure Shaide doesn't fall behind from his injury. Shaide looks at his class leader with concern. Rayn has always been the leader type, but he is also slightly prideful to a fault. He has difficulty admitting when he is wrong, and sometimes it can be difficult to tell if he is following his instincts or is just too stubborn to admit he may be wrong.

Suddenly the passageway begins to smooth out, and they reach a section of rock that has crumbled away.

Rayn looks behind him and shrugs, trying to shine the light further down the passageway. What he sees surprises them all.

This section of cavern looks newer than the rest of the caves. It also looks almost as if it was deliberately made. The ground is much flatter and smoother here, not at all like it was formed by millennia of erosion. The passageway also looks substantially straighter than the caves they have been in, with the rocky ceiling and walls being a mostly uniform height and width.

"What do you guys think?" Rayn asks with a shrug.

Lania looks past Rayn at the curious passageway. "Well, it certainly seems as if we've found…something. We've already come this far, so why not?"

Shaide and Reno both freeze and listen closely.

A strange clicking, rustling sound echoes up the passageway. Rayn looks back and asks, "What's wrong, you two?"

Reno slowly turns around to look behind him, and Rayn's light shines down the passageway.

Eight glittering eyes are crawling towards Reno, and multiple hairy legs are attached to the ceiling.

He yells in shock and punches the apparition twice in the face, causing it to fall from the ceiling. Its legs twitch in the air as it lets out a terrifying screech that echoes through the passageway. Reno roars again and double-hammer blows the wriggling monster in the head, killing it.

Shaide grits his teeth. "Decantulas…"

It's quiet for a moment. The four companions exchange glances as they listen carefully.

The sound of skittering legs echoes up the passageway towards them, growing louder and louder.

Rayn points further up the passageway. "MOVE IT!"

The party of four climbs over the collapsed rock and hauls off up the passageway as fast as they can manage.

CHAPTER 5

IN THE HALL OF THE MOUNTAIN KING

The four survivors of the crash run along a strangely smooth passageway inside of the mountain, trying to flee from the sound of skittering giant arachnids chasing them through the caves.

Shaide's injured leg is slowing them down, but he tries his hardest to push through the pain. Fear and adrenaline work wonders.

Reno suddenly skids to a stop and turns around, punching full force at a decantula right behind him. The blow collides with the giant spider charging at a terrifying speed and knocks it from the ceiling and onto its back. Reno backs away and runs to catch up to the others. The pursuing creatures pile up for a moment as they struggle to skitter past their fellow.

Rayn looks up. "What the hell? Is that light up ahead?"

Lania grabs Shaide by the hand as Reno catches up. "Come on! Let's move! We can fight these things easier in the open!" She hurls a fireball back at their pursuers, and their screeches echo back up the passageway.

Shaide groans in pain as he sprints up the passageway. Sure enough, there is a literal light at the end of the tunnel. Rayn, Lania, Shaide, and Reno burst out of the passageway…

They are momentarily stunned to see sunlight. They are still inside of a cave, but the chamber they are in is massive, easily a half mile across, and above them is open sky. The chamber has no roof. Instead, the walls curve inward, and there is a massive circular opening in the center.

All four jump to either side of the opening. As Reno runs out, Rayn thrusts with his sword and impales the massive spider behind him.

Shaide pulls out his two daggers and slashes viciously at the next decantula to crawl out of the hole. Lania rapidly thrusts her own dagger at the third, but a fourth manages to slip by them. It leaps through the air at Reno, who immediately ducks and swings straight up, punching a hole in its abdomen as a disgusting slime covers his gauntlet.

Several more decantulas skitter out of the hole and spread out. Rayn yells, "Fall back! Get away from the entrance!"

The other three obey, backing away from the opening and trying to keep the giant spiders in front of them. They slash, stab, and punch the oncoming horde, but the decantulas keep coming and coming, driving them back into the middle of the chamber.

Shaide double-stabs and tosses aside an attacker, but then he is immediately jumped on by yet another. With a heavy grunt, he hits the ground, flat on his back, and his daggers are sent flying, several feet away.

He reaches up and grabs the enormous fangs and strains with all his might to hold the creature back off. He roars with the effort as the decantula thrashes and squirms, determined to jam those venomous fangs into him.

Reno throws back a decantula that attempted to jump on him and sees his friend in peril. "SHAIDE!" He tries to reach his friend, but he is interrupted by still another decantula. They are surrounded by dozens of the beasts.

Shaide's arms start to give out, and he draws his legs up and kicks as hard as he can. As the giant spider is thrown off of him, he feels a sharp pain in his injured leg. He ignores the pain and rolls to his feet, stumbling backward, looking for his daggers.

He stumbles into something hard and is momentarily distracted. He finds himself leaning against a large stone statue of a giant eagle that stands on a modest altar.

The dozens of decantulas immediately stop attacking. They seem to stare nervously at the giant statue.

Rayn looks around. "What the hell? What's happening?"

The altar suddenly starts glowing brightly. Reno looks up at Shaide. "Dude!? What did you do!?"

"I don't know!"

A bright column of light shoots into the sky, so blindingly bright that they have to look away. The decantulas shriek and skitter for the cave entrance as a deep rumbling sound fills the cavern.

A glowing golden glyph of some kind rises from the ground in front of the altar. It splits into multiple identical glyphs that form a circle around Shaide and the altar. The glyphs begin to spin blindingly fast around them. Without any warning, the ring expands rapidly outward, picking up Reno, Rayn, and Lania and throwing them against the wall of the chamber, and then it stops twenty feet from the outer wall.

Rayn groans as he climbs to his feet and tries to run and rejoin Shaide. When he reaches the glyph wall, some kind of invisible force seems to stop him from passing. He yells at Shaide, "WHAT THE HELL DID YOU DO!?"

Shaide instinctively reaches down and picks up his daggers. He looks up to see a large yellow glyph forming at the top of the column of light as a thunderstorm builds in the sky above him and swirls around the light.

Without warning, a glowing ball of yellow light rockets through the glyph and spirals down along the light column. Just as it reaches the altar, it flares and opens its enormous golden wings as lightning arcs over its entire body.

It screeches violently, and the lightning stretches across the entire chamber. As the decantulas flee for their lives, they are struck one by one and burned to a crisp by the brilliant lightning storm.

Shaide falls flat on his behind and stares up at the giant eagle standing on top of the altar. It looks just like the statue.

The bird lets out another ground-shaking screech as it looks at Shaide.

Shaide takes a deep breath and has a dawning suspicion of what he is looking at. He takes a battle stance and nods at the giant bird of prey. "If you want to kill me, you'll have to work for it. Come on!"

ETERNAL KNIGHTS OF EDEN I

*   *   *

Aton stands at the open rear hatch of a dropship as they fly in a broad circle through the mountains. They found the crashed dropship around a half hour ago, as well as the bodies of the pilot and two of the students.

They also found seven dead mountain lobos, killed by weapons and blunt force, indicating that at least a few of the students survived the crash.

As Shaide was not among the bodies, Aton is holding out hope that he may still be okay. Unfortunately, they could not find any sign of where the survivors went, so now all of the available air support is moving to the mountains to narrow down their location.

Suddenly the pilot yells, "Ceraph! Take a look at this!"

Aton moves to the cockpit and looks out the windshield. In the distance, a little further up in the mountains, a golden column of light is shooting into the sky. He tilts his head, trying to believe what his eyes are seeing. "No way, it can't be…"

"Can't be what?"

A single swirling storm cloud forms around the column of light, and a column of glyphs forms on the light as well. A brilliant ball of light shoots down out of the sky and spirals around the column.

A.S.GUINN   149

Aton looks at the pilot. "You! Get over there now! And tell every ship in the area to converge on that light!"

The pilot looks at him in shock. "What's happening?"

Aton slaps him on the back of the head. "Get over there! Someone triggered the Altar of Rho! Someone is summoning an angel!"

*   *   *

Rho, the Thunderbird, launches from the altar and streaks at Shaide. Before he has a chance to react, the giant eagle slams into him, knocking him back onto the ground.

He feels a painful jolt of electricity course through him, and he rolls back to his feet. He watches Rho streak around in a large circle at terrifying speed. Shaide notes the direction, and in spite of the pain in his leg, he takes off running the opposite way. He keeps his eyes locked on his opponent as they close in on each other.

Rho turns and rockets directly at Shaide, who mirrors the eagle and runs directly at it. Shaide holds his daggers ready to attack, and a storm of lightning arcs between Rho and the ground.

Rayn yells, "SHAIDE! WHAT ARE YOU DOING!"

Lania activates her perception magic. Her eyes glow green as she observes the fight. Her eyes widen. "Oh, Eden…"

Rayn looks at her. "What is it?"

Lania stares at the bird. "That thing is pure spiritual energy. It's not an ordinary creature."

He looks back at the bird. "Damnit, Shaide…"

Shaide suddenly digs his foot into the ground to stop, and then he leaps backward, away from Rho. His timing could not have been any more perfect…

Rho flies just underneath Shaide as he leaps, and Shaide twists in midair and jams both of his daggers into Rho's back. The bird continues streaking across the cavern, with Shaide now anchored to its back.

Rho screeches in pain from the daggers, and Shaide simultaneously feels a huge charge of lightning course through his body. He resists the pain, pulls out one dagger, and repeatedly stabs it into the bird's back as it turns and angles straight up.

He grits his teeth and yells, "I-AM-HAVING-A-REALLY-BAD-DAY-SO-WILL-YOU-JUST-DIE-ALREADY!?" He punctuates every word with a stab of the dagger, fury on his face as each hit intensely electrocutes him.

The bird slows in the air and then starts to fall backward. Shaide struggles to hold on as Rho twists and turns while streaking towards the ground. The bird spirals violently, and Shaide's daggers become dislodged from its back, sending him flying through the air and to the ground from fifteen feet up.

He tucks into a ball and rolls to absorb the landing, but he still gets the wind knocked out of him. At the same time, Rho pulls an impossibly high-G turn to avoid crashing into the ground and soars across the chamber again.

Shaide lies flat on his back and struggles to draw breath; the impact has stunned him for a moment.

Reno yells, "SHAIDE! GET UP! YOU HAVE TO FIGHT!"

Rayn yells as well, inspired by Shaide's performance. "YOU CAN DO THIS! GO! GET UP AND FIGHT!"

Lania just focuses on the two, a frown on her face.

Rho circles Shaide and then rockets towards him again. Shaide pushes himself to his feet, and a sudden idea strikes him—assuming he can pull it off.

He flips one of his daggers over, grabs it by the blade, and channels his magic energy into it, focusing on a specific effect. He then hurls the dagger at Rho, making it spin through the air.

Rho doesn't even try to avoid the weapon, but when it hits, it sinks hilt-deep into the bird's wing joint, and a sudden starburst of bluish-white spikes erupts from the impact site.

Rho screeches, slams into the ground, and spins towards Shaide. Shaide sprints and jumps on the bird's back and retrieves his second dagger, and then he quickly goes to town, slashing deep into the bird's back as it screeches in pain and rage.

"YEAH! YOU GOT HIM!" cheers Reno.

Lania shakes her head, eyes wide. "No, he doesn't. SHAIDE MOVE!"

Shaide looks up at her, and suddenly a massive wave of electricity explodes outward from the angry eagle. He is picked up and launched through the air, screaming in pain as millions of volts course through his body. He hits the ground nearly a hundred feet away, tumbling and rolling.

Rho stands back up and turns to face Shaide. It spreads its wings wide, seemingly unaffected by the shoulder wound now, and opens its beak. A bright blue ball of lightning forms in front of its mouth and grows and grows. A subsonic screech and thrumming noise fills the air as the ball of energy compresses and intensifies.

Lania closes her eyes and turns away, muttering, "It's over…"

Shaide struggles to his feet and looks at the blinding ball forming a hundred feet in front of him. He raises his daggers in the air.

Rho launches the ball of lightning with blinding speed, and Shaide disappears inside of an enormous sphere of electricity and dust. A bloodcurdling shriek can be heard, and then it suddenly ceases, and all that remains is a giant cloud of dust filling the air.

Lania nods, eyes closed and looking away. She repeats quietly, "It's over…"

Rayn and Reno yell simultaneously, pounding on the glyph wall, "NO! SHAIDE NO! SHAIDE, GET UP!"

Rho seems to be staring at something, but no one notices. A light sparking can be seen inside the dust cloud, and as it clears slightly, the others see that Shaide is still standing, albeit on his knees. He has his two daggers jammed into the rocky ground, and lightning sparks between them. Despite his tattered uniform, the burns covering his skin, and the blood dripping from the corner of his mouth, he has a smile on his face. He grounded the attack, drastically lessening the effect.

Rho launches back up into the air and flaps its wings backward, keeping its eyes on Shaide.

Shaide looks up at it and yells, "IS THAT ALL YOU'VE GOT, YOU BASTARD!?"

Lania looks up in shock.

Shaide yanks his daggers out of the ground and takes off running again, around the outside perimeter and towards Rho.

Rho, meanwhile, shrieks with rage, dive-bombs the ground, and arcs up, rocketing toward Shaide just two feet above the ground, its body arcing violently with electricity. Shaide moves like he is going to jump, and then he suddenly drops his legs out from under him and slides UNDER Rho, flat on his back. He thrusts his blades straight up and cuts deep into Rho's underbelly as the bird streaks over him.

Shaide takes an enormous jolt of electricity as he passes under the bird, and he finds he has difficulty moving when he slides to a stop.

Rho slams into the ground again and spins around, prepared to counterattack. As Shaide lies prone on the ground, the bird lashes out with a bolt of lightning that slams into Shaide. The attack actually picks him up and throws him through the air, screaming in pain, and when he lands, he hits the ground on his injured leg first. His bad leg, already pushed beyond its limits in this fight, gives out, causing him to yell even louder.

Overhead, a single dropship comes into view over the hole in the cavern ceiling.

Reno and Rayn look up and start hollering, "RESCUE! WE'RE SAVED!" Reno even goes so far as to whistle and cheer.

Lania looks out across the cavern at the fight. "Guys. It's not over yet!"

Shaide limps to his feet as he and Rho stare each other down. He yells, "COME ON, YOU BIG OVERGROWN PIDGEON! ONE LAST CHANCE! ONE LAST ATTACK! BRING IT!"

*   *   *

Aton watches helplessly from the dropship, hardly believing his eyes. His fourteen-year-old godson is fighting one of Eden's angels, and he appears to be putting up a hell of a fight. Fliers are a nightmare on the best of days, and here he is, going toe-to-toe with one of the worst.

Even more, there is a certain sense of either irony or destiny about this fight. Of all the angels Shaide could have encountered and activated, it was THIS angel...

As angel trial barriers are completely impenetrable even to capital ship fire, Aton can do nothing but watch helplessly as Rho launches from the ground and flies in a giant vertical loop, picking up speed as it comes down. Its body bristling with electricity, it streaks towards Shaide at maximum speed, and Shaide braces himself with his daggers at the ready.

ETERNAL KNIGHTS OF EDEN I

*   *   *

Reno, Rayn, and Lania watch, their eyes glued to Rho and Shaide as the latter streaks towards their friend, no one in the chamber knowing how this fight is about to end. Shaide has done the impossible and stood toe to toe with a creature they have never seen nor heard of before, and despite the beating he has taken, he is still fighting.

Shaide watches the bird as it comes for him.

There is only one thing to do.

He throws himself forward with all of the strength he can muster from his good leg and thrusts both daggers straight out.

A sickening crunch echoes through the chamber as Rho and Shaide directly collide. Rho shrieks in either pain or rage and slams flat into the ground, Shaide underneath him. When the two slide to a stop, Shaide's daggers are hilt deep in the bird's mouth and neck. Shaide is underneath him, only his head and shoulders visible.

The bird raises a wing and twitches for a moment before collapsing on Shaide.

The thing is, Shaide isn't moving either.

Rho suddenly begins to glow, and without any warning, it becomes a blinding column of light streaking into the sky and back down into Shaide. Shaide's eyes open wide for a moment as he convulses, and then the light fades, and he falls limp once more.

The wall of glyphs fades and sinks into the ground, and the column of light on the altar shoots up into the sky and vanishes.

The altar falls dark.

Reno yells, "SHAIDE!" and sprints to his friend, no longer held back by the glyph wall. Rayn and Lania exchange glances and chase after him.

Reno drops to his knees and skids to a stop next to Shaide "Hey, come on, buddy, don't do this to me now. Come on, dude, breathe. You have to breathe!"

As the dropship glides down to land a few feet away from them, Aton jumps out before it even hits the ground. "SHAIDE!"

He slides to a stop next to Reno and starts frantically checking his godson.

Lania kneels down at Shaide's head and puts a glowing hand on him. Reno, Rayn, and Aton all look at her expectantly as she looks at him with glowing green eyes. A moment later, she closes her eyes, and the green fades, leaving her normal brown eyes behind.

"He's alive. Injured and exhausted, but alive."

Reno and Aton breathe a sigh of relief as three additional Ceraphs slowly walk out of the troop bay of the dropship and come over to meet them.

Lucy puts a hand on Aton's shoulder. "Did Shaide just do…what I think he did?"

Reno looks at the two of them. "Why? What did he do?"

"You don't know what this place is, do you?" says Aton.

Reno, Lania, and Rayn all exchange glances and shake their heads.

Aton sighs and explains, "This is a Trial of Angels. This is one of the chambers where an Angel sleeps, waiting for someone it deems worthy of its attention to arrive. When that person touches the altar, it awakens the Angel and begins the trial."

"And the trial is combat?" asks Rayn.

Lucy shakes her head. "Not necessarily, but in Rho's case, yes. Each angel has its own criteria for who it deems worthy of becoming its partner. Rho just happens to be one of the fighters."

Reno looks down at Shaide, who is barely breathing in front of him. "So, did Shaide pass the trial or not?"

Lucy looks up at Lania. "You, girl. You're a support mage. Is anything different about the boy now?"

Lania jumps when Lucy addresses her. "Umm, give me a minute." Her eyes and hands glow green again, and she uses her magic to assess Shaide's condition. Her eyes open wide as she looks him over.

"It's strange. He has almost what looks like a second aura in him, parallel to his own." Her glow flickers and fades, and she shakes her head. Her own magic aura is depleted from overuse. "What does that mean?"

Lucy looks at Aton, an impressed look on her face. "Like I thought. Aton, your fourteen-year-old godson now has an Angel. Rho, no less."

Rayn raises a hand. "What's so significant about Rho?"

Aton looks at him with a bittersweet half-smile on his face. "Rho was last partnered with Shaide's mother. When she died, Rho came back to his altar like they always do. Two Ceraphs have since awakened Rho, but they were both killed when facing him. My godson here just did what two very strong Ceraphs couldn't. And at his age, no less…"

A deep rumbling sound fills the air as one of the capital ships nears. The pilot of the dropship is standing at the back of his ship, trying to stay out of the way but also unable to resist his own curiosity.

A remarkably short and stocky man wielding a rather large war hammer speaks up. "Ai, Aton? Shouldn't we be gettin' him some medical attention? He don't look too good, to be honest with yeh."

Aton nods. "Yeah, good idea, Bjorn." He scoops up Shaide, stands, and turns to the dropship. "Come on, you three. You've been out here long enough. Let's get you back to where you belong."

Reno, Rayn, and Lania all nod and stand up as well. The pilot is talking with someone on the communications system, but all three teenagers are too tired to pay attention. Rayn, Reno, and Lania take their seats in the back of the dropship, and Bjorn, Lucy, and the unnamed Ceraph sit down opposite of them.

Aton has already taken his seat at the front of the troop bay and is holding an unconscious Shaide in his lap, looking half-worried, and half-proud.

As the dropship lifts into the air, Bjorn looks at the three teenagers. "Ai. Yeh three did right well surviving on yer own out here like ye did. That was no mean feat, lemme tell ye."

Reno smiles with pride, while the other two just lean their heads back, exhausted from their ordeal.

The pilot is taking the flight easy, trying to be gentle on the traumatized teenagers in the back of his ship. Reno glances out the side viewport and notices the gunship escorting them. It looks like they aren't taking any chances after the incident last night.

Less than twenty minutes later, the pilot eases the dropship to a halt and starts its descent. Shortly thereafter, the pilot eases the dropship to the ground and shuts down the engines.

The unnamed Ceraph at the back, a tall Drameri man with dark hair, opens the rear drop hatch. Reno, Rayn, and Lania look out the back as it opens and see all their classmates standing there waiting for them.

Lieutenant Nikola and his junior instructor, Lieutenant Adeline, are waiting in front of the students, looking simultaneously both very anxious and very relieved.

The three teenagers exit the ship first and are greeted by cheers and laughter from their classmates, who are all very happy to see them.

Lieutenant Nikola looks them over carefully. "Are you three okay?"

Rayn looks at the other two and nods. "It's been… I'm just glad it's over, sir."

Nikola pats him on the head and notices Shaide being carried by Aton. He asks nervously, "What…what happened to him?" His eyes are drawn to Shaide's injured leg and the burns covering his body.

Aton shakes his head. "Let me get him to the infirmary first, and then we can discuss what happened. The situation is…complicated."

Nikola nods and turns to the other three survivors. "You three, go to the infirmary and get checked out. I'll be there to see you shortly. Let me get this lot back in the inn, and I'll head that way."

Rayn nods. "Yes, sir. Come on." Reno, Lania, and he all turn and follow Aton to the infirmary, which is actually an old inn repurposed by the military to serve as its hospital.

Reno looks around the town, now seeing it for the first time, and notices the difference between it and the capital. The capital is constructed of many different kinds of buildings, but at their core, most of them share a similar design, regulated by the chamber of commerce to keep the city beautiful and elegant.

The buildings here are of many varying designs and styles. Most appear to have been built by hand, and a number of log and stone buildings look like they were designed to take a beating.

They head into the infirmary, and at the door, they meet a doctor who was standing by for the return of the rescued students.

The doctor looks at Shaide first. "What happened to this one? He looks rather badly burned."

Aton nods. "He got into a fight with the Angel in the mountain."

The doctor stares at him. "This boy fought Rho? And he survived?"

Aton nods slowly. "Actually, he beat him, if you're in the mood for surprises."

The doctor's eyes open wide in shock. After a moment, he shakes himself out of it. "Any other injuries before I began my examination?"

Lania says, "His leg was slashed open by a mountain lobo. I treated him the best I could, but…"

The doctor pulls up Shaide's tattered and burned pant leg and examines the swollen area covered by bandages. He nods. "It seems like you did well for a student. I can take care of him from here. If you would just carry him to this room here…"

The doctor appears to be a young man, but his attitude indicates he has a great deal of experience. He leads Aton into an unoccupied room, and Aton lays Shaide on the bed. The doctor looks at the other students and frowns "I will have to remove his clothes to ascertain the extent of his injuries. Is it okay for them to be here?"

Aton nods. "I understand. You three, wait outside while we check him over."

Rayn, Reno, and Lania all sigh in disappointment and step outside the door.

Aton closes the door behind them. "Alright. Let's see what we're looking at here."

The doctor goes to cut off Shaide's ruined clothes, but they end up tearing and crumbling off easily. The electrical assault fried everything on him. Aton sets Shaide's daggers on the table next to the bed, and the doctor removes his undershirt, leaving him in just a pair of shorts.

The doctor and Aton are both stunned by what they see.

Shaide's body is covered in what is referred to as Lichtenberg figures. A spider-web pattern of intense burns covers his body from nearly head to toe, a series of light purple raised welts that stand out even against the burned skin underneath.

Aton stares at the burn pattern in shock. "Damn… I thought maybe Rho had gone easy on him, but it looks like he was fried alive, doesn't it?"

The doctor undoes the bandages on Shaide's leg and examines the raw skin and the torn muscle underneath. He leans back. "This boy nearly tore his calf muscle in two. I cannot imagine how he fought your Angel in this condition."

Aton looks at him with concern. "Is he going to be okay?"

"Oh, yes," the doctor says with a smile. "Your boy isn't in any real danger. He is remarkably tough. I'll have another healer help me, and he'll be back on his feet by morning. With Rho inside of him, it will be even easier to heal him."

The doctor narrows his eyes at Aton. "You know, now that he has partnered with an Angel, what will happen to him. I've been helping the Ceraphs for four hundred years, and I have learned a few things. I know that it is dangerous to send a fourteen-year-old back to the Academy with an Angel he doesn't know how to control."

Aton shakes his head. "I don't know, Whiteglaive. It's not my call. I was hoping not to drag him into the Ceraphs until he was old enough to make the choice himself, but now we may not have the luxury of choice. We're the only ones who can teach him how to use and control Rho."

Doctor Whiteglaive nods and takes his glasses off. "That being said, I'm curious. If I remember correctly, the last wielder of Rho was your old friend Juvia Darkmoon."

"Yeah, and I already know where you're going. This is her son."

"I see. That is certainly an interesting coincidence. The same Angel with five consecutive generations now…"

Aton nods. "More than that, actually. I'll tell you something not many people know."

Doctor Whiteglaive clasps his hands together and looks closely at Aton. "Oh, please do tell me. I love secrets."

Aton looks at Shaide. "This boy's family has been in the Ceraph Order since its founding three thousand years ago. His distant ancestor was the original order master, and every generation since has produced at least one Ceraph. Shaide is a direct descendant of that line. Rho has never been possessed by anyone outside of his family.

Doctor Whiteglaive looks down at Shaide. "Well, that was something I did not know. It seems this boy has a destiny on his hands. Descendant of the original order master, AND the youngest person ever known to partner with an Angel." He cracks his knuckles "I suppose I better make sure this boy pulls through, then. I'll take care of him. You go check on the other kids."

Aton nods. "Thanks, doctor. I really appreciate it."

He leaves as Doctor Whiteglaive focuses and begins casting a regeneration spell on Shaide. Outside the room, he finds himself surrounded by three anxious teenagers and a couple of annoyed-looking nurses.

Reno asks anxiously, "So? Is he going to be okay?"

Aton has a startled look on his face for a moment, but he relaxes and smiles. "He's going to be just fine. He may have a bit of an unusual scar, but that's it. Now, why haven't you been looked at yet?"

One of the nurses sighs in annoyance. "They refused to leave the door until they knew how their friend was doing."

Aton laughs. "Shaide has some good friends, I see. Well, he's fine, so you three make sure you get better too."

The two nurses usher the boys and the girl into two separate rooms so they can be examined for injuries, and Aton smiles in relief and heads for the door.

On his way out, he bumps into Lieutenant Nikola coming in to check on his students. The lieutenant looks at Aton and asks nervously, "Well? How are they doing?"

Aton leans against a pillar, keeping the lieutenant in suspense for a moment, and then finally answers. "They're going to be just fine. Even Shaide is going to recover. Fighting Rho put him through hell, but that boy is remarkably resilient. All of that, and no real life-threatening injuries."

Lieutenant Nikola nods and sighs. "That's a relief. I get the feeling that's not all, though…"

Aton shakes his head. "No, it's not. Shaide is now partnered with an Angel. The youngest person I've ever known to successfully do so. I don't know if I can safely send him back to the Academy. If he doesn't know how to control Rho, then one bad moment of stress, and BOOM, Shaide could inadvertently unleash a pissed-off thunderbird on the Academy."

Lieutenant Nikola frowns. "So, what do you suggest we do?"

"I'm going to call Master Armstrong, but most likely, Shaide will have to come back to the Citadel with me. Once he is better, of course."

Lieutenant Nikola's eyes open wide. "If he's going back to the citadel, does that mean what I think it does?"

Aton nods. "Yeah. If the master approves it, then Shaide will be joining the Ceraph Order. Or at least, he'll train with us until he can handle Rho."

Aton and Lieutenant Nikola both fall into thoughtful silence, both men feeling a similar mixture of pride and anxiety.

CHAPTER 6

THE SOUTHERN REACHES

Reno wakes up the next morning in a hospital bed feeling remarkably refreshed. He wasn't severely injured, but he received a full medical examination as well as a concoction to help him sleep, and as a result, he got the best night's sleep he's had in a long time.

He thinks back on the events of the past couple of days, and he laments the loss of Bryon and Joslin. While they were not particularly close, they had learned and lived alongside each other for months, and it is with sadness that he accepts he will never see them again.

　　　　　　　　A.S.GUINN

He shakes his head clear and looks over at the door. He appears to be sharing a room with Rayn, who is already putting on his boots and uniform.

Rayn catches sight of Reno and nods to him, saying, "Wow. You actually woke up at a reasonable time, all on your own. Good job!"

Reno sits up and rolls his eyes. "Yeah, yeah, it's known to happen occasionally, you know." He looks beside his bed and is surprised to see a fresh field uniform laid out for him. He grabs it and starts getting ready.

Rayn, Reno, and Lania were all forced to stay in the infirmary overnight after they were treated for minor to moderate wounds. The doctors insisted they rest here and avoid any stress for the night, though this was probably more for their mental health rather than physical.

They were all treated for head injuries and contusions, but for the most part, they were in remarkably good condition considering their ordeal. The doctors performed general full-body curative spells on them, some pretty high-level stuff that left them feeling even better than they had before the crash. The doctors actually had to give them herbal sedatives to help them sleep.

A nurse walks in just as Reno finishes putting his pants on. She looks at the two young men and says, "I was coming to ask how you were feeling, but it seems that you're doing okay."

Reno looks up and asks abruptly, "How is Shaide doing?"

The nurse seems surprised at his abruptness, but she answers, "He's going to be okay. His injuries were much more severe than yours were, but while physically he will be fine, his spiritual energy is nearly completely drained and is behaving erratically. He may not wake up for a few days."

Rayn asks cautiously, "Does it have anything to do with that thing he fought?"

The nurse frowns and nods. "Very perceptive. Yes, when the angel formed the contract with him, it threw his whole spiritual system out of balance. According to the Ceraph who keeps checking on him, it's not a rare occurrence for Ceraphs to sleep for a few days after binding with an Angel. He should be fine once he's had some rest."

Reno tilts his head. "Contract…with an Angel?"

The nurse heads for the door, ignoring the question. "Your instructor is waiting for you in the lobby. When you are ready, go meet him. I'm going to go wake your other classmate." She disappears around the corner.

Rayn looks at Reno and shakes his head, looking mildly bewildered. "Well, that was…enlightening. So, you think Shaide is really okay?"

Reno looks down "I hope so. I don't want to have to get a new roommate."

Rayn laughs. "Yeah. THAT'S the reason you're worried."

Reno finishes putting his new uniform on, and the two boys walk out of the room and down the hallway, heading for the old tavern that serves as the lobby. Despite having been remodeled, the hospital still looks like an old inn.

Lieutenant Nikola is waiting at the counter. Reno raises his eyebrows when he sees Lania is there as well. He could have sworn she got up after they did. She's tapping her foot rather impatiently.

She sees them approaching and stands up a little straighter, a slight smile stretching across her face. "There you are. That nurse said she woke you up first, but it took you long enough to get down here."

Reno glares at her. "Zip it. I'd like to know how you beat us down here."

She sticks her tongue out. "I was already up and dressed when she came in."

"Hey!" says Nikola. "Calm down, you two. We've got business today, now that you're better."

Reno groans and tilts his head back. "Oh, come on, teach. We just spent all night in the hospital after crashing in the wild. Can't we get today off?"

Nikola leans forward. "Cadet Reno Coltide. You enlisted in this academy to serve in the royal military and do what is expected of you. Now that you have recovered, you are expected to resume your duties like you normally would. You're not a child anymore, and you won't be treated as one. Am I clear?"

Reno stands up straight and looks slightly ashamed of himself. "Yes, Lieutenant. I'm sorry, sir!"

Rayn looks down with a smirk.

"That being said, I'm glad you're okay," says Nikola, softening his tone slightly. "It was hard enough losing two students. Unfortunately, we're not on leisure time right now. We are on official business and on a bit of a timetable."

Rayn looks up at him. "Official business, sir?"

Nikola nods. "Yes, official business. I will explain more thoroughly once we meet up with the rest of the class."

"And Shaide…" Reno asks timidly. "How is he really, sir?"

Nikola contemplates Reno for a moment before responding. "Shaide is going to be okay, but do you understand the significance of what he's done?"

Reno and Rayn exchange glances, and Lania's eyes dart from one to the other.

Nikola sighs. "That thing in the cave was an Angel. One of the children of the planet. Typically, as I understand it, once a Ceraph is strong enough, he or she will go face one of these Angels in order to form a partnership. They have to undergo some kind of test to prove their worth to the Angel, and then it agrees to form a contract and bind itself to them for as long as they live, enhancing their power and coming to their aid in times of need."

Reno stares blankly at Nikola.

Seeing the confused on his student's face, Nikola sighs and continues. "It is incredibly rare for someone outside of the Ceraph Order to possess an Angel. Shaide is also the youngest known to have ever done so. We don't really know what will happen to him."

"Will the Ceraph Order take him, sir?" asks Rayn.

Nikola shrugs. "I honestly do not know, kid. Even his godfather doesn't know what will happen to him. Not yet, at least."

Rayn nods. "I think I understand, sir."

Reno and Lania just remain quiet.

"Alright, then," says Nikola, straightening up, "if that is all the questions, then, as of now, you have officially returned to duty. Follow me, and we will meet up with the rest of the class."

As Nikola turns to leave, Rayn follows behind. Lania looks at Reno and shrugs before falling in line behind Rayn. Reno stands still for a moment and then glances down the hallway where Shaide presumably lies, feeling a twinge of disquiet. Then he falls in behind Lania and marches out of the hospital.

They step outside and see the town in proper daylight for the first time. It was rather ominous and intimidating last night when they returned from the mountain, but now, in the daylight, Broadspring appears to be a rather charming rural village.

The wooden and stone buildings have a hardy but welcoming appearance. The streets are paved with light gray stones quarried from the nearby mountain, and they are remarkably smooth and flat. The town definitely has an older feel to it, and it provides an interesting contrast to the warships hovering overhead.

The section of town they are in seems to be predominantly devoted to the royal military. There are a few civilians around, operating food stalls and similar roadside stands, but most of the people on the street are fellow military personnel.

Reno looks straight up and sees an impressive sight: the heavy cruiser floats directly overhead, its massive size casting a long shadow over the land. Reno looks behind him and sees the carrier not too far outside of town.

Lania hisses, "Reno. Look forward. You look like a tourist."

Reno snaps his eyes back to the front. "Sorry."

They find their junior instructor and classmates waiting for them near an archway leading into the main town. Their classmates exchange whispers when they see the number of those returning is down to three.

Nikola sees their confusion and decides to head it off. "Darkmoon is going to be in the hospital for a couple of days, but he is going to be fine. Don't worry yourselves too much about it. You have a job today, and you will need to be fully alert to ensure your safety. Jarvis, Coltide, Howler, form up with the others."

Rayn, Reno, and Lania form up with the other fourteen classmates and wait patiently for Nikola to continue.

In silence, they stand in a relaxed parade stance for a couple of minutes, waiting. Finally, twenty soldiers who don't look like the main garrison troops make their way up the street and come to a stop in front of the students. Their outfits bear the markings of the Alastair Royal Army, but they don't look like standard uniforms.

The one leading the group walks up to Lieutenant Nikola, and Nikola salutes him. The leader returns the salute and says, "I'm Major Jordan Stryder, Alastair 13th Ranger Detachment. I have been assigned to allow your students to shadow my men for a few days in the field."

Lieutenant Nikola nods. "Yes sir. I have seventeen cadets for this week's training mission. Darkmoon is still in the infirmary from the…incident."

Major Stryder tilts his head. "Did you say Darkmoon?"

Nikola looks confused. "Yes sir. Why?"

"My old captain was named Darkmoon. He was killed in action about four and a half years ago down by Highwatch. Saved my life."

Nikola nods and lowers his voice. "Yes, sir. That was likely Shaide's father. He was killed down there several years ago."

Major Stryder raises his eyebrows. "I'd love to talk to him later, if I have the chance. I'm sorry he cannot come along. I'd be interested to find out if he is anything like his father. From the sound of it, he certainly seems to be."

ETERNAL KNIGHTS OF EDEN I

Lieutenant Nikola shrugs. "I didn't know his parents, sir. I can only speculate."

"No need. I'll determine for myself when I have the time." The major steps back. "Cadets, I am Major Jordan Stryder. I am the company commander for the 13th Ranger Detachment, Alpha Company. My company will be taking you out on a patrol deployment for a few days, and you will learn firsthand how things are done in the field."

He looks around at the cadets, who all seem to be mildly excited at this news. "We will not be babysitting you. As members of the Alastair Royal Military, you will be expected to fight alongside your temporary squadmates, and aid in our mission to repel corrupted influence in the area and keep them away from the town. It is going to be very dangerous, and you will not have the home comforts that you are accustomed to in the academy."

He looks at the students very seriously. "I cannot stress enough how important it is that you follow your squad leader's instructions to the letter. These men know how to survive out here. If you follow their instructions, you will make it home in one piece. If you ignore or disobey their orders, you very well may not make it home at all. Do you all understand?"

A chorus of "Yes, sir!" echoes from the seventeen students in formation.

Major Stryder turns to Lieutenant Nikola and gives him his orders. "Lieutenant, divide your cadets into four squads who will work well together, and I will assign them to one of my squads."

Lieutenant Nikola nods and starts calling out names to group up the cadets. "Coltide, Jarvis, and Howler. You three obviously work well together. Celeste Wyatt, you will join them as well."

A tall, athletic girl with long, pure white hair and ice blue eyes walks over to them. She is the tallest girl in the class, and in fact, she is even taller than most of the boys. She is carrying an unusual weapon for a student: a bluish-silver halberd slung across her back. She nods and stands beside them without another word.

Reno and Rayn exchange glances. Celeste was always extremely quiet and reserved. She has the best grades in the class, on par with Shaide and Rayn, but no one really knows much of anything about her—aside from the fact that her martial arts skills are beyond terrifying.

Lania nudges Celeste and winks, and Celeste returns a rare, subtle smile.

Major Stryder also carries a halberd, and he seems to take notice of Celeste. He walks over to Rayn's squad. "You, girl. Wyatt, is it?"

 A.S.GUINN

"Yes, sir."

He looks at her halberd with interest. "A halberd is an unusual choice of weapon for a trainee. It's usually suited to someone with more combat experience. Can you handle it correctly?"

"Yes, sir," Celeste replies proudly. "I am very proficient with my weapon."

Major Stryder takes a few steps back and unshoulders his own halberd. He looks her in the eyes and says, "Show me. Try and hit me. I promise you won't hurt me."

Celeste looks uncomfortably at Lieutenant Nikola, but he shakes his head and says, "You have your orders, Wyatt."

Celeste unshoulders her halberd and stretches out as everyone backs away, watching with interest. When she gets the nod of approval from Major Stryder, she performs a series of high-velocity spins and twirls with her halberd, gracefully running it around her arms and under her legs.

Major Stryder takes a more serious defensive stance. "Okay, Wyatt. You can handle the weapon, but can you fight with it?"

Celeste yells, "YAH!" and lunges forward with remarkable speed, narrowly missing Stryder with her first thrust as he turns sideways. She draws back and rapidly thrusts forward several times, forcing him to turn and back up as he avoids her attacks. She punctuates each attack with a "YAH!"

Major Stryder deflects her last attack sideways away from him with his own halberd. Surprisingly, she takes his block in stride and violently swings the halberd around from the other direction. When he blocks it again, she aggressively swings at him from the left, then right, then left again several times, forcing him to backstep as he blocks her aggressive attacks.

He blocks her from the left again, and she feints, acting like she will swing from the right but then changing direction and performing a low sweep from the left. Stryder jumps into the air to avoid it, and she follows through seamlessly, swinging the polearm behind her back and bringing it straight over her head for a powerful downward attack.

Stryder doesn't have time to move, and he raises his halberd up horizontally above his head, catching her attack at the last possible second with a loud CLANG!

He yells, "STOP!"

Celeste draws back her own halberd and stands it up beside her, looking slightly out of breath as well as a little disappointed.

Stryder surveys her carefully for a moment and then says something very unexpected. "You did very well, Wyatt.

You will be a hell of a Ranger someday with that natural proficiency. If the rest of your classmates are half as talented as you, I think you will all be just fine."

Celeste looks confused. "But…sir? You blocked or avoided everything I threw at you."

Stryder smiles and closes his eyes. "Wyatt, I am over four hundred years old. I have been serving in the military for the past hundred." He opens his eyes. "I have experience that you simply do not have. The simple fact that I had to block your attacks instead of casually dodging you is a testament to your natural talent. Keep working at it, and you will be a fine warrior. I'm sure you all will be."

The unexpected encouragement gives the students a small boost in morale. They all look ready to go now.

To Celeste's group, Major Stryder says, "You four, I want you with my squad. You showed the resilience to survive in the mountains after crashing, and Ms. Wyatt here is obviously proficient as well. I'm confident you can handle what we are planning to deal with."

Reno and Lania both look slightly unnerved at this statement.

The other three groups pair up with their corresponding Ranger squads and get to know each other for a moment before deploying.

As three other Rangers walk over to join them, Reno says to Major Stryder. "Can I ask you a question, sir?"

"Of course. What do you want to know?"

Reno asks tentatively. "You said you were over four hundred years old. Does that mean you are a Mitera, like my friend Shaide?"

Stryder smiles at his shyness. "Yes, boy, I am. Descended from some of the original soldiers who fought in the great war, if that interests you. It has no bearing on our mission, though. I was born in Alastair, and we are all here to defend our great nation, so do not treat me as if I am special. When we are in the field, we are brothers."

Reno raises his eyebrows at Stryder's rather long answer, but nods. "Yes, sir."

Stryder glances at the squad members beside him. "Cadets? This is Kimball, Bull, and Jax. I have served with them for a few years now, and they are among the finest soldiers you will find anywhere."

Kimball is a white-haired tomboy looking woman carrying an interesting looking rapier. She looks almost as if she could be related to Celeste. Bull is a massive tank of a man standing over seven feet tall and wielding a huge battle axe. Jax, on the other hand, is the direct opposite of Bull, standing not much larger than the teenagers. He carries a pair of daggers, a strange but stout-looking black bow, and two quivers full of wicked-looking steel-shafted arrows.

Rayn steps forward. "I'm Rayn Jarvis, swordsman and cadet company commander. This is Reno Coltide, martial artist." Reno punches his fists together as Rayn continues. "Lania Howler, swordswoman and support mage, and you've already met Celeste Wyatt."

Everyone exchanges greetings, and then Major Stryder turns to address everyone. "Squads, you already have your orders for this mission. Head out and commence operations."

He turns to his own squad as the other three groups start heading into town. "Alright, we are going to check out a drake nest that was spotted by scouts about a week ago. I don't want to tangle with them if it's not necessary, so our initial mission is to assess the threat and decide if it needs to be eliminated or not. Understood?"

The members of his own squad reply in unison, "Yes, sir."

Rayn nudges Reno, and the four cadets add, "Yes, sir," a moment later.

Major Stryder grins slightly. "Relax. I'm not going to put you in the thick of a fight with a nest of drakes. If it comes to it, we will handle the extermination, and you will provide support. Drakes are nasty. Even if you could handle them, it is too risky."

Reno looks visibly relieved that they will not be facing the drakes themselves. In contrast, Celeste looks mildly disappointed.

Major Stryder pulls out a region map and lays it down on the ground, and they all squat down around it. Stryder points at the map. "We will be following this course to the area we are gathering intel on. It's a long trip, and if everything goes as expected, we should be there in a couple of days."

Reno gives an uncomfortable look to Lania and Rayn, but neither of them seems especially perturbed by the news of the mission length. Rayn asks casually, "Sir? What is our anticipated mission window?"

"We're expecting six days. Two days en route, two days recon, and two days return trip. If it becomes an extermination operation, the mission time could increase."

"Understood, sir."

Bull hands out four backpacks. He explains in a deep voice, "These are your supplies for the mission. We were instructed to prepare survival supplies and provisions for our shadows. Those packs have everything you will need." He looks at an extra pack with confusion.

ETERNAL KNIGHTS OF EDEN I

Stryder says, "Oh yeah, that. There were originally going to be four squads of five, but with the incident…well, we have fewer students than anticipated."

Bull looks at the pack. "Do you still want me to bring it? It would be a shame to let it go to waste."

Stryder shrugs. "If you want to bring it, you may. It's time to go."

He turns and leads the seven followers through the archway and out onto a winding path leading through the mountains. The heavy gate swings closed behind them, and with a loud, reverberating clang, it latches.

As they make their way down the path out of the town, they appear to be in some kind of shallow canyon or valley, and they walk for quite some time before they see the path open up in front of them.

The path flattens out, and the rocks bracketing the road drop away, revealing an awe-inspiring view. Reno's mouth hangs open slightly as he takes in the scene. Lania mirrors his reaction, looking around with great interest.

The road they are on is still slightly elevated up on the mountainside, and it provides them with a tremendous long-range view of the southern plains. Reno's eyes sweep the view as he takes in miles upon miles of plains. Hills of varying sizes dot the landscape, as well as lakes and ponds, and to the west lies a massive forest.

Reno and Lania exchange approving nods. Kimball catches sight of this and raises her eyebrows in amusement. "You two think it's a pretty view, don't you?"

Lania nods. "Yeah, it's amazing."

Kimball smiles rather sadistically. "And that beautiful view you see is filled with so many horrible things that can and will kill you in a second that it really makes you contemplate the correlation between beauty and danger."

"She's right," says Jax. "There is nothing more dangerous in this world than a beautiful woman."

Celeste winks and says, "I can agree with that."

Rayn coughs, indicating he does not wish to become involved in this conversation.

Major Stryder points off to the southeast. A lake is visible far in the distance, and Reno feels like it is the lake they were shown on the map. The major says, "That is Lake Blackwyrm. The drakes we're going to investigate are supposedly nesting in a cave on the far side. As I said before, it's about a two-day journey, so we're going to pace ourselves and not burn energy unnecessarily."

"I have a question, sir," says Lania. "If you know exactly where you need to go, why don't you take an airship to check it out? Wouldn't it be faster?"

"That is an excellent point, but for the Rangers, there are two reasons we do this on foot. The first reason is simply that the airspace here is too dangerous for small unescorted airships. Look at what happened to you, for example."

The three survivors of the crash exchange nods.

Major Stryder continues. "The second reason is far more practical in nature. Although we have mission-specific objectives, our job is far more than that. We travel on foot so that we are constantly familiarizing ourselves with the land and looking for any additional threats to the safety of the settlements out here."

They set off along the road, heading south. Major Stryder says, "Keep your eyes open at all times. The kingdom south of the mountains is nothing like it is to the north. Up north, the military is present in force, and they do a good job of keeping the areas around the major population centers clear. It's true that you still have dragons and even behemoths up there, but as long as you stick to the civilized areas, you're more or less safe. That's not the case south of the mountains."

"South of the mountains," adds Kimball, "you have lobos, drakes, decantulas and megantulas, nekoshin, basilisk, trolls, ogres, giants, snapjaws, and even wild behemoths and dragons. And that's just the start. The corrupted versions of these monsters keep drifting north in larger and larger numbers, and they are at least twice the nightmare of their more natural counterparts."

Jax shudders. "I HATE nekoshin. Great, big catlike beasts that are like a smaller cousin to the behemoth. They are mean, fast, smart, and stealthy, and even worse? They can use magic to some degree, which makes them a bitch to fight."

Major Stryder coughs and raises his voice slightly. "Anyways! What I'm trying to say is to remain alert. This is a very dangerous region, and I want all eight of us to make it back to Broadspring in one piece."

Their first day en route to Lake Blackwyrm proves to be quite eventful. First, they get ambushed by a pack of plains lobos and promptly dispatch the threat without issue. Then they encounter a pair of basilisks, gigantic venomous serpents, near the creek bed when they resupply their water, and Major Stryder and Kimball each take one out. And near dusk, they even encounter a very curious behemoth that follows them for a while, making them very nervous.

Behemoths are among the most dangerous beasts to dot the plains. They did not appear until Eden first came to this namesake planet, and many people speculate that they are actually divine in nature. Their level of power and intelligence certainly seems to indicate this.

The behemoths resemble gargantuan, buff, hairless lions with large horns coming out of their heads. A full-grown behemoth stands over sixty feet long nose to tail, with some of the greater varieties growing even larger than that. It is difficult to estimate, but the average behemoth seems to weigh somewhere around twenty to thirty thousand pounds. They are so powerful and tough that it is generally advised to call in capital ships to neutralize them from the air.

The good thing is, because of the behemoth's intelligence, they almost always avoid populated areas, and they prefer to be left alone. They are very territorial, however, and they do not like strangers passing through their runs.

The group reaches the bank of the lake that runs alongside the road they are following and set up camp for the night. Bull and Reno gather firewood as Kimball and Celeste fish in the lake. Jax and Rayn scout the area for any nearby threats, and Major Stryder looks over their maps to see if they can improve their route and try and save some time.

Lania ends up pouting because there is nothing left that needs doing, which leaves her sitting alone at the campsite, snacking on some fruit they picked up on their trek. They brought enough food to last the whole trip, but the Rangers know the value of preserving provisions and trying to live off the land whenever possible.

Eventually, Bull and Reno return to the campsite, and Lania starts laying the wood for the campfire while Reno stacks the spare wood.

When Lania has the firewood ready, she raises a hand, and a glowing orange ring appears around her arm. A split second later, a ball of fire launches from her hand and ignites the firewood.

Lania looks slightly proud of herself and sits back, resuming her snacking.

Not too long after getting the fire started, Jax and Rayn return to the campsite and report that the area seems deserted, and then Celeste and Kimball return with enough fish to feed the whole party.

Lania helps Celeste and Kimball set up the fish to cook while Major Stryder and the boys all joke about the day's travels.

Jax leans back on a log and sighs. "Man, when that behemoth spotted us, I thought we were dead for sure. That one was unusually patient to let us go."

Stryder laughs. "Yeah, I was getting worried when he started following us. I just thought to myself, 'Just keep moving. Let him know we are just passing through.' I don't think we could have taken him if he got mad."

Bull scoffs. "Nah, I could have taken him, sir."

Kimball looks up with her eyebrows raised. "And that is why we call you Bull, because you're so full of shit. You may be big, hell, you may be outright huge, but you cannot take on a ten-ton behemoth alone."

Bull huffs again "Nah, I could do it."

Stryder laughs. "You know, we could go back if you want to fight him that badly."

Bull closes his eyes and leans back. "No thank you, sir. I don't want to backtrack and waste time."

"Nice cop out..." Jax mumbles.

Everyone in the camp laughs uproariously at this, and as Kimball wipes the tears from her eyes, she says. "Again, this is why we call you Bull."

Reno mutters to Rayn, "These guys are a lot more laid back and fun than I was expecting. I thought they'd be more, you know, mean and serious."

Rayn opens his mouth to answer, but Jax beats him to it. "We may be career military, but you have to have a sense of humor to survive out here. If you spend all day every day fighting on end but never relaxing and having a good time, you start to lose track of what you're fighting for."

Stryder nods. "Around the other military personnel, we remain serious and professional. However, it is very important for a squad to be close and friendly. When you spend every day looking death in the face, your squad becomes like your family. You learn to look out for each other, you learn each other's ticks, you learn how to make each other laugh, and you learn how to piss each other off. You learn everything about each other, and when the time comes, you fight as one unified team, and then you all go home."

"You may not like everything about the people you fight alongside," adds Kimball, "but as long as you do so, you are family. Learn to value your brothers and sisters in arms. Trust each other, and you will almost always come home."

The four fourteen-year-old students nod, listening with rapt attention. Here they are, out in the field in the southern frontier lands, working alongside some of the best the military has to offer. This is what they are all hoping to do someday.

Kimball starts passing out the fish. "Alright, everyone, eat up. We've got a long day tomorrow, and you don't want to go to sleep on an empty stomach."

The eight companions, the four teenagers and four veterans, eat their dinner quietly, enjoying their first hot food of the day. The fish is actually quite tasty. It's not a variety that

ETERNAL KNIGHTS OF EDEN I

Reno has ever seen before, but it is full of flavor and falls apart in his mouth.

When they finish eating, Stryder gives out some last orders for the day. "Okay. Cadets? You all go to bed. We'll handle guard duty. I'll take first watch for two hours, then Kimball, then Jax, and then Bull. Understood?"

"We don't mind helping with the watch, sir," says Ryan.

Stryder shakes his head. "Your enthusiasm is appreciated, Jarvis, but your well-being is one of our priorities. We learned long ago to function effectively on low sleep. You cadets are growing teenagers, and sleep is vital to your effective performance." He nods approvingly. "No, it is appreciated, but we will handle the watch. Get some sleep."

Stryder climbs a tree and watches the plains as the other seven lay down, using their packs like pillows, and drift off to sleep.

Reno does not realize how tired he really is until he lies back to relax. He finds himself thinking that Shaide would be enjoying the time of his life out here if he were not still in the hospital, and then he dwells on that fact for a few minutes. Before he knows it, he drifts off to sleep.

CHAPTER 7

THE HORNETS' NEST

Reno wakes up the next morning before sunrise. He sits up and surveys his surroundings for a moment, noticing that Stryder, Kimball, and Jax are all still asleep. He looks around and sees Bull sitting against a tree, staring off into the distance.

Reno is wide awake, his senses fully alert. He is privately amused that for once, he is the first one to wake up. For some reason, he slept unusually soundly, and he finds himself feeling well rested. He quietly gets to his feet and walks over to where Bull is sitting against the tree. He is amused to see that even sitting down on the ground, Bull is huge.

Bull looks at him as he approaches and says in a soft voice, "Morning person?"

Reno shakes his head and laughs quietly. "No, I'm usually the hardest one to wake up, actually. What time is it?"

Bull looks at the eastern horizon, where the sky is ever so subtly beginning to lighten, and answers, "I'll be waking everyone up in just a few minutes."

Reno looks out across the plains, noticing movement in the dim morning light. He squints, trying to identify what he is seeing.

Bull notices him looking. "Lobos. They know we're here, but they don't want to come near the water's edge, so they're staying back."

Reno tilts his head. "Why don't they like water?"

"Snapjaws love eating lobo," Bull replies with a smile. "The lobos out here on the plains have learned over the years, so they stay clear of the water."

Reno raises his eyebrows in alarm. "Are WE safe near the water?"

Bull nods. "Snapjaws don't like our campfires. We burn herbs that repel them, so they leave us alone."

Reno is deeply impressed by the knowledge of these Rangers. They truly have learned the land and how to survive out here. They are as home out here on the plains as the wildlife is. Maybe even more so.

A few minutes later, Bull stands up. He picks up a rock and loudly bangs it against his oversized battle-axe, making a loud ringing sound that echoes across the plains.

Rayn and Lania sit bolt upright, looking around in alarm, while Celeste just casually sits up, glaring at the source of the noise. Meanwhile, Jax, Stryder, and Kimball all calmly wake and rise, pushing themselves to their feet.

The octet eats a relaxed but quick breakfast out of their provisions, mostly fruit and dried grains, and within the hour, they are back on their feet and resuming their long trek through the wilds.

As they get farther southeast, the frequency of wildlife encounters gradually increases. By noon, they have encountered two packs of lobos, an ill-tempered nekoshin, several hungry basilisks, and even a swarm of angry vespids: flying insect-like creatures that greatly resemble the giant wasps found north of the mountains.

By noon, the students' nerves are heavily frayed as the increasingly frequent attacks are beginning to wear them down, especially since Stryder has them join in the fighting. They have discovered one thing, and that is that they are not yet in the physical condition they need to be in.

ETERNAL KNIGHTS OF EDEN I

The lone exception is Celeste, who is proving to be an especially proficient fighter. She twirls gracefully around her prey, striking with terrifying speed with her bladed halberd. She seems to be an experienced fighter, and her physical conditioning far exceeds that of her three classmates.

When noon rolls around, Stryder stops and very carefully surveys their surroundings. Reno imitates him, but he doesn't see anything anywhere near them. Stryder seems satisfied, and he turns around and drops his pack. "Okay, now is a good time to eat lunch. Everyone close ranks and relax for a few minutes. I advise fruit and vegetables for lunch, but it's up to you."

As they sit down to eat, Reno overhears a worried-sounding Kimball speaking with Stryder. He listens carefully, wondering what she is concerned about.

"Don't you think the concentration of monsters is strange?"

Stryder looks around subtly. "Yeah, it's true. We don't usually encounter the wildlife this frequently. They were getting awfully close to that behemoth's territory. That's unusual."

"Yeah," whispers Kimball. "I feel like something is driving them north, out of their normal territories. These are fierce beasts, Jordan. It's not easy to drive them out of their lands."

Major Stryder nods. "I know. Maybe those drakes are causing more of a problem than I thought."

Kimball puts her hands on her hips and tilts her head skeptically. "Come on, Jordan. Do you really believe that a nest of drakes is enough to do this?"

Stryder shakes his head. "No, I don't. But until we know what's causing it, we just have to keep moving."

Kimball nods "Understood, sir."

Reno returns to his lunch, mulling over what he just heard. The Rangers seem to think something is wrong out here. Is it safe for them to be here?

Rayn notices the worried expression on Reno's face and leans over. "Hey, Reno, is everything okay? You look like something is bothering you."

Reno frowns and decides to carefully repeat what he heard. "I dunno, dude. I feel like we've been getting attacked more than we should be. I know we're out in the wilderness and all, but we can't go more than an hour without fighting SOMETHING."

Stryder looks over at him. "You noticed it too, huh?"

Reno nods slowly.

Kimball sighs and butts in. "Yeah, this is exactly why we're down here. That drake nest is strange enough on its own, but the monsters out here are behaving oddly too. We're going to figure out why."

Reno nods and finishes eating his fruit. He finds himself missing the creature comforts of home. At the academy, they are fed well, and the food is healthy. But the students also go into town every weekend and end up stockpiling on sweets and snack foods. . With the meat and sweets that Reno is used to eating, this diet of fruits and grains is making Reno homesick.

Stryder gets to his feet. "Alright. Everyone pack up. We're moving out. Because it is getting increasingly dangerous, we're shifting to a precious-diamond formation."

Rayn tilts his head. "Sir?"

Bull moves to the head of the pack, Jax takes the rear, and Kimball and Major Stryder take position on either side of the students. Kimball explains. "Precious-diamond is an escort position. You four are most likely to be targeted by stray hungry fauna, so you will stay in the center while we take up a four-point position around you, each of us responsible for monitoring our respective sectors for danger."

Rayn nods. "I get it. Because we're younger and smaller than you all, a hungry lobo might get some ideas if we're outside the pack."

"You catch on quick," Kimball says with a smile.

Celeste frowns, looking a bit put out. "I can handle myself, you know."

Major Stryder's voice rings out sharply. "Cadet Wyatt!"

Celeste stands up straight. "Sir!"

The major rings out in a drill sergeant voice, "What were you told to do before setting out to join us in the field?"

Celeste thinks for a moment. "To follow orders and trust you, sir!"

"That's right. If you do what we tell you, then you will make it home in one piece. If you do not, then you probably will not make it back. So, do you have a problem with the orders I have given, cadet?"

Celeste looks slightly ashamed for a moment. "No, sir!"

Stryder relaxes his stance a bit. "Good. It is incredibly dangerous out here. Trust me, and I will get you home. Bull? Move out."

The party sets off once again. Their route branches from the main road, and they follow this path for another five hours. At first, they are forced to stop frequently to fight native wildlife that takes exception to their presence, but then the attacks strangely cease altogether.

As the sun begins to set on the horizon, Kimball grows increasingly uneasy. Reno can't really understand why. He'd have thought that not being attacked anymore was a good thing, but when his eyes drift to Bull, he sees the giant of a man is gripping his battle-axe tightly. Although his head is pointing straight forward, Reno has the distinct impression that his eyes are darting around wildly.

They come to a stop on the edge of a plateau overlooking a large lake. Stryder looks around and says to the group, "Alright, our target is just around the lake, in that cavern over there." He points at a cliff overlooking the lake, on the other side.

Reno squints. If his eyes are working right, then it looks like there is some kind of cave in the cliff wall down at ground level, near the water. He looks around, surveying the area.

The plateau that they are stopped on wraps around the eastern half of the lake and tapers down to ground level as it moves west. The westernmost quarter of the lake is open to the plains, creating an interesting little cove that Reno can understand being appealing to the drakes.

Stryder issues his orders, "Same drill as last night, but this time, stay close."

The party of eight follows the same routine as the night before, with everyone going out to complete their various tasks. A short time later, they are all eating dinner and going to bed, with Stryder taking the first watch.

Reno is exhausted from fighting all day and then climbing the incline of the plateau while working their way through the brush. He falls asleep as soon as he lays his head down.

Lania looks at Reno in amusement. She finds herself thinking about how he is not your typical military student. He is kind of lazy and socially awkward at times, but after the ordeal in the mountains and fighting alongside him here on the plains for a couple of days, she finds herself thinking he isn't so bad. She leans her head back and fades into sleep.

Celeste lies on her back, staring at the stars overhead, appreciating how beautiful the night sky is out here. She pulls her halberd close, and after some time passes, she closes her eyes and drifts off to sleep.

Rayn is a bit different from the others, and his anxiety over their mission gnaws away at him while he lies on the ground. Reno made a good point earlier, and something doesn't seem quite right. The Rangers aren't saying anything, but Rayn can tell they are nervous. He can also tell they aren't the kind to get nervous easily. He lays his head back and tries his best to go to sleep, but it is some time before he drifts away.

All this time, Major Stryder is observing the students as he simultaneously watches their surroundings, forming his own opinions over them and deciding who will and won't make a good soldier in the future.

*   *   *

The next morning, the party of eight is split up into four pairs positioned along the ridge overlooking the drakes' den. Stryder is paired with Rayn, Celeste is paired with Kimball, and Lania is paired with Bull, which leaves Reno paired with Jax.

Reno and Jax are looking out across the valley from near their campsite. Reno is lying on his belly while Jax is in a low kneeling stance, looking through a monocular scope at the den.

Reno shoots a glance at Jax. He is the most mysterious of the Rangers they are with. He's smaller than the others, honestly no bigger than fourteen-year-old Reno himself. He's mostly quiet, like Bull, but he seems very energetic most of the time.

He is also equipped differently than the others. His bow is made of a very stout metal rather than wood, and his arrows also seem to be some kind of metal. In spite of this, they seem to fly even faster than wooden arrows, and Reno has seen them hit like a truck.

Now, however, Jax is kneeling in an uncomfortable position, sitting as still as a statue. Despite his usually energetic nature, he is very focused now that it is time for business.

He glances over and catches Reno looking at him. He casually points at his eyes, and then back across the valley, telling Reno to watch their target.

Reno shakes his head clear and goes back to watching the den. In short order, his attention is rewarded. Just as the sun crests the ridge to the east, several large lizard-like creatures shamble out of the cave. Jax taps Reno on the shoulder and hands him the monocle.

Reno zooms in on the lizards and sees the drakes just like they were described in his textbooks. They are very large four-legged lizards with backward-pointed horns on top of their heads and short spikes running all the way down their backs and tails. They're an odd green and brown color, clearly evolved to blend in with the local terrain. If Reno had to guess, they are likely somewhere around five feet tall at the shoulder and around twenty to twenty-five feet long nose to tail. Reno shudders when he considers dealing with them.

He hands the monocle back to Jax, who looks at him in amusement. "Big, aren't they? I bet you've never actually seen a drake before."

Reno shakes his head.

Jax looks through the monocle at their target and suddenly zooms in. "Whoa, hey now. That's new. Explains a lot too. Here, take a look. The big one." He hands it back to Reno.

ETERNAL KNIGHTS OF EDEN I

Reno looks through the monocle again, and his eyebrows go up in surprise. There is another drake-like creature with them, but it looks different than the others. It's about twice as big and jet black in color. It also looks mildly deformed, as if it has mutated in some way. It looks like something has distorted its appearance somehow.

Reno zooms in on it further and notices something else that's different. It has some kind of wings folded flat against its back, but they don't quite look natural. Their skeletal structure is exposed, and the black leathery webbing looks rotted and necrotic.

Reno looks over at Jax in alarm. "What is that thing? It looks kind of strange to be hanging around those drakes."

Jax takes the monocle back. "That, my dear boy, is what we were afraid we'd find: a corrupted drake. It looks like it is pretty severely corrupted too. A big drake like that would certainly explain the odd behavior of all the fauna down here. Even the behemoths would think twice before messing with it."

"What does that mean?"

Jax frowns as he watches a second, slightly smaller corrupted drake shamble out of the den with the others. "It means we are going to have to exterminate them. Or at least we'll have to take out the corrupted ones."

Reno looks at him with concern. "You're going to try and take out those huge drakes?"

Jax nods. "Probably. Standing orders are to handle normal wildlife incursions as we see fit, but all corrupted beasts must be taken down at all cost before they can have a chance to threaten local settlements. Those two big drakes definitely qualify as a threat."

Reno shudders again.

Jax pats him on the shoulder. "I reacted the same way when I was your age. You get used to the danger. If you trust Stryder and do what he says, you'll make it. You may be scared out of your mind, but you'll make it."

"You lost Shaide's parents a few years ago…" Reno says skeptically.

Jax stares at the ground. "I wondered how long that would take to come up." He looks at Reno. "You need to understand something about that. What I'm about to tell you is classified, so don't repeat it, okay?"

Reno nods, interested now.

Jax looks out over the valley as he recounts his story. "We were facing a large population of formers, or humans who had been corrupted to the point they lost their humanity and basically became feral monsters. The thing was, these weren't your run-of-the-mill formers. When we went in force with the

ETERNAL KNIGHTS OF EDEN I

Ceraph Order to clear them out, we were met with an overwhelming amount of resistance. These formers were organized and armed. They weren't like the mindless zombies we fought before."

Reno listens intently. He has never heard this story before.

Jax continues. "They were threatening the village of New Watch, near the border. For generations, we had advised the people living there to move north. While we were trying to clear out the ruins of the old city of Highwatch, one of the the border cities from before the war, some of the formers, along with a large swarm of corrupted beasts, attacked New Watch and forced us to divide our forces."

Jax looks down and shakes his head. "Major Stryder told Darkmoon's squad to fall back and wait for help, but Darkmoon's wife, your friend's mother, was in that village, fighting a losing battle to give the villagers time to evacuate. Darkmoon and his squad disobeyed orders and stormed the village. The two-pronged counterattack gave the villagers the time they needed to evacuate, but shortly after, every Ceraph and trooper that was in that village was overrun by enemy forces, and we lost them all. Shaide's parents were heroes, but they cost the lives of many good soldiers, including their own, because they disobeyed orders."

Reno sits quietly, taking in all this information. He wonders if Shaide knows all of this.

"Did they do the right thing?" Reno finds himself asking before he can stop himself.

Jax looks at him with an unreadable expression for a moment as he considers the question. Finally, his expression softens, and he answers "They disobeyed orders and cost the lives of quite a few soldiers, along with their own, but his disobedience saved the lives of nine-thousand civilians. Personally, I believe they are heroes, but I can't really say. You can decide for yourself whether they did the right thing or not."

Reno frowns. "They saved a lot of people, but I don't know if Shaide sees it that way. He lost his parents."

Jax shrugs. "I couldn't tell you. I don't even know if he knows what happened."

They continue to observe the drakes for a while, trying to get a feel for what they are dealing with. Around the ridge, the other three pairs are doing the exact same thing, so that there are eight very nervous Alastair personnel watching their quarry.

Sometime around noon, Reno catches sight of something glinting in the distance. He squints and asks Jax. "Hey, what is that?"

Jax looks through the monocle and sees Major Stryder flashing a signal mirror at him. He fumbles in a pouch and reflects a signal back, and the glinting stops.

Reno looks up at Jax with a confused expression.

Jax holds out his hand to him. "Come on. We need to meet up with the others."

Reno takes Jax's hand and pulls himself to his feet. "What was that about?"

Jax pulls out the mirror again. "Signal mirror. Nice and subtle way to communicate."

Reno is mildly impressed as the two of them set off around the lip of the plateau. It takes them twenty minutes to reach the place where Major Stryder signaled to them, and when they arrive, Lania and Bull are already waiting for them with the major and Rayn.

Rayn nods as they approach and bumps fists with Reno. "Hey, Reno, did you see what we are dealing with?"

Reno nods, slightly pale. "Yeah. A bunch of big ol drakes, and a couple of even bigger corrupted ones."

"And Bull is threatening to wrestle them," Lania says with a shudder.

Bull looks down at the big drakes below. "I can take 'em."

Stryder shakes his head in amusement. "I'm sure you could, Bull. But we all want in on the action, so be considerate, okay?"

Bull pretends to look disappointed. "Yes, sir."

"So," asks Reno, "we're really going to have to take out those things?"

"Yes and no," replies the major. "WE are going to take out those things." He indicates himself, Bull, and Jax. "But you will hang back and stay safe. I believe you are strong, but you are still inexperienced, and a couple of corrupted drakes are going to be a bit much for you to handle. Second, we don't have to take out all of them. If we can eliminate the two big corrupted ones, the ordinary ones shouldn't be a significant threat. We'll play them by ear."

"Don't feel bad, Reno," says Lania. "Those things scare the hell out of me too."

Reno looks a bit taken aback, and he sputters. "Afraid? Who said I was afraid?"

Lania smiles and looks away. "It's okay. No one blames you."

"The big drakes make me nervous too," says Stryder. "No shame in it, Coltide. The secret isn't not to be afraid. The secret is overcoming it."

Reno nods and shrugs slightly. He looks around. "Hey? Where are Celeste and Kimball?"

Rayn points across the gap. "They were farther away, so we'll have to wait a few minutes."

Lania sidles over next to Reno and asks quietly, "So, how was it hanging out with Jax all morning?"

Reno immediately thinks of the story he told him. "It wasn't bad. For how squirrelly he is, he is remarkably calm when he's focusing on something."

Lania nods "Yeah, Bull is really quiet. Like, REALLY quiet. He just watches like a hawk. He'll answer if you talk to him, but he really doesn't say much. He's nice, though."

Reno nods thoughtfully. "This isn't a bad trip so far. I kind of miss home, though."

Lania giggles. "You're weird, Reno. You know that?"

"What on earth makes you say that?" Reno says, looking slightly offended.

Lania gives him an amused look. "When you're at the academy, you're always anxious to get out and about as much as you can, but now that we're actually out, you just want to go home. I didn't say it was bad. You're just a little weird."

Reno pouts slightly "I miss my food and my pillow. That's all."

"Yeah, I understand that," Lania says with a sigh. "We got spoiled by the good food at the academy and in the capital. Camp-style living is a bit of a jarring change for me too."

Reno tilts his head "Then why are you making fun of me?"

Lania giggles again. "Because your reaction is cute." She realizes what she said, and she coughs and turns away in embarrassment. Reno narrows an eyebrow and shakes his head.

Meanwhile, Jax and Bull watch the exchange with amused grins. Jax looks at Reno, jerks his head at Lania, and winks with a grin. Reno just raises his eyebrows and mutters, "Okay then…"

A few minutes pass, and two white-haired women come into view. More accurately, a white-haired woman and a white-haired teenager. Reno is mildly amused by the sight of the twin white heads approaching.

Celeste has her halberd slung across her back as she walks over to join her classmates.

Rayn asks her, "How was your morning with the scary lady?"

"She's not bad," Celeste replies with a shrug. "She's actually really nice. She let me kill a couple of megantulas that tried to creep up on us." She smiles and sighs. "It was fun."

Reno shudders. Forget Kimball. Celeste is pretty scary too.

Kimball walks up to Stryder and asks, "Alright, what's the plan, Jordan?"

Stryder looks around and nods. "There are two corrupted drakes down there. Standing orders are the elimination of all corrupted beasts we encounter. The two corrupted drakes are our primary targets. The elimination of the remaining drakes is not necessary, and they are to be considered targets of opportunity. Do not engage them unless forced to."

To the students, he says, "You four will remain out of range, and you will not approach under any circumstances. Do NOT attempt to engage the drakes. While I feel that you may be able to handle them, my priority is your safe return, and I will not risk you coming to harm."

Celeste bites her lip in disappointment, holding her tongue. She resigned herself to following orders after being chewed out by the major. Lania and Reno share a matching expression of relief. Rayn, meanwhile, doesn't look like he has an opinion either way.

Stryder turns back to his squad. "Bull, you take point on the smaller of the two corrupted. Jax, you support him and watch his back. I'll run point on the larger corrupted. Kimball, you support me from my six and make sure the smaller drakes stay out of the way."

Kimball chews her lip for a moment, looking uncomfortable with the order, but her trust in the major is absolute, and she replies, "Yes, sir."

Stryder isn't the company commander for nothing. He notices Kimball's discomfort and turns to her. "Speak your mind, Sierra. What's wrong?"

Kimball frowns "Jordan, those drakes are bigger than any we've dealt with before. I don't know if a one-plus-one assault will be enough against these things."

Stryder closes his eyes and smiles. "When have you ever failed to jump in and save me if I was in over my head? Same for all three of you."

Bull, Jax, and Kimball all nod.

Stryder opens his eyes. "I trust your judgment if you feel like you need to step in and offer support. We've always taken care of each other, and we won't stop now."

"You're right, Jordan," says Kimball, relaxing a little. "These corrupted drakes just make me nervous. That's all."

"Understood. Besides, I feel like the kids won't just sit back if we're really in trouble." He gives Celeste, in particular, a serious look.

Celeste coughs and rubs her neck awkwardly.

"Is everyone ready?" the major asks.

A chorus of "Yes, sir" reaches his ears.

"Alright, let's move out. I'll take point." He moves to the head of the pack, and they set off around the south edge of the plateau. The walk is long because they have to go all the way to where the land levels out and then turn around and walk back into the cove at ground level. Stryder considered just scaling the cliff side, but then decided against it to avoid getting backed into a corner.

They take their time, sticking close to the cliff wall while approaching the drakes' den. Bull stays behind the students while the other three Rangers take the lead.

Rayn mumbles to himself, "I'll say this, the drakes are keeping the other monsters away, at least."

Stryder looks over his shoulder and replies in a low voice, "Yeah, it does make the trip a little easier." He slows down and shushes the party.

Up ahead, the drakes come into view. The biggest is leaning over the water, drinking. Behind him, the other drakes are milling around, play-fighting or lying in the sun. The group's second target is, unfortunately, on the far side of the smaller drakes. This could make their job a little harder.

Reno whispers to Bull, "What makes the smaller drakes so dangerous? They don't look a whole lot bigger than lobos."

Bull whispers back, "Their hide is like armor. They are very hard to injure. In addition, they are extremely fast and agile. They can grab you real fast."

The big corrupted drake by the water suddenly turns his head and watches them approach. Stryder eyes the drake warily as it snarls and bares its teeth, smoke coming from its nostrils.

"Well," he mutters, "this is going to be fun. Follow the original plan and try and get to the corrupted drake on the far side. Retreat as soon as you take down the target. No need to stick around. We'll meet back up where we did before if we get separated."

Bull walks over to Jax and nods, and Kimball draws her rapier and stands next to Stryder. The major looks over his shoulder and says, "You four stay back, and follow the plan. Do not get involved, okay?"

Four heads nod to him, acknowledging his order.

Ahead of them, the drake claws at the ground, and its kin all watch the group angrily. Stryder's halberd begins to glow faintly, and it arcs with electricity. "Wait for an opening and then go for the second corrupted drake."

Stryder roars "UNGH!" and he takes three wide, violent swings at the big drake. Each swing emits an arc of electricity that flies out and slams into the big drake at lightning speed, rocking it back and enveloping it with crackling energy. In response, it lets out an earsplitting roar, although whether from pain or anger, they cannot tell.

Kimball leaps forward, her sword glowing light blue. She viciously thrusts her blade forward in an inhumanly fast barrage of stabs, piercing the drake's hide and making several blossoms of ice crystals erupt from its side.

The drake turns its head and snaps its monster jaws at Kimball, but she leaps clear of the attack.

Bull and Jax take advantage of the drake's distraction to run past it. Jax pulls three arrows and simultaneously notches them, a light blue glow emanating from them as he leaps over the big drake and parkour-runs across the backs of several smaller drakes between him and his target.

Bull, meanwhile, true to his name, charges forward at a surprising speed given his size and simply uses his oversized battle-axe to bludgeon any conventional drakes out of his path.

Reno, Celeste, Rayn, and Lania watch in awe as the two Rangers in front of them take on the corrupted drake, moving in ways they did not know was humanly possible.

As Kimball leaps back out of the way of the drake's bite, Stryder leaps forward and gets under the drake's head. His blade still arcing with electricity, he spins around and slashes at its chin, knocking its head away from Kimball. He then hits it with an upward swing and then leaps into the air above it and slams its head down with a full-extension, two-handed swing, each hit releasing a blast of lightning magic.

The downward blow slams the drake's head into the ground. Stryder comes down on its head from above to impale it and end the fight quickly. The drake, however, reacts far more quickly than Stryder anticipated, and it spins around hard, catching him in mid-air with its tail.

Stryder's eyes open wide from the impact, which sends him through the air and skidding along the ground. A curious subtle flare of light emanates from his body with each hit.

Kimball doesn't miss a beat, leaping forward and launching a second barrage of thrusting ice attacks, knocking chunks of the drake's scales loose as the ice blossoms erupt beneath them.

As Kimball leaps back, Stryder leaps forward again from his spot on the ground. A trickle of blood drips from his mouth, but he seems otherwise unharmed. He hurls his halberd at the drake and impales it in one of the vulnerable areas where Kimball blew its scales off.

The drake rears its head back in pain as the halberd buries itself a foot deep. A split second later, Stryder grabs the halberd mid-leap, and the force of his impact drives it even deeper.

Kimball seems to be reading her commander's mind, and she leaps forward, thrusting her rapier deep into the drake's chest, next to Stryder's halberd. She releases a large ice bloom just as Stryder releases a huge thunder-blast from his blade, causing the drake's body to light up with the water-amplified internal lightning attack.

The drake cranes its neck back and looks down at them, smoke pouring from its mouth. Stryder and Kimball both simultaneously yell, "Uh-Oh!"

Reno sprints out of nowhere and slams into them both from the side, knocking them and their blades loose from the drake's chest. Just a split second after they are clear, the drake spews a jet of flames from its mouth, scorching the ground beneath where they had been just a second before.

The three of them skid along the ground and roll to their feet. Stryder and Kimball look at Reno in surprise. Reno looks down, expecting a reprimand, but instead, Stryder simply says, "Thank you."

Stryder doesn't waste another second. He leaps through the air and buries his halberd in the corrupted drake's neck, forcing its head away as it releases another burst of flame intended for them. Kimball leaps in behind Stryder and thrusts her rapier into its neck below Stryder's halberd. Stryder uses the blossom of ice from the wound as a springboard and launches himself up into the air.

Kimball drops to the ground and leaps up at the drake from beneath, jamming her ice-charged rapier into its neck and setting it up for Stryder's next attack.

With perfect timing, Stryder comes down from above and buries his halberd in the drake's head, right behind its eyes. He releases a massive burst of lightning from his blade, and the drake roars in pain, collapsing to the ground.

Kimball runs over and thrusts her blade at Stryder, allowing him to jump on it, and then she uses it to hurl him up into the air. She leaps back and hollers, "You're clear! Do it!"

At the peak of his inhumanly high jump, Stryder throws his halberd down into the drake's head, burying it deep in the scaly flesh. A ball of supercharged blue lightning forms in his hands, and he puts them together. A split second later, intense blue lightning streaks into his halberd as he dives from mid-air, and the still-living drake howls in pain.

Just before he lands, Stryder grabs onto the halberd, driving it THROUGH the drake's head, and releases a massive blast of the blue lightning into its body, causing it to erupt through the flesh and arc out into the air and the ground.

The big corrupted drake's eyes roll back into its head, and it moves no more.

ETERNAL KNIGHTS OF EDEN I

This whole time, curiously, the normal drakes kept their distance, choosing not to interfere as their larger corrupted kin fought the Rangers. Stryder pulls his bloodstained halberd loose and jumps down. "Okay," he says to the students "fall back. We're done here."

Reno looks over at the others. "What about…? Oh."

Bull is leaning against his battle-axe buried deep in the smaller corrupted drake's neck as Jax retrieves his arrows from its hide. Bull gives Stryder a thumbs up as the smaller drakes back away and cower in fear. Evidently, they are not unintelligent and can tell that this would not be a wise fight. Several of them are injured where Bull bludgeoned his way through them.

They are starting to get agitated, though, which means it's time for the group to go. Stryder points up the cliff. "Fall back! Meet us at the RV!"

Bull pulls his axe out, and he and Jax run off in the opposite direction. Stryder, limping slightly, points back the way they came, and the six of them jog back out of the canyon as the drakes start walking around the corpse of the big corrupted drake and glare at them angrily.

Celeste looks longingly at the drakes, craving a fight, but she remains with the group as they retreat.

Rayn asks Kimball as they jog away, "Why didn't you just clear out the regular drakes too?"

Stryder slows down to a fast walk as they get out of range of the drakes, and Kimball answers. "It's a delicate matter taking care of threats. When it regards native wildlife, we try not to kill any more than we must because it can upset the ecosystem."

Stryder nods, still limping slightly from the tail hit. "Drakes are dangerous, but they aren't inherently bad. They help control the local herbivore populations, and they are especially helpful at keeping boar populations down. If we take out TOO many predators, then the herbivores overpopulate and damage the flora balance."

"I see," says Rayn. Thank you, sir, ma'am. We have learned a lot over these past few days."

"That's why we do these annual exercises with you academy students," says the major. "You'll be doing our jobs someday, and we want you to be prepared. Don't stop paying attention now, though. The trip back is the most dangerous part."

"How so, sir?" asks Reno as he power-walks alongside Rayn.

Stryder raises his eyebrows and chuckles. "That right there is exactly why. Rookies, and sometimes even veterans.

have a tendency to relax after their main objective is complete. They aren't as alert on their return trips and end up getting hurt or killed by something trivial."

Reno looks back behind them, and something catches his eye. A person, dressed in black, is standing on the cliff, looking down on them. He seems to have a kind of haze around him as he looks down, and although it is difficult for Reno to tell at this distance, he seems to have a distinct look of displeasure on his face.

Reno taps Kimball on the shoulder. "Hey, ma'am, who is that?" He turns around and points to where he saw the strange figure, but the man is no longer there.

Kimball frowns. "Who is who?"

Reno shakes his head "I swear I just saw someone standing up there. All in black."

"I think the adrenaline still has you overexcited, Coltide. No one should be out here on their own. It's just your eyes playing tricks on you."

Reno looks behind him again at the now empty cliff. "I swear I saw someone."

They meet Jax and Bull at their previous rendezvous point and make their way back to their campsite from the night before. They rest there for the night to recover their energy and allow Stryder's sprained leg to rest slightly.

Experienced fighters like Stryder and his Rangers actually have the ability to use their magic energy like a sort of shield, forming a protective aura around their bodies that can absorb a limited amount of damage. Using this aura is very draining, however, and tends to wear out fighters afterward. Unfortunately, it doesn't absorb everything and behaves more like a cushion most of the time. Severe impacts like a twenty-ton drake's tail can still cause moderate injury.

They leave in the morning, beginning their two-day trip back to Broadspring. True to Stryder's prediction, their return trip is nearly as exciting as their journey to the objective. They are forced to fight several packs of megantulas, lobos, basilisks, nekoshin, and a handful of other creatures that see them as a potential meal. Now more confident of the students' abilities, Stryder allows them to gain some valuable experience against these creatures.

They spend the first night next to the lake where they made their first camp, and this is when the Rangers inform them that they have a number of campsites they like to use throughout the southern lands because they have proven in the past to be quite defensible.

The following morning, they begin the last leg of their journey back into town, and along the way, they experience the same routine of encountering dangerous beasts. The students get

     A.S.GUINN

tired from fighting all day, but they also gain a great deal of experience that will be very valuable in their future careers.

Just before nightfall of the second day of their return journey, they enter the small canyon leading up into Broadspring.

The guards at the gate look down as they approach, and one calls out, "Identify yourselves. OH! Major Stryder! I'm sorry sir, let me get the gate open. We weren't expecting you until at least tomorrow!"

Stryder looks up. "The objective went more smoothly than expected. The kids aren't half bad either."

The gate swings open, and the guard says, "I'm glad to hear it, sir. Welcome back."

The eight companions re-enter the town of Broadspring. The students had a hell of a time, but they are now happy to be returning to the safety and comfort of civilization. Reno makes a mental note to go visit Shaide as soon as he is given leave to do so.

CHAPTER 8

CITADEL

[Three days after Shaide's battle with Rho]

Shaide wakes up in an unfamiliar room, looking at an unfamiliar ceiling. He lies still for a few moments, trying to recall what happened, and where he is. He feels like he has been asleep for too long, and his head is heavy.

When he focuses on what he can remember, he recalls a handful of details. The dropship crash and the subsequent struggle for survival are the first things to come to mind. As he walks himself through what he remembers, he recalls the cave, the decantulas, and the massive chamber.

He remembers the great altar in the chamber and the thunderbird.

He is distracted from his thoughts when a man's voice speaks to him from beside his bed. "Shaide? I see you're finally awake."

Shaide turns his head and sees his godfather sitting in the corner of what he now realizes is a hospital room. Aton appears to have been reading a book when he happened to look up and notice Shaide's eyes were open. Shaide slowly sits up and watches his godfather get out of his chair.

Aton walks over and kneels next to the bed, an uncharacteristic look of concern on his scarred yet handsome features. "How are you feeling, kiddo?"

Shaide looks down at his bare chest and his arms and legs. He is surprised to see that his injuries are all healed. He looks back up to his godfather and replies, "I feel…not bad considering what happened. How long was I out?"

Aton pulls the chair over and sits down. "Three days. Fighting that angel really did a number on you."

Shaide tilts his head, his suspicions confirmed. "So that WAS an angel?"

Aton nods. "You did the impossible, Shaide. At your age, you passed an Angel's Trial. Rho the Thunderbird is with you now."

Shaide raises his eyebrows. "Umm… Come again?"

Aton sighs "I need to explain from the beginning, don't I?"

Shaide nods slowly. "Yeah, I've heard the stories, but I don't really get it."

Aton leans forward. "Okay. There are a number of godlike beings that were raised by Eden when he came to this land. No one is entirely sure where they came from, but their altars dot the land. We call them the Angels. They are sentient manifestations of spiritual energy guarding the planet."

Shaide nods slowly "I get that much, and the Ceraphs work with them somehow."

"Yes. Whenever a potential Ceraph is deemed ready, the order selects an angel that they believe to be a good match, giving them the greatest chance of success in pairing with it. When they touch that angel's altar, if the angel deems him or her worthy of its attention, it will awaken and put the Ceraph through a trial, usually combat, though occasionally something stranger."

Shaide nods, following so far.

Aton continues. "If the Ceraph fails the trial, well, they usually die. In fact, dying is often precisely how they fail. But if they pass the trial, the angel will grant them its power, leaving its altar to bind itself to the Ceraph's soul, granting him a drastically increased potential in ability, and even the ability to summon the angel into this world in times of need."

Shaide's eyes open wider. "When you said they bind to the Ceraph's soul…"

Aton nods. "The Angel literally lives inside you, as part of you. This isn't without risk. If the host isn't strong enough, the angel will gradually erode his soul over the years, and his sanity and sense of self may eventually decrease, but most Ceraphs don't live long enough for that to happen."

Shaide tilts his head the other way, his confusion growing. "But I'm not a Ceraph. I'm just a student."

Aton nods, seemingly amused. "Yet, Rho deemed you worthy of his attention, and apparently rightly so."

Shaide looks blank. "Rho? You said that before."

Aton nods. "The angel now residing in you is named Rho. Angel of Storms. The Thunderbird. Would you like to know more about him?"

Shaide nods.

Aton continues again. "Rho is a unique angel in a couple of ways, the biggest being that he seems to be attached to your family. Since the formation of the Ceraphs, he has only been possessed by your direct ancestors, back to the first Ceraph himself. For three thousand years, he has served the Edenkin bloodline."

Shaide blinks in confusion. "Edenkin?"

Aton nods. "Alexander Edenkin was the first Ceraph selected by Eden to fight against the corrupted and the Fallen in the great war. Edenkin was not his original family name, mind you. It has been lost to the records for millennia, but Eden granted him this new name when he entered into his service. Since that day, Rho has only ever served his descendants."

Shaide frowns. "So, my family has always been destined to have Rho?"

Aton laughs. "That would be something, wouldn't it? But no, I think it is more likely that Rho personally feels attached to your family and simply refuses to serve anyone else. I don't think it's a matter of he CAN'T serve someone else. He simply won't."

Shaide looks down at his hands. "What will happen to me now?"

"I cannot say," Aton replies with a frown. "I've been ordered to return you to the Citadel to speak with Master Armstrong once you have recovered. There it will be determined if you will become a Ceraph, or if you will return to your life. Personally, I cannot say. It isn't up to me."

Shaide tilts his head "You mean I don't have to become a Ceraph? I thought the angels only served you lot?"

Aton shakes his head. "Oh, lord no. There have been a handful of incidents in history where non-Ceraphs end up with an angel as their partner. Most of the time, they are military or Rangers, but they can be anyone. They are usually given a choice. If they choose to resume their normal lives, we give them the necessary training to interact properly with their angel and avoid losing control, and then we let them go."

Shaide nods "I see. I think… I don't know."

Aton pats him on the back. "Take it easy, boy. You've got time to decide."

Shaide looks at him suddenly. "My friends! Are they…?

Aton ruffles his hair with a smile. "Relax. They're fine. Your little bunch is actually out on an exercise with Major Stryder, your dad's old commanding officer, right now. I'm sorry to say you will probably not get to see them before we leave."

Shaide looks both relieved and disappointed. "When do we leave?"

"As soon as you feel better. An unprepared teenager with an angel could be dangerous. We need to make sure you can handle him before we have an…accident."

Shaide nods, swings his legs out of bed, and stands up.

Aton rises too. "Whoa, Shaide. Take it easy."

Shaide flexes his hands and lifts his legs a couple of times. Then he turns to face his godfather. "I think I'm good to go, Dad."

Aton chuckles to himself. "You can really be impatient sometimes. you know that?"

Shaide shrugs. "Maybe. I just… You said I could be dangerous. I don't want to wait if I'm putting others at risk. That's all." He looks around. "Where are my clothes?"

Aton sighs, still chuckling to himself. "You really do remind me a lot of your mother sometimes. As for your clothes, they were pretty much destroyed in your fight. Do me a favor. Get back in bed and rest for a bit. I'll find your lieutenant and see if I can't get you another field uniform, okay?"

Shaide grinds his teeth for a moment and then lies back in bed.

"I'll go find him, and I'll see if I can't get you some food while I'm at it. After three days without food, you've got to be starving."

Shaide's stomach seems to grumble in response to Aton's statement. As Aton looks at his godson in amusement, Shaide looks down, slightly embarrassed. "Umm, thanks…"

Shaide leans back against the headboard as Aton leaves the room. Not long after, a pretty military nurse in her twenties

　　　A.S.GUINN

walks in with a tray of food. Shaide can smell meat and potatoes and some kind of bread.

The nurse sets the tray down beside the bed and starts looking him over. "I'm glad to see you're finally awake. How are you feeling?"

Shaide tries not to blush awkwardly as the pretty young woman feels him over and gets close to his face as she examines him. "I'm, uhh, I'm feeling okay. I can't believe I was out for three days."

She stands straight. "Well, everything seems to be fine. Go ahead and eat. Do you need anything?"

Shaide's eyes drift across the pretty nurse for a moment, and then he shakes his head. "No thank you. I think this will be enough."

She nods and smiles "If you're still hungry after that, let me know. We always take really good care of our Ceraph friends here."

Shaide nods, and she leaves the room.

A Ceraph, huh? He knew about his mother, and he spent the last several years being raised by Aton, but he never really thought about being one himself. It always seemed like something that was above him somehow. Like it was something for people more special than him. Now, however, it seems like he may very well be on his way to becoming one after all.

And Rho… According to Aton, his family has been Ceraphs for generations. Since the very beginning, in fact. He never knew that before. Maybe this is something he is destined to do?

But he will have to leave all of his friends. He remembers having to leave Amari behind when he found out about his parents. He never got to see her again, and he still misses and thinks about her sometimes. He has his friends, Reno, Rayn, and Lania. He even gets along with Celeste pretty well, even if she scares the pants off of him sometimes.

He can't forget Nyu, his little Nekomata…friend? Girlfriend? What IS she exactly, anyway? He laughs to himself. He'd be leaving a lot behind to go to the Ceraphs. He doesn't want to leave his friends again…

He looks down in surprise to see he has already emptied his plate. Sure enough, as the nurse predicted, he is still rather hungry. Almost as if she were expecting it, she comes through the door with some extra food at the exact moment this thought crosses his mind.

She looks down at his tray and smiles. "I thought you'd still be hungry, so I went ahead and brought you some extra. Just between us." She winks and leaves the extra food with him.

"Thank you…" he says as she walks away. She simply responds with a wave.

A short time later, the door to his room opens again. This time, it's Aton and Lieutenant Nikola.

Nikola pushes past Aton and looks closely at Shaide. "How do you feel, Darkmoon?"

Shaide sets his tray aside. "I'm okay, Lieutenant. I feel fine."

Lieutenant Nikola sighs and relaxes. "I see. They took good care of you here. Aton already told me the situation, so I have new official orders for you."

Shaide tilts his head. "Sir?"

"You are to report to the COV *Black Pegasus* and return to the Citadel with Ceraph Atondier Norvus for evaluation. When evaluation is complete, you have leave to choose whatever path you see fit. You are welcome, however, to return to the Alastair Royal Military Academy after evaluation if you so choose."

Shaide notices the emphasis the lieutenant placed on the part about returning, and he smiles slightly. "Understood, sir."

Lieutenant Nikola places a folded uniform and some fresh boots on the side of the bed. "You'll be needing some fresh clothes, so I brought you a new field uniform."

"Thank you, sir. Can I ask you a favor?"

Nikola looks up at him. "What is it?"

Shaide frowns. "Can you, uhh, tell my friends that I said goodbye? I think we'll be leaving before they make it back."

"Of course," Nikolas replies with a smile. "I'll give the class your regards. Take care of yourself, Darkmoon. I'll leave the two of you to it for now. Excuse me."

Nikola ducks out of the room and heads down the hallway, returning to his duties.

Aton watches him leave. "He's not exactly what I expect from an academy instructor, but he is dealing with first-years, and he is young, after all."

Shaide starts getting dressed. "He's not so bad. I heard that the instructors get harder as the years pass on, allowing you to prepare over time for service instead of breaking you in all at once. I guess a bunch of first-years aren't held to the same standards as seniors."

Aton laughs. "Yeah, that makes sense. If you're too strict on a bunch of fourteen-year-olds, it won't end very well. They like to rebel, like I did."

Shaide looks at him in amusement. "You were rebellious?"

"Yeah, and pretty bad about it, too. I'll tell you when you're older. I shouldn't encourage you."

Shaide straps up his boots, grabs his gear from the nightstand, and turns to Aton. "Alright, I'm ready."

"We probably won't be leaving for a while, but we can head up to the corvette when you're ready."

"Yeah, I don't want to sit around here any longer than I have to." Shaide was already getting a feeling of cabin fever from being cooped up in the hospital.

"I understand that. I don't like hospitals much either." He opens the door. "After you."

Shaide walks out of the room and turns automatically towards the waiting area. Aton walks alongside him, steering him in the right direction.

The first thing Shaide notices is how the hospital looks more like a repurposed inn. The waiting area looks like an old tavern that was converted into a reception area, and although they've done a good job of fancying up the place, Shaide can still tell.

Aton leads him up to the reception counter and addresses the pretty receptionist. "Yes, ma'am. I am Atondier Norvus of the Ceraph Order. I need to check out Mr. Shaide Darkmoon."

The nurse looks up at him in amusement. "Smartass. You don't have to be so formal, Aton. So, he finally woke up, huh?" She looks over at Shaide. "Handsome young man, aren't you? Very well. I will file the paperwork for his release. You're free to go."

Aton jokingly salutes. "Thank you, ma'am. Much appreciated."

The receptionist sighs. "I can't tell if you're flirting with me or mocking me… Take care, you two."

Aton chuckles as he walks Shaide out the door. "I may have gotten drunk at the tavern and hit on her last time I was here."

"I kind of figured that," Shaide replies, rolling his eyes.

Aton's eyes go wide as though he is offended. "What does that mean? I'm always a perfect gentleman around the ladies."

Shaide looks straight ahead. "I don't think the word 'gentleman' means what you think it does."

Aton has the decency to look mildly ashamed of himself. "Sometimes I think I may have let you see more than I should have. I think your mom would hurt me if she knew what I'd let you see over the years."

Shaide sighs and looks around. It's his first time seeing the town, and the fortified buildings are a definite change from the elegant architecture of the city. Nevertheless, he rather likes the rustic feel of this place, and he makes a mental note to come back and visit someday.

Aton speaks up rather abruptly. "You know? If you DO become a Ceraph, you just might be able to arrange a visit to your old girlfriend in Erita. What was her name…Amari?"

Shaide blushes slightly when Aton mentions her name, and Aton grins at his reaction. Shaide sighs and looks down. "I haven't seen her or even spoken to her in over four years, Aton. I'm not sure she'd even remember me now."

Aton frowns. "I wouldn't be so sure about that. I remember the look on her face when you had to leave with us. I don't think she'd forget you that easily." He coughs "She MIGHT be mad at you, but I can almost promise she would be happy to see you. If you get a chance, of course."

"If you say so," Shaide says uncertainly.

Aton leads him to the dropship pad and approaches the Ceraph Order dropship parked slightly away from a small pool of Alastair Royal Military dropships and gunships. The pilot is already waiting for them.

"Do you need a ride back to the *Black Pegasus*, Aton?"

Aton nods. "Yeah. We'll be departing shortly, so you should probably remain on board. The COV *Light of Eden* will remain here to provide support."

The pilot climbs into his dropship. "Well, come on board. We'll take off shortly."

Shaide sits in one of the jump seats at the back of the dropship as Aton waits for something. Just a moment later, a blonde Mitera woman whom Shaide is quite familiar with climbs into the back with them.

Lucy looks at Aton in mild annoyance. "I could have used a LITTLE more warning before we set off, you know. The others are staying behind to support local operations. Just in case."

Aton coughs. "Sorry…"

Lucy looks at Shaide. "So. You awoke Rho, eh? Not bad at all, especially for a teenager. If you're anything like your parents, I'll be damn glad to have you on board."

Shaide looks down awkwardly. "Umm… Thanks auntie."

Lucy laughs and pulls Shaide into a slightly provocative hug, squishing him against her chest. "Poor boy. You still get shy around pretty women. That'll change as you get older. Don't worry. A handsome young man like you will have the girls all over you in a couple of years."

Shaide pulls himself free and leans back in the seat, looking down awkwardly.

Aton slaps the cockpit door, the dropship's turbines spin up, and it rises into the air. He scolds Lucy "Good lord, sis, how many times do I have to tell you not to traumatize the boy?"

Lucy seems to be a lot more relaxed now that the incident in the cave is over. "Oh, come on. What teenage boy doesn't want attention from a hot woman like me?"

Aton narrows his eyes. "I don't like my sister talking like that, you know. Besides, You're thirty-five, and he's fourteen. That's just…wrong."

Lucy laughs. "Oh, come on. For Mitera, that age difference is nothing. Besides, you both know I'm just screwing around. It's been a harrowing few days. I've earned the right to unwind a little."

Shaide starts laughing to himself. His uncle Aton and his twin sister were always like this. And likewise, she was always giving Shaide a hell of a hard time whenever they had time to relax. She had a weird obsession with jamming his face into her chest, and he still isn't exactly sure why.

In truth, she only did it because it embarrassed him. She's helped look after him almost as much as Aton for the past few years.

A couple of minutes later, the inertia shifts, and the dropship lowers into the small hangar bay of the corvette. Ironically, this is the same corvette that picked Shaide up from Erita a few years ago. It seems to always correspond with some major life change for him.

The pilot drops the troop hatch and gets up. "Alright, communications say we'll be departing in fifteen minutes. Go ahead and get comfy."

"Hey, Lucy," says Aton, "can you take Shaide to the crew quarters? I'm going to speak with the shipmaster. And DON'T do anything weird to him."

Lucy rolls her eyes at Aton. "Jesus, he IS a kid. What do you think I would really do to him?"

"I don't even want to think about it," Aton mumbles. He turns and walks the opposite way as Lucy leads Shaide back to the crew quarters located behind the stuffy hangar bay.

The hangar bay of the frigate is spacious enough to house several single-ships comfortably, but the corvette's hangar bay is small, only big enough to house four dropships, and they cannot lift off very high to exit the hangar. The ship was designed to be small and agile, and space was not a huge priority in its construction.

Lucy leads him into the troop quarters, where the actual Ceraphs stay on their trips. They have been allotted more accommodations than the ship's normal crew due to their status as Eden's warriors, but the quarters are still cramped, with eight bunks squished together along the walls.

Lucy sits back on a bed. "Get comfortable. I promise I won't do anything weird to you. Nothing TOO weird, anyway." She chuckles and pulls out a book from a pouch.

Shaide leans back and starts to consider everything that has happened again. Now that the adrenaline and excitement are wearing off, he is starting to feel nervous. What IS going to happen to him?

A few minutes pass, and a deep subsonic hum thrums through the warship. The inertia shifts slightly, and Shaide can tell the corvette has begun to move. They're on their way to the Citadel.

A few minutes later, Aton steps back into the Ceraph quarters and sits down on one of the beds. "We're about seven to eight hours from the Citadel, depending on how the shipmaster decides to fly it. Get comfy."

*   *   *

The journey back to the Citadel is a long one. Over a thousand miles separate it from Broadspring, including the equatorial Heartland Mountains, which stretch over fifteen thousand feet above sea level.

Shaide, Lucy, and Aton play cards in the Ceraph quarters of the ship for the last few hours of their journey. Initially, Lucy suggests they play strip poker as a joke, but Aton firmly reminds her that, one, he is her brother, and two, she is terrible at poker and would probably be the one to lose and end up naked.

She quickly retracts her suggestion, and they ended up playing without any stakes. Aton and Lucy are very different in many ways, but also very much alike. They both have two sides to their personality. Like Aton, Lucy is very serious and focused when it comes to their work. She is likely among the strongest Ceraphs alive, and it comes from years of dedicated service.

On the other hand, she is also a very gentle and fun-loving individual. She views Shaide as a kind of adopted nephew of sorts, and she plays the part of the fun aunt quite enthusiastically. Her flirting with the young man is entirely innocent and lighthearted, but Aton still worries sometimes that she might take it too far someday. Lucy has a bit of a reputation of being TOO friendly, and she has gone home from the bar with strange men more than a few times over the years.

In spite of his protectiveness over his godson, Aton is little better than his sister. He behaves himself around Shaide, but he is pretty well known in certain districts of Corallina as a bit of a womanizer.

True to Aton's warning, Lucy has lost several hands in a row by the time they feel the ship decelerating to dock with the spire at the Citadel.

Aton feels the inertia shift and looks around, gathering the cards. "Okay, I think we're just about home. Let's get our things and meet in the hangar bay. We'll go see Master Armstrong first thing."

Lucy frowns and says, "Boo. I haven't had a drink in days…"

Aton glares at her. "Lucy, I really wish you wouldn't act that way in front of Shaide. He's still a kid."

She winks at Shaide. "Come on, Aton. He's on track to become a Ceraph soon. He's earned the right to be treated like an adult. Besides, it's nothing he hasn't seen before."

Shaide coughs. "Lucy…I think I've seen more of you than I probably should…"

"That was ONE TIME, and in my defense, I was very drunk," Lucy says, rubbing her neck.

Aton remembers the incident where she fell in the living room and accidentally tore her shirt off, and he rolls his eyes. "That was more than I wanted to see too. And sis? Being drunk is not a good defense, just for the record."

Lucy picks up her bag and sighs. "Yeah, I know. C'mon, kid. Let's go see the headmaster so I can go home and unwind."

Shaide follows Aton and Lucy through the corridor and out into the hangar bay. When they walk out, they see that the bay doors on one side are already open, and a wide tower is in view. This tower is encircled by numerous pylons jutting out from the center, serving as docks for airships too large to land

The corvette drifts slowly to one of the pylons with a pair of crewmen on it, and it eases over to dock against the walkway. A moment later, the turbines spin down and shut off, leaving the ship airborne on nothing but the gravity cores.

Aton raises his eyebrows. "Whoa. I think Armstrong was waiting for us."

Shaide follows his godfather's gaze and sees a familiar man he hasn't seen in some time. The man appears middle-aged but in good physical condition, with a short white beard and neatly trimmed hair. This is Master Orville Armstrong, the commander of the Ceraph Order's operations.

Aton walks out of the hangar bay onto the gantry, Shaide and Lucy following close behind.

The old man holds out a hand, and Aton shakes it. "Atondier. It is good to see you made it back safely. Lucy? You as well. I presume the other two remained behind?"

"Yes, Master Orville," says Aton. "They chose to remain behind and continue assisting the Alastair Broadspring Battalion with their operations while we handled this matter."

Armstrong nods, looks behind Aton at Shaide, and extends a hand. "Well, son. It seems like you've made one hell of an accomplishment. How are you feeling?"

Shaide nervously walks out from behind Aton and shakes hands with Armstrong. "I feel okay, sir. Still a little tired, but okay."

"That is to be expected. Binding to an angel is no small feat, and your body will take some time to adjust to the changes. Come with me, all of you. Let's discuss this somewhere more comfortable."

Armstrong turns around and walks towards the tower itself, and the three arrivals follow close behind.

Shaide takes this opportunity to observe their surroundings. They are on the bottom level of pylons, but they are still easily over a hundred feet from the ground. Several warships are docked against the tower above them, and several more are floating above the citadel further away.

Beneath them, however, is the real marvel. The Citadel is a massive fortress that, in ancient times, served as a royal stronghold. When Eden formed the Ceraph Order, it was gifted to them by the Alastair royal family, and it has since been upgraded into the modern fortress they stand in today.

The outer wall is a perfect circle almost exactly one mile in diameter. The outermost wall is solid stone, over six feet thick and just over fifty feet high, with a dozen towers spread equidistantly around the perimeter. The inside wall has multiple structures attached to it, including multiple housing additions that allow the members of the Ceraph Order to live in reasonable comfort.

The old chapel on the north edge of the Citadel now serves as the Ceraphs' dedicated chapel, and Master Armstrong's office and home are in its bell tower. Like many of the structures, the chapel is connected to the Citadel's wall from the rear, providing a connected system of facilities and corridors inside the Citadel itself.

Out on the Citadel grounds are multiple freestanding structures, ranging from a small housing district to the markets and even to multiple training and recreational facilities. A massive open training ground is situated almost directly in the center of the Citadel grounds, and the road leading to the gates on the south wall connects directly to it.

The spire, where they are located, sits on the northeast area of the Citadel, on the outer wall connecting directly to the chapel. This was among the structures added later, and it serves as the airship docks for the entire Citadel.

As Shaide looks around the fortress, he notices that the Ceraph Order Dreadnaught, the COV *Final Judgement*, is conspicuously absent. The twelve-hundred-foot-long vessel is one of the largest warships ever made, and by far the most powerful, with multiple high-tech railguns capable of destroying entire villages with a single salvo.

They enter the spire itself and approach an open-walled mechanical elevator that lowers them down to ground level. Armstrong leads them out of a side door into the chapel and up the spiral staircase leading to his office. Shaide catches a glimpse of the inside of the chapel, and for the second time in his life, he is awed by the beauty of the white stone and gold-trimmed architecture reminiscent of Erita.

He feels a slight pang as he remembers the Tamiel family and his old friend Amari. It really has been far too long since he has seen her.

Armstrong holds open the door to his office, and Shaide, Aton, and Lucy walk in.

His office is more modest than the chapel outside, but no one can say it isn't elegant. The floor is laid with a deep red hardwood, and the walls are covered in some kind of lighter wood paneling, with white curtains over the windows. It is quite beautiful in its own way.

Armstrong sits behind his desk, and the other three follow suit and sit across from him. He looks at Shaide for a moment, and the young cadet feels some discomfort at the amount of focused attention he is getting from such an important man.

"What do you remember about that day, when you encountered Rho?" Armstrong finally asks. "Tell me everything you remember."

Shaide thinks back. "Well, sir. We were moving through the caves where we had taken shelter from the weather. We were trying to find some high ground to make a signal fire. We ended up finding a section of cavern that looked like it had been deliberately made, but we also stumbled across a decantula nest. The drove us back into this massive open-roofed cavern. At some point, I accidentally touched this…altar-looking thing, and…well…"

Armstrong is listening intently. When Shaide hesitates, he encourages him "Go on. I want to hear everything."

Shaide swallows and nods. "Yes, sir. When I touched it, this bright golden light shot into the air, and these weird glyphs rose out of the ground. They started spinning and suddenly spread outward, forming some kind of barrier. Next thing I know, this giant golden eagle, arcing with electricity, drops out of the sky and attacks me. I fought for my life against the bird, and somehow…well, somehow I came out on top. Then this golden light struck me. I felt a strong burning sensation, and then…"

ETERNAL KNIGHTS OF EDEN I

Aton, Lucy, and Armstrong are all looking at him intently.

"I remember having a strange dream. The bird was there, and it spoke to me. It called itself Rho, and it said it would fight alongside me. He said something about an Eternal Knight too, but it was kind of fuzzy. After that, I just remember waking up in the hospital with Aton."

Armstrong sits back and nods to himself. "That sounds about right."

"I hadn't heard that part yet," says Lucy. "We arrived right at the end of it."

"What do you want to do?" Armstrong asks Shaide. "Assuming everything works out the way I would like and you are able to make your own choice, what would you like from us?"

Shaide frowns. "What do you mean, sir? Like, do I want to be a Ceraph?"

Armstrong nods "Yes. Are you interested in joining the Ceraph Order? If you would prefer to return to the academy, we can arrange this. We would train you to interact with and control Rho, and you would return to your class as soon as you were ready. However, you also come from a long line of Ceraphs, and as far as I am concerned, you are welcome to join us, although, at your age, it would be quite some time before you were allowed on missions on your own. What do you think?"

Shaide looks around, feeling a bit uncomfortable with having this decision thrust upon him. "Is this… Is this a decision I have to make right now?"

Armstrong smiles and shakes his head. "No, I suppose not. There's little point in making your decision before you are ready anyway. Just have your decision ready when you finish your training. I would like you to do something for me, however."

Shaide tilts his head.

Armstrong stands up. "Follow me, all three of you. I would like to see something, and I would show you something as well."

Aton, Lucy, and Shaide get to their feet and follow Armstrong. He leads them out of his office and further up the spiral staircase, and they circle around Eden's Bell before emerging onto the top of the bell tower itself.

Shaide looks out across the Citadel and sees what Armstrong wants to show him.

"There are currently forty-six true Ceraphs in the Ceraph Order," says Armstrong. "In addition to that, there are over four hundred prospective Ceraphs and over ten thousand combat and support personnel in this corps. We all live together and work towards a common goal, hoping to ultimately rid the world of the legacy of Belial and grant peace to our people once again."

Shaide leans over the rampart and sees a Nekomata and a Drameri sparring in the courtyard. "Is that even possible?"

Armstrong nods. "Eden says it is. Rho is one of sixty known angels like him. But there are also three angels that are considered special. The Archangels. Eden gave us a prophecy nearly three thousand years ago stating that if anyone could gather the triad and bring them to the temple of Bahamut, then Bahamut could be awakened, and his cleansing light would purge all that was not of the world, returning it to its natural state. Translated? Anyone who can summon all three Archangels at the lost temple will be able to cleanse the corruption in the land and save everyone."

Armstrong leans back from the ramparts. "That has been the Ceraph Order's true purpose since the end of the Great War, although we don't broadcast it. Throughout history, we have found a single Archangel, but we have never gotten any further than that. Currently, he has no master and lies in wait."

Shaide nods. "I think I understand."

Armstrong looks at Shaide. "Good. Now I would like to meet Rho. Summon him for me if you can. Show me what you have accomplished."

Aton and Lucy back away to the edge of the rooftop, giving Shaide some room.

Shaide looks around and asks. "Umm…how am I supposed to do this?"

"Focus on that other presence inside you," says Anton. "Raise your hand to the sky and ask that presence to come forward, and then focus your spiritual energy. You'll know when you have it right."

Shaide stands nervously in the middle of the rooftop. "Okay…here goes nothing…"

He closes his eyes and feels out that strange foreign presence inside him. It's a warm, pleasant feeling, like he is not alone, but a feeling not native to his spirit. He raises his hand above his head and tries to speak to that presence.

Rho, please come forward. I would like to meet you.

An intense sensation surges through his arm, and suddenly a bright light erupts from his hand. He opens his eyes and jumps slightly as the light forms a golden glyph circle in the sky. Every person in the Citadel stops what they are doing to look up.

An eagle's earsplitting screech echoes across the plains, and a golden ball of lightning dives through the glyph circle, directly towards Shaide. At the last possible second, its wings flare out, and a powerful blast of wind forces everyone to take a

     A.S.GUINN

couple of steps back. The majestic thunderbird lands gently on the ramparts of the tower and looks directly at Shaide.

"Did I do this?" Shaide asks, his eyes wide with shock.

Armstrong nods "That is your angel, Rho."

Shaide carefully approaches the bird. "Rho…"

The Angel nods and makes an odd chirping noise. He leans his head forward, and Shaide instinctively rubs his beak. Electricity arcs from the beak to Shaide's hand, but oddly, it does not hurt him. In fact, it feels almost pleasant.

Aton says quietly, "I have seen this angel several times, but I will never quite get used to him…"

Rho turns his head and seems to nod to Aton in greeting.

Aton says nervously, "Do you recognize me, old friend?"

Rho chirps at him.

Armstrong steps forward. "Rho, my old friend, it is truly an honor to have you among us once again. Can I ask a simple favor of you?"

Rho turns to Armstrong and seems to nod.

Armstrong smiles. "Take good care of our young friend here. He is strong but inexperienced and naïve. I will depend on you to protect and look after him."

Rho spreads his massive wings and squawks pleasantly.

"Thank you, old friend."

Shaide looks up at his new companion in awe. Rho chirps at him and then looks at the sky as if asking something.

Shaide tilts his head. "Are you asking what I think you are?"

Rho nods and then lowers his head to the ground. Shaide looks at Armstrong and Aton uncertainly. Armstrong, however, simply says, "Go on. Rho wants to bond with his new partner and show you the world through his eyes. We will be here when you return."

Shaide nods and straddles the back of Rho's neck. Shaide looks around for something to hang onto, but instead feels a painless electrical surge and like he is almost magnetically attached to Rho's neck.

Rho spreads his wings wide and suddenly launches into the air. Shaide cannot help but yell out a loud, "WOOHOO!" as Rho streaks over the top of the citadel and up into the air.

To the west, Shaide can see the capital city, Corallina, in the distance. Rho turns east however and streaks high across the land. Shaide has been in airships many times, but none of them came even close to the feeling of flying with Rho. Shaide almost has this strange feeling that the angel can sense his thoughts, because whenever he sees something he likes, Rho turns and gives him a better view of it. He soon realizes that he and the thunderbird really are connected, and this feels as natural to him as walking.

Rho climbs into a building thunderstorm, and Shaide nervously leans against his neck as lightning arcs around them. When a bolt of lightning strikes the angel directly, Shaide yells out in shock, but he quickly realizes there is no pain. While he is connected to Rho, the storm cannot hurt him.

After some time passes, Rho turns back towards the Citadel. For the first time, Shaide is able to really see the giant fortress that houses the protectors of Eden. He sees the fleet of warships below him and the surprisingly symmetrical layout of the fortress from above.

Rho circles around and comes down towards the bell tower, where Shaide sees Armstrong, Aton, and Lucy waiting for him. On the grounds below, dozens of people outside look up at him in shock and awe as the giant thunderbird flares up and lands gently on the ramparts of the bell tower roof.

Shaide eases himself off of Rho's neck and then rubs him behind his head. The angel chirps and then spreads his wings and launches himself into the sky, vanishing into a golden glyph that forms for a split second and then fades away.

Aton looks up jealously. "Yeah…mine doesn't fly."

Armstrong looks at Shaide, who now feels much more at ease. "Let us go find something to eat, and we can discuss what to do with you. We can also introduce you to some of our comrades whom you may not know yet."

Lucy watches the sky in awe as well. "Shaide, I have never been so jealous of a teenager in my life."

Shaide smiles, and the four of them climb down the bell tower and head to the Citadel's dining hall, where they can share a meal and discuss Shaide's future in further detail.

He has always felt a bit out of place, but he finally feels at home.

CHAPTER 9

ENDINGS AND BEGINNINGS

Reno and his squad of classmates have just made it back to Broadspring after a five-day mission in the southern plains, shadowing a group of Alastair Royal Army Rangers. They spent five days in the wilderness, living off of their provisions and what food they could scrounge up, living like real Rangers. When they returned, Reno wanted to tell his friend Shaide all about their adventure, but then his instructor informed him of the circumstances.

Reno looks at Lieutenant Nikola in stunned disbelief. "What do you mean Shaide is gone? I thought he was laid up in the hospital!"

Rayn and Lania both look upset as well. Shaide is their friend, after all. They at least wanted to check on him. Even the usually cool Celeste Wyatt looks mildly disappointed.

Lieutenant Nikola frowns slightly at Reno as he explains, "When he woke up two days ago, the Ceraph Order decided they wanted to take him for a classified purpose. It has something to do with that angel you all came across in the mountains. Captain Rockwell, the highest-ranking officer present, cleared Shaide for an indefinite release until such time as the Ceraph Order deems they no longer need him and that he can return to duty. That's all I can tell you."

Rayn puts a hand on Reno's shoulder. "Let it go, Coltide. There's nothing we can do about it. If the Ceraphs want something, they get it. Just let it go."

Reno throws Rayn's hand off his shoulder. "No! I will NOT let it go! Damnit! We crashed in the mountains, lost two of our friends, stumbled into an angel's lair, Shaide gets put in the hospital, we go on a dangerous mission, and when we get back, my best friend is just gone without any explanation? I think I've earned some damn answers, Rayn!"

Lieutenant Nikola yells sharply, "Stand down, Coltide! NOW!"

Reno jumps to attention, anger still etched into every line of his face.

ETERNAL KNIGHTS OF EDEN I

The lieutenant stands in front of him, his brow furrowed. "Reno! I understand you are upset about Darkmoon being gone. I didn't exactly like them taking off with one of my students myself. But we are members of the Alastair Royal Military! We do what is needed for the good of the nation whether we like it or not! And right now, the Ceraph Order needs him, and we must respect their wishes! So, for the love of Eden, take your attitude and cram it, cadet! This isn't about you, and the sooner you understand that and stop acting like a spoiled brat, the better off you'll be!"

Reno's eyes open wide in surprise. The truth behind his instructor's words stings. He knows he is being selfish. He has had a stressful few days, though, and he feels like he's earned some selfishness. However, he's also caught off guard by Nikola's attitude. The lieutenant has never lost his temper on them like that before, and Reno realizes he has crossed a line.

"I'm sorry, sir."

Lieutenant Nikola relaxes a little. "Alright, you four. We aren't expecting everyone back until at least tomorrow, so if you can keep your attitudes in check, you are free for the evening. You are welcome to check out Broadspring and enjoy everything it has to offer. Be back at the barracks by nine, and for the love of Eden, do not leave the safety of town."

The cadets nod their assent, and the lieutenant says, "Dismissed."

Rayn grabs Reno by the arm, and the four of them walk through the archway separating the makeshift military compound from the town proper. Rayn looks at Reno like he wants to say something, but surprisingly, Celeste intervenes.

"Follow your own advice, Rayn. Let it go."

Rayn looks at Reno's defiant face and sighs, letting go of his arm. He tries to act casual as he asks, "Okay, what do you all want to do?"

Lania raises her hand. "Well, I, for one, would like to eat some actual, proper food for once. It's been provisions, fish, and fruit for days. I want something good."

Reno sighs and reluctantly relaxes a bit. "Yeah, I could go for a proper meal myself."

"Yeah," adds Celeste. "I could really go for a steak."

Lania looks at Celeste's slender, athletic figure and frowns. "Girl? Where do you put all that food you eat? I have to watch what I eat, or I get soft. You seem to eat non-stop, and you stay all skinny and muscley."

"It's a gift," Celeste replies with a shrug. "Now, are we going to go eat or what?"

Rayn sighs. "Yeah, I'm in. Let's go find a café."

"I wish I could eat whatever I want…" Lania grumbles quietly to herself.

Reno nearly chokes trying not to laugh.

The four cadets find a nearby café and order themselves their first real meal in several days. Reno picks at his food disinterestedly, not really joining in the cheerful conversation of his friends. He is worried about Shaide, wondering what will happen to him.

The following day, the last of the students return to Broadspring, and by seven that evening, all of the surviving cadets of Lieutenant Nikola's first-year class are loaded back onto the frigate and flying back north to the capital city of Corallina.

*   *   *

Major Stryder watches the ARV *North Star* disappear into the distance over the mountains to the north, and then Kimball taps him on the shoulder.

"What is it?" he asks.

Kimball's face quirks into a small grin. "What did you think of our cadets? Miss them already?"

Stryder stretches and sighs. "They are an interesting lot, I will give them that much. I think some of them have some serious potential given enough time, and maybe some growing up."

"They're fourteen years old. Honestly, I'm impressed that they can do what they did at their age. I think they'll be fine."

Stryder nods "Yeah, I'm sure you're right. Still, we do this every year, and they are definitely one of the more interesting groups I've seen."

Kimball laughs. "Yeah, they're characters, that's for sure. They feel like people you'd read about in a bad book. I think they'll be fine, though."

"So," says Stryder, "we're off for the evening. What do you want to do?"

"Go drinking?" Kimball replies with a shrug.

"Yeah, sure. Why not?"

Kimball smiles at her commanding officer and friend. "That's the spirit. Come on, let's go celebrate killing two corrupted drakes."

The two set off down the street and find her favorite bar: a little tavern-like place on the same street as the military compound.

As they walk in, the barkeep looks up. "Hey, Captain. The usual?"

Kimball raises her hand in greeting. "Yeah. Jordan is with me too, so make it two."

The barkeep raises a mug in response.

"Hey, Nat, Major! Come join us!"

Stryder looks up and sees Bull, Jax, and a few other Rangers from Stryder's company at a table in the corner, and he and Kimball decide to join them. They walk over and have a seat.

Jax looks at his commanding officer. "Fancy seeing you two out here. I don't see you unwinding a whole lot, Major."

Stryder shrugs. "We just spent most of a week babysitting teenagers. I'm not complaining, but it is an exhausting task. I think we all earned some R&R."

The group of Rangers spends the evening drinking and visiting. Major Stryder has a good relationship with all of them, not just the ones he works directly with. They have a good time until sometime past midnight, when Stryder and Kimball decide it is time to leave.

Kimball stumbles slightly as she stands. "Alright, boys and girls. Your friend Captain Kimball needs to go to bed. It's been a long week, and I'm ready for some proper sleep."

Stryder waves goodbye to his men as he walks out the front door with her. The two of the make their way back up the street to the military compound and head for the Ranger's barracks.

Kimball looks at Stryder and says in a slightly slurred voice, "You know, Jordan, if the boys are all going to be out late, you and I could… Hey, are you listening?"

Stryder stops walking suddenly, staring at something up the street.

Kimball follows his gaze and focuses her eyes. A lone man is standing in the middle of the street, just watching them. He doesn't look like military. He has long hair and is wearing a ragged, long black coat. In the dark, it is difficult to make out details, but Stryder is sure this man doesn't belong here.

He decides to say something. He approaches the man and hollers out, "Hey, buddy! Come here a moment. I need to speak with you."

The man turns his head to look at Stryder, and a grin seems to cross his face in the pale light. Without warning, his right hand glows red, and he points it at one of the nearby barracks. A jet of red flame streams from his hand into the building, and a split second later, the whole building explodes into flames.

"Holy crap!" Stryder waves his hand, summoning his halberd out of thin air, and behind him, Kimball does the same with her rapier. They charge the man, but he just smiles and slams his hand into the ground.

ETERNAL KNIGHTS OF EDEN I

The stones beneath Kimball and Stryder's feet explode, and they are thrown onto their backs as flames erupt from the ground.

Stryder groans and pushes himself to his feet as the man dances in a circle, flames streaming in all directions, igniting the buildings all around him. Army personnel are streaming out of their burning buildings, struggling to figure out what is happening.

Stryder gets to his feet and is moving towards the man again when something streaks through the air towards him. He moves to block the projectile, but…

It is too fast. He feels a ripping pain and a thud, and he looks down to see a large serrated dagger impaled deep in his chest. The dagger glows with red energy, and before he can even fully register what has happened, it releases an explosion of red flames.

Stryder falls onto his back and struggles to remain conscious as Kimball stands over him, screaming something at him and looking frantic. His eyes register some kind of purple glowing glyph in the sky, and he hears what sounds like terrifying, maniacal laughter.

A cackling, insane sounding voice calls out "You arrogant heretics believe you won, but we will not be silenced so easily. We will take this world that is rightfully ours, and you will not be here to stop us. Asmodeus! Do your thing!"

As he bleeds out rapidly on the ground, he doesn't know if he is hallucinating or actually seeing it, but what looks almost like a winged Daemon descends through the purple glyph in the sky.

A moment later, with his friend Natalie Kimball holding his hand, a bright purple light erupts before his eyes, and he no longer feels anything at all.

*   *   *

Shaide Darkmoon has been at the Citadel for several days now. After receiving a proper tour of the fortress from his godfather, Aton, and spending a couple of days acclimating to the environment, he is now sitting in the medical lab with a young woman doctor who is performing a number of tests on him in order to assess the stability of his spiritual power after fusing so suddenly with Rho.

Ceraphs who attempt to join with an angel typically undergo some kind of preparation before doing so, as the sudden addition of such a powerful spiritual force to the body and soul can be overwhelming and even dangerous to the unprepared. The doctor is quite surprised that such a young and unprepared teenager even survived the process.

A.S.GUINN

Nevertheless, he did, indeed, survive, and now it is her job to assess his condition and compatibility with his new partner. She has several wires and leads attached to him, measuring his body's response as she asks him to perform various magic tasks.

As he channels lightning energy into a special magicore stone designed to absorb it, she watches the gauges with interest. She mumbles to herself, "He has a remarkably high constitution for his age. Rho is fully integrated into his nervous system, but he is showing no sign of overload or fatigue. His spiritual aura seems remarkably similar to Rho's."

She looks up and addresses him directly. "Oh, Shaide, you can stop now. Have a seat and relax."

Shaide, wearing nothing but a pair of canvas shorts, lets go of the stone and walks over to a nearby chair to sit down. His immature teenage figure is somewhat scrawny but still remarkably muscular. He's trained harder than most of his classmates, and it has him in exceptionally good physical condition.

Dr. Shepard walks over to him and starts removing the leads and the IV, casting a gentle healing magic over him as she does so to prevent bleeding. She is an attractive young doctor, only in her late twenties, and Shaide finds himself again feeling slightly shy and uncomfortable with an attractive young woman touching him.

This does not go unnoticed by Dr. Shepard, and she smiles a bit. "You know, if you're going to be a real man, you're going to have to get past your shyness around pretty girls."

Shaide looks up at her and turns red when he realizes her face is about an inch from his. "I, uhh…well…"

She looks him right in the eyes and mock-sighs. "You know, if only you were a few years older, I could maybe teach you how to be a real man, but alas, no. You're too young for all that right now." She struggles not to crack a grin as he turns bright red.

He can't close his eyes, and he stares right into her emerald green eyes as she stares him down, and he has no idea what to do or say. She is reminding him a lot of how Lucy behaves inappropriately around him.

Dr. Shepard stands up and laughs. "You really do need to loosen up a bit, Shaide. Lucy told me to do that to you. She said you always got uncomfortable if a woman gets too close to you."

Shaide leans his head back and sighs. "Can I put my clothes back on now?"

"Yeah, I'm all finished. As best as I can tell, your body is acclimating well to Rho. Better than most Ceraphs acclimate to their angels, actually."

As Shaide starts getting dressed, someone knocks on the door. Dr. Shepard calls out, "Come in!"

Shaide sputters, "Hey! I'm not finished getting dressed yet!"

The door to her office opens, and Aton comes in. He stops when he sees Shaide getting dressed and shakes his head. "You could have told me to wait a minute. If it'd been Lucy, she'd have had a field day walking in on him getting ready like this."

Dr. Shepard shrugs. "I didn't see the harm in it. He's still wearing SOME clothes, after all."

Aton shakes his head and chuckles. "Anyways, how is he? Any problems with him and Rho?"

Dr. Shepard sits down and leans back. "Nope. His body has acclimated remarkably well to Rho's presence. He seems to be Rho's natural vessel. Their compatibility is among the best I've ever seen."

Aton raises his eyebrows, impressed. "That's rare even among properly prepared Ceraphs."

"Yep. Well, he's good to go. What's next? He is kind of an unusual case, so I'm curious what you have planned."

Aton looks at Shaide. "Do you feel up to a combat test?"

Shaide finishes putting on his top and tilts his head at the question. "Combat test?"

Aton nods. "We're trying to figure out how much control you really have over your new abilities. I want to take you out onto the plains and have you hunt some tough game using your power. I want to see how much of a difference it makes."

Shaide stretches his shoulder. "Yeah, I guess I'm good to go. What do I need?"

Aton turns around, indicating Shaide should follow. "Everything you would normally have in the field. No need to bring anything fancy."

Shaide follows Aton out the door and into the residential district of the Citadel where Dr. Shepard has her office. She is a medical doctor, but she specializes in spiritual research, which is why her office is separate from the Citadel's hospital.

Aton leads Shaide to his small house, where Shaide has been staying with him. The proper Ceraphs are afforded slightly better living conditions than the daily troops, but they still live modestly.

ETERNAL KNIGHTS OF EDEN I

Aton and Shaide walk in the front door, and Shaide picks up his field harness, checking his daggers and field gear. Once he has all of the straps tightened down and the snaps fastened, he meets Aton back in the living room.

Aton looks up at him. "Okay, are you ready?"

Shaide nods.

Aton walks out the door. "Okay. We'll be riding sleipnir out to where I want to go. It's going to be an all-day trip, so make sure you're ready."

Shaide rolls his eyes. "I'm ready. Sitting around and waiting is what kills me."

Aton nods approvingly as he starts out the door. "Good. We'll head to the stables and take a couple of the sleipnir out onto the plains."

Shaide follows Aton out onto the Citadel grounds, and they leisurely stroll to the main gate. He looks around at the Citadel as they go, still feeling slightly in awe about the ancient fortress. Even though he spent some time here growing up, he was primarily raised in the capital. While it is true that Corallina is very grand and impressive, there is still something special about this ancient fortress.

He also seems to be attracting a lot of attention as they walk to the stables. All of the personnel they pass seem to watch him with interest, and a couple of them lean over and whisper something to their neighbors as they watch him.

Shaide looks at Aton and asks uncomfortably, "Is there something I'm not getting here? Why is everyone looking at me?"

Aton looks around and nods in understanding. "It looks like it didn't take long for word about you to get around."

Shaide tilts his head in confusion. "I don't get it. What word?"

"Your incident with Rho is kind of a big deal around here," Aton replies with a chuckle. "I wouldn't be surprised if a lot of our comrades thought you were special in some way. Like I've told you, doing what you did at your age has never really happened before. That kind of makes you a big deal to some."

Shaide looks around nervously.

Aton ruffles Shaide's short hair and laughs. "Of course, to me, you're still just a little squirt. Don't worry about it."

Shaide frowns and mumbles, "I don't want to disappoint anybody."

Aton slows his pace and walks alongside his godson. "Take it easy, kid. You don't have to impress anyone. Just do what you can. That's all anyone can really ask of you. In the life of a Ceraph, anytime you just make it home alive is a good day. Don't stress about it."

Shaide nods, feeling a little better. He still feels that creeping unease about everyone's expectations, but the nausea is gone, at least.

Aton walks up to the stablemaster, a Drameri man named Armolas. "Good afternoon. Can we borrow a couple of steeds for the day?"

Armolas looks up from his book and nods. "Of course. Any particular reason or just going for a ride?"

Aton looks at Shaide next to him. "I'm taking the new guy out onto the plains to see how well he fares with his new companion at his side."

Armolas looks far more interested now. "So, I presume this is our new young comrade. Shaide, I believe it is?"

Shaide nods and holds out his hand, and Armolas shakes it. "Yes, sir. I'm Shaide Darkmoon. It's a pleasure to meet you."

Armolas lets go of Shaide's hand and leans back in his chair. "I remember your mother. She was a fine Ceraph. Very strong and driven. I was sad to hear of her passing."

Shaide nods awkwardly, uncertain as to how to respond. Aton stands there silently for a moment, not really sure how to break the awkward tension.

Armolas shakes his head and seems to snap out of it. "Well, anyway, please help yourself to the steeds. Aton, you already know what to do."

Aton bows. "Thank you. We should be back after dark, so don't wait up for us."

Armolas nods in response "Eden watch over you, Aton. Shaide."

Aton turns and walks back to the paddock out behind the stable house and leans against the wooden fence. Shaide follows behind him and leans on the fence next to him. Aton winks at him and then turns back to the paddock and whistles loudly.

In response two sleipnir trot over to them: one chestnut brown, and the other a deep midnight black. The six-legged equines have been raised from birth to work alongside their Ceraph masters, and in spite of the ever-growing popularity of magicore-powered transportation, they remain a vital part of the Ceraphs' lives.

Shaide has spent a fair amount of time around sleipnir, so he reaches up to rub the black steed's head without any fear or hesitation. The sleipnir seems to sense that he is trustworthy because it leans its head forward in response. It bares its sharp, pointed teeth slightly as it snorts at him, looking content.

Aton looks at Shaide in amusement as he rubs his own steed's snout. "I see you still have your way with the sleipnir. They can be a bit picky with people sometimes, but she seems to like you."

Armolas walks up behind them. "Well, this wasn't what I expected."

"What do you mean?" asks Shaide.

As Armolas approaches Shaide's sleipnir, it watches him warily. "Twilight here doesn't usually like anyone. I was starting to worry I would have to just turn her loose in the wild and hope she would be okay. I suppose I shouldn't be too surprised. Her mother was your mother's personal steed. Perhaps she can sense who you are."

Shaide looks back at the mare, Twilight, and rubs her snout. She leans her head forward and seems completely at ease. "Huh. Does that mean she isn't rein trained?"

Armolas chuckles. "Don't worry. I've trained her to ride. She just doesn't seem to like most people. She's not even fully grown yet, about a year old, so she may just be being stubborn, but I'm glad to see she likes you, at least."

Shaide frowns. "Wait, how is she only a year old? My mother died several years ago."

"Your mother's sleipnir is still here in the stables. She didn't take her with her on the mission when we lost her. In fact, she is still here to this day. We've retired her, but she is happy and healthy."

Shaide raises his eyebrows and nods.

Aton had slipped away at some point while they were talking, and he approaches with a pair of saddles and reins. "Come on, kiddo. We're burning daylight here. We need to get moving."

Shaide hops over the fence, and Aton hands him the riding gear. Shaide promptly begins setting up Twilight for the ride, putting her saddle and reins on. A moment later, he steps on the stirrup and swings his leg over her back, resting comfortably on the saddle.

Aton enters the paddock and saddles up his own steed while Shaide waits patiently. Once he climbs on the back of his sleipnir, Armolas nods approvingly.

"It looks like you know what you're doing. I'll get the gate for you." Armolas leads them along the fence line to the closed gate, and he opens it to let them out. "Alright, boys. Take care of my friends here. Bring them back in one piece."

Aton raises his hand as they ride out the gate and onto the road leading out of the citadel. The two companions are quiet for a time as they ride out onto the main road.

Shaide has never actually been out in this part of the country on the ground before. He looks around at the wide-open plains with interest. Off to the east, he can see the capital city, where he spent most of his life. There isn't a whole lot in the way of trees around the Citadel, but he can see a dense forest to the west. In fact, the forest seems to be where Aton is leading them.

Aton looks over at Shaide. "Let's pick up the pace a bit. I want to try and be back to the Citadel by nightfall, and I have quite a bit I want to do with you before we head back."

Shaide nods and leans forward, squeezing his legs against Twilight's sides. Understanding her rider's desires, she digs her feet into the ground and starts galloping rather rapdly. Shaide is caught slightly off guard by the unexpected acceleration. Twilight is a lot faster than he anticipated. He hangs on tight and looks over his shoulder to see Aton falling behind. Not wanting to leave his godfather behind, he pulls back on the reins slightly, slowing her down.

A minute later, Aton catches up and eases off a little to ride alongside Shaide. He yells to Shaide with an amused expression, "That is a fast girl you've got there. I always thought Ruby was one of the faster rides, but your girl there left me in the dust."

Both sleipnir gallop along on all six legs at a rapid thirty miles per hour. The ride is much smoother than one would expect on the back of an animal. Their six-legged stance allows them to move along much more smoothly so they don't jar their riders too badly.

The sleipnir have incredible stamina and are able to maintain their pace for a half-hour until they reach the border of the forest and their riders ease the pace down to a trot.

Shaide takes this opportunity to say, "Hey, old man."

Aton raises an eyebrow. "Who are you calling old?"

Shaide smirks. "So, you haven't told me the plan yet. What are we doing here?"

"Yeah, I guess I have kept you in the dark. There are some nasty critters here in the forest, dangerous but not overwhelming. It's a good place to see what you're actually capable of."

Shaide nods, accepting the explanation. "Okay. What do you want me to do?"

Aton looks around through the increasingly dense trees. "When we find a critter, take it down. Try and tap into Rho's power and use it to aid you in the fight. You should find yourself a bit stronger than before."

Shaide nods again and scans their surroundings as they trot along. They ride down the forest trail for nearly ten minutes before movement reaches Shaide's ears. He pulls back on Twilight's reins and brings her to a stop as his ears pick up something moving through the dense brush to his left.

ETERNAL KNIGHTS OF EDEN I

He stares into the dark brush, watching for any sign of movement. Meanwhile, Aton hangs back, watching him carefully.

Shaide's hands drift to his daggers, waiting for an opportune moment. The sound stops, and Shaide's eyes lock onto a single leaf that he saw move. Aton watches in silence, waiting anxiously for something to happen.

Without warning, a large nekoshin leaps out of the bushes, directly at Shaide. Shaide is prepared, however, and knocks the oversized cat back with a well-timed shockwave spell. He immediately backflips from Twilight, drawing the cat's attention away from the sleipnir.

Without hesitation, he dashes forward and delivers a rapid series of lightning-infused dagger slashes, leaving deep cuts in the cat's face and neck. The nekoshin is apparently accustomed to fighting its prey, however, and it hits Shaide with a heavy paw bigger than the young man's head.

Shaide hits the ground with a grunt, but he quickly recovers, rolls back to his feet. He hesitates for a moment when he realizes that it didn't hurt as much as he would have expected. A lightly shimmering aura flickers over his skin. He sees movement, and his attention snaps back to his quarry.

The nekoshin leaps at him, razor-sharp claws extended and dagger-like teeth bared. Shaide drops flat to the ground and lets the cat pass directly over him. He rolls sideways to face the nekoshin and hurls his daggers at his opponent. The big cat turns sideways in time for both daggers to bury themselves hilt-deep in its side.

Shaide summons a lightning aura in both hands and hurls twin bolts of lightning at the nekoshin. The twin bolts connect with the daggers, creating an internal arc of electricity, stunning the oversized forest cat. Shaide immediately sprints forward and jump-kicks his opponent, knocking it over onto its side. He grabs his daggers and pulls them out, kicking off into the air.

The nekoshin groans a little as Shaide backflips and slams both of his daggers into the cat in a heavy finishing blow. The nekoshin groans one last time before falling still.

"Not bad, kiddo."

Aton rides up alongside him, looking down at the giant forest cat. Like the nekoshin of the southern reaches, this cat is the size of their sleipnir and is not an opponent to be taken lightly. Nevertheless, Shaide took it down with relatively little effort.

Aton looks down at his godson. "I was worried when he hit you, but I didn't know your aura had grown that strong either."

Shaide tilts his head. "My aura?"

Aton nods and explains "When your spiritual energy grows to a certain level, your excess energy forms a kind of protective barrier over you that absorbs some degree of impact and magical damage."

Shaide's eyes open wide with dawning comprehension. "Oh, that's what that was. I'd learned about it, but I was under the impression that it was rare for someone to have it."

"It is. Usually, only Ceraphs, and especially powerful mages or warriors, possess aura barriers. The recent addition of Rho has evidently granted you the necessary reserves to raise it subconsciously."

Shaide whistles, and Twilight trots back over to him. He quickly pulls himself back up onto her back with a grunt before responding. "So, what now?"

Aton leads him along the forest road. "We keep going. I want to see what you're capable of, and one nekoshin, although a formidable opponent, is not enough to see your abilities."

Shaide tilts his head to the side in confusion. "So, what are you looking for, then?"

Aton rides leisurely down the path, stopping every so often to have Shaide fight with some beast that crosses their path. In the course of four hours, Shaide defeats two nekoshin, three packs of forest lobos, and even a stray drake that tries to ambush them. All the while, Aton sits back and evaluates his godson's performance.

Shaide has just performed a rather aggressive spiral swing, decapitating an oversized serpent, when Aton rides up beside him.

"Alright, Shaide, I think that will be enough for today. I was hoping to come across some of the bigger nasties out here, like the quillbulls, but it's getting late, and we should be heading back."

Shaide sheathes his daggers and pulls himself up onto Twilight's back. "So, did you see what you needed to see or not? I'll be kinda ticked if I did this for no reason."

Aton smiles and shakes his head. "I didn't see what I hoped, but I saw what I need to. The academy taught you well, and you seem to be adapting well to Rho's amplification. Give it some time and plenty of experience, and I think you'll make a fine Ceraph."

Shaide nods, and they turn back the way they came. This time, they travel at a much faster pace, no longer seeking a fight, and it isn't long before they emerge from the western edge of the forest and onto the open road.

Shaide looks up at the sky and watches curiously as what appears to be a heavily damaged corvette flies towards the Ceraph Citadel. Aton sees it as well, and he frowns.

He turns back to Shaide. "Hey, we should pick up the pace. Let's get back to the Citadel. I have a bad feeling all of a sudden."

Shaide nods, and the two riders push their sleipnir as fast as they can manage. It doesn't take them long to reach the gates, where they find an unexpected person waiting for them.

Lucy looks up as they come to a stop at the checkpoint. "Come on, both of you. Armstrong needs to see us as soon as possible."

Aton slows down to a trot, and Lucy walks alongside him. He looks down at his sister and asks, "What happened? We saw the corvette limping back in and figured something was wrong."

Lucy shrugs. "I don't know. Zaene came and told me to wait for you at the gate and then proceed straight to Armstrong's office. That's all I've got."

Armolas walks out to meet them as they trot up to the stables and dismount. "Good to see you all made it back in one piece. Even picked up Lucy on the way."

Aton nods and hands the reins over to him. "Hey, can you do us a favor and put these two up for us? Armstrong sent for us, and it seems urgent."

Shaide hangs back a bit, looking weary. The tension in the air is making him uncomfortable. Armolas walks over, takes

Twilight's reins from him, and says "Yeah, go on ahead. If Armstrong needs you, it's best not to keep the old man waiting. Don't start expecting this special treatment, though. Next time you put your own steeds away. Got it?"

Aton nods gratefully. "Thank you, Armolas. We better hurry."

Armolas is already walking away from them and leading the two sleipnir back into the paddock.

Lucy taps her foot impatiently, in serious mode right now. "Come on, you two. We should hurry."

Aton, Lucy, and Shaide rush across the courtyard and into the chapel, quickly running up the staircase until they reach their master's office.

When they step through the door, they see a disheveled shipmaster and a somber-looking Armstrong waiting for them, as well as several Ceraphs standing randomly around the room.

Aton looks at Armstrong and asks, "What happened, Orville? What is all of this?"

Armstrong looks at the shipmaster and their fellow Ceraphs and sighs, hesitating a moment before explaining. "There has been a serious incident that I believe you should all be made aware of. Shipmaster August, tell them what occurred."

ETERNAL KNIGHTS OF EDEN I

The middle-aged shipmaster turns around and addresses the room in a subdued tone, "A few hours ago, we were on maneuvers a few dozen miles from Broadspring, where we were stationed. We received a short-band distress signal from the fleet over the village and high-tailed it over in response. When we arrived, I could not believe what I saw."

He hesitates for a moment before continuing. "The entire village was either leveled or burning. Corrupted beasts and a remarkable number of formers were overrunning the village, and the entire air fleet had somehow been taken down."

Aton raises a hand. "Whoa, whoa. Hang on. You said the fleet was brought down? How is that possible? There was at least one heavy cruiser and a carrier down there. What could have brought them down?"

"Let him finish, Norvus," says Armstrong. "There is more."

August continues with his story, shaking as if he is still in shock. "There was no sign of any survivors. Everyone seemed to have been overrun by the corrupted and formers swarming the area. Before we could even make a thorough assessment of the situation, we were set upon by a swarm of corrupted wyvern and even a small dragon, and we ended up taking heavy damage even as we fled the region to bring word back."

Lucy and Aton just sit there for a moment, mouths open in shock. Aton hesitantly asks, "Dai and Kiro?"

August shakes his head. "I'm sorry. We found no sign of survivors before we were forced to flee."

Lucy puts her face in her hands and takes several deep breaths. Aton balls his hands into fists as he tries to process the loss of his two teammates.

Shaide raises a hand and hesitantly asks, "What about the ARV *North Star* and the students from the academy? Were they brought down as well?"

August shakes his head. "I do not believe so. They appear to have departed a couple of hours before we received the distress signal."

Shaide lets out a slight sigh of relief and leans against the wall.

Aton looks at August and Armstrong, clearly thinking about something important. He suddenly asks, "What could have done all of that? That's not something a bunch of corrupted monsters and formers could have done on their own. Their numbers in the region were not nearly high enough to take the town, so what the hell happened?"

Armstrong shakes his head, no answers coming to him. Then he says, "Aton, I wish I had an answer for you, but the truth is this. Nothing I know of could have pulled off what happened except possibly an Angel. As I find it absurd that the only Ceraphs in the area, Dai or Kiro, might have done something like this, I have no answers as to who or what is behind this. Rest assured, we will be making it a top priority to identify and stop whoever or whatever is behind it."

He lowers his head "And I offer my condolences for the loss of your two friends. I cannot help but feel like we are losing Ceraphs and friends far too often these days."

Aton and Lucy maintain identical looks of disbelief as they let the news of their friends' demise, as well as the entire village of Broadspring, sink in. Their fellow Ceraphs around the room also have their heads bowed in respect and mourning at the loss of two of their own. Even Shaide lowers his head. He may not have been close with them, but he knew them for years, and he even kind of liked them.

Armstrong looks up and says to Shaide, "This is why we need you, Shaide. There are not very many true Ceraphs, and those like you, to whom this seems to come naturally, are essential if we are to keep the corruption at bay. If you still wish to join us, we will begin right away preparing you for what is out there."

Shaide nods, not really sure how to answer.

Armstrong seems satisfied. "Go back home for now, and we will discuss your future at a later time. Get some rest and be ready for when we need you."

Shaide nods and gets to his feet. He pauses, putting a hand on Aton and Lucy's shoulders, and waits until they both look up at him and nod. Then he turns and walks out the door.

Behind him, he hears someone say, "Is that the kid who picked up Rho?"

Armstrong's voice reaches Shaide as he walks down the stairs. "That's him. I have a lot of hope for his future."

Shaide walks out of the temple and onto the Citadel grounds, contemplating everything he's just heard.

Thousands of people dead in such a short span of time, all apparently at the hands of these corrupted beings. This is the reason he chose to join the military and why he is now considering choosing to join the fight with the Ceraphs.

With the loss of his parents, along with countless others, Shaide cannot sit idly back knowing he is capable of making a difference. When he first learned he could fight just a few years ago, there was no longer a question as to what he wanted to do with his life. Even at such a young age, he knew what he had to do.

Lost in thought, he jumps when he realizes he is already at the door of Aton's house. He lets himself in and proceeds to his bedroom. He takes his gear off, setting it neatly on his nightstand, and sits on the bed as his thoughts stray off into the past.

He remembers an adorable Elmeri girl with unusual pink hair who had a huge impact on his life, both being the first real friend the other ever had. He thinks of his friend Reno, whom he spent the last several months fighting and learning alongside with. He thinks of Nyuralisiania, his unexpected Nekomata…friend. And he thinks of everyone else he has formed some kind of relationship with.

These people are the reason he chooses to fight, because he wants to create a world where they can be happy and free.

He heads into the kitchenette and makes himself a snack as he waits for his godfather to come back home, and he makes his decision.

CHAPTER 10

ACT TWO: GUARDIANS

Two years have passed since the incidents at Broadspring. Shaide Darkmoon is now a very active Ceraph acolyte. He is still fairly young, and his partnership with Rho is unusual for an acolyte, but Shaide is well known for being the exception to many norms.

He can frequently be found accompanying more experienced Ceraphs on their own missions, learning from them and aiding them in their various objectives. Shaide has already directly helped save two villages from corrupted infestations in addition to aiding in the hunting down of multiple corrupted beasts that threaten the southern reaches of Alastair.

 A.S.GUINN

ETERNAL KNIGHTS OF EDEN I

He occasionally corresponds with his old friends from the academy when he has downtime. Even Celeste makes a point of writing to him from time to time. They weren't especially close, but she is fascinated by the Ceraphs and loves reading and hearing his stories. He takes pains to visit his old friends on the rare occasions he makes it to the capital.

Unfortunately, his little Nekomata girlfriend, Nyu, was heartbroken when she learned about him joining the Ceraphs because she realized she wouldn't be able to see him anymore like she wanted. She had been looking forward to seeing him every weekend. Shaide felt bad about it, but there was little he could do.

Reno expressed alternating feelings of envy and displeasure at Shaide's joining of the Ceraphs. He is proud of his best friend for joining the most elite group of warriors responsible for defending the world itself, but he is also rather upset that his best friend will not be around much anymore. Nevertheless, on the rare occasions when they do get to spend time together, they enjoy themselves.

Celeste has started hanging out with Reno, Rayn, and Lania. After eliminating the drakes with them, the usually introverted girl became very close to them. Celeste and Shaide get along especially well whenever he drops in, and she seems interested in joining the Ceraph Order herself in the future.

Sadly, Shaide has not been able to make it to the capital in over six months. He spends nearly all of his time out on missions these days, and he has quickly become one of the Ceraphs with the highest percentage of field time. Every time he comes back from a mission, within a couple of days, he is usually heading out with another Ceraph, determined to get as much experience as possible.

Finally, two days ago, Master Armstrong directly ordered Shaide to take two weeks off and stay home and relax to give his body and mind time to recover from the enormous workload he has been taking on. When Shaide protested, Armstrong explained to him that if he spent too much time in the field, then he might lose sight of what he is fighting for. He also reminded him that he is still training and that it is important to take time off and reflect on one's experiences. Shaide was unable to argue with the master's logic and agreed to take a couple of weeks off. Despite his unwillingness to do so, he is really looking forward to going into Corallina today to see his friends again.

His greatest frustration so far has been that, despite his vigilance, he has not come across any missions that take him to the Erita capital city of Sora. He made a promise long ago to come back and see Amari, but to this day, he has been unable to keep that promise. The guilt has been eating at him for some time. Nevertheless, he perseveres and fights on, doing everything he can to make a world where she and everyone else he cares for can live safely and happily.

The Ceraphs have no official uniform to speak of, even though their support forces do, so Shaide puts on the usual field outfit that he uses these days, as he currently does not own any casual clothing that fits him. He traditionally wears black leather armor over a black gi-style outfit, with black boots and a black hood. He feels like it makes him more intimidating, which is important as he fears his young age will cause people to take him less seriously.

He has also grown considerably over the past two years, now standing nearly six feet tall and still growing, with a lean and muscular build. His godfather, Aton, is certain that he will be a very strong individual, and Lucy makes a point to behave rather inappropriately when he happens to be around her. Fortunately, Shaide has gotten used to her behavior, and it makes him significantly less uncomfortable. Nevertheless, lately, his godfather has been growing concerned that she is not entirely joking anymore.

Once Shaide finishes putting on his field outfit, he sheathes his sword across his back and heads out the door. As Shaide grew bigger, he began favoring a longsword over his daggers, and while he still carries them with him, his single-edged longsword is his weapon of choice for most missions these days.

After making sure he has his Ceraph Order medallion, he makes his way to the stables to get his mare, Twilight, to ride to the city. The once troublesome sleipnir has grown very attached to Shaide, and now she will not allow any other sleipnir to even approach him, determined to be the only one he rides.

Armolas looks up as he approaches. Twilight sensed his approach and is already waiting for him by the fence line, alerting Armolas to Shaide's presence.

Armolas sighs as he approaches. "Are you heading out on yet another mission? You really need to take a break once in a while."

Shaide chuckles. "No, Armolas. I'm headed to the capital for a bit of R&R. Armstrong is forcing me to take some time off, so I figured I should go see my friends from the academy."

Armolas nods approvingly. "Good. Even the toughest warriors need some time off occasionally. You work too hard. and you'll work yourself into an early grave."

Shaide hops the fence. takes the saddle from Armolas, and quickly preps Twilight for departure. To her credit, she waits patiently as he sets her up.

He rubs her snout. "How're you doin', girl?"

She snorts happily as he takes his hand away and climbs onto her back.

Armolas opens the paddock gate and stands aside as Shaide slowly rides out of the pen. "Have a good weekend, my friend. See you in a couple of days."

Shaide laughs "I feel like you're trying to get rid of me."

Armolas just waves and laughs, and then he walks back into his house.

After their exchange, Shaide rides Twilight out of the front gates and, after a short talk with the guards, sets off for the capital city of Corallina. It's a lengthy ride, but on Twilight's back, it is less than two hours. He pats her on the head, and then she kicks off a high speed, carrying him west to the city.

The ride is completely uneventful today. After around twenty minutes, he relaxes and enjoys his surroundings. It is a mild spring morning, and there is nothing but green grass and multicolored flora as far as the eye can see, with the occasional glistening of a lake or pond in the distance.

About three-quarters of the way to the capital, Shaide has Twilight slow down and stop for a break by a lake that sits only a scant two hundred feet from the road. He climbs down from her back and lets her go to the lake's edge to get a drink of water as he relaxes on the shoreline for a while.

This lake is one of the larger ones surrounding the capital and its suburban villages, easily over a dozen miles across. It tends to be a major tourist spot for people getting out of the city, and sure enough, he can see several camps of people enjoying a weekend excursion. Scattered around the lake, he can also see multiple squads of soldiers on patrol to ensure the civilians' safety.

Once Twilight seems like she has had enough water, Shaide climbs back onto her back and ushers her towards the city. He glances over his shoulder at the lake behind him and smiles to himself. He and his fellow Ceraph Order members from the Citadel have worked hard to keep the region around the capital safe, and it warms his heart to see the people enjoying themselves without a care in the world.

Shaide rides up to the south gate to find a small contingent of guards warily observing his approach. Anytime you see an armed man ride up to your gate, it is reasonable to be a little cautious. As Shaide slows to a stop, one of the guards approaches.

"Good afternoon, sir. May I see your identification and ask your business in the city? Especially armed as you are?"

Shaide nods and hands over his citizenship card and his Ceraph medallion. The guard looks at the medallion for a moment and then hands it back.

"My apologies, sir. I did not realize. If it is okay, may I ask your business?"

Shaide nods. "I'm here on a personal visit. I used to attend the Alastair Royal Military Academy, and I am coming into town to visit some old friends whom I no longer get to see very often."

The guard nods and writes down a note, mumbling under his breath, "Social…visit…to…academy. Got it." He looks up. "Sorry for the inconvenience, sir. Please, go on in."

Shaide nods and replies "No need to apologize. I understand. Thanks."

A moment later, Shaide rides through the gate and onto the main south road, heading up to the Mu district. He keeps Twilight at a fast trot to avoid injury to any bystanders as he observes the city around him. He hasn't spent much time here in the two years since he joined the Ceraph Order, and he sometimes finds himself feeling a bit homesick for the place. Even before his parents' deaths and his subsequent enrolling in the academy a few years later, Shaide was basically raised in the capital. It was his home.

He checks a small package he has with him, making sure it is still securely fastened to Twilight. This package contains something sentimental that he has held rather dear to him for a long time, and he needs to have some work done to it.

As he climbs the hill through the various tiers of the city, he attracts a few looks. Sleipnir, while allowed in the city, aren't used very often as personal transport anymore. They are mostly used to pull cargo carriages whenever helicars aren't practical. On top of that, midnight black steeds like Twilight are extremely rare, and many onlookers seem impressed by her beauty.

Shaide looks over his shoulder at his sword. There is also the fact that he is riding through town relatively heavily armed. He reasons that this is likely also attracting a lot of attention.

A short time later, he reaches the Mu district, and the academy comes into view ahead of him. He has a stop to make first, though, so he turns off into the commercial district and slowly rides to the tailor's shop he had grown fond of during his time at the academy.

He hops down from Twilight's back and secures her to a pillar, where she stands and waits patiently. He rubs her snout and feeds her some of the meat he brought for her. Then he unfastens the package and enters the shop with it.

 A.S.GUINN

As he walks in, he sees a familiar old man standing at the counter. A broad smile stretches across his face as he approaches the counter.

The old man looks up at him and asks, "Hello, young man. How can I…help…you…" He squints and leans closer. "You look very familiar, young man, but I cannot quite place the face. Have we met before?"

Shaide bows his head and smiles. "Mr. Wellsley, it has been too long. I'm Shaide Darkmoon. I used to attend the academy, and I came to you for all of my clothing needs."

Mr. Wellsley blinks a few times, looking at Shaide's chest and then up his face a few times. After a moment, a wide smile crosses his face, and he reaches out and shakes his hand.

"You got big, boy. Where have you been?"

Shaide points to the Ceraph medallion on his chest, and Mr. Wellsley leans forward and examines it before looking up at Shaide's face in surprise.

"You joined that lot? At your age?"

"Yeah, there was an…incident a couple of years back. I ended being basically conscripted into the Ceraphs afterward due to a series of unusual circumstances. It has been hard for me to find time to come back to the city since then."

Mr. Wellsley nods in understanding. "Saving the world seems like a full-time job these days." He frowns and tilts his head. "By 'incident,' you aren't referring to the disaster at Broadspring, are you?"

Shaide shakes his head. "No. While my incident did happen near Broadspring, as best we can tell, it wasn't connected to the disaster."

Mr. Wellsley sighs in relief. "You had me worried for a minute, boy. So, what can I do for you today? I doubt you came all this way just to see an old man."

Shaide holds out the package. "My old favorite outfit is way too small now. I was wondering if you could work your magic and tailor me a new outfit of similar design."

Mr. Wellsley smiles. "I suppose I can. Come into the back here, and I will get your new measurements. I'll even make sure to leave enough extra fabric to let it out as you grow. Lord knows you aren't done yet."

Shaide follows Mr. Wellsley into the back and drops his gear, allowing the old man to take updated measurements. After a few short minutes, they are finished, and Shaide puts his gear back on and meets the man back at the front counter, where he finds him drawing up a new outfit based on the one he bought with Amari all those years ago.

Mr. Wellsley looks up when he reaches the counter. "Well, Mr. Darkmoon, I should have this done in about a week.

I know you'll be busy, so just come back for it when you get a chance, and keep yourself safe, alright?"

Shaide nods. "Thank you, Mr. Wellsley. I'm going to head out and see if I can find my friends. I haven't seen them in a long time. I'm hoping they're out in town."

Mr. Wellsley waves as Shaide walks out the door. "Good to see you again, boy. Don't be a stranger!"

Shaide unties Twilight, climbs onto her back, and rides her up to the academy. There is a stable house just outside the academy entrance where students can check out a sleipnir if needed, so Shaide rides up to the stablemaster.

"Excuse me, but could I trouble you to look after my sleipnir for a few hours? I have business with a few of the students, and I need a place to keep her."

The stablemaster turns around and spots the medallion on Shaide's chest. He also frowns at his face for a moment, realizing he looks familiar. After a moment, he shakes his head clear and answers, "Ceraph Order? Of course, it would be my pleasure to look after such a beautiful steed if you can cover expenses."

Shaide climbs down and hands him some silver. "I appreciate it. I'll be back in a few hours for her."

The man waves his hands. "No rush. These beauties are my life, after all."

Shaide rubs Twilight's snout and whispers, "Be good. I know you don't know him, but you can trust him.'"

She snorts slightly as he hands the reins over to the man. "Thanks again, mister."

Shaide walks up the road a little further to the academy gates and approaches the guards. They watch the Ceraph a little warily as he asks. "Excuse me, but can you tell me whether or not a particular individual is currently on academy grounds?"

The constable looks at Shaide's medallion and nods. "Of course. Who am I looking for?"

"Reno Coltide."

The constable scans his sign-in sheet and shakes his head. "I'm afraid Mr. Coltide is currently not at the academy. He checked out a couple of hours ago for recreational purposes. Is he in trouble with the Ceraphs?"

Shaide smiles and shakes his head. "No, I used to attend the academy, and he is an old friend of mine."

The constable tilts his head. "I thought you looked familiar. So, the Ceraphs took you after all, huh?"

Shaide nods. "Yeah. It's been interesting. If you'll excuse me, I'll try and find him in town."

"Of course. Have a good day, Ceraph."

Shaide turns and walks back down the street on foot, noting the road to the spring off to his right. He smiles as he remembers some of the better days when he lived here.

He reaches the commercial street and heads for his old favorite café, where he plans to have lunch. When he walks onto the patio, he recognizes several familiar heads, and a smile stretches across his face as he walks over to greet them.

Reno is animatedly talking to his friends, saying, "…and then freakin' Celeste just ignores orders entirely and charges headlong into the pack of cockatrice, wiping them all out singlehandedly before Sergeant Mills has any idea what is happening! I'll always remember how good we ate that day."

Everyone else at the table breaks out laughing, and no one immediately notices the young man standing behind Reno. Rayn Jarvis looks up over Reno's head and blinks for a minute.

Reno sits up straight. "Sergeant Mills is right behind me, isn't he?"

Rayn shakes his head and smiles. "Someone else."

Reno turns his head and looks up at the smiling face of his best friend. He blinks for a minute before standing up abruptly, kicking the chair over by accident.

"SHAIDE!"

Reno spins around and grabs Shaide in a rib-crushing bear hug. Shaide looks at Rayn with watering eyes as Reno squeezes the life out of him.

After a moment, Reno lets him go and says in exasperation, "I didn't know you were coming into town today! I haven't seen you in months, bro! How are you doing! Holy CRAP, you got tall!"

Shaide sits down in a chair next to the attractive young woman with white hair, whom he does not immediately recognize. "I'm doing well. Armstrong is finally forcing me to take some time off, so I thought it was a good time to come into town for the weekend."

The young woman next to him smirks. "You look good, Shaide. You've grown up."

Shaide looks at her for a moment, and then his eyes open wide in shock. The little flat-chested tomboy has grown up substantially in the year since he last saw her. He blinks a couple of times before responding. "Oh, uhh… Thank you, Celeste."

She looks down in disappointment for a moment before sighing. "You didn't recognize me, did you?"

He coughs and rubs his neck. "Well, uhh… I haven't seen you in about a year. You've…grown…a lot."

Lania on the opposite side of the table frowns and glares at Celeste's chest. "Yeah, no kidding. I think I'm jealous of her."

"Hey Lania, Rayn," says Shaide, changing the subject. "How're you two doing?"

Rayn smiles. "Good to see you again, Shaide. I'm good. The academy has been sending us out on lesser hunting missions recently, and we've been recounting some of our more interesting little excursions."

"I notice you recognized Lania right away," mumbles Celeste.

Lania lets out an explosive sigh. "Well, maybe because my chest hasn't grown like a freakin' pair of balloons over the past year like yours."

Celeste coughs under her breath. "*cough* Washboard *cough*"

Lania looks down ashamedly. Between the two, Celeste has definitely grown, while poor Lania still looks like she is about twelve. Rayn and Reno seem to be holding in their laughter. This argument appears to be a frequent occurrence.

A familiar young woman walks over to the table. "Oh, a newcomer. Can I get you something to drink, sir?"

Shaide looks up and blinks. The café owner's daughter is looking him in the face, and she is now a stunning eighteen-year-old beauty.

He shakes his head to clear it. "Uhh, yeah, Ashlie. Let me get a hot tea, if it wouldn't be any trouble."

She squints and suddenly recognizes him. She stands up straight in surprise. "Shaide? Oh my Eden, is that you? Lord, you've gotten big. Where have you been?"

Shaide rubs his neck shyly. He always had a crush on the girl, but he's still shy around women. The fact that she's now a grown woman doesn't help.

"I left the academy two years ago. I've been working with the Ceraph Order, so I haven't gotten to come into town as much as I'd like." Ashlie was always off work every time he managed to come into town, so he hasn't seen her in a while.

She nods, looking impressed. "I see. Well, I suppose that is a pretty good excuse. What do you want to eat? It'll be on the house. All of yours."

Reno looks up. "Really?!"

She nods. "We don't see Ceraphs through our café very often. I know Daddy would like to show his appreciation."

Shaide looks surprised too. "Well, if you're sure it's okay." He places his order, and she walks back to the kitchen with a big smile on her face.

"And of course, I'm still invisible while you're around," Reno says with a sigh.

Shaide looks at him in confusion. "What do you mean?"

Rayn leans back and laughs. "Shaide, you are absolutely clueless with girls, aren't you? The waitress is clearly into you."

Shaide frowns and looks down slightly. "There are times I wouldn't mind getting a date, but the life of a Ceraph doesn't exactly leave much time for a personal life."

"Well," says Lania, "your parents found time, didn't they? If they did, so can you."

Reno chuckles. "He still has a crush on that Elmeri girl he was friends with as a kid."

Shaide looks at him and shakes his head. "No, it's not like that with her. I haven't even seen her in six years. No, she was the first real friend I ever had. I'm just sad that I never got to see her again."

Reno raises his eyebrows "You're telling me you still haven't gotten in touch with her? What the hell, man?"

"Saving the world is more important than my personal desires," Shaide replies with a shrug.

Celeste smiles and raises her glass. "A fellow workaholic. A man after my own heart."

Rayn leans forward and asks, "Is there anything interesting you can tell us?"

"No," says Shaide, "it's been oddly quiet lately. We've had all of the usual incursions, but nothing out of the ordinary has occurred since the destruction of Broadspring."

All four of Shaide's friends look down sadly as they recall the incident in which twenty-one thousand people perished in one day, including the Rangers they had made friends with.

Rayn sighs and looks up. "We lost some of our best people that day. And we were very nearly among those lost. I still can't believe what happened."

"Did your people EVER come up with an explanation as to what happened that day?" Celeste asks Shaide.

He shakes his head. "No. All they ever figured out was that something immensely powerful destroyed the town. All of the evidence suggests one single being was behind most of the destruction, and the swarms of corrupted came later. They're thinking possibly a corrupted dragon, but one hasn't been seen since before the incident, so it's just a theory."

The quartet seems lost in thought for a moment, but they are interrupted by Ashlie bringing out their food. With five hungry bellies, this is more than enough to distract them from their discussion.

"Thanks, Ashlie," says Shaide. "Tell your father we said thanks as well."

Ashlie smiles and winks at him. "Daddy says you are always welcome here when you have a chance to come through. I'll leave you to enjoy your meal. Let me know if you need anything." She drifts away to help the other customers, her smiling gaze lingering on Shaide for a moment before she turns away.

Reno points in frustration. "See? I'm invisible."

"Who WOULD look at you next to him or Rayn, chubby?" mumbles Celeste.

"Hey, you wanna take this outside, missy?" replies Reno, staring at her in mock anger.

Celeste looks around. "We're already outside, idiot."

Rayn puts his face in his hands. "Will you two cut it out? I swear, we can't take you guys anywhere!"

Lania is holding her gut as she tries her hardest to restrain her laughter, while Shaide just has his face in his hands, laughing so hard he's about to cry.

Before long, they've finished up their dinner and are walking out of the café. Reno asks Shaide, "What do you want to do now? You're the one who doesn't get to come into town very often."

Shaide stops and considers Reno's words. What DOES he want to do now that he's here?

Rayn asks him "Do you want to go hang out at the spring for a bit? It's not like we have anything better to do."

Shaide nods. "Yeah, sure. Let's relax and let some of this food settle a bit."

The Ceraph and his friends set off up the road towards the favorite Academy hangout in the nature reserve.

*   *   *

Several thousand miles to the east, in the Erita capital city of Sora, a very different scene is occurring at the Tamiel family mansion.

A silver-haired Elmeri in a general's dress uniform is standing in the family garden next to an ornate casket, his hand on the white stone finish as tears flow freely down his face. This man is Koraru Tamiel, brigadier general of the Erita Royal Army. The woman in the casket is his wife, Aria Tamiel.

Beside him stands a young Elmeri woman with pink hair and red eyes, and tears run down her face as she listens to the Elmeri priest give his sending to the gathered family members. Amari Tamiel feels his words pierce her, providing no comfort for the loss of her mother.

The priest's words ring out to the gathered family and friends. "We cannot understand why the goddess would take

ETERNAL KNIGHTS OF EDEN I

Aria from us so soon. We cannot fathom why the goddess would see fit to strike a loving mother down with illness, taking a mother from her children and a wife from her husband. We can only take comfort knowing that Aria has returned to the goddess's loving embrace and that when the time is right, her family and friends will see her again. We offer our prayers to the protector Eden and the goddess Shizune to carry the soul of our lost Aria to the eternal paradise, where she will wait for her loved ones to see her again."

The priest bows and walks away, leaving the family to grieve their loss.

Aria Tamiel fell inexplicably ill after a vacation trip to the Gulf of Shizune at the far south edge of Erita. Everything on the trip was fine until the day they left, when Aria began complaining that she was not feeling well.

In just over forty-eight hours, Aria progressed from mild headaches to pain wracking her entire body, with fever, chills, and hallucinations rapidly escalating in severity. Two days ago, her heart stopped without warning, and she was gone.

The doctors could not understand what was wrong with her. Her illness seemed to have been nothing more than a moderate cold, but the symptoms were more severe than anything they had ever seen, and no matter what treatments they tried, she wouldn't respond. Strangely, the illness did not appear contagious, as no one else showed any symptoms at any time.

Six men on Aria's side of the family pick up her casket, and the family escorts them as they carry her to the family mausoleum, where she will find her final resting place.

Amari and her father watch silently as Aria's father slides the mausoleum door closed with a somber look on his face.

Yania, the Drameri maid, walks up and puts a hand on Amari's shoulder. She whispers quietly, "Come on, we should return to the house. You could use something to eat, and your father needs to be alone right now."

Amari looks up at her father, who is staring blankly at where his wife is now entombed. She looks back at Yania and nods, and then she follows her to the house.

As they walk, she says, "I don't understand, Yania. How could this happen?"

Yania shakes her head. "I do not know, Amari. I've looked after this family for quite some time now, and I've nursed all of you through illness at some time or another. I've never seen anything like this, though. I'm sorry. I don't have the answer you seek."

Amari looks down and nods.

Yania shakes her shoulder gently as they walk into the house. "Why don't you write to Shaide again and tell him what happened? I'm sure speaking to him will make you feel a little better."

Amari looks somehow even more downcast. "He's never written back, Yania. I don't think he cares about me or even remembers me anymore."

"Now, girl, you know that's not true. Your father told you some time ago that the Alastair military was not allowing him to contact you. I'm sure he has not forgotten about you. I'm sure he is thinking about you just like you think about him."

Amari looks up at her housemaid and friend, pain and grief etched into her face. "Do you really think so?"

Yania nods, keeping Amari's mind on Shaide and off of her mother "I'm sure of it. You two were very close. He will not have forgotten you so easily. Now, let me get a pen and some parchment, and you can write to him and tell him what you're going through and how you feel. Even if he cannot respond, I am sure that your thoughts are reaching him."

Amari nods and sits down at the dinner table, watching as Yania walks to the neighboring office and returns with a sheet of parchment and a pen.

"Now, write what you feel, and I will prepare some dinner."

Amari sits and contemplates what to say for a moment. Then she puts her pen to paper and writes the letter. She looks it over for a moment and, satisfied, folds it up.

When Yania brings in her dinner, Amari hands the letter to her.

Yania takes it and smiles. "I'll speak to your father when he is feeling better, and I'll see if he cannot help me find where to send this. I'll make sure this reaches where it needs to go.

Amari smiles weakly and nods. Still sitting in her chair, she reaches over and hugs Yania around the waist. "Thank you, Yania. No matter what happens, I can always count on you, can't I?"

Yania smiles "Of course, girl. I've helped raise you since you were a small child. You are like a sister to me, although I would never say so in front of your father. I will always be here for you."

Amari nods and eats her dinner quietly, grieving over the loss of her mother but feeling an odd comfort at the same time. It takes her a moment to realize it, but Yania was right. Writing a letter to Shaide, even not knowing if he will read it, has still made her feel better about what she is going through. She smiles to herself slightly, glad that she has Yania to support her. She feels a pang of guilt as well, knowing her father does not have anyone he is close to like that. Her mother was his whole world outside of work, and she knows it is hitting him far harder than it is her.

After dinner, Amari heads up to her bedroom and changes out of her formal clothes and into a revealing but comfortable athletic outfit. She picks up her mage staff from her dresser and looks it over.

The design of this staff is very familiar, and for a good reason. When she began formal training as a war-mage, she had her own staff custom made. Cosmetically, it is a copy of the replica that Shaide bought her years ago: a purple pole with gold inlay, with heavy golden rings around the head of the staff. The staff functions as both a spiritual catalyst to amplify the caster's magical ability as well as a highly effective melee weapon in the right hands.

Amari holds it in front of her and focuses, channeling her spiritual energy into it as she harnesses her emotions. The letter to Shaide crosses her mind as she focuses, and a slight smile crosses her face.

CHAPTER 11

RETURN

At the end of Shaide's second week of vacation, as he walks with his old friends back up to the academy gates, Celeste pesters him about giving her a sparring match, and Reno makes some rather inappropriate jokes about her just wanting to be all over him. Being the coolheaded girl that she is, she ignores his quips entirely.

Rayn reaches the gate first and is checking everyone in when he sees Lieutenant Nikola approaching the gate with something in his hands. As the lieutenant reaches them, Rayn sharply barks, "Sir!" and salutes across his chest.

Lania follows suit, and Reno and Celeste promptly cease their bickering and salute as well.

Shaide's eyes open wide with glee. "Lieutenant Nikola!"

The lieutenant returns the salute and looks at Shaide with surprise. "Is that who I think it is? Relax, you four. Shaide! As I live and breathe, I wasn't sure I would ever see you again after the Ceraphs took you."

As his friends step back and out of the way, Shaide walks forward and shakes the lieutenant's hand. "I came into town to visit with my friends for a few days since Master Armstrong is forcing me to take a vacation."

Nikola nods in understanding. "I suppose you have been working hard. I actually have something for you, believe it or not." He hands Shaide a small handful of letters. "These have been coming for you since just after you left, actually. The postmaster saw that you weren't a member of the academy anymore and just stashed them away. Another one apparently came in yesterday, and they gave them all to me to decide what to do with them."

Shaide looks through the letters and sees that they are all from Amari. He feels a slight jolt of joy as well as guilt. "Wow. I didn't know she had been writing me…"

Lieutenant Nikola coughs and asks, "So, how have you been? I haven't heard much about you except that you have been staying extremely busy."

Shaide shakes his head and looks at the Lieutenant "Yeah, I've been shadowing on missions every chance I get. That's actually why I was forced to take a vacation. I guess he knew I would never take a break on my own.

Nikola nods and smiles. "You have to remember to take a break once in a while. What's the point of fighting if you can't take time to enjoy what you're protecting?"

Shaide looks down and sighs. "Yeah, I know."

"Well, come on you lot," Nikolas says to the other four. "We have some prep to do before your mission tomorrow." Then, to Shaide, he adds, "Good to see you, Shaide. Come by more often."

Shaide waves at him as he turns to head back into the academy.

Reno steps forward, shakes Shaide's hand, and pulls him into a brotherly hug. "See you soon, I hope. Don't be a stranger."

Celeste tightly hugs him as well. "Don't forget about us, oh holy one. Come and see us whenever you can."

Shaide nods and laughs. Lania pulls him into a tight hug too. "We really do miss having you around, you know. You and

Reno's antics when you were together made life a lot more interesting."

When Lania lets go, Rayn reaches out and shakes his hand. "Same thing they said. Make sure you come back and see us more. Don't wait six months like last time."

Celeste grumbles, "I didn't even get to see you that time."

Shaide laughs as they walk back into the academy. "I'll do my best. See you guys later!"

He turns and heads to the stables to pick up Twilight, and a few minutes later, he is on his way back to the Citadel. When he reaches the fortress, he hands Twilight off to Armolas, and after a short conversation, he makes his way to the house he shares with Aton and Lucy.

As he walks across the Citadel grounds, he looks at the sealed letters from Amari. The first one is dated just a week after he left the academy to join the Ceraphs. The most recent one is less than two weeks old.

He walks into the house, and begins opening the letters in order, smiling when he sees that she does indeed remember and miss him, and thathe seems to be doing well. The letters make him feel progressively happier while simultaneously making him miss her all the more. When he reaches the last letter, however, his face falls, and his heart drops.

Dear Shaide,

I don't know if my letters have reached you or not, since you have never written back, but I hope that they are and that you are happy to read them.

We buried my mom today. She fell ill just over a week ago, and they were unable to treat her before she passed away. It's been really hard on my dad and me, but we're getting by somehow.

Meeting you six years ago changed my life. You gave me the confidence I needed to stand up to my bullies. Although no one really bothers me anymore, I still don't have many friends, and I really miss you a lot of the time.

I've been attending the elite military academy here in Sora. My father is making sure I receive the best possible education, and I have been excelling at my spiritual studies. When I think of you, it makes me happy, and I use that to power my magicks. They say I am one of the strongest mages they've seen in years, and I could even be a viable candidate to join the Ceraphs someday if my father would allow it.

I've even been practicing my martial arts since you left, and I am now nearly as strong as the instructors who teach me. I'd really like to show you sometime if I ever get to see you again.

How are you? If you are able to write me, I'd really like to hear what has been happening with you since you left. You should come to Erita and visit us sometime, if you are able. My father and I would really like to see you again.

I'll let you go for now. I miss you, and I am thinking of you. Take care.

Amari

Shaide sets the letter down and puts his face in his hands. Aria Tamiel looked after him like a mother, and she was a very good woman. It breaks his heart to find out about her passing. He can also sense the pain in Amari's words even though she did her best to appear strong.

It has been far too long, and he decides he has to go and see her no matter what the cost. Just as he comes to this conclusion, Aton and Lucy walk through the front door, both looking tired and exhausted but satisfied. Their mission must have gone well.

Aton tilts his head when he sees Shaide. "What's wrong, kid? Who died?"

Shaide closes his eyes and hands him the letter.

Aton reads it and winces when he realizes his insensitivity.

Lucy snatches the letter from his hand, reads it quickly, and then shakes her head. "Smooth. I'm sorry to hear that, Shaide."

"I need to find a way to Sora," Shaide says to Anton. "I made a promise to her years ago, and it's time I kept it."

Aton raises his eyebrows. "That actually may be possible. If you go talk to Armstrong and request to join them, we actually have a medical team going to Sora in a few hours. They're going to investigate reports of a mutant virus that is resistant to all treatment, and the Sora crew isn't prepared for this type of investigation. Armstrong might let you escort them."

Shaide jumps to his feet. "Thanks, Aton."

Lucy calls out to him as he heads for the door, "Hey, handsome, if things go well with your girl, I'll make sure to teach you all about how to make her happy when you get back." She winks at him as he shakes his head and hurries out the door.

Aton looks at his sister and shakes his own head. "You really have issues, you know?"

Lucy shrugs. "Oh, come on. Why can't I have a little fun with the kid?"

Aton closes his eyes. "That depends on what kind of fun you're referring to. Sometimes I'm worried you're not kidding."

She laughs but doesn't respond.

*   *   *

Shaide knocks on Armstrong's door. He waits until he hears a "Come in," and then he proceeds inside.

Armstrong looks up at Shaide and waves a hand at a chair opposite his desk. "Well, this is a surprise. How has your time off been?"

Shaide sits down, trying to suppress his anxiousness. "It was good. I spent two weekends with my old friends from the academy and got to catch up with them." He coughs and rubs his neck. "I was NOT expecting them to look so different. Especially the girls…"

Armstrong chuckles quietly to himself. "You kids do like to grow fast. So, what brings you here today?"

Shaide sighs, glad to get to the point. "If it is okay with you, I would like to escort the research team that is going to Sora to investigate this virus they've discovered out there."

Armstrong leans forward, a suspicious look on his face. "How did you even find out about the research team? It was supposed to be top secret."

Shaide hands Armstrong the letter from Amari. The order master scans it and sighs.

"Mrs. Tamiel is indeed one of the victims of this mysterious illness, I'm afraid. Now I see. You want to go and see your friend, but you also want to find out how she died and put a stop to it, am I correct?"

Shaide nods, holding his breath.

Armstrong leans back and rubs his temples for a moment before looking up. "Very well. I will authorize you to join the research team as their escort. I would rather you not go, but I can see it is very important to you. I have a feeling you would find your way out there anyway. However, I need you to understand something, so listen very closely."

Shaide leans forward, listening intently to the order master.

Armstrong looks him straight in the eyes. "I do not have anyone I can send with you. You will not be shadowing another Ceraph this time. You will be on your own. Your actions will be your own responsibility. If you get into trouble, you won't have anyone there to help you. Do not do anything reckless. Just keep the research team safe and make the Ceraphs proud. Understood?"

Shaide nods. "I won't do anything crazy, Master."

Armstrong looks down and sighs. "That's exactly what your mother said before her last mission. Just…" He looks up. "Make sure you come home in one piece."

Shaide stands up and nods. "I will, sir. Thank you. When do I leave?"

Armstrong looks at his clock. "They leave in just a couple of hours. They should be meeting at the COV *Last Beacon* in about an hour. Grab what you need and meet them there."

Shaide nods. "Thank you, sir."

He leaves the office and heads back to his house to check and gather the rest of his gear. He realizes he never actually answered Armstrong's question. When he showed Armstrong the letter, the order master must have figured out that Aton had told him.

He'll also get to see Amari for the first time in six years. He feels slightly nervous now that he thinks about it. What will he do? What will he say to her? She must have changed since then. Is she even the same person he knew? Anxiety and doubt plague his mind as he rushes home.

Before he knows it, he is standing at his front door. He was so absorbed in thought that he didn't realize his feet were automatically carrying him home.

He walks in and finds Lucy sitting alone in the living room. Aton is nowhere to be seen. She looks up as he walks through the door and immediately asks, "Well? How did it go? Is Armstrong letting you go with them?" She knows this is serious and is behaving herself.

Shaide nods. "Yeah. Armstrong is actually sending me by myself to escort the research team. I'm kind of nervous, and for more than one reason."

Lucy gets up, walks over, and pulls him into a hug. "I'm proud of you, Shaide. Armstrong is sending you on your first solo mission." She squeezes him and sighs. "You know, there was a time I could squish your face in my boobs, but now you're all grown up. It kind of makes me sad when I think of it."

Shaide chuckles to himself. "I'm not just nervous about the mission. What do I do when I see her, Lucy? I haven't seen her in so long. Is she even going to be the same person I knew before?"

Lucy looks up at his face and smiles, shaking her head. She's a tall woman, but she's still a few inches shorter than Shaide, coming up to his nose. She pats him on the head and says, "You'll be okay, kid. You're a good guy. Just be you when you see her, and everything will be fine."

Shaide takes a breath and nods. "Thanks, Lucy."

She steps back. "Now, get your gear and go take care of business. We'll be here when you get home. I'll tell Aton where you went."

Shaide heads to his room and begins packing his field bag for an extended trip. As usual, there is no set timeframe for this mission, and there is no telling how long he will be gone. He makes sure to pack his new casual outfit he had made in the extremely likely event he has some downtime.

Fifteen minutes later, he is armed, armored, and carrying his bag to the front door. Lucy walks over and hugs him again, pulling herself against him a little harder than is probably necessary. She steps away and smiles. "Good luck with your mission, and good luck with your girlfriend."

Shaide sighs. "You know, she's not really my girlfriend."

"Uh-huh, sure," Lucy says with a grin. "Keep telling yourself that. If you're not hers, then I just might have to take you for myself." She winks and closes the door behind him.

Shaide tilts his head in confusion, thinking for a minute. Then he shakes his head and sets off for the spire. Although he is extremely nervous, he also feels a certain sense of elation, both at getting his first mission and at the prospect of seeing his old friend for the first time in so many years.

He enters the tower and inquires with the security desk regarding the location of the COV *Last Beacon*. The receptionist looks up the ship and gives him directions, and he guides the mechanical lift to the appropriate level. When he steps out, he spots the guards at the *Last Beacon's* docking pylon. He is worried for a moment that he may have trouble getting on board, being a last-minute addition, but he approaches anyway.

Fortunately, it seems that Armstrong sent word ahead that he was to join the crew, because they appear to be waiting for him.

They look up as he approaches. "Ceraph Shaide Darkmoon?"

"Yes, I am him." replies Shaide, surprised at the reception.

The guard nods. "Welcome to the *Last Beacon*. You may board."

Shaide pulls his bag up higher onto his shoulder. "Thank you. Have a good day." Then he proceeds across the catwalk and into the frigate's hangar bay. The shipmaster, an old Elmeri veteran named Corolas, approaches him as he boards.

"Mister Darkmoon, I am shipmaster Corolas. I believe we have met before."

Shaide sets down his bag and bows in greeting. "Yes, I've been on your vessel a few times before when shadowing senior Ceraphs."

Corolas bows back and smiles. "We weren't initially going to have a Ceraph escort for this mission. I am pleased to see that Armstrong changed his mind."

                              A.S.GUINN

Shaide debates how much to tell Shipmaster Corolas, but he finally settles on the truth. "I am close to the family of one of the casualties, so Armstrong decided it was worthy of more personal attention."

Corolas nods. "I understand. I'm just glad to have you aboard. From what I hear, you are young but capable. I certainly feel better having you here."

Shaide looks around "Is the research team on board yet?"

Corolas shakes his head. "Not yet. They should be arriving shortly. Go ahead and get comfortable in the Ceraph quarters. I'll have them come speak to you when they've boarded."

Shaide picks his bag up and nods. "Thank you, Corolas." He turns and heads for the Ceraph quarters, which, on this particular ship, are adjacent to the hangar but in the front half of the ship. He exits the hangar into the corridor and enters the quarters to his left.

He is very familiar with the Ceraph quarters of the COV vessels, and he immediately stashes his gear in one of the bunks. He is the only Ceraph on this mission, which is unusual in many ways, but it means he has the whole room to himself unless the research team joins him in here, which is unlikely.

He lies back in his bunk and pulls out a book from his bag to entertain himself while he waits to depart. It's an interesting story that was suggested to him by Reno, about three friends who are very different from one another yet who all seek to serve their god and protect their world any way they can.

The first friend follows the way of creation and seeks to create a world where all can live in harmony and with no conflict.

The second friend follows the way of balance, believing that all things must have a beginning and end, and seeks to preserve the present, believing the world they live in is the only world that can exist.

The third and final friend follows the way of annihilation. He believes simply that the only way they can save their world is to indiscriminately eliminate all who threaten their way of life.

Despite their differences, the friends are able to live in harmony with each other. The first friend sets out to help build new homes and settlements and encourage people to start families, aiming to fulfill his beliefs and create a better world. He gathers a great following and is beloved by those he serves.

The second friend sets out across the world, helping to preserve life as it is, healing the ill and defending those who cannot defend themselves. He gathers a great following among those who seek to help others, and he becomes a shining monument to the sanctity and preservation of life.

The final friend sets out alone, seeking out those who would harm the innocent and purging them without mercy. Like the other two, he acquires a great following, but his followers believe the future lies with strength. His army marches across the land, eliminating all who would threaten the world.

The three friends, each following their own ways of life, keep the world in a bountiful era of peace. They help create and preserve society, and they eliminate any threats to the innocent people they protect.

When a powerful being arises one day, seeking to end all that the three friends have sought to protect, they gather their forces and march to find this being. The three friends find that their power alone is not enough to stop this terrible being. Their followers are slaughtered one by one as they fight in vain to stand against this being of insatiable malice.

Then the three brothers have an idea. They stand for the three aspects of the universe: creation, existence, and destruction, so they focus their thoughts and spiritual power, praying to the universe itself to lend them aid. To their shock, their prayers are rewarded. Their souls are lifted from their bodies, and they are bound together, transforming into an entirely new being of tremendous power.

This being stands against the invading force, and with a single swift act, it purges the invader from the world forever. And once the final battle is over, the being descends into the planet to slumber, never to be seen again.

The three friends are no longer mortal, and they can no longer exist among their people. As they float, disembodied, above the battlefield, a voice speaks to them, telling them to sleep far away from civilization and silently watch over the planet as the society they gave rise to follows its own path.

As Shaide reads his story, there's a sharp knock on the door to his quarters. He closes his book and asks, "Who is it?"

A muffled voice says, "We're from the research team. May we come in, or is it a bad time?"

Shaide sits up. "Yeah, come on in."

The door slides open, and three individuals walk through the door: an Elmeri man, a human woman with glasses, and what looks like a little girl.

The man tips his glasses and introduces himself. "I am Vargas Amaranthine, the leader of the biology research team heading the investigation in Erita regarding the recent string of unusual illnesses. Can I safely assume you are Shaide Darkmoon, the Ceraph who has been assigned to escort us while we work?" His voice is slightly haughty and proud, and Shaide is certain the Amaranthines are one of the noble families of Elmeri society. He seems pleasant enough, however.

Shaide stands up and bows out of respect for Elmeri custom. "Yes, I am Shaide. Master Armstrong assigned me to escort you at the last minute."

Vargas nods and waves his hands down slightly. "No need for such formalities, Shaide. I may come across like an Elmeri nobleman, but in truth, I haven't been home in over twelve hundred years. I did not leave on the best of terms with my family, and I chose to conduct my research with the Ceraph Order in peace."

Shaide rubs his neck. "Right, sorry. I have a friend in Sora who is Elmeri, and I spent some time there as a child. Old habits die hard."

Vargas smiles and shakes his head. "No need to apologize. You are Mitera, am I correct? It pleases me that Armstrong not only saw fit to assign us an escort, but an experienced Mitera warrior at that."

Shaide coughs and looks down. "Well, in truth, I'm only sixteen. This is actually my first mission with the order on my own."

"Oh, I see," Vargas replies with raised eyebrows. "As the Mitera age at around the same rate as my own people, it is difficult to discern one's age sometimes. Nevertheless, he would not have sent you along if he did not believe you were up to it. I stand by my statement that I am pleased to have you along."

Shaide nods, feeling slightly better. "Thank you, Vargas. It's nice not to be treated as a child for once."

The young human woman steps forward and leans in uncomfortably close to Shaide. She closely scans nearly every inch of his body as he stands there uncomfortably.

He looks at Vargas and asks, "Umm, what is she doing?"

"Amber?" Vargas says to the young woman, "At least introduce yourself to the young man before you invade his personal space. What are you even doing?"

She looks up. She has long deep red hair and ice-blue eyes. Her glasses are round and surprisingly thin for how wide the lenses are.

She steps back and says in a rapid, excited voice, "I'm sorry, I shouldn't be so rude. I am just so excited to meet you after all this time. You're a bit of an anomaly among the Ceraph Order, but I wasn't around when Doctor Shepard examined you, even though I was so absolutely excited to find out that such a young specimen had successfully merged with an angel with no negative side effects to speak of. I am SO happy to meet you. Would it be too much to ask you to strip off your clothes and let me thoroughly examine your body? I am so curious to find out what makes you so special among the other Ceraphs, and it is just so exciting to have such a rare opportunity to study such a perfect example of angel compatibility, and especially such a cute one! Most of the Ceraphs I get to meet are rather rugged men with bad attitudes and heavily scarred bodies, and such a pristine and youthful example is just so hard to come by and—"

"AMBER!" Vargas barks. "Calm down and introduce yourself. You're scaring the poor man."

The woman takes a breath and calms herself for a moment. Her speech is slightly slower as she introduces herself. "I'm so sorry. I've been studying your case ever since you came to the Ceraphs, and I have been desperate to meet you for a long time. And I'm sorry I'm rambling again. My name is Amber Cyrus. I have been the chief analyst on the team for a couple of decades."

Shaide tilts his head as she shakes his hand. She still seems to be trembling with excitement. "Well, I, umm… I'm Shaide Darkmoon. It is a pleasure to meet you."

She nods rapidly and says excitedly, "Of course I know who you are. I know we have business here, but I would LOVE to spend some time alone with you and find out what makes you special before we have to part ways, but this mission should have us spending quite a bit of time together and—"

Vargas puts a hand on her shoulder. "AMBER! Calm down, girl! You'll have plenty of time to talk to him. Ronoa, introduce yourself."

The person Shaide took for a little girl steps forward and says in a surprisingly mature and professional tone, "Greetings. I am Ronoa Firestone. I oversee managing and maintaining our equipment and machinery. While I personally believe an escort is unnecessary for this mission, I am nonetheless grateful that you were willing to accompany us. I look forward to a productive business relationship."

Shaide bows, realizing she must be a Termer, also known to the less polite as a dwarf. "It is a pleasure to meet you. You seem to have a well-rounded team."

Ronoa looks at Amber with disdain. "I could do with a slightly less hyperactive co-worker, but yes. I am pleased to say we have a talented team of researchers, and we are prepared to handle nearly any situation that may arise."

Amber, who is still kind of fidgety, asks "So, can I talk to him now, please?"

Vargas sighs and shakes his head. "Good goddess, girl. I haven't seen you this wound up in a long time. Shaide, do you feel like going over the plan for our mission now? Or would you prefer to wait until we arrive?"

Shaide waves at the couches secured between the bunks and says, "I have time now, if you would prefer to get it out of the way."

Vargas nods and sits down across from him. Ronoa sits down next to Vargas, while Amber sits down with surprising elegance next to where Shaide is standing. Vargas looks at him apologetically as Shaide sits down next to Amber."

Vargas begins. "When we arrive, we will first set up our laboratory at the Ceraph outpost at Sora's Our Lady Shizune Medical Center. Next, we will be going to have dinner with the Tamiel family to get a firsthand account of Lady Aria's illness and find out if there is anything we missed. They live conveniently close to the hospital, and I would like to begin as soon as possible. Afterward, we will return to the laboratory, and we will spend the next several days locating and interviewing family members of those we have confirmed shared this same illness. Once that step is completed, we will begin reaching out to families of those who died of similar illnesses to see if they are connected. All this time, Amber and her team will be analyzing any and all samples of anything related to the illness. Once we complete this initial round of investigation, we will decide from there how to proceed. Any questions?"

Shaide looks around as the feeling of inertia of the frigate lifting off settles, and then he replies, "Nope, I believe that pretty much covers it. Throughout all of this, where would you like me to be?"

Vargas nods "I would like you to escort me while I am interviewing the families. While I am at the laboratory, I will have little need of you, and I have no problem if you simply do as you please. Technically, you are the ranking individual on this mission as a Ceraph, so I will defer to your judgment."

Shaide waves his hands. "Oh, no. You are by far the more experienced here. I will follow your lead as long as it doesn't put anyone in harm's way."

"I am pleased to see you are humble and reasonable," Vargas says with a smile. "Several of the Ceraphs I have worked with in the past proved rather arrogant and hardheaded. I believe we will get along just fine. Now, are there any further questions?"

Shaide shakes his head. "I'm not here to step on toes. I think I know everything I need to for now."

Vargas and Ronoa stand up. "If you'll excuse us, then. We will rejoin our team and prepare while the airship travels."

"Do you mind if I ask you some questions while we travel?" Amber asks Shaide. "I promise to try and behave myself. I just really want to know about when you merged with your angel."

Vargas looks at him with mild exasperation. "It's your call. As I said, technically, you're in charge here. I can tie her up if you need me to."

Shaide is honestly slightly intimidated by this woman's remarkable energy, but he doesn't want to be rude either. He nods. "Yeah, it's fine. I might get a chance to learn something too."

Amber stands up and wrings his hands. "Oh! Thank you thank you thank you thank you! I really appreciate this! Now—"

Vargas cuts her off. "Remember. Be calm. I know you are excited to meet your study subject, but he is a person. No dissecting him while he is still alive."

Amber takes a breath and calms herself. "I will behave, Vargas. I know I can't cut him open."

Vargas mumbles to himself as he walks out the door, "I should probably prohibit her from any physical examinations either, but..." He closes the door behind him.

*   *   *

Three exhausting hours later, Amber finishes her interview with Shaide and thanks him for his time. She tried to convince him to take his clothes off so that she could perform a comprehensive investigation of his body, but he declined.

Vargas finally comes and gets her, telling her that they need to go to bed for the evening. The frigate is moving at a decent pace, but they will still not be arriving until early morning, and they need to try and get some sleep. Shaide also suspects that Vargas did this to save him from her and give him some time to himself.

Shaide lies back in his bunk, puts away the book he has been reading, and thinks to himself about his meeting with his old friend tomorrow. He feels significant anxiety because he still doesn't know what to say or do when he sees her. Will she even recognize him?

He does his best to cast away this doubt and anxiety and then closes his eyes. Vargas was right: he will need his rest. Assuming he can get any.

*   *   *

A few hours later, Shaide is in the middle of a pleasant dream. He is back at the academy with his old friends Reno, Rayn, Lania, and even Celeste. Bryon and Joslin are still alive and hanging out with them. His old "friend" Nyu is there as well.

They are all just hanging out at the spring, enjoying their day and being carefree. Shaide knows this isn't a memory.

                    A.S.GUINN

ETERNAL KNIGHTS OF EDEN I

They were never ALL together like this. But it is a pleasant experience, nonetheless.

A strange dark feminine figure with horns and yellow eyes rises from the water in front of him. No one else seems to see her, but her eyes are locked onto him, as if they are boring into his soul. Suddenly, she stretches out towards him, and he feels himself moving…

With a start, he shoots awake and looks around the dorms. He feels the inertial shifting indicating the frigate is decelerating. That must mean they are arriving at the base in Sora. He climbs out of bed and checks all of his gear, and then he grabs his bag and steps out of the Ceraph quarters.

He turns to his right and walks through the bulkhead into the open hangar bay, where he sees the bay doors on his side of the ship have already been opened. He walks out to the edge of the ship and looks out at the stunning view he has not seen in years.

Sunshine glitters over the vast architecture of the Elmeri city of Sora, the capital city of the Erita empire. The white marble-like buildings with their golden trim stretch out as far as the eye can see as they slowly fly over the city. When Shaide looks towards the bow, he can see they are heading for the military base in the core of the city, more specifically, its towering docking spires.

The research team walks out behind him, carrying their personal gear on rolling carts. In addition to the three individuals he met in his quarters, there appear to be nine additional members of the research team who work under their respective leaders. While the medical facility here in Sora has some of the best medical equipment available, the research team chose to bring their own specialized equipment along that they developed personally and that they felt was superior to some of what Sora had.

The frigate eases to a crawl as it drifts right up next to a dock on the great tower, and a crewman in the hangar handles the ship's controls from a console by the bay doors, easing it against the docks.

Shaide notices that these docks are different from the ones back in Alastair. The walkways are covered and shielded from the elements, and when they are in place, an extendable gantry comes out and settles into the hangar bay, giving them access to the dock.

A pair of Elmeri men stand at the entrance to the docks and bow as Shaide approaches. He notices they bear Ceraph medallions as well, and he remembers that each nation does indeed have a small contingent of Ceraphs permanently stationed there, even though the bulk of their personnel are in Alastair.

Then men bow to Shaide, and one of them says, "Good afternoon, brother. We only just got word that you would be escorting the research team while they were here. Allow me to welcome you to the Elmeri city of Sora. I am Naliel, and this is my partner, Parlas. It is my pleasure to welcome you to Erita."

Shaide bows respectfully, somewhat familiar with their culture. "I'm Shaide Darkmoon. It has been many years since I have been to Erita, and it feels good to return."

Naliel tilts his head in thought. "Darkmoon? Are you related to the late Juvia Darkmoon, by chance?"

Shaide bows his head, stung by the unexpected reference. "Yes. In fact, she was my mother."

"My condolences," Naliel says, bowing his head respectfully. "I was saddened to hear of her passing six years ago. It pleases me to see you honoring her legacy by carrying on her work. May the goddess watch over you as Eden guides you by his light."

Shaide nods and completes the edict: "And may we one day return to her as our ancestors' memories guide us, shining bright."

Naliel looks impressed. "I see you indeed are familiar with our culture. You are most welcome, Shaide Darkmoon."

The research team walks up behind him, looking amused at the interaction between Shaide and the local Ceraphs.

Shaide, however, is not paying attention to them anymore. An Elmeri man in an extraordinarily ornate military officer's uniform is walking down the docking pylon towards them, flanked by two lower-ranking officers. This man has not aged in the six years since Shaide last saw him, and Shaide stares at him as if he cannot believe his eyes.

The man approaches and greets the two Elmeri Ceraphs first. "Naliel, Parlas. I'm sorry I am late. Would you please introduce me to our guests?"

The shipmaster walks up next to Shaide and bows respectfully to the high-ranking Elmeri officer as Naliel introduces everyone.

"Guests from the Ceraph Citadel in Alastair, allow me to introduce you to Brigadier General Koraru Tamiel. He is the general in charge of Erita's special operations regiment and one of Erita's most esteemed military officers."

Shaide's eyes linger on Koraru, barely containing the joy he feels at seeing this man once again. The shipmaster shrugs and introduces himself first. "I am Shipmaster Corolas of the Ceraph Order's logistics and support division. Please allow me to thank you for having us in your nation's capital to perform our duty to the people of Eden."

Vargas shrugs and steps forward, looking at Shaide curiously when he still doesn't introduce himself. "I am Vargas

Amaranthine, General. It is my pleasure to return to Erita after so many years away."

Shaide takes a deep breath and steps forward, bowing deeply. "General Koraru Tamiel, I am the Ceraph Operative assigned to escort the research team while they conduct their operations. My name is Shaide Darkmoon. I am very, very pleased to see you again."

CHAPTER 12

THE PROMISE KEPT

General Koraru Tamiel remains stock still, staring at Shaide with a stunned look on his face. Shaide, for his part, remains bowed down, waiting for some kind of reaction. Koraru, however, just looks down at him, not sure if he believed his ears.

Finally, after a moment, he says, "Did you say your name is Shaide Darkmoon?"

Shaide stands up straight, smiling slightly as he looks back into the face of the man who took care of him so long ago. "Yes, sir. It has been far too long since I made the promise to come back and see you someday. I was finally able to keep it."

ETERNAL KNIGHTS OF EDEN I

Vargas steps forward. "Shaide?! You know General Tamiel?"

Koraru answers for him, the slightest smile gracing his previously expressionless features as he explains, "When Shaide here was a child, he spent two months living with us while his parents were busy conducting an operation. I was friends with his parents, after all, and it was my pleasure to look after him. He and my daughter were very good friends."

Vargas looks at Shaide. "Now I see why Armstrong changed his mind and had you accompany us. This mission is personal for you."

Shaide nods and looks up at Koraru's face, hesitating before asking, "Is it true? Did she really pass away from this illness?"

Pain crosses Koraru's features as he replies, "Yes, I am afraid so. Amari is taking it hard as well. I know it will cheer her greatly to see you again, if you wouldn't mind visiting her."

Shaide smiles sadly. "Her letters finally reached me. I made a promise back then that I would come back and visit. I plan to keep it."

Koraru nods, his expression becoming blank again. Shaide suspects he is hiding a great deal of pain under years of military discipline. "Shaide, you are welcome at my house anytime. Please, if you are able to get away from your duties, come by the house tonight for dinner. I will keep it a secret from her so you can surprise her. For now, I regret that I must return to my duties. I simply came to greet our honored guests, and I was not expecting to find you here."

He pauses as he turns away and mumbles, "You got big, Shaide."

Shaide watches as General Tamiel walks away down the pylon, and then he suddenly realizes he is being stared at from all directions, and he jumps slightly. "What is it?"

Shipmaster Corolas is the first to explain. "You really have no inkling how special it is that you are on such personal terms with General Tamiel, do you? No one else outside his family could speak to him so casually. No one except you."

Shaide is a bit taken aback. "I hadn't considered it, honestly. To me, he is basically Uncle Koraru."

The shipmaster shakes his head and turns away. "Well, I will leave you to your business. We will remain docked here until further notice in case you need anything. Good luck, all of you."

"Well, umm, *Master* Darkmoon," says Vargas, "shall we proceed to our research facility?"

The research team starts pulling and pushing their carts past them onto the docking pylon as Shaide gives Vargas an amused smile. "Master Darkmoon?"

Vargas turns to follow his team, Shaide right next to him. "Of course. If you were raised by General Tamiel, you are basically part of the duchess's family. You should have told us you were so important!"

Shaide looks at him suspiciously, not sure if he should take him seriously. "I'm NOT important. My family and his were just friends before their passing. It's no big deal."

Naliel leans over next to him. "I had no idea you knew the general. I would have prepared a better welcome if I had known."

"Aren't the Ceraphs loyal only to Eden?" Shaide says, frowning. "Why is he such a big deal to you?"

"We may be Ceraphs of the Order," says Parlas, "but we were still born here in Erita. We spent many years of our lives here under Elmeri culture. Even if we no longer owe allegiance to Erita, we still respect how important and influential some people can be."

"Yes, that's right," adds Naliel. "As a Ceraph, you learn to navigate some of the treacherous political climate on top of your duties as a protector of the people. It's not all about fighting monsters, you know?"

As they board a cargo elevator powered by some invisible force, Shaide thinks about this. He never considered the other aspects of the Ceraphs. He just trained to fight and never gave it a second thought.

When they reach the bottom of the tower, the fourteen of them step out and walk across the ground floor to the checkpoint, manned by a small contingent of uniformed Elmeri and Drameri personnel carrying halberds across their backs. After verifying everyone's identities, they give them a "Have a wonderful day" and usher them outside, where they find several dropship-like transport helis waiting for them.

As his team loads their gear onto the three cars, Vargas turns to Shaide. "When we get to the laboratory, you should go see your friend. She just lost her mother very prematurely. Seeing a friendly face would do wonders to cheer her. We'll meet you there after dinnertime."

Shaide feels that sense of anxiety again, and he also starts to second-guess his decision to come along. "Are you sure? I'm here to escort you, after all. Perhaps I should wait until you are ready to head over and come with you."

Vargas puts a hand on his shoulder. "Fights monsters for a living but scared of a girl he hasn't seen in a few years. That is honestly quite adorable, my friend. No, go ahead and head over once we reach the laboratory. You're simply scouting ahead to make sure everything is safe for us, after all."

Shaide sighs and smiles slightly despite his anxiety. Vargas seems to be a good man. "Thank you, Vargas. I sincerely appreciate it."

Vargas shrugs. "We were prepared to have no Ceraph escort at all. I think we can get by for a couple of hours. She IS the daughter of one of the victims. In truth, having you help ease her mind and put her in a better mood will make our job easier."

Vargas leads Shaide to the front cargo car, and they take their seats in the passenger compartment. Amber and Ronoa sit down behind them.

Naliel leans in the door. "We will not be accompanying you, I am afraid. We have some business to take care of, so we may not see you again while you are here, depending on how successful you are. Take care, all of you. Master Darkmoon." He bows ironically and taps the roof of the car, letting the driver know to take off.

Shaide sighs. "That's going to stick, isn't it?"

Amber smiles from the back. "Oh, of course it is. I kind of like calling you Master Darkmoon. It makes the prospect of examining you even more exotic and exciting."

Shaide shudders. The woman is actually quite attractive, but he finds her extremely intimidating. Then there is the fact that she is way older than him, even if she doesn't look like it.

The convoy of cargo helicars lifts into the air and flies off in an orderly line. An Erita gunship drifts to the head of the convoy as they travel the mere mile to the nearby Our Lady Shizune Medical Center, and when they arrive, they settle down onto the rooftop.

As they land, a middle-aged human woman walks out onto the rooftop out of a waiting cargo elevator. She is wearing a lab coat, and she seems to be their greeting party.

She walks up to Vargas and holds out her hand. "Vargas Amaranthine, It has been far too long, old friend."

Vargas takes her hand and shakes. "Melody Green. It seems like only yesterday I was teaching you at the Alastair Institute of Medicine. It is indeed good to see you again."

Dr. Green gives him a sharp look as she replies, "Yeah, I suppose fifteen years is nothing to an elf who lives thousands of years, but to us short-lived humans, it is a long time."

Vargas bows apologetically. "I am sorry, Melody. It is uncomfortable for me to return home, as you know. I really should have come to visit, though."

"Yes, you should have," Dr. Green replies, nodding sternly.

The two continue their exchange as the research team unloads their equipment onto the elevator. As Shaide follows them, Vargas turns to him and holds out a hand. "Shaide? Don't you have an appointment you should be getting to?"

Shaide shakes nervously; the prospect of seeing her after all this time is growing more and more terrifying.

"Go," Vargas says sternly. "We will catch up with you later."

Dr. Green looks at Vargas, confused, but he just shakes his head at her. Before the door closes, Amber hollers, "Good luck!" and the doors slide shut.

Shaide walks back to the now empty cargo helicars and climbs into the front one.

The driver looks over at him. "Sir? Where can I take you?"

"I need to go to the Tamiel residence," Shaide replies in a slightly shaking voice. "I need to meet with them before the research team gets there."

The driver nods and looks back forward. "Very well. Relax, and we will be there shortly." He lifts off the helicar and flies slowly to the east. As it turns out, the estate is only a mile from the medical center as well, and they arrive in just under two minutes.

The driver eases the car down into the main courtyard, next to the motor pool, before getting out to open the door for

Shaide. "Here you are, Master Ceraph. I believe someone is coming to greet you."

Shaide looks up in surprise to see another familiar face that hasn't aged a day: Yania. She approaches him with a confused but pleasant expression on her face. Shaide walks over to meet her, and she greets him warily.

"Good afternoon, sir. How may I… Oh!" She spots his Ceraph medallion. "Master Ceraph, this is an unexpected surprise. We weren't expecting you until after dinner. Is everything okay?"

As Shaide looks at the familiar face, fond memories flash through his mind. He says, "Yania, don't you recognize me?"

She frowns and looks at him closely, examining his face intently, and then it dawns on her. Her eyes open wide as she steps back and says breathlessly, "There is no way… Shaide? Is that really you?"

He smiles and nods. She steps forward and hugs him, putting her arms around his neck as she says, "I didn't recognize you. What are you doing here!?"

She lets go and steps back, and Shaide replies, "I know, Yania. It's been entirely too long. I received Amari's letters yesterday, and when I saw what happened, I went to the order master right away to find a way to come here, and he actually assigned me to escort the research team here for…Mom…" Shaide's face falls slightly.

Yania, now only coming up just past his shoulder, puts both of her hands on his face. "Don't you mind that now. Please, come on in. Amari will be beyond thrilled to see you."

Shaide follows her as she leads him up to the house. The helicar pilot waves and takes off again, heading back towards the medical center.

Yania leads Shaide through the door. "Wait here. I will bring her down. I'll let you surprise her."

Shaide stands there awkwardly for a moment as Yania walks out a side door and disappears for a few minutes. He begins to fidget nervously as he waits, feeling short of breath and, in fact, moderately panicky. What will he say!?

He hears footsteps and sees a young Elmeri woman he does not recognize walk into the foyer with mild confusion on her face. She looks at him and says, "I'm sorry, Master Ceraph, we weren't expecting you for some time. I'm afraid my father, General Tamiel, won't be home for a few hours. Is there…anything…I can…"

She squints and looks at him for a moment. "Do I know you? You look incredibly familiar."

His eyes open wide with surprise as the realization hits him. The unique pink hair, the pink eyes, the shape of the face… He almost did not recognize her. She's so different from the little girl he used to know. The grown young woman in front of him, however, is in fact…

"Amari? Is that really you?"

Her eyes open wide as she slowly walks across the room, a stunned and disbelieving expression on her face. She stands in front of him, examining him closely for a moment, and then her jaw drops. Yania stands in the doorway where Amari came in, watching with a smile on her face.

Shaide mumbles quietly, "It has been way too long…"

Without warning, Amari's suddenly looks extremely angry. Before Shaide can react, she slaps him across the face. Hard.

He keeps his head turned away for a moment from shock. Inwardly, however, he thinks, *I might have deserved that…*

"I waited SIX YEARS for you to come back and visit," she yells as he slowly turns his head to face her, "or at least write me, or ANYTHING!"

Shaide looks down in shame. "I know… I'm sorry."

Her lip trembles for a moment as she struggles with herself. Shaide is worried another slap is coming, but instead, she throws her arms around his neck and jumps on him, knocking him flat on his back. She rests her head on his shoulder and cries.

"When my dad said they wouldn't let you visit, I wrote you over and over, but you never wrote back. I thought you'd forgotten me. And now Mom is gone, and you come back to me now, of all times…"

Shaide groans from landing on his sword and dagger, and he pats her on the head. "I know it's no excuse, but I never received any of your letters until just yesterday… I read about Mom, and I made sure to come right away… I'm so sorry, Amari…"

Amari sniffles a few times as she squeezes his neck, both of them still flat on the ground. After a moment, she seems to realize where she is. She pushes herself up, bright pink in the face, and then she realizes the awkward way in which she is sitting on him.

Her face turns even redder, and she says, "Oh…sorry…" as she pushes herself to her feet. She reaches out, and Shaide takes her hand, letting her pull him up.

She looks at him and asks the all-important question: "Why are you here, anyway? And you're wearing a Ceraph medallion."

Shaide looks down at it and nods. "I'm a Ceraph now. It's a very long story, but it is why I was even able to come visit you in the first place. I met your dad at the docks, and he told me to come early if I could."

Amari looks crestfallen. "So…you only came because it was on business…"

Shaide shakes his head frantically. "No. I mean, I AM here on business, but that's not WHY I came. It just gave me the opportunity to. I came to…well…" He hesitates, feeling nervous again.

Amari looks back up at him. "Yes?"

"Well, I came to see you…" He can feel his face getting hot.

Amari looks like she is cheering up again as she says, "Did you really? Do you promise?"

Shaide nods. "When I read about…Mom…I went straight to Armstrong and asked if I could join the research mission coming here. I told him about her, and he agreed to let me come and escort the researchers."

Amari smiles, looking significantly happier. She turns around. "Come on. Let's go to my room. There's so much I want to talk about."

Shaide coughs and follows her awkwardly as she leads him upstairs. Yania calls out, "Don't do anything you wouldn't want me or your father to see!"

Amari turns red-faced and yells, "Yania! Seriously!?"

The sound of Yania's laughter follows them all the way to Amari's bedroom. Shaide stands awkwardly at the door for a minute as she walks in.

She turns to face him. "Come on in. It's okay."

Shaide cautiously walks into her room and examines his surroundings.

The room is drastically different than it was six years ago when he was here. It looks like it belongs to a young woman now rather than a little girl. There's a poster of some rock band on the wall, and several trophies are on shelves by the door. Shaide leans close to read them and realizes they are all champion trophies for martial arts and magic competitions. If these awards are any indication, Amari is actually an accomplished fighter.

He looks at a case above her dresser and realizes with a start what the staff inside it is. He turns to her and points at it. "Is that what I think it is?"

She turns pink and nods. "Yeah. It's very special to me. I made sure to keep it and take care of it all this time."

Shaide turns and looks back at it, lost in a memory for a moment. He was worried that she might have forgotten him, but it seems she missed him at least as much as he missed her. It makes him feel even worse for taking so long to come back.

As if she can read his mind, she blurts out suddenly, "I really, really missed you, you know?"

There's a slightly hurt look on her face, but after the briefest moment, it is gone, and she is looking him up and down.

"You look good. You're all grown up now."

Shaide glances around awkwardly, not really sure how to respond to that, his face burning from embarrassment.

She looks at him expectantly. "Well? How do I look?"

Shaide stares at his feet, having trouble responding to that. He ends up blurting out without thinking, "Amazing."

He freezes as he realizes what he said, and she looks flattered and stunned at the same time. The tension in the room is so thick that it feels like he might suffocate.

Suddenly, without warning, she bursts into laughter, tears coming from her eyes. Shaide loses control and starts laughing right along with her. The tension disappears all at once, and they spend a good minute trying to regain control of themselves.

Finally, she manages to catch her breath. "I don't know what I was expecting, but that was definitely not it." She has a wide smile on her face.

Shaide gets his laughter under control moment later, and he takes a few deep breaths so he can talk again. "Really, though, you look good. Really good. I wasn't expecting to see a woman when I got here. I still remembered the little girl I knew." He realizes what he said and turns slightly red again.

Amari seems slightly embarrassed too, but she also seems pleased. "I'm glad you think so. Everyone still thinks I'm weird, even though they are too afraid to pick on me now. But you? You never did judge me by how I look. You always just treated me as if I were no different."

Shaide sits down in the armchair across the room and smiles, thinking about the couple of months when he stayed here. "To me, you weren't different. You were just Amari."

She tilts her head. "Were? And now?"

Shaide pushes through the embarrassment. "I think you're better than the others now." He frowns. "Did that come out weird?"

Amari giggles unexpectedly. "I really, really did miss you. It was always hard to be sad when you were around."

Six years have passed, and yet it feels as if it was no time at all. Their two personalities mesh perfectly, so talking quickly becomes as easy for them as if they have been together for years rather than apart.

"So, what HAVE you been doing for the past few years?" asks Amari.

Shaide sits back and relaxes. "Well, I went back to live in Corallina after Mom and Dad passed away. Aton, my godfather, kept me in a dorm at the private school I attended until I was fourteen. My mom and dad were both big deals in the military world, and my tuition was waived for my whole stay. When I was fourteen, I went to attend the Alastair Royal Military Academy, although I was only there for a few months, because…"

He goes on to explain the incident where they crashed in the mountains and how he came to fight, and subsequently partner with, Rho. As he tells her of his return to the Citadel and subsequent joining of the Ceraph Order, her expression becomes increasingly awestruck.

She doesn't interrupt him, however, and he finishes his story with his exploits over the past two years, ending with him coming to Sora.

By the end, her eyes are as round as dinner plates. She lets out a low whistle and says, "I thought I had seen a lot for my age, but everything you have seen… Just, wow…"

Shaide nods "I honestly don't know how I feel about everything I've seen so far, but it isn't all bad. It let me come back and see you, even if a little later than intended."

Amari sits back on her bed and sighs. "I've been seriously considering joining the Ceraphs myself when I am able. My teachers have all said I am a prodigy at nearly everything I do, and I especially excel at nearly anything related to combat. Daddy, though…"

She pauses for a moment, looking troubled. "Since Mom died, he has gotten extremely protective of me, and he even said he doesn't want me even going into the military. He wants me to take a job where I am safe. But…"

Shaide looks at her, waiting for her to continue.

"I still want to join the Ceraphs, especially now that I know you're with them. Hearing your stories firsthand is really inspiring."

Shaide hesitates. "It's not all it's cracked up to be. I enjoy it greatly, knowing I spend every day of my life trying to make a difference, but really…it's rough and miserable more often than not."

Amari looks over at him with an amused grin. "Still trying to protect me, I see. I know that it's basically going to be a living nightmare most of the time, but once I knew I was capable of protecting other people, there was no real question as to what I wanted to do. You know?"

Shaide inwardly agrees with her words, remembering the feeling when he realized he was capable of something bigger. Part of him wants her to stay safe and happy as well, but another part remembers them playing as kids, promising to save the world together someday, and he realizes that saving the world with her might not be such a bad thing.

Amari gives him a confused look as he is lost in thought. "Hey, Shaide? What do you think about that?"

Shaide shakes his head and sighs. "Honestly, I'd much rather you stay safe as well, but I can't help but remember our promise to save the world together either. I can't say I would mind that."

Amari smiles as he says that. "I was wondering if you even remembered that."

Shaide looks up at her in surprise. "Of course I remember. I could never forget that. We spent nearly every day pretending to save the world."

Amari sighs. "How long are you going to be here?"

"Honestly?" Shaide frowns. "I don't know. I'm here with them as long as they are researching this bizarre illness, so I imagine I will be here for quite a while."

At this, Amari smiles again. "Would it be okay if we spent some time together while you're here? I know you'll be busy, but I'd like to see you whenever you have time."

Shaide looks at her, now with amusement on his own face "Of course I'd like to see you. I didn't come all this way to say hi once and then disappear, you know."

She smiles and then looks down, seemingly embarrassed for some reason. She asks shyly, "Would it be okay if I hung around with you while you're working here? I'd also like to see what you do while you're here."

Shaide chuckles slightly to himself. "Well, they keep insisting I'm the guy in charge, so if you're really sure you don't mind being bored out of your mind, I don't see why you couldn't accompany me, at least locally."

She looks as if Shaide has just completely made her day. Of course, her real motivation is to spend more time with him, but she really is curious about the Ceraphs, and it couldn't hurt to see for herself.

They spend the next hour or so chatting about anything and everything. She tells him all about her martial arts training and her spiritual studies. She shows him the real staff she had made to replicate the one he bought for her so long ago. They spend the whole time together just enjoying each other's company.

Finally, Yania knocks on the door. "Are you decent? I don't want to come in and catch you two at it!"

Amari turns bright red and yells, "YES, YANIA! WE'RE JUST TALKING!"

Yania opens the door and walks in. "Dinner will be ready in just a moment. Your father wants to talk about the arrangements for your wedding as soon as possible."

Shaide's and Amari's heads snap to Yania with looks of absolute shock on their faces. Amari yells as loudly as she can, "WHAT WEDDING!?"

Yania bursts out laughing so hard she that she has to clutch her side and lean against the doorframe for support. "I'm…I'm just joking with you, young lady. Don't take me so seriously…" She wipes a couple of tears away, actually crying from laughing so hard.

Amari pouts for a moment as Yania catches her breath.

Yania finally says, "Really, though, dinner is about ready, Amari. You two should come on down and say hi to your father."

Amari and Shaide climb to their feet and follow Yania down the hall and downstairs to the dining room. After a quick washing of the hands, they are sitting down next to each other at the table when Koraru walks in.

Shaide gets to his feet again. "General! I'm glad to see you again."

Koraru sighs. "You really needn't be so formal in my home, Shaide. As far as I am concerned, you are family. Please, sit back down and be comfortable."

Shaide shrugs and sits. A moment later, Yania comes into the dining room with a roast, which she sets down on the table. She makes a return trip, this time coming back with a platter of cooked vegetables and spuds.

"You know you are always welcome to join us, Yania," says Koraru. "Please, eat with us. You missed him as much as we did, I am sure."

Yania smiles and takes a seat. "Master Tamiel, you know it is improper for me to join you without invitation."

Koraru sighs. "I suppose that the standing invitation doesn't count…"

Amari puts food on Shaide's plate for him, leaving him surprised and awkward. Yania smiles to herself as Amari serves Shaide dinner. Even six years later, she is all about the boy.

Dinner is a pleasant affair. While they eat, Koraru asks Shaide what he has been doing since he was gone, and Shaide retells the story he told Amari. Koraru seems impressed with everything Shaide has done.

"Shaide, I'm proud of you, child. After your parents' deaths, I was concerned you wouldn't have it very easy, but I am proud to see you persevered and really made something of your life."

Shaide looks stunned and pleased at the same time. "Oh, well… Thank you. That means a lot."

Koraru nods "I mean every word of it."

Once dinner is finished, Amari looks at Shaide and jerks her head, indicating that she wants him to follow her. She leads him on a short walk into the garden and sits on one of the brick posts bracketing the many flowerbeds and vegetable patches. She stares out across the garden in silence for a moment.

Shaide looks around, remembering the two of them playing here as children. The sun is setting to the west, and the garden is only lit by a dim orange glow on the horizon. As he watches, the decorative stones housed in lanterns begin glowing, emitting a soft light to illuminate their surroundings.

"My dad is broken, you know? When he lost Mom, he kind of just shut down. His life is all about work now, and he is terrified of me doing anything that could put me in danger. He isn't the same man he used to be."

Shaide walks over and sits next to her, thinking carefully about his next words. "Give him some time. They were together for centuries, I imagine. He won't recover from a loss like that overnight." He looks at her, gauging her own condition. "How have you been doing?"

Amari looks up at him, sadness in her eyes. At the same time, though, a strange strength shines behind her gaze as well.

　　　　A.S.GUINN

"It hurts. I really miss her. I'm not sure that it has even sunk in that she is gone yet."

She drops her gaze for a moment, thinking, and then she looks him straight in the eyes, a renewed determination in her voice. "I do not believe that Mom would want me to sit around mourning her and refusing to move on, though. She would want me to stand up and keep moving forward. She would want me to follow what I want in life."

Shaide nods, approving of her resolution. "A few thousand years is a long time to do nothing."

She quietly takes this in and then, a moment later, says, "Can I ask you something?"

Shaide looks at her in surprise and nods.

"Why IS the Ceraph Order investigating this illness? Your order typically only gets involved when the corruption has something to do with what is happening. So why ARE you here?"

Shaide stops for a moment and considers her words. He never stopped to think about it. When he saw the opportunity to come along and help, he just acted. Now that he considers it, though, she is right. They wouldn't be here unless they thought there was more to this than a simple bug.

She looks at him expectantly as he considers her question. Finally, he replies, "I never considered it until now. I saw the opportunity to keep a promise I made, and I never thought about why we were coming. Now that you put it that way…"

The furrow in Amari's brow grows deeper. "Tell me the truth. Do you think your order would be here if the corruption wasn't in play?"

Shaide hesitates, worried that his answer might spark something reckless. When he sees her intense, curious gaze, though, he finds himself unable to lie to her.

"I think you're right. We wouldn't be here if they didn't think the corruption was involved."

Amari relaxes and leans back on her hands. "That's what I've been afraid of from the moment I found out that Ceraph researchers were coming. My dad questions why I want to join the Ceraphs when the answer is right in front of us."

It is now Shaide's turn to feel curious as she explains, "For three thousand years, the corruption has been taking lives, destroying families, and making people afraid to leave their own homes. Many of my people living here in Sora believe that we are too far from the Deadlands to have anything to be afraid of, but here we sit, my mother taken by an inexplicable illness, and Eden's servants believe the corruption is involved."

She looks over at him. "Three thousand years, and my people still haven't learned. They held a false sense of security during the war and refused to get involved, believing it wasn't their problem. And now, today, people are dying from the corruption once again, and my people refuse to face the truth and do anything about it."

She looks him in the eyes. "Six years ago, you made a promise to me that you would come back to me, and you've kept that promise. Will you keep the other promise we made?"

Shaide stares back at her with great curiosity. *Other promise?*

Amari looks him in the eyes and asks him "Will you keep the promise that you and I would save the world together?"

CHAPTER 13

FINDING INDEPENDENCE

Shaide looks at Amari for a moment, processing what she just asked him. "When you say together, do you mean…?"

Amari sits up straight and waves her hands. "Oh! No, I just meant that we would work together and save the world. I didn't mean that we would, well, uhh…" Her face is a bright burning red as she gets completely flustered from embarrassment.

She is saved by the sound of an approaching helicar. As the two look up, they see a helicar with the Ceraph logo on the side landing in the motor pool adjacent to the garden.

Koraru and Yania walk out of the house and into the garden, and Shaide and Amari get to their feet to follow as they walk over to meet the two members of the research team who came to speak with them.

Vargas and Amber step out of the vehicle and wait as Koraru approaches. They bow as he stands before them, and then they both greet their host.

"Koraru Tamiel," says Vargas, "it is a pleasure to see you again, although I wish it were under better circumstances."

Koraru bows halfheartedly. "Come on in, and I will answer any questions you may have."

Vargas and Amber stand up. Amber looks at Shaide and winks. "So, this is your little girlfriend, I take it?"

Shaide rolls his eyes and ignores her. Amari, on the other hand, turns bright pink and asks him, "Did you tell them I was your girlfriend?"

Amber cuts Shaide off before he can say a word. "Oh yes! He went on and on about how you two were committed to be married, and how he absolutely could not live without you, and how you went on and on about wanting to have as many babies as he could give you, and—"

Shaide turns his head and growls, unamused, "Hey, Amber? Do you think Armstrong would say anything if you were to just disappear and never be seen again?"

She is not intimidated by his threat and continues poking fun at him. "Are you saying you want to make me your slave and keep me in your basement? Wow, I didn't know the two of you were like that! Are you sure your girlfriend wouldn't mind sharing you with me like that? Or would it be more like you were sharing me with each other? That could be fun and—"

"AMBER! SHUT IT!" barks Vargas.

Amber shuts her mouth abruptly. "Yes, sir!"

He glares at her. "We are here on professional business, and do not forget, she is the daughter of General Tamiel, who is right in front of us. I am certain he does not appreciate you joking about his daughter like that."

Amari unexpectedly pipes up, saying, "Actually, we are getting married next week. Didn't he tell you?"

The shock of this unexpected joke successfully stuns Amber into silence for a moment, and then she exclaims, "Do WHAT!?"

Amari, absolutely red in the face from embarrassment, faces forward, refusing to meet Shaide's gaze. Yania has a slight smile on her face, but Shaide cannot see Koraru's expression.

Yania opens the door and lets them inside, and Koraru leads them into the dining room, where the table has been cleaned off from dinner and a handful of small but tasty looking snacks have been laid out for them.

Koraru turns around, his expression stony and empty once again. "Please, have a seat."

Vargas and Amber sit down on one side of the table, while Shaide and Amari take their places where they sat at dinner. Meanwhile, Yania and Koraru take their places at opposite ends of the table.

Amber's gaze darts from Shaide to Amari, an expression of shock still on her face. Shaide is beginning to think she doesn't realize Amari was joking.

Koraru is the first to break the uncomfortable silence. "Allow me to begin by asking a single but vital question."

"Of course, General," says Vargas, nodding respectfully.

Koraru leans forward, hands together, and locks gazes with Vargas. "Why are the Ceraphs investigating this illness? Do you believe the corruption played a role in my wife's death?"

Vargas frowns, and looking to Shaide, he asks, "May I tell him what we know?"

Shaide is momentarily taken aback. He forgot he was the de facto leader of the research team while he was here. He says, "They deserve to know everything."

Vargas nods and turns back to Koraru, who is waiting expectantly. "Yes, sir. While we are still attempting to confirm this, we believe that the virus that claimed your wife's life, along with several dozen other Elmeri and Drameri lives, was, in fact, a once non-threatening cold virus that came in contact with some source of corruption, and as a result, it mutated into a virus that our people's bodies are incapable of fighting."

"Has ANYONE survived this illness?" asks Koraru.

Vargas looks at Amber, who jumps when she realizes everyone in the room has followed suit. She clears her throat. "Umm, yes, actually. One. We know of one single case where the infected individual actually survived the illness and recovered. They are unable to walk, and they suffer from terrible shaking and pain, but their body was somehow able to fight off the infection."

"Are you certain it was the same illness?"

"We believe so, although, as we have not identified the pathogen, we cannot yet be sure. The symptoms were identical, however, even in severity. Somehow, by means we are not yet certain of, they regained consciousness and are currently in quarantine in the medical center."

Koraru nods and relaxes slightly. He says to Vargas and Shaide, "I am issuing you an official authorization on behalf of the Erita Royal Military. Although it is unnecessary, as the

ETERNAL KNIGHTS OF EDEN I

Ceraphs have international jurisdiction, I hereby authorize you to take any steps you deem necessary to contain and combat this illness."

Vargas nods. "Thank you, sir."

Koraru closes his eyes for a moment, as though steeling himself for something.

"Proceed with your questions. I will aid in any way I can to make sure no one else suffers the way my family is suffering."

Vargas bows his head respectfully. "Thank you, General. I know this will be very painful, but it is vital we hear it firsthand to make certain we understand. Please describe everything about your wife's condition, beginning with where you were when she fell ill."

Koraru takes a deep breath and begins. "We were vacationing at the Gulf of Shizune. Despite its proximity to the Deadlands, there has been no sign of corrupted activity in the region for centuries, as you know. We swam in the ocean, ate the local food, and simply enjoyed our time together for a while."

He continues, looking slightly pale. "The day before we were due to return, she began not feeling well. She had a slight fever, and she complained of a headache and mild chills. We came home the next day, and she rapidly took a turn for the worse. First came the shortness of breath, then the muscle spasms, and then everything just went wrong at once. Every symptom you can imagine wracked her body until she became comatose, and then it was over…" As he recounted his story, his face became paler and paler, and his stony expression fell into misery.

Amari gets to her feet, walks over to her father, and puts her arm around his shoulders, her expression full of grief and sorrow. In spite of her own obvious pain, she comforts him, saying, "Hey, Dad. It's going to be okay…"

Vargas carefully asks, "While you were down at the gulf, can you think of ANYTHING out of the ordinary that occurred or that only she would have come into contact with? Anything at all, no matter how small."

Koraru shakes his head, looking at the table in front of him.

Amari raises her hand and looks up. "Well, there was one thing…"

As five stunned pairs of eyes lock onto her, she looks surprised at the sudden attention she is receiving. She hesitantly explains, "On the beach, the day she fell ill, there was this strange man. He was running down the beach, and he ran into mom, knocking her over and landing on her. He got up and helped her to her feet, and then he was gone a moment later."

Koraru whispers to her, his expression shifting to anger, "You never mentioned this before. Why?"

Amari lowers her gaze. "I never thought it was important. People run into each other all the time."

Amber is the one to lean forward now. "This man. Can you describe him?"

Amari nods and says, "He looked like a young adult, human, I'm sure, or Mitera. Long black hair and a strange outfit. Even though we were on the beach, he was wearing something with long black sleeves. And I think he had a scar of some kind across his cheek."

Vargas and Amber exchange glances but don't say anything.

"Do you think he is connected in some way?" asks Amari.

Koraru is now looking up again, tight-lipped as he suppresses his anger and waits for their answer.

Vargas shrugs. "We don't have enough information yet to be certain, but this is the second time so far that we have heard of this man. I wonder…"

Koraru sighs and takes a breath, regaining his composure. "Is there anything else we can help you with this evening? It is getting late, and I don't want to upset my daughter and housemaid any further than I must."

Vargas gets to his feet and bows. "No, General. You have given me more than enough. I do not wish to trouble you further. Thank you."

Shaide sighs and gets to his feet, and Amber follows suit.

"Are you all heading back to the medical center now?" asks Amari.

Shaide looks at Vargas and answers, "Yes, I think we probably should. They have a schedule to maintain, after all."

Amari looks at her father as he climbs to his feet, and then she looks back at Shaide. "Would you like to stay the night here? It's been so long since we've seen you…"

"Truly?" Shaide shakes his head and sighs. "I would like that, but I have to stay with the research team. I've been entrusted with their lives, so I don't have the luxury of choosing what I want to do."

Vargas raises his eyebrows at this display of Shaide's integrity, as though he believed Shaide was only here for personal reasons.

Amari looks slightly downcast, but she immediately asks, "Well, would it be okay for me to come see the laboratory with you and just stay the night there? I really don't want to say goodbye yet."

     A.S.GUINN

"Amari Aria Tamiel, Koraru says in a raised voice. "I do not want you getting too involved in the Ceraphs' business. It is too dangerous, and I do not want you getting in their way!"

Amari rounds on him and counters "Dad, it's just a research laboratory. We are not going into battle! How much trouble do you really think I can get into? Besides, I have a powerful Ceraph looking out for me, so I'm certain that I will be just fine!"

Shaide, Vargas, and Amber watch this exchange nervously. They are certain there is more going on here, and as for Shaide, he's fairly certain he knew what it is.

Koraru slams his fist down on the table. "I don't want you spending too much time around them and getting any funny ideas about running off and trying to 'save the world.' You are sixteen years old, and I will not let you do something so reckless!"

Amari yells back, her spiritual aura crackling around her from her anger, "I'm just going to spend some time with Shaide, whom I haven't seen in years! It's not like I'm running off to join the Ceraphs! Besides, it is my future, and if I want to join the Ceraphs and make a difference rather than cowering here in the capital, ignoring what is happening out there, then, by the love of Eden, I will join them if I damn well please!"

Yania quietly says to Koraru, "Master Tamiel, please. She just wants to spend some time with our old friend, whom we all, including you, missed dearly. Is that really so bad?"

Koraru grits his teeth, but he looks Shaide dead in the eyes and says, "If anything happens to her on your watch, there is not a god alive who can protect you from me. Do you understand?"

Shaide sighs and lowers his head. Doesn't he get a say in this? "Uncle Koraru…I'm a Ceraph, sworn protector of Eden, and you are also family to me. The only way anything will happen to her is if it takes me out first."

He raises his gaze to meet Koraru's, and the two lock eyes for a moment. Finally, Koraru relaxes and says in a much softer tone, "Just take care of her, Shaide. My daughters, and dear Yania of course…they are all I have left."

Shaide nods. "Of course."

"Hey, are you really okay with this?" Amber whispers to Vargas.

"Shaide is the only Ceraph here," Vargas whispers back. "His word goes. Also, she seems very knowledgeable and intelligent. Having her with us could prove useful."

Amber shrugs. "If you say so."

Koraru turns and walks to the dining room door. "Yania, please show them out. I am feeling tired, and I need to be alone."

Yania nods understandingly. "Of course, master. If all of you would please follow me." She leads them out into the garden, and they follow her along the path to the motor pool. The sky is dark now, as the sun set some time ago. It was already sunset, after all, when the researchers arrived. The garden is now illuminated by luminescent stones housed in decorative casings.

Amari sounds slightly embarrassed as she says, "I'm sorry you had to see that. Dad has been rather overprotective since Mom died."

"He said daughters. Plural," says Amber.

Amari nods. "Yes, I have an older sister, but she isn't around much. She is a special operative with the National Security Council, and she is usually busy with work."

"I see. So, uhh, is your dad okay with you two getting married? He doesn't seem too keen on Ceraphs."

Amari tilts her head. "Married? What are you... OH!" She forgot about the joke she had made earlier. "Oh, no I was just messing with you. Shaide and I are just really old friends. He lived with us for a while when we were little. We're just close!"

Amber drops her head. "You were just messing with me? Damn… I made a bunch of plans for what I would do at the wedding!"

Shaide sighs. This woman is exhausting to be around.

Yania stops as they reach their waiting helicar. The driver took a nap while he waited, and now he is sitting and warming up the car for takeoff. She looks at her young charge and says, "Alright, be careful, Amari. Keep Shaide safe and out of trouble."

Shaide tilts his head. "Why are you telling her to keep ME safe?"

Yania chuckles. "You take care of her too." She hugs him around the neck and says, "It really is good to see you again. Really good. Don't stay gone so long next time."

Shaide pats her back and laughs. "You know I'll have to bring her home, right?"

Yania looks at him with an odd pitying look in her eyes. "Of course you'll be bringing her home. I guess I forgot about that."

Shaide looks at her suspiciously as she lets go of him, and he says, "And we'll be here for a while. I'll be coming by to visit whenever I have a chance."

Yania smiles. "Of course, how silly of me. Well, take care, Shaide."

She leans into the bushes behind her, pulls out a luggage case, and hands it to Amari, who takes it and looks at Yania with confusion. "What's this?"

Yania pulls her into a hug and smiles. "I suspected you might want to leave with him, so I packed some things for you earlier and hid them out here just in case." She hugs Amari more tightly and adds, "Take care of yourself. Come home safe whenever you're ready."

Yania releases her hug, and Amari looks suspicious as she backs away. "Okay, I will. Thanks, Yania."

Yania nods. "Okay, you all should get going. May the goddess bless you in your endeavors."

Amari climbs in the backseat of the helicar, leaving room for Shaide to sit down beside her, leaving her between him and Amber. Both women are fairly small, so the backseat is comfortable with three people.

Vargas sits in the front, next to the driver, and says to him, "Okay, take us back to the medical center. No need to rush."

The driver nods, and a moment later, the helicar lifts off the ground. Shaide and Amari wave to Yania as the car flies away, until she is out of their view.

The flight to the hospital is short and uneventful. Just a couple of short minutes later, they are landing on the rooftop of the main building, the top floor of which houses the Ceraphs' medical research center.

Once the car eases to a landing, the driver pops the doors, allowing everyone to disembark. As Amber climbs out of the opposite side, Shaide takes Amari's hand and helps her out of the car. She goes around the back and retrieves her luggage bag, and a moment later, they are all standing in the elevator, going down one level to the research center.

When the elevator doors open, Shaide is dazzled by the bright light in front of him. The research center is extremely well lit, with white floors, walls, and ceilings, but there's no sign of where the light is coming from. It seems to be self-illuminating somehow.

Vargas leads them down the hallway, and Shaide takes note that even this late in the evening, there are a handful of researchers actively working, either sitting in their labs or walking up and down the hallway.

Shaide asks Vargas, "Do these people ever sleep?"

Vargas chuckles, "We have two to three shifts of researchers, depending on what they are working on. We are working around the clock to try and find the solution to this illness problem."

Shaide frowns "Well, if we find the source and put a stop to it, is all of this really even necessary?"

Vargas looks at him and shakes his head. "IF we can find a definitive source and IF we can stop it? Then, no, this is probably not necessary, but just in case we don't find it in time and an outbreak occurs, or even just to have a plan in case we stop it and it comes back later, we are researching around the clock to find a countermeasure to treat anyone who is infected with this illness."

"Oh, now I see."

Vargas leads them through a set of double doors into a more subdued and comfortable-looking section of the building. Just inside the doors, he points to the left and right. "These two suites are the Ceraph dorms. They are rarely used since we have no Ceraphs personally assigned to this research institute, so no one should bother you here. Ms. Tamiel? Why don't you go ahead and put your luggage away and get comfortable? That looks heavy."

Amari nods and looks at the others suspiciously, and then she goes into the dorm behind Shaide.

Shaide slaps himself in the face. "Oh, crap. I left my bag in the cargo heli earlier…"

"No worries," Vargas says with a laugh. "When it came back, I unloaded your bag and put it in your dorm." He leans over and looks behind Shaide. "Actually, the dorm behind you. Where she went."

Shaide bows and says, "Thank you."

"Now, I have a question. What do you make of what Ms. Amari said about the man who bumped into her mother?"

Shaide looks at him "I really don't know much about biology, but all of the victims have been elves, right?"

Vargas nods "Yes. There are no known cases of any infection other than Elmeri and Drameri citizens. We inquired with the Alastair and Termer branches, and there are no cases reported among the other races."

Shaide nods, putting the logic together. "And she said the man looked human. Maybe we're dealing with a human or humans who strayed too close to a corruption-rich area and brought back a mutated virus that only affects Elmeri and Drameri?"

"While I don't know if it was accidental or not," says Vargas, "your assessment would seem to favor our current theory, that someone immune is carrying the bug and transmitting it to our people."

Shaide looks at the dorm behind him and has further misgivings about bringing Amari along. "Is it safe for any of your people to be around the research if it only affects your people?"

Vargas shakes his head. "Don't worry. From what we've seen, the illness is not contagious for some reason. How they are contracting it is hard to say, but it doesn't seem to spread from person to person. We are taking precautions, of course, but so far, the evidence says we are safe as long as we don't come into contact with the source."

Shaide nods and relaxes a little.

Vargas notices and says, "On a personal note, I noticed Ms. Tamiel seems to have an interest in joining the Ceraph Order, judging from the fight with her father. Have you considered taking your girlfriend back to the Citadel?"

Shaide looks at him with raised eyebrows. "Really, Vargas, she is not my girlfriend. There is no romantic involvement between us. She is like family to me."

"So you say, but I feel like she may be interested in a different kind of family relationship, just so you are aware. But that wasn't my question."

Shaide sighs. "I hadn't considered it, honestly. I chose the life I'm leading. I chose this knowing that I would not get to see my full lifespan. Admittedly, Rho was thrust upon me without my consent, but I know that my life will end one of two ways. I don't know, however, if I can bring myself to lead HER into that life."

Vargas shakes his head at this but stays silent.

Amber is the one who speaks the important truth: "Shaide, if she chooses to join the order, that is her choice. If she does, she will probably do so with or without you. People who feel that calling always find their way to our order. The question is, would you rather her join on her own, with no one she trusts to guide and protect her? Or would you rather keep her close so you can teach her, guide her, and make sure she is safe?"

Shaide opens his mouth, but no words come out.

Amber nods. "Exactly. Just think about it."

Shaide feels a bit uncomfortable discussing this any further. So he changes the subject. "What do you need from me right now?"

Vargas looks over his shoulder. "I don't think we need anything at the moment. We are going to confer with Ronoa about what we learned, and then after we check on our research teams, we will be going to bed. You should go get some rest too."

Shaide nods and turns to face the dorm behind him. "Alright. Have a good night. Let me know if you need me." He walks into the dorm and closes the door behind him.

Inside, he sees that the dorm appears surprisingly comfortable. There are four bedrooms on one wall, and in the middle is a full master-style bathroom with shower and bath. He is standing in a small lounge area with two comfortable couches and a couple of padded rocking chairs, and at the far end of the suite is what appears to be a small kitchenette.

Amari comes out of the second room from the end and walks up to him. "This is a lot more comfortable than I would have expected. Someone's bag is in the room on the end, so I grabbed the room next to it."

Shaide frowns, walks past her, and peeks in the last room. It is a cozy bedroom with a basic but comfortable-looking bed and a wardrobe on the wall. Now that he looks closely, he sees that the rooms are actually connected by a single door between them.

He spots his bag in front of the wardrobe and nods. "I thought so. I guess that's my room. They brought my bag in earlier."

Amari giggles for some reason. "Yay! Our rooms are right next to each other, like when we were kids!"

"Don't get so excited," Shaide says, rolling his eyes. "It's not THAT big of a deal."

She gives him a fake-serious look. "No peeking on me. I know I'm not much to look at, but I also know boys are perverts. I still want my privacy."

He sighs and glances at her well-developed figure before turning to his bag and beginning to unpack his away-from-home kit. "I don't know why you're saying you're not much to look at. I think you're remarkably pretty, myself." Distracted by his unpacking, Shaide doesn't realize what he said.

Amari doesn't respond, and he turns to see what she is doing. He is surprised to see a beet-red face and slack jaw staring at him. He tilts his head and asks, "What did I say?"

Stuttering, she says, "Y-you think I-I'm…p-pretty? R-really?"

He feels the heat rise into his face, and he resumes unpacking. He responds with his back to her. "Well, of course I do. Why wouldn't I?"

She explains in a quiet voice, "The other kids don't really mess with me anymore, but I can tell they still think I'm weird. No one ever compliments how I look. Maybe my clothes, but not me."

Shaide remembers that she had always had trouble with bullies. He didn't think that it was still a problem. He turns to face her and asks, "Are your hair and eyes really that unusual?"

She nods, still red as a tomato from embarrassment. "Yes. We Elmeri have a wider range of natural hair and eye colors than you other races, but in either case, pink is still pretty much considered the trait of a freak or a mutant. Especially both at the same time. Red or white maybe, but not pink."

Shaide frowns. "You know? I wouldn't think you looking different like that would be a bad thing. I'd personally think such a unique-looking woman would be prized, not shunned. Like you're special."

Amari just stares at him silently for a second. Then she walks over to him, kneels down, and pulls him into a tight hug. "Thank you, Shaide. This is why I missed you so much."

He hugs her with one arm, confused. "What do you mean?"

She hangs onto him as she says "You never treated me as if I was different. You never treated me like the colonel or general's daughter. I was always just Amari to you. I never had to worry about what you thought of me."

Shaide nods, understanding somewhat now. "Well, to me, you're just Amari. You're you."

"Thank you. Really." She lets go of him. "Are you hungry? I checked, and it looks like they keep some preserved food stocked here."

Shaide and Amari enjoy a snack of preserved meat and nuts and stay up for a couple of hours talking about everything and nothing. To anyone watching them, it would be clear that they are natural friends. In fact, despite the years that have passed, Shaide still gets along with Amari at least as well as he gets on with Rayn and even Reno. Maybe even better.

Finally, just before midnight, they finally decide that it is time for bed. Shaide lies down and finds himself thinking that these are the times when giving his life to Eden's service is worth it: when he can enjoy being with his friends because of the sacrifices made by him and his fellow Ceraphs.

Amari, on the other hand, finds herself thinking happily to herself that after years of praying to Eden and the goddess Shizune, the best friend she's ever had has finally come back to her. At the same time, she feels a confusing mix of emotions rising inside her when she thinks of him. It is entirely pleasant, however, so before long, she drifts off to sleep with a smile on her face for the first time in a long time.

*   *   *

Over the next two weeks, Shaide does a great deal of traveling alongside Vargas and Amber. They spend their days going out and interviewing the families of those who they knew had contracted and perished from this illness. Shaide finds it a bit unnerving that nearly all of their stories are far too similar.

Throughout these couple of weeks, Amari comes with them on several of these research interviews. She goes home every few days for a few hours and tells her father that she is learning about medicine and healing magic from the researchers at the hospital. The best part about this is that she isn't lying to him, as she is legitimately studying the medical uses of spiritual aura when Shaide is busy.

She even gets Shaide to sign a document stating she is studying with the Ceraph Order under an actual Ceraph to get her released from her academy classes. Here in Erita, the Ceraphs are held in just as high esteem as they are in Alastair, and if a Ceraph requests something, they usually get it.

Over those two weeks, Shaide and Amari's friendship cements quickly. The two spend nearly all their free time together, even though their friendship is strictly platonic.

The researchers begin to notice a disturbing pattern among those who were infected. Several of the families recall seeing the same person the very day their family member or friend fell ill. They all describe him in exactly the same way, including him running into the victim or coming into close contact with them.

It becomes increasingly clear that this is not a natural occurrence and someone is intentionally spreading this infection.

A solid month after the Citadel research team's arrival, Vargas and Amber knock on Shaide's dormitory door. He hollers, "Come in!" and the two enter to dorm to find him and Amari sitting at the kitchenette table, playing cards.

Shaide looks up. "What is it?"

Vargas walks over and hands him a map of Erita with a bunch of red marks drawn on it. Shaide looks at it and then back up at Vargas. "What is this?"

Vargas explains, "We've compiled the information we've gathered about every known case of infection in the country and charted it on this map. Tell me what you see."

Shaide looks at it closely. Amari gets up and leans over his shoulder, examining it closely as well. She points at the area around the Gulf of Shizune and says, "That's where we went for vacation. There's a lot of these marks in this region."

"Good eyes," says Vargas. "We've established a pattern, and every single person who contracted this illness had been within this region within forty-eight hours of showing symptoms. Every known sighting of our mystery man also occurred within this region. What do you think, Shaide?"

Shaide looks closely at the pattern and nods. "I think I may have even more than that. Not only are the cases focused on this particular region, but they seem to be focused around this particular spot here, in the mountains. What is this place?" He points at a spot on the map and shows it to Vargas.

Amari answers the question before Vargas gets a chance. "That's the volcano Mt. Kasai. It's been dormant since before the great war, but it's a popular tourist spot."

Shaide thinks to himself for a moment. Why does Mt. Kasai sound so familiar? He shakes his head. "I feel like if we want to find the source of this illness, or at least the man spreading it, this is a good place to start."

Vargas nods. "I believe that I agree with you. How would you like to proceed?"

Shaide opens and closes his mouth several times, trying to find words. He is still getting used to them treating him as if he is in charge, but he seems to have made all the right decisions so far, and they have grown to respect his opinion on a more personal level.

Amari waves her hand in front of Shaide's face. "I vote we go south and investigate the area. It's the only way we can find anything new, as far as I can guess."

Shaide slowly turns and looks at her. "You said 'we'?"

Amari nods and crosses her arms stubbornly. "Well, I AM the only one of us who has ever actually been down there. You'll need a guide, and I would rather do it myself than entrust you to some local idiot that could be in on this dastardly plot."

Shaide rubs his temples. He has grown very fond of Amari's presence. Having her around makes him not miss his other friends quite so much, or at least, he doesn't feel lonely. However, he really doesn't want to take her and endanger her either. He is certain her father would murder him with his own hands if ANYTHING happened to her.

She leans on his shoulder. "I can look after myself, Shaide. And I can look after you. Please, let me come with you. I promise, from the bottom of my heart, you will not regret it."

Shaide sighs and relents. "Fine. You can come." He turns to Vargas. "I guess contact the COV *Last Beacon* and arrange for us to relocate south to Mt. Kasai. He should already know, but make sure Shipmaster Corolas notifies the Citadel of our operation plan."

Vargas nods and bows. "Understood, Master Ceraph. If it is okay, I would like to bring the entire research team on board with skeleton equipment. I don't plan on running any extensive tests in the field, but I want to at least be able to run a basic analysis of any samples we find."

Amber winks at Shaide. "I love how much more confident you've become since you joined us. It makes you so much more intriguing. Ms. Amari, you had better be careful, or I may have to steal your young man from you and just eat him up myself! I've been dying to give him a more thorough examination, you know what I mean?"

Shaide cuts her off. "Amber, first, we AREN'T together. Second, I'm only sixteen. I think I'm a little young for what you have in mind. Third, we have a job to do. Cut it out. If you want to act like a frustrated schoolgirl, do it after we complete our mission."

His rebuttal doesn't curb her enthusiasm, however. It seems to just encourage her. "Oh my. You are becoming so much more take-charge. Perhaps I would rather you give ME a, umm, medical examination."

Shaide and Vargas simultaneously yell, "AMBER! SHUT IT!"

Amber actually recoils from both men yelling at the same time. Vargas grabs her by the shoulder. "I will make the arrangements for our departure. Come on, Amber, we have work to do." He steers her out of the room as she pouts.

"You know," Amari says with a sigh, "I'm really not sure whether I like her or not."

Shaide laughs. "Honestly? Me either."

"She's a lecherous old lady. I don't like the idea of her touching you in, uh… Well…I don't like the idea of you being alone with her."

"She may be upwards of…well…, fifty, sixty, seventy years old? But among elves and Mitera, that is barely more than a child. She barely looks older than a teenager, to be fair."

"Are you saying you're actually attracted to her?" Amari asks a confused and, oddly, hurt look on her face.

Shaide is a bit taken aback by her reaction. "No! I'm just saying she's not really that old. My aunt Lucy is only in her thirties, and she acts almost as bad as Amber does! And…wait, why am I defending myself? And why are you upset?"

The hurt look on Amari's face gives way to full confusion. "Huh…? I…I don't know. I guess I shouldn't be. I just felt really… I don't know. I just didn't like her acting like that."

Shaide chuckles, and then he rapidly gives way to laughing uncontrollably. As the tension in the room disappears, Amari's mood lightens up, and she joins him in laughing loudly for several minutes.

When they finally catch their breaths and calm down, Shaide shakes his head and says, "I don't have any interest in her anyway, so let her make her creepy, inappropriate jokes. It won't make a difference."

Amari blurts out without thinking, "Is there anyone you ARE interested in?"

Shaide looks at her, wondering why she would ask that. He thinks about it for a moment. She IS extraordinarily beautiful. Her dark pink hair, pink eyes, smooth face, and… He shakes his head to clear the thought. She's a very dear friend. He would be INSANE to think that way.

He shakes his head and answers, "I don't know. I don't exactly spend much time around girls my own age, you know."

She chuckles, but it has an oddly hollow sound to it. "I was just wondering. What do I need to bring with me?"

"Are you absolutely sure you should come with us?" Shaide asks, frowning. "I mean, you are probably vulnerable to this illness. I don't think I could take it if something happened to you, you know?"

Amari smiles and rubs his hair. She gave him a haircut a couple of days ago, and his short borderline buzz cut is very soft under her hand. He feels a slight chill run down his spine as she rubs his head.

"I'll have you there to protect me, so I'll be fine."

Shaide looks down. "I think you might be putting just a little bit too much faith in my abilities. I'm just saying."

"Well then," Amari says with a giggle, "I want to make sure you have me there to protect you. I really can take care of myself, you know."

Shaide sighs and stands up. "Yeah, I know. I'm still worried, though. Don't forget, this is my first mission without anyone guiding me. And now there's a chance I'm going to end up having to try and bring someone in. Either that or bring them down. It's a little bit scary, you know?"

Amari unexpectedly hugs him and pulls him close. She hasn't done this since the day he first came back. "Hey. You'll be okay, Shaide. I'm a little nervous too, but we'll work it out."

She lets go. "Come on. Let's pack up our stuff and make sure we're ready when it's time to go."

CHAPTER 14

ANGELS AND DAEMONS

It is the next morning before the research team and the COV *Last Beacon* are ready for departure. By the time the research team had all of their equipment loaded on board the frigate and received authorization to operate in the south of the country, night had fallen, and even Shaide agreed that it would be better to depart first thing in the morning.

Now Shaide is standing on the bridge of the frigate, looking out over Erita with intense interest. He's never gotten to see this part of the country before, and he is surprised at how drastically it differs from Alastair.

The nation of Alastair has a broad range of terrain, including a massive mountain range, open plains, marshlands, vast forests, and deserts. Shaide has experienced each of them at some point or another.

Erita has a different feel to it. It is essentially divided into strips that are easily identified on a map. In the farthest northern reaches, it is adjacent to the Dorim Mountains. The weather here alternates from mild and temperate to overwhelming blizzards. Very little of the population lives in these reaches, as Elmeri don't adapt well to the extreme cold.

South of this area is a strip of perpetual plains and rolling hills, where the capital city of Sora and the smaller city of Farendell are located, as well as a number of scattered farms and villages all throughout the plains. A strong military presence keeps this region moderately safe and quiet, allowing the people to live in little fear.

South of the plains lies the Lorien Mountains. A drastic contrast from the relatively safe plains in the north, the mountains are home to a great number of savage monsters and beasts that make traversing them by foot or anything short of a warship hazardous. Nevertheless, there are a handful of patrolled roads that allow some manner of travel when necessary, although it is still a great risk.

ETERNAL KNIGHTS OF EDEN I

South again is the Great Armaros Desert, a vast, inhospitable wasteland situated between the Lorien Mountains to the north and the Galandel Mountains to the south. The two mountain ranges meet on the eastern edge of the continent, preventing any rainfall from reaching the wasteland. The Great Armaros Desert has no officially sanctioned settlements in its vast dry sands, and it is home to many of the most vicious beasts to be found on Eden. These beasts are widely considered to be more dangerous than most of the corrupted beasts found in south Alastair, and the only reason the land has any significance at all is the inexplicable presence of multiple Angel altars used by the Ceraph Order when ascending new Ceraphs.

The Galandel Mountains are a stark contrast to the Lorien Mountains, with several large-walled cities built along its south face overlooking the Gulf of Shizune. Mt. Kasai is situated nearly in the center of the mountain range, and while the rest of the Galandel Mountains are remarkably hospitable, the region around Mt. Kasai is home to a number of beasts nearly as nasty as those in the desert. Tourists are advised to remain on designated heavily patrolled channels through the region, and even then, a few dozen tourists wind up perishing every year.

In the southernmost reaches lies the almost paradise-like plains adjacent to the Gulf of Shizune. Dozens of small cities populate this region, and many of them have no perimeter defenses to speak of. Despite the proximity to the Deadlands, the southernmost region has next to no dangerous fauna roaming its plains, and the strong military presence based out of Valencian City handles what few beasts dare stray near populated areas.

Most traffic out of the north would be heading for the southern hub city, but the COV *Last Beacon* is not making the trip all the way to Valencian City. They will be meeting with an Erita Empire destroyer stationed over the southern face of Mt. Kasai and coordinating their search for the individual in question.

Inwardly, Shaide is feeling some concern over whether Master Armstrong would actually approve of this course of action. Nevertheless, he feels that this is necessary, and he sincerely hopes that the repercussions of his actions will not be TOO severe. In all honesty, he is not certain whether he is more concerned about Armstrong's reaction or Koraru's.

It is too late for regrets now, however, so Shaide turns to Shipmaster Corolas and asks him, "How long before we make contact?"

Corolas consults his chart. "I give it just under thirty minutes. You'd best go gather your team and prepare to make contact with the garrison."

　　　　　　　　A.S.GUINN

Shaide bows. "Thank you, Shipmaster. I appreciate your assistance."

Corolas bows in return, a slight smile on his face. "I exist to serve the Ceraphs, whether it be a two-thousand-year-old veteran or a young man just starting out. When you are trying to save the world, I am more than happy to help."

"What did Armstrong say when you sent the cross-continental transmission?" Shaide asks hesitantly.

Corolas chuckles. "I didn't get a response before we departed. I'm sure Armstrong will have some words with you when you return, but I know what you are trying to do, and I will happily help you in stopping a disease that threatens the entirety of my people. Ask for forgiveness later."

"Thanks," says Shaide, and he laughs uncomfortably. Then he leaves the bridge and heads down to the hangar bay.

When he left the Ceraph quarters, Amari lay down to take a nap. When he walks into the hangar, however, he sees everyone present is watching something. He follows their gaze and sees something that catches him by complete surprise.

An Elmeri woman is practicing some kind of elegant martial arts routine with a purple and gold staff. With a start, he sees the pink hair and realizes he is watching Amari practice her combat skills. His eyes are glued to her as she displays incredible skill and precision. She is both highly elegant and terrifying at the same time.

She is performing a series of spins and twirls, swinging her staff aggressively like a war hammer, and performing elegant acrobatic kicks, seeming to completely defy gravity as she performs half of her moves completely inverted.

She sees him out of the corner of her eye, and for a brief moment, she increases her speed, and then she lands gracefully on her feet without a sound, her staff smoothly returned to its position on her back.

Everyone in the hangar bay, men and women alike, applaud her performance cheerfully. She looks surprised to receive such praise and applause, and Shaide suspects that although she saw him approach, she may have been unaware she had an audience.

He walks over and notices she is dripping with sweat. She was not holding back with her practice. He is still in awe as he says to her, "That was incredibly impressive. I knew you were a top-class martial artist, but I had no idea you could move like that. It was like you were simply ignoring gravity."

Amari smiles at the unexpected praise. He cannot tell if she is blushing, however, because she is flushed from the workout. "Now do you believe I can take care of myself?"

"I never doubted you. I was simply concerned for your safety."

Amari cocks an eyebrow "Why were you concerned for my safety if you didn't doubt that I could handle myself?"

Shaide tilts his head. "Don't you worry about me or your dad?"

"Of course I do," she replies rather haughtily. "I care about you, and what you do can be dangerous."

Shaide gives her an amused look. "Don't you also trust that we can handle ourselves, though?"

She puts her hands on her hips, and her attitude becomes borderline sassy. "Of course I trust that you can handle yourselves, but I still worry… Oh. Okay, I think I see your point." She drops her head and looks mildly embarrassed again.

Shaide pats her on the head and laughs. "I don't know how I ever got by without you. Now, come on. We need to gather the research guys and get ready to meet the garrison at Mt. Kasai. Speaking of which…"

She looks at him curiously as he hesitates.

Shaide asks worriedly "Won't your father be pissed if he finds out you're here?"

Amari giggles. "Well, Dad is in Dorim on a trade negotiation meeting with the Termer, so he won't even be back to find out for a few days, even assuming anyone tells him. And why would they? I'm being accompanied by a Ceraph."

Shaide thinks for a minute and admits she has a point. In the month since he came back to Erita, he has noticed that everybody seems to accept what the Ceraphs do without question. As the chosen servants of Eden, their word is considered law in most cases, and the people of Erita simply let him do as he pleases, assuming he is on some kind of holy mission.

When he was accompanying other Ceraphs on their various assignments, he had just assumed that cooperation had been arranged in advance. Now he sees this isn't always the case.

They walk back into the corridor where the forward crew quarters are located. The research team is housed in two of the unoccupied crew quarters. Shaide knocks on the door and waits for a response.

Vargas opens the door. "Hey, Shaide. What do you need?"

Shaide points back over his shoulder. "We'll be arriving at the rendezvous shortly. You all should come with me to meet the garrison and explain the situation."

Vargas nods "Of course, Master Darkmoon. Amber's right. That IS kind of fun to say. Huh."

Shaide rolls his head back and sighs. "You're really not going to drop that, are you?"

"Afraid not," Vargas says with a laugh. "We only pick on you because we like you. You know that, right?"

Shaide chuckles despite himself. "Yeah, I suppose. Just get ready to meet me in the hangar bay."

"Will do, Master Darkmoon."

Shaide's eye twitches, still mildly annoyed by the whole "master" nickname. He's not anyone's master, after all. If he is honest with himself, he is still a green rookie, all things considered.

Amari looks over at him as they emerge back into the hangar bay. "You know, you kind of have a natural leader thing going. People can't seem to help but trust you."

Shaide shudders slightly, nervous about meeting with the garrison forces. "I don't know why. I know what we have to do, but I can't say I'm really confident about actually doing it, you know?"

Amari puts a hand on his shoulder and squeezes. "Relax. We'll be fine. One step at a time. Just deal with the situation as it unfolds."

Shaide nods and takes a breath. "Right. One step at a time." He feels himself calming slightly. "Thank you."

Amari gets some water from one of the crewmen working in the hangar to rehydrate herself from her workout, and the two of them sit quietly for a while. About ten minutes later, Vargas, Amber, and Ronoa enter the hangar bay to wait with them as the warship gently decelerates.

Shaide walks over and looks out the bay doors as they approach a lone destroyer hovering low to the ground. He looks down and sees the rocky crater of Mt. Kasai beneath them. There is no glow of lava on the surface as the crater capped itself many centuries ago.

Shipmaster Corolas walks out into the hangar bay to join them just as they pull alongside the destroyer, maintaining around five hundred feet between them.

This destroyer is scarcely larger than their frigate, but its hull is bristling with magicore cannons, and the vessel is extremely heavily armored. Its turbines are nearly twice the size of those on the frigate, allowing the more heavily armored vessel to maintain a similar level of mobility. The white steel hull is decorated with gold inlay similar to that of their buildings, giving the massive war machine an elegant, dangerous appearance.

Amari pulls her hair back into a ponytail and pulls a hood over her head to make her distinctive pink hair less obvious. Shaide gives her an amused look as she is clearly worried about someone recognizing her.

A single Erita dropship lifts off from the destroyer's hangar bay and flies across the gap in between them. The dropship hovers outside of the bay doors for a moment before casually drifting inside and landing gracefully on the deck. This dropship bears a similar design to its parent vessel, with a sleek white hull that is far more aesthetically pleasing than the bulky, angular dropships of Alastair or Dorim.

Two Elmeri men and a woman step out of the dropship's loading ramp and walk over to them. The woman in front wears a fancy and highly decorated white officer's uniform, and Shaide recognizes the insignia as that of an Erita Army colonel. She is looking at Vargas with some manner of disdain for some reason. Vargas is looking down at the ground in what almost appears to be shame.

The two men behind the colonel are carrying bladed spears, and they stare dead ahead, as professional and graceful as can be.

Shaide steps forward and bows. "Colonel, it is my pleasure to make your acquaintance. I am Shaide Darkmoon of the Ceraph Order."

The colonel takes her eyes off Vargas and bows politely. "Master Ceraph, it is our pleasure to host your presence, although I cannot say the same for everyone in your company."

Shaide stands up straight and says in confusion. "Colonel?"

Amari looks unnerved and uncomfortable. For a moment, she wonders if SHE is who this colonel is referring to.

Vargas bows his head. "She is referring to me, Master Ceraph. Allow me to introduce you to Colonel Evania Amaranthine. My sister."

Everyone who is present looks between them in surprise. Now that it has been said, there is indeed a family resemblance.

Colonel Evania shakes her head. "Vargas, I am only tolerating your presence because our Ceraphs here have brought you along, meaning they must need you for something. Do not mistake my stance on this matter. That being said, I do not wish to waste any more time on you. Master Ceraph? I have a troubling update regarding our situation that you nonetheless may find useful."

Shaide looks at Amari for a moment. Thankfully, Colonel Evania seems to believe Amari is also a Ceraph, so she is paying her little attention or interest. He turns his gaze back to the colonel.

"Forgive me, Colonel. Are you aware of the reason we are here? I wasn't aware you had been told we were coming."

Colonel Evania curls her lip in mild disdain as she says, "Master Ceraph, do not underestimate my experience. A human former is running around in the Mt. Kasai region, and a mysterious illness is spreading throughout the region, and now the Ceraph Order is present with a warship and a research team. I am one thousand and twenty-one years old. It is not difficult for me to ascertain why you are here."

Shaide bows again. "My apologies, Colonel. I am still young, and I have limited experience with the elegance and grace of the Elmeri. I spend most of my time with the impulsive and short-lived humans, after all."

Although this was nothing more than a thinly veiled ruse to flatter the colonel and remain on her good side, she nonetheless proves susceptible to his flattery. She bows and accepts his apology.

"Your lack of experience is forgiven. I believe you intended no offense. Now, as for my updates regarding the situation, I believe this human former who is running loose in the mountain is responsible for the rash of illness that has spread in the area. I have eleven men and women who are very ill after coming into direct contact with this man while attempting to apprehend him. It is my belief that this infection only affects Elmeri and that it can only be contracted through direct contact with this man."

Vargas refuses to look up, but he says, "This is consistent with our findings in the laboratory. It would seem our hypothesis is correct, Master Ceraph."

Colonel Evania nods her head at Amari. "Mistress Ceraph, for your safety, I would highly recommend you exercise extreme caution when seeking this man. Your Mitera leader here may possibly be immune to this illness, but as one of our people, you may be susceptible to it."

Amari keeps her head bowed as she says, "Thank you for your concern, Colonel. I will heed your advice and remain vigilant and careful. Could you do me the courtesy of describing this man?"

The colonel nods approvingly. "I see not all who leave Erita lose their manners. Of course. He is a human male the height of Master Darkmoon and of similar build. He has long, straight black hair and a scar across his cheek."

Amari turns her head to Shaide. "That sounds like the man I saw."

Shaide nods to her before addressing Colonel Evania again. "Colonel, we have determined that the illness is not contagious from those infected, only from the source. Would you be willing to have your infirm transported here for our

     A.S.GUINN

research team to look at? They have been studying this illness, and they may be able to treat your men, or at least find a countermeasure against future infection."

Colonel Evania looks at Vargas with great displeasure for a moment, and then she closes her eyes and says, "I do not wish to entrust a certain individual any more than I must, but if the agent of Eden believes it is best, I will not question the will of the great savior." She opens her eyes. "Very well, Master Ceraph. I will heed your request and entrust my men to the care of your people."

Shipmaster Corolas has remained oddly silent throughout this whole encounter. It seems that his presence is not necessary, and he is simply observing.

Shaide turns to Vargas, Ronoa, and Amber, addressing them more formally than normal. "I have instructions for the Ceraph Order research team. You are to remain on this vessel to evaluate the incoming victims and take advantage of the live specimens to find a way to treat this infection."

Amber looks at him suspiciously. "You said remain on this vessel. May I ask, what do you plan to do, Shaide?"

Shaide points over his shoulder at the sword on his back. "I am going on a seek-and-destroy mission. I will find this man and capture him to ascertain the nature of this infection and find a possible means of stopping it. Failing that, I will eliminate him and bring the body back for study." Shaide is finally getting a chance to do what he does best, and his nervous anxiety is now giving way to a cold, confident focus.

Vargas shudders slightly. "Master Ceraph, you are truly intimidating when you prepare to do, well, what you Ceraphs do best. Good luck. Do you have any instructions should the worst happen to you?"

"Remain here and contact the Citadel for further instructions when able. Shipmaster Corolas will be in charge in my absence."

Shaide turns to Amari and opens his mouth, but she interrupts him before he can say what he wants to say.

"No, Shaide. I will not remain behind while you go on a seek-and-destroy mission alone. I will not do it. You will need my help."

Shaide feels a sense of alarm as he looks into her pink eyes. "You are vulnerable to infection. I cannot risk your safety by taking you up against something we KNOW will kill you!"

Amari puts her hands on her hips. "He can only infect me if I let him touch me, right?"

"She is correct," says Vargas.

Amari nods over Shaide's shoulder. "Thank you, Vargas. So, Shaide? All I have to do is make sure he doesn't touch me."

Shaide lowers his head and growls, "You make it sound so simple."

Amber walks up beside Shaide. "For the record? You know that if you leave without her, she will just find a way to catch up. You better just take her with you so you can protect her, you know?"

Colonel Evania is watching this rather unprofessional argument with an amused expression. Shaide had been starting to wonder if she was capable of any expression other than disdain.

He sighs and looks into her eyes. "Very well. You can come with me on one, single condition."

Amari relaxes a bit and nods. "Of course. What is that?"

He locks gazes with her. "If I tell you to do something, no matter how much you don't like it, you have to promise to do what I say, no matter what."

She nods again. "I promise."

Shaide repeats himself. "No. Matter. What."

She nods more exaggeratedly. "I know. I promise."

He sighs. "Okay, good." He turns to address Colonel Evania again. "Can you tell me where and when the last known sighting of this man was?"

Colonel Evania politely indicates her dropship. "If you would like, Master Ceraphs, I can do better. I can take you to where he was seen just before your arrival."

Shaide looks back at Amari. "For the record, this is still a really bad idea."

She smiles nervously. "Shaide, the world was built on bad ideas."

Colonel Evania leads them to her dropship, and they board behind her bodyguards. "You know, Master Ceraph. The young lady isn't wrong."

Vargas hollers across the bay, "Good luck, Master Ceraphs!"

Shaide waves as the dropship rises from the deck and flies out of the hangar bay.

The colonel yells at her pilot, "Take us to grid RW-213 and land near the cavern entrance. We have to drop our Ceraph guests off for a little former hunting."

Shaide leans forward. "Colonel, if this is too personal, I understand, but curiosity is getting the better of me. Can I ask you something?"

The colonel looks down her nose at him for a moment. "Is it about my dear younger brother and me?"

Shaide nods gingerly.

"You're right," she says, sighing. "That is personal. But I will tell you anyway because I appreciate your respect for our culture." She pauses and then explains, "My family has all served in our military for over fifteen thousand years. We have all seen service since before the official founding of Erita. Vargas not only turned his back on fifteen thousand years of tradition, but he left our proud nation of Erita to join your order as a SCIENTIST. He abandoned everything our family held dear, and he has not even spoken to a member of our family in centuries. Then he just turns up out of the blue. So perhaps you can understand my displeasure at my brother's sudden, unexpected return."

Shaide bows his head and decides to respond sympathetically, although, in fact, he does NOT understand. "I can see your point of view. My family has been in the Ceraph Order since its founding three thousand years ago. I cannot imagine there was any other path for me."

Colonel Evania nods "Thank you for your understanding. This is why we respect the Mitera. Your respect for family, honor, and tradition are much like our own in many ways."

She looks pointedly at Amari. "Dear girl, when serving with your companion here, do not forget that our people consider it a great honor to bear a Mitera child. Just a thought for when you reach the age of matronage."

Shaide's eye twitches as he feels a sense of confusion. At sixteen, isn't she technically at sexual maturity? And is the colonel actually trying to tell her she should have his child? What the hell is with this woman?!

Colonel Evania's keen eye catches Shaide's confused look, and she says, "Master Darkmoon, is it possible you were not aware of this aspect of Elmeri biology?"

Shaide looks over at her "Colonel? What do you mean?"

Amari groans. "No…don't…"

An amused look spreads across the colonel's face. She is proud of her people, and she seems more than eager to educate others about them.

"You see, Master Darkmoon. While Elmeri females reach physical maturity at the same time as what humans call puberty, and become fully capable of having adult relations, an Elmeri female does not become capable of bearing children until closer to one hundred years of age, and even when we do, the times we can do so are few and far between. We believe it was Shizune's way of ensuring our population remained manageable, considering the long lifespans that we have relative to other races."

Amari has her face buried in her hands in embarrassment.

Shaide, meanwhile, has his eyebrows raised high. He just received a sexual education lesson from an Erita colonel in the back of a dropship. He isn't sure how to respond to that.

Colonel Evania looks at Amari with amusement. "Judging from the girl's deference to you, and her timid reaction to me educating you, you must be no older than sixteen to twenty and have likely never experienced intimacy before. I commend you, Master Ceraph. Restraining yourself around her must be difficult."

Shaide coughs as Amari buries her head in her lap. "Colonel, please. She is a childhood friend in addition to my responsibility. Although everyone keeps thinking otherwise, we are not romantically involved."

The colonel leans back. "Very well, I can see I am making you uncomfortable. For the record, I believe you should consider it. A Mitera-fathered child would be very strong. In fact, I suspect young Mistress Ceraph here has Mitera heritage herself."

The pilot calls back, "Ma'am? We will be arriving in two minutes."

The colonel looks to the front and yells, "Thank you, Gejios."

Shaide leans over to Amari and whispers, "Hey, are you okay?"

Amari nods her head in her hands and sits up, looking away from him. He suspects she is still feeling embarrassed from the biology discussion from a moment ago.

The colonel looks back at Shaide. "Do you have a plan to find him, Master Ceraph?"

Amari responds to the colonel's question before Shaide can. "Well, Colonel, I suspect that since he is infecting our people, he would find a single Elmeri girl with a single escort to be an easy target and will likely come to us."

Colonel Evania nods, her amused expression giving way to respect. "Using yourself as bait to lure him out. Gutsy plan."

Shaide looks at Amari with considerable alarm on his face. "Are you sure? This is an extremely dangerous and reckless plan."

Amari nods. "Yes. If he does get me, just make sure you kill him before he can get away."

Shaide closes his eyes, a sick feeling in his stomach. He doesn't like this plan, but he suspects that he doesn't really have a choice in the matter.

A moment later, the dropship descends and touches down onto a level clearing where Shaide sees six Erita soldiers guarding the entrance to a cavern.

When Colonel Evania departs the dropship, all six men and women jump to attention and say, "Ma'am!"

She addresses them. "Soldiers. What is the current situation?"

One of the men drops the salute and replies, "Ma'am, Sergeant Pendolas took a squad into the cavern to pursue the target. We are currently under orders to guard this entrance and make certain he does not come out this way!"

Colonel Evania nods. "Very good. Men, these are Ceraph Special Operatives of the Alastair Citadel. They are here on a holy mission to detain or eliminate our quarry. Offer them any support you are able, but otherwise, stay out of their way. Understood?"

"MA'AM!"

Colonel Evania steps to the side and allows Shaide and Amari to depart the dropship. "Master Ceraphs, these men are at your disposal. Please do not waste their lives if you can help it."

Shaide nods. "Thank you, ma'am."

She bows in a standing prayer pose. "May Eden and the goddess Shizune watch over you as you perform the work of our savior."

Shaide returns the pose. "His will be done."

Colonel Evania boards her dropship once again, and a moment later, they lift off and disappear into the distance.

The Erita soldier who responded to the colonel now turns to Shaide. "Orders, sir?"

Shaide gulps, feeling the pressure of having the responsibility of these men's lives in HIS hands now. He makes a decision. "Continue with your existing orders. Do not enter the cavern. You are only to make sure our quarry does not escape through this route. No matter what you do, do NOT let him touch you."

The soldier salutes in response. "Sir! Understood!"

Shaide looks Amari in the face and hesitates.

"I'm coming with you, Shaide. Stop wasting time."

Shaide nods, and then he heads into the cavern with Amari right beside him. They proceed deep down the main shaft, and as the light fades, Amari takes her staff in her hands and makes it glow, granting them light to guide their steps.

*   *   *

Shaide and Amari have been in the cavern for nearly an hour, slowly advancing down the winding shaft. Amari has proven to be indispensable on this mission, as her spiritual ability far exceeds his own and the glow from her staff's guiding light also illuminates the trail left by the Erita soldiers. She even pointed out that one of the trails is slightly different, indicating that it belongs to their quarry, or at the very least, that it does not belong to the soldiers.

They can see that the soldiers and their quarry remained in the main cavern shaft. Despite having encountered several branches in the tunnels, the trail continues straight down the largest one.

Shaide has also noticed a distinct lack of any native fauna in the tunnels. He is uncertain as to whether there are simply no inhabitants in these caves or if they were cleared out intentionally.

They proceed deeper and deeper, and finally, Amari taps Shaide on the shoulder. "Check out these rock formations on the walls," she whispers.

Shaide follows her gaze and notes the porous-looking rocks around them and the carbon-rich surface of the walls.

"I think these are old lava tubes," Amari says. "These caves must go all the way to the volcano's core."

Shaide shrugs. "Well, you DO like warm places, after all."

Amari sighs "I don't think I want to be THAT warm."

Shaide chuckles as they proceed further into the magma tubes. They've been in the tunnels for a total of an hour and a half when Amari suddenly takes a sharp breath. "Look! Ahead!"

Shaide follows her gaze and sees a white boot on the ground. He and Amari run up the tunnel and find a half-dozen Erita soldiers lying on the ground, blood all over the walls from deep slash and stab wounds.

Amari looks around in horror. "What happened here?"

Shaide looks at the precision of the attacks. Every blow is to a critical area. He feels a sense of foreboding as he realizes something important. "This was no former…"

Amari looks at him quizzically, "What do you mean?"

Shaide squats down and looks into one of the men's unfocused eyes and then at the stab wound directly through his heart. "Formers are borderline mindless. They may have some level of intelligence left, but they are essentially berserkers. They leave a total mess. This? This was done by someone very skilled."

*Cough!*Cough!*

Shaide and Amari turn to the sound and see one of the soldiers is still moving. They exchange glances and run over to him.

Amari points her staff at the man, and a greenish glow illuminates his wounds. Shaide kneels down and looks him in the eyes. "Soldier! What happened here?"

The soldier wheezes weakly. "Our target…we were pursuing him and caught up. When we did, he had a sword. We

attempted to take him down, but his speed and strength…
cough"

Shaide glances up at Amari. She is focusing hard on trying to heal this man.

"It was inhuman… *cough* I've never seen anyone move… *cough*"

The man's eyes lose focus, and he falls still. Amari focuses harder, tears running from her eyes as she tries desperately to heal him.

Shaide stands up, turns away from him, and puts an arm around Amari. "We can't help him anymore. Come on. We can't stay here."

She lowers her staff and nods. Her guiding light shows a single trail still moving away from the carnage, leading into a glowing cavern up ahead.

They follow the path, and Amari shuts off her glowing staff to preserve the element of surprise. They reach the edge of the tunnel and put their backs against opposite walls, looking into the cavern.

It is a massive open space with a remarkably flat floor, almost certainly formed by cooling lava. All around the edge of the chamber is a river of molten rock, flowing in and out of the walls and down channels in the floor. In a handful of places, the lava periodically fountains up out of the ground, splashing the area around with molten red.

The heat coming from the chamber is unbelievable.

In the middle of the chamber, walking away from them, is the man the soldier described: black outfit, long black hair, tall stature, a black sword of some kind on his back.

Shaide looks at Amari and takes a deep breath. "No matter what happens, stay back. Do not let him get near you. If something happens to me, run. Run like hell and don't look back."

Amari locks eyes with him. "I did promise to do whatever you said."

Shaide looks at her suspiciously, but he can't risk arguing with her with their target so close. He focuses inside himself and taps into the presence of Rho, sleeping deep within him. He thinks, *Hey, Rho. Been a while. I could really use your help right now. Grant me your strength, so I can purge a corrupted asshole. Okay?*

A surge of spiritual aura wells up inside him, and he feels his strength, speed, and focus increase drastically. He plants his foot on the ground and prepares to launch himself forward.

He looks at Amari and says, "Wish me luck."

"Good luck." She hesitates. "Don't die."

Shaide focuses all of his strength, and then he sprints across the cavern, hurling himself into the air at his unaware target.

Or so he thinks.

The man suddenly spins around and draws his sword, deflecting the charge and forcing Shaide to throw himself over the man to avoid the instantaneous counterattack.

The man looks at him for a moment and frowns. "You're no elf. Why are you here?" His gaze finds the Ceraph medallion on Shaide's chest. "Oh, I see. The order finally got wind of my experiments and sent an assassin to take me out. I am quite flattered. Really!"

Shaide gauges the man carefully. He's met a handful of formers before, and something isn't right here. This man is far too coherent and steady to be a former. What is he?

"What do you want here, former?"

The man laughs derisively. "Former? I am no former. Do not lump me in with those mindless pieces of cannon fodder. I am far superior to them."

Shaide feels a chill forming in the pit of his stomach despite the blistering heat. "You didn't answer my question. What do you want? What are you doing here?"

The man smiles. "Me? I am doing my lord's work, of course! I am developing an incurable virus that can rapidly convert thousands of unenlightened maggots at a time into free members of our dear flock! The problem is, it is not yet complete, and it keeps killing them instead of converting them. Quite a bother, really."

Shaide tilts his head suspiciously. "And why are you telling me this so freely?"

The man outstretches his arms to the sides as if it were obvious. "Well, because I know you will never tell anyone what you saw and heard here! Dead men cannot speak, after all!"

He suddenly lunges forward with terrifying speed. Inhuman isn't even the appropriate word to describe it. He slashes aggressively with his blade, attacking so quickly and ferociously that it is all Shaide can do just to dodge and parry his assault. He cannot even think long enough to look for an opening to counterattack.

Blades clash together repeatedly, the sound echoing in the vast cavern. Shaide finally manages to raise a foot and kick the man away from him, giving him a moment's reprieve from the relentless assault.

The man isn't even winded. "I must say, I am quite impressed. You are the first I have met who has been able to withstand my blade. It looks like you may be more fun than I anticipated. What is your name, Ceraph? You have earned my respect."

Shaide responds, stalling the man so he can catch his breath. He shouldn't be this winded. Something is wrong. "I'm Shaide Darkmoon. Descendant of one of the original Ceraphs of the Great War."

The man bows respectfully. "Ironic, for I have been on the opposite side of the coin for nearly as long. I am Justice Whitebear, and I am the man who will kill you."

In a lightning-fast motion, Justice stabs his blade into the ground, and a fan of flames erupts beneath Shaide, striking him before he can react and blasting him off his feet. His aura crackles as he lands on his back inches from a pool of lava, his hair singeing from the heat.

He backflips across the pool and hits it with a summoned ball of water, causing a violent eruption of steam as Justice leaps across the pool after him.

Justice grabs his eyes and yells, "OH, CLEVER BITCH!" as the steam scalds and blinds him. Shaide lunges at him with his blade as the man hits the ground, but he only manages a glancing cut to his leg, and the man lashes out with a kick and strikes Shaide in the face, making stars pop in his vision and bloodying his nose.

Shaide lands on his back and grabs his face. Then he sees a black cloud of smoke swirling violently as archaic glyphs appear on the ground and in the air. His eyes open wide in shock.

Justice yells, "In the name of our father, Belial, I summon you Taurus! Daemon of the First Circle!"

With an ear-splitting bull roar, a massive minotaur wreathed in flames and wielding two massive battle-axes materializes from the smoke.

Justice yells, "Finish him, Taurus! Fulfill your father's will!"

The bull rushes forward and swings its twin axes down on Shaide.

Milliseconds before Shaide is split asunder, from out of nowhere, a ball of ice flies across the cavern and blasts Taurus away from him.

He doesn't question the aid, but rolls to his feet and raised his hand. "In the name of the Father of Light, Eden, I summon you! RHO!"

A golden glyph appears in the ceiling, and the earsplitting screech of an eagle erupts through the massive cavern as the thunderbird Rho streaks through a portal and across the cavern. Taurus gets to his feet just in time to be struck by the angry golden eagle of lightning.

Shaide looks back at Justice and points his sword at him. "Hey! Asshole! We aren't done yet!"

Justice climbs to his feet, and his face splits in a horribly sadistic grin. "It's a shame. I think I am actually beginning to like you, boy."

They leap towards each other and begin another violent exchange of blows. The sounds of swords clanging together, a bull roaring, and an eagle screeching fill the cavern as the intermittent sound of lightning and tremendous thuds punctuate this orchestra.

Shaide strikes the ground in front of Justice, missing his foe but causing an eruption of thunder behind him, blasting him over Shaide's head and flat on his face. Shaide spins around and raises his sword to deal the finishing blow.

THKT

He freezes as pain fills his body, and he sees the man looking at him, eyes full of disappointment. He looks down and sees the blade piercing his chest by his sternum, and a feeling of numb shock overcomes him.

Justice climbs to his feet and pulls his blade from Shaide's chest, catching him as he collapses. "It's a shame, really. If you weren't serving the wrong god, you could have accomplished so much more with your life. Instead, it ends here. A damn shame."

In the background, Rho fades from the cavern as his summoner can no longer maintain him.

"NOOOO!"

The pattering of footsteps gets louder, and Justice turns around to discover the source.

WHAM!

With tremendous force, a golden staff hits him across the face and slams him to the ground.

He groans in anger and yells, "Where did you come from!?"

Shaide coughs, blood coming from his mouth, as he tries to say, "Amari…No!"

Amari violently twirls her staff around, overpowering Justice's attempts to parry and regain his balance, striking him over and over again. Then he throws himself backward, making her take a wild swing and putting her off balance.

He reaches out, his hand emitting a strange black haze, and attempts to grab her. His hand passes a mere inch from her face as she recovers and vaults herself in the air with her hands, going over his head and striking him in the back of the head with her staff.

Taurus comes barreling through the cavern, and Amari freezes for a moment at the sight of the twelve-foot-tall burning bull sprinting towards her. She throws up a barrier at the last possible second, just before Taurus slams into it. The barrier shatters, and she is sent flying into the lone stone pillar in the center of the cavern.

Shaide rolls over on his belly and tries to drag himself forward as blood fills his lungs. He promised her he would protect her. He promised he wouldn't die. So many promises he is determined not to break.

Justice slowly walks over to her, sleeve pulled back to expose a whole arm emitting that strange black haze. Shaide realizes with a start this must be how he infects his victims.

"You know, I COULD kill you now. He was fun, but YOU are just annoying, girl. So, how about I infect you with my new and improved handy dandy curse here and let you suffer and die over the next, oh, few days."

Shaide pushes himself up on one arm and pulls one of his daggers from its sheath. With a roar of effort, and all of the strength he has left, he hurls the dagger at Justice before collapsing flat to the ground.

CLANG!

Justice spins and deflects the dagger with his sword. "Oh! Still alive! Wow, you are REALLY one tough young man. Color me impressed."

"UNG!" Amari uses the distraction to push herself to her feet and kick Justice hard in the back, sending him forward into a pool of lava.

His earsplitting screams fill the cavern: "OH! IT'S HOT! OH HELL, IT'S HOT! IT BURNS! IT! BURNS!"

He rolls out of the pool and thrashes on the ground, but something new grabs the attention of Amari, Taurus, and the half-conscious Shaide.

The entire cavern begins to rumble, growing more and more violent as it continues. Justice pushes himself to his feet. He is covered in burns "WHAT IS HAPPENING!?"

The rock suddenly crumbles behind Amari, revealing a statue of some kind of bird wreathed in flames and a stone altar. A moment later, a beam of red light shoots into the roof of the cavern, and a tremendous explosion rocks the ground itself.

*   *   *

Colonel Evania looks around the hangar bay of her destroyer as a deep rumbling fills the air. The other personnel in the hangar look around in confusion as well as the sound of rumbling fills the air, growing louder and louder. Several of the men walk to the edge of the hangar bay and look at the volcanic crater in the distance.

The colonel walks over to the edge of the hangar bay as well and follows their gaze. The mountain itself seems to be trembling as the rumbling makes it impossible to hear anyone speak.

"What are those Ceraphs up to?" She wonders aloud.

ETERNAL KNIGHTS OF EDEN I

Suddenly a bright red light erupts from the center of the crater, and a second later, every bit of the rock in the crater explodes upward, filling the air with ash and debris, and reveals a massive chamber underneath. The immense chunks of rock disintegrate in midair as the crewmen of the destroyer run for cover in case the debris comes to them.

The beam of red light is coming from something in the center of the massive chamber.

The colonel stares in wonder. The events of the next few minutes will be something that she has never seen in her thousand-year life.

*   *   *

Amari screams as the roof of the cavern explodes over their heads, the giant chunks of stone simply disintegrating in midair above them. A wall of red glowing glyphs forms around her and the newly uncovered altar, and in one swift motion, they expand outwards, picking up Shaide and Justice and hurling them to the edge of the cavern.

By some miracle, Shaide misses the boiling pool of lava, but Justice lands in the flowing river around the outside of the chamber, and if he is alive, his screams cannot be heard over the sound of the chaos in the cave.

Amari looks up as a column of glowing glyphs erupts into the sky. A swirling firestorm forms at the top, and then a ball of fire streaks from the sky right towards her.

She screams and manages to run before it flares just above the altar, revealing a bird shrouded in flames. With a start, Shaide suddenly realizes why Mt. Kasai sounded so familiar.

"There are many places in the world where a Ceraph must be incredibly careful," says Aton, "because they are home to lost angels that could awaken at any time."

Shaide looks at his godfather with confusion. "What are lost angels?"

"Lost angels are those that have not had a Ceraph in so long that the have been deemed dormant or too dangerous and are sealed away to prevent unnecessary casualties."

Shaide inquires curiously "Where would these places be?"

Aton explains "At Mt. Kasai in Erita, a great angel of flames sleeps beneath the mountain. Theta, the Phoenix."

As this memory flashes before Shaide's dying eyes, he thinks about Amari, Koraru, and his uncle Aton. "I'm sorry I couldn't keep my promises," he whispers, and then he ceases to move.

Amari looks at the angry burning bird in front of her and then glances at Shaide, who is unconscious or dead near the wall of the cavern. She wants desperately to go to him, but she is certain this bird in front of her will not allow her to leave.

The only way out of here is to defeat him. If that is the case, so be it.

"I'm coming for you, Shaide. One way or another, I'll be with you soon."

She spins her staff around aggressively and screams at the phoenix, tears rolling down her face. "BRING IT!"

The bird screeches at her as flames erupt throughout the now open cavern and shoot into the sky.

CHAPTER 15

PHOENIX SONG / AFTERMATH

Amari performs a series of acrobatic backflips, nimbly dodging violent eruptions of flame as the angel known as Theta the Phoenix launches wave after wave at her. Theta seems unable to land a hit due to her agile movements, but at the same time, the sheer intensity of his assault is preventing her from getting close.

As her frustration builds, she decides to take a chance. Shaide is severely wounded, and she doesn't have time to dance with this thing. She sprints forward, dashing from side to side to dodge the incoming flames as rock melts inches room her and her clothes singe from the heat. With a tremendous leap in the air, she twirls her staff and sends a barrage of giant ice spikes at her enemy.

Leaping into the air proves to be a huge mistake. At the exact moment she launches her barrage, the phoenix simultaneously releases a volley of fireballs. Robbed of her mobility in the air, she is unable to dodge the attack.

As she is struck by the searing flames and blown further into the air, she also hears the bird screech and a series of thuds as her assault finds its mark. She hits the ground hard and flinches from the pain of the burns now covering a good portion of her body. The pain is so intense that she cannot move for a moment, and tears run down her face.

Now angry from Amari's attack, the phoenix launches into the air and begins circling the cavern. When Amari manages to get to her feet, the bird screeches and makes a beeline for her.

Amari braces herself and then erects a canopy of ice just before impact. The phoenix's flames are so intense that they instantly boil the ice into steam. The resulting explosion smarts on her already burned skin, but it successfully shields her from the flames. Amari anticipated this, however, and she has her next move planned. With a wide twirl, she slams her staff into the ground, and spikes of ice erupt from the ground in a fast-moving line.

The phoenix is not prepared for this, and the spikes catch up from behind, spearing its wings and bringing it crashing to the ground. The bird screeches in pain, and the sound echoes through the cavern.

Amari sees her chance and sprints towards her quarry, pushing through the pain. She strikes the ground, launching a second volley of ice without breaking stride.

The phoenix screeches as its body is impaled a second time, but the legendary beast will not go down so easily. It screeches again, this time in anger, and a massive wave of fire explodes in all directions. Amari hurls herself behind a large boulder and screams as the flames rush around her, blistering her already burned skin.

The phoenix launches itself straight into the air, flying high into the sky. Amari stands and watches the clouds, feeling a sense of dread as the flames covering the phoenix's body intensify. It reaches the arc of its climb and hurls itself towards the ground, streaking towards Amari like a meteor.

Amari summons all of the spiritual energy she can manage. Summoning this degree of power risks overloading her body, but she has no choice. She focuses as hard as she can and channels all of her magic into a single point. She aims carefully, knowing this will probably be the last thing she ever does, but she will not let that thing near Shaide.

With a scream of effort, a massive spear of ice forms in midair, and she hurls it into Theta's path. A satisfying thunk echoes across the crater as the spike finds its mark, and the bird's wings open wide just a hundred feet from the ground. The massive spike blossoms and explodes, erupting all over Theta's body.

But she was too late.

Theta slams into the ground at over seven-hundred miles per hour, and a massive fireball erupts from the kamikaze attack, sending Amari flying through the air like a ragdoll and slamming her into the glyph barrier just inches from where Shaide lies on the other side.

Her flesh blisters, and she feels multiple bones break. She sees Shaide's hand just inches from her own, and she struggles to reach for it, unable to pass the barrier. Tears run from her eyes as she struggles in vain to touch him one last time, but she collapses, all of her strength gone. She finds comfort only in that the great bird sacrificed itself in its last attack.

A column of flames erupts from the center of the cavern, and the phoenix rises from the ashes once again.

Amari growls, "You have GOT to be kidding…"

She rolls on her back and struggles to push herself into a sitting position. The phoenix gently glides over to her and lands at her feet.

Amari sits up against the glyph wall, shielding Shaide. She is trembling with rage and fear, but she gives the bird a determined stare. "You can kill me, but leave him alone! I won't let you touch him."

Theta stretches out its wings and flies back. It opens its beak, and a great ball of flame begins building in its mouth. A great rushing sound fills the air as the phoenix draws in all of the heat and spiritual power in the cavern, focusing it into a single ball of super-compressed flame that burns so brightly that everything else seems to go dark in comparison. A high-pitched screech fills the air, growing higher and louder as the bird prepares its final attack.

Amari closes her eyes and stands in between Shaide and the bird, summoning every scrap of power left in her body. She whispers, "I'm sorry I couldn't keep my promise…" And puts up the strongest barrier she can muster around him, sacrificing her safety to protect him.

The cavern goes silent for a moment, and then the loudest explosion she has ever heard in her life fills her ears. A great wave of pressure hits her, and she feels the intense heat burning every inch of her body. But the pain she expects does not come.

A feeling of numbness washes over her as the heat abates, and she collapses to the ground. She finds herself thinking, *Am I dead?*

She senses movement nearby, and she opens her eyes. She is lying on the floor of the cavern, and Shaide is just outside the barrier from her. He's wounded, but the phoenix flames did not touch him. She rolls over onto her back and freezes in fear at the sight of the great bird standing over her.

Theta just looks at her for a moment, and then it lets out an unexpectedly soft squawk. A moment later, it begins singing a soothing, gentle melody. A soft green glow envelops Amari, and she suddenly feels her pain ease and then disappear.

She looks down at her burned flesh and watches her burns fade into nothing. She looks up at the bird and pushes herself to her feet, standing between it and Shaide. "Why are you helping me?"

It just squawks and then bows its head to her. It doesn't seem to desire a fight anymore.

Amari glances down at Shaide; there is a huge pool of blood underneath him. She looks at the phoenix and asks desperately, "Please…help him too."

The phoenix stares at her, and for a moment that feels like an eternity, it does nothing. Then, just as she fears it will not help her, it resumes its song.

In front of Amari's very eyes, Shaide's chest wound seems to close and heal itself.

Theta sings for nearly a minute, finishing Amari and Shaide's healing, and then it collapses to the ground, exhausted.

Amari looks at it, tears running down her face, and says, "I don't know what you are or…why. But thank you…"

Suddenly the phoenix dissolves into a burning column of red light. Amari jumps back in shock, and a second beam of light strikes her. Theta's entire essence streams into her, forever becoming a part of her soul.

She screams in pain and shock. The sensation of the angel invading her body is overwhelming. Then, as suddenly as it begins, it is over. She coughs and stands frozen, unable to move from shock.

Moments later, the glyph wall fades, and her legs give out beneath her. She drags herself over to Shaide with all of her remaining strength, struggling to remain conscious, and manages to lay her head on his leg before passing out.

*   *   *

The crews of both the ERV *Spear of Erita* and COV *Last Beacon* watch this battle below in shock and awe. No one breathes as everything suddenly becomes almost eerily peaceful.

One of Colonel Evania's bodyguards asks her, "Ma'am? What the hell just happened?"

The colonel, in all her years of experience, has never seen anything like what has just unfolded before her eyes. For the first time in centuries, she is equally as confused as everyone around her, and she just stares at the open crater.

The Ceraph frigate is already moving towards the opening in the distance, and her bodyguard asks, "Ma'am? Orders?"

Evania shakes herself out of shock. "Those Ceraphs may need our help. Inform Commander Qorosel that I need her to reposition over the crater and prepare for support and rescue operations. Go!"

"Ma'am!"

As her men scatter to prepare the dropships, she stands at the edge of the hangar bay, processing what she's just witnessed.

*   *   *

Two days pass before Shaide regains consciousness. He stares at the ceiling of yet another unfamiliar place, trying to recall exactly what happened. He's feeling very groggy, and his brain seems to only be running at half-speed.

Then, his memories suddenly return all at once. He reaches up for his chest, looking for the stab wound from the Fallen in the volcano.

His chest is completely unmarked. He frowns and looks at where the wound was, confused and slightly disoriented. He has a fluid IV running to his arm, but he is otherwise not hooked up to anything.

A flash of Amari and the phoenix comes to mind, and he leaps out of bed. He pulls the IV out of his arm with a flinch and walks out of the room in his hospital gown. He stops a passing nurse, who nearly jumps out of her skin when he grabs her.

"Excuse me, ma'am, is there a young Elmeri woman in here? Pink hair, pink eyes, would have been brought in by military or Ceraph forces?

The nurse looks confused for just a moment before realizing who he is. "The Ceraph girl who was brought in with you? Yes, she is in the next room over. She is—"

"Thank you, ma'am."

"Excuse me, sir? You shouldn't be… Oh, never mind."

Shaide goes into her room and sees her lying unconscious on the hospital bed. When he kneels down next to her, he notices that she doesn't appear injured, but she is in a gown and has an IV, nonetheless.

An Elmeri doctor enters the room behind Shaide. "Relax, young man. Your partner should be just fine. We consulted with the medical team that brought you in, and they said she is simply suffering from joining fatigue, a common condition when a Ceraph first merges with an angel."

Shaide's eyes go wide. "Merges with…what? She beat that thing? She won?"

The doctor shrugs. "I do not know if she 'won' or not, but your biology expert looked her over and said her condition was simply due to a massive amount of spiritual energy being suddenly infused into her system, so she is just resting now."

As he says this, Amari groans and starts to move.

"Amari? Hey, are you okay?"

"Shaide?" she mumbles and opens her eyes, looking around groggily. Her gaze falls on Shaide, and she looks at him in surprise for a moment.

"You're okay!" she cries out. She rolls over in bed and hugs him around the neck, and he pats her back in surprise.

Shaide nods "Yeah, I'm okay. I'm good."

She pulls back and frowns. "What, um…what exactly happened to me? What was that giant firebird?"

Shaide thinks for a moment, and then he responds carefully, "I think part of you already knows the answer."

She looks at him for a good minute, still regaining consciousness after being out for two days. She finally asks, "Was THAT an angel?"

Shaide nods and pats her hand, feeling a tremendous sense of guilt over bringing her along. "You did say you wanted to become a Ceraph…"

Amari blinks and stares at him for a moment, and then what he says sinks in. "I'm a Ceraph now!?"

He chuckles at her excited reaction and shakes his head. "Well, no. Not yet. But this is literally how I ended up joining. So if you really, really want to, I'm sure it can happen. What are you going to tell your father?"

Amari looks down, embarrassed. "I'm actually surprised you haven't figured it out already."

Shaide looks at her, nonplussed.

"When I left home to work at the hospital with you, and especially when I came here with you, I made the decision that I wouldn't go home. If I want my own future, I can't do it with my dad breathing down my neck. I have to be free to make my own choices. So, I decided that I would return to Alastair with you and build my own future my way."

Shaide blinks a few times and then he says, "Oh. I, uhh… I see."

Amari looks slightly hurt as she asks, "Do you not want me coming with you?"

Shaide shakes his head. "No, that's not it. Being able to see you more than, you know, once every few years sounds like a really great thing! I just don't want you to be in danger like that all the time. You know?"

Amari looks thoroughly downcast "You're not going to let me come back with you. Are you?"

Shaide looks at her for a moment and then sighs. "I want you to be safe, and I want you to stay where you can have a long and happy life. But it isn't my place to tell you how to run your life. If you want to save the world, I guess I'll just have to save it with you."

Amari's stares blankly for a moment, and then a wide smile breaks across her face, and she hugs him around the neck once again. "Thank you…"

A voice comes from behind him. Amber. "Oh, you two are awake! Nice butt, Shaide."

Shaide is confused for a moment. Then a gentle breeze brushes his back, and he realizes these gowns have no backs to them. He jumps to his feet. "I'm, uhh, going to get dressed."

Shaide rushes back into his room, and surprisingly finds his clothes and gear on the table beside his bed. Someone has even cleaned them and patched the hole in his shirt from the stab wound.

He looks at the leather chest piece; there's a hole running clean through it. The armor will have to be replaced. He puts on his clothes and damaged armor, and then he walks back into Amari's room.

He looks at Amber as she explains the situation to Amari.

"…technically finished our mission here in Erita. You two found the source of the illness and eliminated it, which means our work is done. We'll be heading back to the Citadel basically whenever Shaide is ready."

Amari asks her, "Am I able to come with you?"

Amber sits back and thinks. "Well, technically, Shaide is the officer in charge. The decision on whether to bring you back is ultimately his. I'm sure if you do a couple of, umm…private personal favors for him, if you know what I mean, you could convince him to bring you back."

"Private personal… NO!"

"Amber!" barks Shaide. "Stop torturing her!"

Amber looks at him in amusement. "Hey. I was trying to help you, you know. Get you a little action."

Shaide drops his head and looks straight down. "Why…why did I get stuck with you of all people, Amber…"

Amber responds pointedly "Because I'm the cutest and best damn biologist in all of the Citadel?"

Shaide sighs. She has a point. "Anyways, is it really my decision whether to bring her back or not?"

Amber nods "She meets all of the qualifications to come back for evaluation. You weren't the only person to become a Ceraph this way, Shaide. Just the youngest."

Shaide looks at Amari, who's watching their conversation with interest. "Before me, who was the youngest?"

Amber thinks. "Actually, your mother, now that I think about it. She stumbled across Rho at only sixteen years old. But a handful of young adults have stumbled across angels over the years. Military trainees begin operations at sixteen a lot of times, so a few accidents have happened over the past three thousand years."

"So, she wouldn't be unusual?"

Amber shrugs. "It's rare but not earth-shattering. Her birthday is a month before yours, so she's closer to seventeen anyway."

Amari looks at him with round, adorable, puppy dog eyes as she asks, "Shaide, will you please take me back to the Citadel with you? Especially now? There is no way my father will ever let me leave the house again after this…"

Shaide sighs. She's probably not wrong. Plus, this is basically the thing she wants most in the whole world. It would be beyond cruel to deny it to her.

"Yes. You can come back with us."

Amari puts her hands together and yells, "Yay! Thank you! Where are my clothes?"

Amber coughs. "Well, your clothes were mostly incinerated in the battle. I'll have to get you something, but it might be a little tight in the chest." She looks down at her own chest and then back at Amari. "Seriously, kid, what has your maid been feeding you?"

Amari crosses her arms over her chest self-consciously.

Shaide lowers his voice. "We would really appreciate it if you could loan her something…quickly…"

"Aww, you're no fun," Amber says with a sigh. "Okay, let me go see what I have. If it's not your style, though, don't come whining to me."

She walks out of the room.

Shaide wonders out loud as she walks away, "You know? I'm almost scared of what kind of outfit she'll bring back."

Amari is blushing hard when Shaide turns around. He sighs. "Relax. I won't let her make you wear anything weird."

 A.S.GUINN

Amari shakes her head. "It's not that. When, umm, when my clothes burned off, did you, uhh…see…anything?"

Shaide bows his head and chuckles. "I was unconscious until a few minutes before you woke up. Relax, I didn't see anything."

She looks at him with relief.

"Speaking of which…how am I even alive right now? I was pretty sure he stabbed me in the heart or lung."

Amari shrugs. "I think it was the bird. After it quit fighting, it did something and healed my wounds, and then it healed yours. You must have still been barely alive. I passed out right afterward, though."

Shaide nods "So…you ended up saving my life after all."

Amari blushes again. "I promised I would look after you. We'll look after each other, right?"

Shaide nods. "You know I'm going to make sure not to let you out of my sight after this whole mess, right?"

"I'm fine with that," Amari says with a smile.

"Oh, just kiss already."

Shaide and Amari turn to see Amber walking back into the room.

"That was fast," says Shaide.

Amber shrugs "I'm sleeping here in the hospital while I look after the Erita soldiers who were infected by the weird illness. My suitcase was in the room just up the hall."

Shaide spins around. "Oh! How are they doing?"

Amber tilts her head "It's the weirdest thing. Ever since whatever the hell happened in the crater, they've actually been recovering, and quickly at that. We are beginning to theorize the infection was actually a type of curse, and you must have taken out the caster, so the curse is fading."

Amari remembers the man being swept away by lava. "Yeah, he kind of got boiled alive on a river of lava. I think it's safe to say he's gone."

"Exactly."

"How did you know that?" asks Shaide.

Amber coughs. "We, uhh, found his deep-fried body not far from you. Easy to figure out what happened."

"Good point."

Amari pulls her IV out, and a brief green glow lights the hole, stopping the bleeding after only a second. "I'd like to get dressed now. I don't like this hospital gown."

"I'll wait outside," says Shaide. "Amber, don't do anything to her. That is, uhh, a direct order."

Amber wiggles provocatively. "Oh, I just love it when you get all bossy."

As he leaves, he says, "I really hate you sometimes…"

Amber laughs as she shuts the door behind him. "Oh, come on. You know you love me."

Click

Shaide leans against the door and smiles to himself. Amber may be an annoying total pervert with a disturbing obsession with him, but he can't deny that she has become his friend. He's actually gotten used to her constant inappropriate behavior. It reminds him of home.

He keeps drawing the gaze of various hospital personnel, and he is again reminded that the Ceraphs attract a lot of attention and respect from the people of Erita. The stares still make him uncomfortable, though, and he is glad when the door clicks open a few minutes later.

"Okay, you can come in now."

Shaide walks back into the room, and when he sees Amari, he involuntarily freezes for a moment.

"What do you think?" asks Amber.

Amari's outfit is…interesting but not unpleasant. Her top stops just above her midriff, and it has short sleeves and slightly exposed cleavage. The bottom half is an armor-paneled thigh-length skirt, with white leggings and knee-high boots. The whole outfit is in a dark blue and pink theme. She actually looks extremely cute, enough so to disarm Shaide for a moment, at least.

Amber shrugs. "It doesn't show any cleavage on me, but what can I say. The girl looks good in it."

"You're staring…" Amari says, embarrassed. "How do I look?"

Shaide coughs and turns away. "Sorry. It looks good. I wasn't expecting her to bring you something like that. That's all."

Amari nods "Can we get out of here now?"

"Come on. Amber, Are you sure we're done?"

She nods. "I'm actually going to be staying here for a few more weeks to study the men who survived the affliction and see if I can't work out a countermeasure of some kind. Everyone else is just waiting on clearance to return home."

Shaide nods and pats her on the head, perhaps a little harder than necessary as retaliation for her torturing him with perverse jokes. "Take care, then. We'll see you back at the Citadel whenever you make it back."

She waves as he walks away. "And hey, if girly here hasn't put out by the time I get back, I'll kidnap you for a few hours and show you a REAL woman!"

Shaide grits his teeth and grumbles, "Damnit, Amber…"

Amari looks slightly jealous for some reason. "You know, I'm not sure she's kidding. I might HAVE to do it just to save you from her."

Shaide stops and turns his head sideways, a look of alarm on his face. "I think I let you spend too much time around her."

Amari looks confused, and suddenly her hand jumps to her mouth. "I didn't mean to say that out loud! I was just thinking!"

Shaide looks around awkwardly. "I…I think that might be worse."

Amari coughs "Let's uhh… Let's keep moving."

They continue up the hallway in silence until they see another familiar face.

Colonel Evania Amaranthine turns to greet them as they approach. "Ceraphs, it is good to see you again. I was worried that you may not recover from such an ordeal, but here you are, on your feet."

Shaide bows. "Colonel, it is a pleasure to see you again."

She bows in return. "I wanted to thank you for completing your mission and saving my men. I have seen and met many Ceraphs over the years, and you never fail to impress me. It pleases me to see Eden has such capable followers to carry out his will."

Shaide bows again. "It is simply our duty to protect the people of Eden from the corruption and all that would bring them harm. Thanks are not necessary."

"Perhaps," Colonel Evania replies, "but I am certain that it is still appreciated."

Shaide rubs his neck, slightly embarrassed. "It…does help morale a little."

The colonel looks at Amari. "Mistress Ceraph, you never did tell me your name. I would like to know, if you do not mind, the names of both Ceraphs who saved my men, and possibly all of our people."

Amari looks down in embarrassment. "I am Amari Tamiel."

Colonel Evania's eyes open wide. "Wait. You are Brigadier General Koraru Tamiel's daughter?! I have been speaking with the general's daughter this whole time, and I did not know?" She suddenly looks very alarmed. "Ma'am, I am so sorry that I spoke to you with such casual disrespect when suggesting… Please forgive me."

Amari shakes her head and smiles. "No, it's okay. I, uhh…well, you only spoke the truth. Our people DO view the Mitera favorably, and…well…"

Colonel Evania still seems embarrassed at disrespecting the general's daughter. "Come to think of it, he never spoke of you being with the Ceraphs."

Amari is bright red at this point. "He umm… He's going to be very angry when he finds out. He did not actually know I was on this mission…"

Colonel Evania looks stunned. "Oh. Well, I will not interfere with Ceraph business, so do not be concerned. What ARE your plans now, Master Ceraph?"

Shaide raises one hand. "Please, just call me Shaide. We are returning to the Citadel to rest, recover, and await further instructions—aaand get a possible butt-chewing from the Deadlands for departing on this mission without approval."

Colonel Evania smiles broadly, extremely amused now. "Well, Mast…Shaide. As I said, you Ceraphs certainly never fail to impress or amuse me. I hope to work with you again someday."

Shaide and Amari both bow. "Goodbye," they say in unison.

*　　　*　　　*

Shaide and Amari walk onto the bridge of the COV *Last Beacon* and approach Shipmaster Corolas, who quickly greets them.

"Master Darkmoon, Mistress Tamiel. It is a pleasure to see you well again. Vargas already informed me of your mission completion and of our impending return to the Citadel. We will be ready to depart whenever you give the order."

"Is everything and everyone accounted for?" asks Shaide.

Corolas nods "Everything except the weird hyperactive one, Amber, I think, is her name. She is remaining here and will return later via commercial transport."

Shaide nods. "As far as I am concerned, head back to the Citadel when ready. I also need you to send a carefully worded transmission to Brigadier General Tamiel."

Corolas looks at Amari and then back to Shaide, seeming to understand.

"Tell him the Ceraph Order has need of Amari, but that she will be well taken care of."

"And tell him I said I love him," adds Amari, "but I have to choose my own future, and that future isn't in Erita. It's where I can help everyone, not just our own people."

Corolas nods. "Very well, I will send the transmission. We will be departing within the hour."

"We'll be down in the Ceraph quarters if you need us," says Shaide.

　　　　　　A.S.GUINN

Corolas waves dismissively. "You've done more than enough. Leave the rest to us. We'll get you home."

Shaide and Amari leave the bridge and climb down to the Ceraph quarters on the bottom deck. When they enter their room, Amari lets out a long sigh.

Shaide looks at her with concern. "What's wrong?"

Amari looks at him with a complicated expression. "I'm just nervous. I've never even left Erita before, and now I'm leaving home, possibly forever, to start a life I've dreamed of for years." She unexpectedly walks over and wraps her arms around his back, resting her head on his chest.

Shaide reciprocates, wrapping his arms around her and patting her back. "It's going to be okay, Amari. I imagine it's scary for everyone to leave home for the first time. The Ceraphs are good people. Mostly. My aunt is a little nuts, but I can't help that."

Amari giggles, some of the tension releasing.

Shaide continues. "You'll do everything at your own pace. Armstrong values our lives. He never makes us do anything we can't handle. You'll have more than just me. You'll have all of us taking care of you. It's like a big, weird, messed-up family."

Amari smiles and lets go of him and then sits down at the table. "Thank you, Shaide."

He shrugs and sits down across from her. "You know, if you WANT to go home, I can always have Corolas stop in Sora first."

"No," Amari replies, shaking her head frantically. "I WANT to do this. I'm just nervous. I'm not doubting my decision at all!"

Shaide chuckles. "Relax, Amari. I'm just messing with you."

"Okay. So, what do you want to do until we get back?" She yawns

Shaide laughs "I don't know. I know I could REALLY use a shower, but I never could get comfortable using the ones on these ships. Always seemed…weird."

Amari raises her arm and sniffs, and then she lowers her arm subconsciously. "Actually, I think I need one too. We could probably both shower after all that happened."

Shaide nods absently.

Amari's eyes suddenly open wide. "I didn't mean we should both shower TOGETHER. I just meant we both probably need…"

Shaide busts out laughing. "I didn't say a WORD, Amari. YOU'RE the one who thought that. I think you really DID spend too much time with Amber."

      A.S.GUINN

Amari buries her face in her arms and says in a muffled voice, "I think you also spent too much time around Amber."

Shaide leans back and sighs. "Yeah, you're probably right."

Amari gets up. "I'm going to go take a shower, now that you've mentioned it."

"Me too. I'll be all self-conscious if only you are clean."

Amari's eyes open wide. "You mean together? Well, I... I GUESS it's okay, since we..."

Shaide pats her on the head as he walks past her to grab his travel bag. "Relax, Amari. Our ships aren't as fancy as the Erita warships, but we still have separate male and female bathing facilities."

Amari looks straight forward. "Oh. Right. Sorry, I...don't know what I was thinking."

Shaide frowns at the sight of her red face as she digs in her bag. "Did you WANT to shower together? You almost look disappointed."

Her head snaps up and she shakes her head "No, I... It has been a REALLY long couple of days. My brain is all kinds of screwy right now."

He shakes his head and laughs. "I'm just jacking with you. Relax."

She quickly regains her composure and says, "I really, really did miss you, you know? Even back then, I knew that no matter what I did with my life, it would be better if you were in it."

He looks down, feeling a little embarrassed at the mushy feeling stuff, but he nods. "I know I was terrible, and I never wrote or contacted you, but I missed you too. I thought about you pretty much every day, and I kept an eye open for a chance to come back and see you."

There's a knock at the door.

"Come in," says Shaide.

A crewman walks in. "I'm bringing you a message from Shipmaster Corolas, sir."

"What is it?"

The crewman responds. "He said we will be departing within five, and he also has a message for you from General Tamiel, sir. General Tamiel says, and I quote…" He looks down at a slip of paper and reads, "You promised me you would look after my daughter, and I am going to hold you to that promise. If anything happens to her, however, the corrupted will be the least of your problems. No angel will be able to save you from me if anything befalls her or if you do anything to hurt her. That being said, remember, I love you both. Take care of yourselves.

My door will always be open." He closes the letter and looks up. "That is all, sir."

Shaide nods. "Alright. You're free to go."

The crewman ducks out and closes the door.

Amari looks amused. "That was unexpected." She turns and hugs Shaide tightly "Make me one last promise?"

He looks down at her in surprise.

"Promise me that no matter what happens, you will never leave me again. Can you promise me that?"

He puts his arms around her back and nods. "I promise. As long as you need me around, I will be there."

She smiles. "Thank you."

She closes her eyes and enjoys his company. The future is very uncertain, but as long as they can face it together, she is sure it is a future she can look forward to. For the first time in a long time, she feels like all is right with the world.

CHAPTER 16

A NEW BEGINNING

"DO YOU HAVE ANY IDEA HOW RECKLESS YOU WERE?!

Shaide, Amari, and Vargas are standing in Master Armstrong's office after they returned to the Citadel. Aton and Lucy are there as well. Armstrong looks absolutely livid as he tears Shaide and Vargas a new one at the top of his lungs.

"I CLEARED YOU TO GO TO SORA AND RESEARCH THE ILLNESS! I DID NOT TELL YOU TO GO ON A BLOODY FORMER HUNT!"

Shaide and Vargas cast their eyes to the ground in shame as Amari stares at Armstrong, shocked at his reaction.

 A.S.GUINN

ETERNAL KNIGHTS OF EDEN I

"YOU TOOK MY FRIGATE, TOOK IT DOWN TO MT. KASAI, TAKING THE GENERAL'S DAUGHTER WITH YOU, NO LESS, AND PROCEEDED TO AWAKEN A GODDAMN ANGEL AND BLOW THE LID OFF OF THE MOUNTAIN!"

"Master Armstrong, sir," Amari says indignantly, "I made him take me along with him. He tried to talk me out of—"

"YOU SINGLE-HANDEDLY CHASED DOWN A FORMER, KILLED HIM, AND SAVED AN ENTIRE NATION. DO YOU KNOW WHAT?"

Shaide and Vargas look up in confusion as Armstrong's tone softens.

"What you did was exactly what the Ceraph Order stands for." Armstrong lowers his head and continues. "Do not misunderstand. What you did was incredibly stupid and absolutely beyond reckless, but your actions saved countless lives. You saw a threat, recognized the urgency, and took action. I should be putting you under house arrest and never letting you leave again, but I can't bring myself to punish you."

Shaide relaxes, letting out the breath he has been subconsciously holding.

Armstrong leans forward. "Do not misunderstand, though. If you ever do something that reckless again, there will be consequences. Do you understand?"

Shaide nods. "Yes, Master Armstrong."

Armstrong turns to face Amari, who seems uncomfortable and very nervous. He looks her up and down for a moment, assessing her.

"So, this is Amari Tamiel. I received a very unhappy transmission from your father a few hours ago, you know. He basically threatened to level the Citadel if anything happens to you, and he also promises to make sure Shaide suffers greatly before he lets him die."

"That sounds like my father," Amari says with a sigh.

Armstrong stands up and walks around the desk. "So, you're the young lady who broke the seal on Theta's altar and somehow convinced the bad-tempered phoenix to partner with you?"

"Technically," Amari replies nervously, "our target threw me into the altar and broke the seal, sir."

Armstrong chuckles. "So he did. Nevertheless, you were the one who awakened him. That makes you a very special young woman. Did you know a similar occurrence brought Shaide here into our order?"

"Yes, sir. He explained how he joined when he found Rho completely by accident."

Armstrong nods "When an angel chooses a partner, it is tantamount to Eden himself choosing you to be his servant. In nearly every situation where someone outside of the order has awoken an angel, they are offered a chance to join our order and devote their lives to Eden's service and to protecting the people of Eden."

Amari keeps her eyes locked forward, waiting.

Armstrong looks at Aton "From the report given by Vargas here, and Shipmaster Corolas, what is your assessment of our young Elmeri friend, Aton?"

"Well, Orville, she seems to be very talented, strong in both spiritual and martial skills, and she is clearly full of courage and loyalty. I think she would be a great addition to our order."

"I agree. Ms. Tamiel, you are welcome to remain here at the citadel with us. If you choose to remain, you will stay with a sworn Ceraph, who will be responsible for your safety as they supervise and train you, preparing you for a future with our order."

"I would like that, Master Armstrong," Amari replies without hesitation.

Armstrong nods and smiles. "I suspected you would. Speaking of sworn Ceraphs, Shaide?"

Shaide looks nervously at Armstrong, worried about another butt-chewing.

Armstrong continues. "I feel like it would be a bad idea to separate the two of you. You work well together and clearly have an unshakable bond of trust and loyalty. Keep her close and ensure she is safe and well taken care of as we prepare both of you for your future with us. Understood?"

Shaide nods. "Yes, sir. I had already planned to look after her."

"Very well. Ms. Tamiel, I would like you to return to Shaide's home with him while Mr. and Ms. Norvus and Mr. Amaranthine and I discuss some important business. I will have Mr. Norvus arrange an apartment for you later this evening."

"Thank you, sir."

"You may go. We will discuss your futures in more detail later."

Shaide and Amari bow and walk out of Armstrong's office, looking extremely relieved that things turned out as well as they did.

Armstrong gives them time to get out of earshot and then asks Aton, "So, based on everything we were told, what do you think about the 'Former' they dealt with on Mt. Kasai?"

Vargas looks at Aton with interest, wondering about the answer will be as well.

Aton glances at Lucy, who nods as if she agrees with whatever he is thinking. "Well, I'm not so sure what they dealt with was a Former, Orville. Formers are typically strong but dumb. They aren't capable of complex strategic plans like this one. They certainly aren't able to go toe to toe with a Ceraph alone, even a young one. And then there was the Daemon he summoned. Shaide did not seem to realize the significance of it, but a Daemon has not been seen in over twenty-eight hundred years. Not since the last Fallen was hunted down and eliminated."

Armstrong nods. "Yes, that's exactly what I was thinking myself. A mere Former could not summon a Daemon. Only a Fallen empowered by Belial could summon such a creature."

Aton and Lucy exchange alarmed looks.

Vargas raises a hand. "Excuse me, Master? What does this mean, exactly? I don't understand."

Armstrong sits back in his chair and sighs, rubbing his temples. "We have suspected for years that Belial may not have perished in that final battle but rather simply went into hiding, biding his time while he recovered his strength and came up with a plan. The ever-increasing flow of corrupted and formers coming from the region in recent years, combined with the occurrence of several unexplainable catastrophic events, has all been pointing to one thing."

Aton lowers his head and nods. "The enemy is on the move again."

Armstrong closes his eyes. "The return of the Fallen is an omen, a sign that something powerful is brewing deep within the ruins of Temenos. Whether our old enemy is awakening once again or whether the millennia of corruption poisoning the land has given birth to some new enemy, something is happening down there."

"What does this mean for us?" Aton asks nervously.

"I will speak to Eden and find out what she thinks of our recent developments. I have not sought her guidance as much as I should recently because her lack of action has been bothering me. Perhaps it is time I sought her counsel once again."

Aton nods, and Lucy asks, "What would you like of us in the meantime?"

Armstrong considers the question for a moment. "Those two youngsters may be the key to our future. Never have I seen anyone to whom this comes so naturally, and young Amari shows great promise as well."

"If I may ask, Orville," says Aton, "why did you insist that those two stay together? It seems to me that both of their training would go more smoothly if they were to be separated, free of distraction."

     A.S.GUINN

Armstrong smiles. "There are patterns that have occurred throughout the history of our order. One of those patterns involves Theta."

"I don't understand, sir," says Lucy.

Armstrong explains "Throughout history, in the rare instances that Theta has chosen a partner, that person has always been close to the partner of Rho. Whether the order's master put them together or they simply found their way on their own, they've always been two sides of the same coin. When the two are together, they accomplish very great feats unimaginable to those who did not witness them with their own eyes. I do not feel like separating them would be the right option when history shows they should be together."

Aton nods in understanding, but a look of concern shadows his features as he says, "I just hope that we don't put more on their shoulders than they can handle. Juvia put a great deal of trust in me to take care of her son, and her soul would never let me rest if he dies before me."

Armstrong chuckles quietly to himself. "Honestly? I do not believe her spirit would ever let me rest either if anything happened to him if there was anything I could have done to prevent it."

Aton repeats his previous question: "So, what should we do?"

Armstrong looks back up at him. "Make sure they are ready. I sense a great change coming on the horizon, and for better or worse, we are going to need their help if we expect to survive it. The time will soon be at hand when the future of Eden will be decided. Let us make sure we are ready for that day."

*   *   *

Shaide walks Amari across the grounds of the Citadel, towards the residential district, where he resides with his godfather. The two walk in silence for a few moments as Amari takes in her surroundings.

Shaide finally speaks up. "How are you feeling?"

Amari looks at him. "I feel nervous, but I think I am mostly excited. Sitting at home, doing nothing but training and studying, I always felt like I was just wasting my time. I shouldn't be sitting around worrying about petty things when I could see the peace under which I had been living was a lie. Now that I'm in a place where I can do something, and make a difference, I just feel excited."

Shaide nods and chuckles. "Don't get too excited. The Ceraphs are probably not the romanticized perfect priests of order you read about in your history books. In fact, they can kind of be a rough bunch. A lot of them are heavy drinkers, and well…they kind of behave like Amber, if you get my drift."

                              A.S.GUINN

ETERNAL KNIGHTS OF EDEN I

Amari looks at him with concern "You mean the Ceraphs are a bunch of alcoholic perverts?"

Shaide smiles as he looks at the ground. "A lot of them are. But they are also the toughest, most loyal family and friends you can ever hope for. Their eccentric behavior is just a way to cope with the horrible things they see in the course of their work."

Amari nods slowly. "I guess I can see that. They must have seen a lot of people die. I always wondered how they dealt with the memories of people they couldn't save."

"Indeed. The support crews that are here are an amusing bunch as well. For an order devoted entirely to the service of Eden, they are certainly an interesting group of people."

As they continue on their way, Amari stares in awe at her surroundings. The chapel and the air tower stretch majestically behind them. The high walls in the distance marking the perimeter of the fortress are an impressive sight in the setting sun, and she cannot help but watch as the last slivers of orange drop below them.

She looks at Shaide, impressed by how comfortable and at home he seems. She always felt in the back of her mind that he belonged in Sora with her, but now she sees that this is where he really belongs. She just hopes that she belongs here with him.

They drift into the residential district, and Shaide leads them up to his door, unlocking it and standing back to let her in. "My house is your house. At least until they get your apartment set up."

Amari frowns. "Couldn't I just stay here with you?"

Shaide thinks for a moment, but then he sighs and shakes his head. "There isn't any space. The beds are all singles, and there are only three. You'd have to sleep with one of us, and it would be kind of cramped. I don't think you'd be comfortable here."

"I've just never REALLY stayed alone before," Amari says with a sigh. "I mean, I've been on my own for a few days on trips before, but I've always had someone around, like Yania, or my mom or dad, or even my sister sometimes."

Shaide ruffles her hair a little. "It'll be okay, Amari. You're always welcome to visit. I'll try and visit as much as possible too. Besides, we'll likely be out on missions most of the time, so I'll be around. And you'll make new friends here too. They won't judge you for looking different. Everyone here is a little different, after all."

Amari smiles and nods "I know. Thanks, Shaide."

"Tomorrow is the weekend. Maybe I can take you into Corallina to meet my friends from the academy. Reno is a great guy, even if he is a little lazy. And Rayn is great too. A good leader. He'll go far in the army. Lania is real smart, although she's kind of shy and self-conscious, and Celeste is quiet, but she may be almost as good a martial artist as you."

Amari giggles. Shaide is getting excited at the prospect of introducing her to his friends, and he reminds her much more of the little boy she made friends with when he acts like this. "I think I would like that. You'll have to show me around the city too. I've never seen Corallina before. I've never even been in Alastair."

Shaide gives her a look like she's said something incredibly obvious. "Well, of course I'll show you around. The faster I can get you settled in, the happier you'll be. At least, I hope, anyway."

Amari sits down on the couch as Shaide goes into the kitchen. She peruses the bookshelf, and when he returns with some water for both of them, she asks him, "Hey, what's that book you've been reading? I never asked you about it."

He reaches into his bag and pulls it out. "Oh, *The Immortal Triad*? I'm actually finished with it now. Why?"

"Can I read it?" Amari asks, looking embarrassed for some reason. "You seemed really into it, so it must be good."

Shaide nods and hands it to her gingerly. "Just please take care of it. It apparently belonged to my mother."

Amari takes it and sets it on her lap. "You always mention your mother, but you never really talk about your father. Why not?"

Shaide frowns. "Well, truthfully? I never really knew much about him even when he was alive. He was so mysterious. He was some kind of special forces soldier with the army, but he and Mom never spoke about his work. He was strong, and fun while he was around, but I don't think I ever really knew him. All I really knew was that he was descended from one of the daughters of the Emperor of Temenos when the nation fell, the only member of the royal family to survive the war. He and my mother never actually were married for some reason, but they remained together as if they were."

Amari raises her eyebrows. "Wow. I never knew that."

"We never really spoke of it. I actually have relatives on his side of the family somewhere, but there was some kind of rift in his family, and I've never met them."

Amari isn't really sure how to respond to that, and after a few minutes, Shaide nods off into a nap, so she begins reading his book about the three friends who save the world.

After about an hour, Aton and Lucy come in the door, and Shaide jerks awake.

"Hey, you two," says Aton. "We've got an apartment set up for you, Ms. Tamiel."

Amari stands up as Shaide tries to wake up real fast. "Thank you, I guess."

"I think she's nervous about living alone," Lucy says with a smile.

Aton kicks Shaide's foot to get him awake faster. "Come on, we'll show you where you'll be staying."

Shaide climbs to his feet and follows Amari, who, in turn, halfheartedly follows Aton.

Her apartment winds up being only a few hundred feet up the street, on the first floor. Aton leads them to her front door and unlocks the apartment for her.

"Welcome to your new home." He hands her the key.

They walk inside to find the apartment is actually fairly nice. Like the house, there is a full kitchen and living room and a pair of bedrooms that share a common master bathroom. The military-inspired design utilizes the limited space to create a very efficient but comfortable layout.

Amari sees the second bedroom and asks, "Who is going to use the other bedroom?"

Lucy looks like she is trying to suppress a grin. "I suggested that we move Aton into here with you so I could have the house alone with Shaide, but…"

Aton lowers his head and rolls his eyes. "No, you didn't, Lucy. Don't pick on the poor girl like that."

"Okay, I didn't," Lucy says with a sigh, "but it sounded funny. I'll be staying with you. I will help mentor you on adjusting to life with the Ceraphs, and I will keep you company and make sure you have everything you need. In truth, I won't likely be here at the same time as you very often, so we won't really be in each other's hair much."

"And you are welcome to come visit at the house anytime you feel like," adds Aton. "I know Shaide certainly won't mind."

Shaide nods. "Lucy may be a borderline alcoholic pervert, but she's good. Don't worry about her. Just…don't let her teach you any bad habits."

"You mean I can't start a competition to see who gets a piece of you first?" says Lucy, pretending to pout.

Amari looks at her with alarm on her face, and Aton shakes his head. "Come on, Lucy. That's just cruel. Don't pick on the girl like that."

Amari mumbles under her breath, but loudly enough for everyone to hear, "I bet I would win, old lady…"

Shaide looks at Amari with shock on his face as Aton gives her an amused look. Amari smiles even as she turns pink from embarrassment.

Lucy, meanwhile, whistles low, with an amused expression to match her brother's. "Old lady? I think I'm actually starting to like you, girlie. You've got some spunk. I think we'll get along just fine. So, what's the bet?"

Shaide recovers from his shock and yells, "Whoa, whoa, WHOA! NO ONE is getting a piece of me. Especially not THAT way. What the hell, Amari?"

Amari's face is burning red with embarrassment. "I learned with Amber that it's kind of fun to play this game. I have to protect you from all of these older women, you know."

"Older women?" Lucy chuckles. "You know I'm only about twenty to thirty years older than you, right? That's like…a few days for long-lifers like us."

Amari buries her face in her hands. "Oh no… What have I started…?"

After an amusing hour of moving all of Lucy's things to the apartment and taking Amari to the supply exchange to get her some basic necessities, Amari and Lucy are set up in their new apartment. Despite their bickering, they seem to get along well, although Shaide is still not sure this is a good idea.

Lucy goes to her room to celebrate having her own place finally, so Shaide and Amari take the opportunity to visit at the front door before he goes home to catch some sleep himself.

She leans against him and puts her head on his shoulder. "I've gotten so used to having you around. I don't know if I'll be able to sleep now."

"It'll be okay, Amari," he says, patting her head. "You'll get used to it in time. I'll take you to Corallina tomorrow and show you around. We'll also get you some better living stuff than the supplies from the exchange."

The two separate, and Shaide walks back to his home, lost in a train of thought.

Something is happening that he doesn't fully understand. That former they encountered in Mt. Kasai wasn't normal. Shaide has fought and even killed Formers before, but none of them were like this. No, this one seemed like he had a plan. And that Daemon he summoned reminds Shaide a great deal of their angels...

Then there was that curse. That wasn't something a mindless rogue crazy would come up with. There was also what he said about his "master." Something is wrong...

Shaide feels like there is something dark in the background, something that plots against them as they remain oblivious to its presence. Something is happening, and he intends to find out what.

Despite all the bad, however, there is some good happening too. He found his old friend Amari again, and he even gets to spend his days working with her. He still feels a sense of grief at allowing her to put herself in danger, but at the same time, he remembers the promise they made. To save the world together.

That's a promise he can get behind.

It seems like the last month has been an eternity. While it may seem like they foiled a horrible plot to end the Erita nation, and saved millions of lives, he knows that their fight is far from over.

No. Their fight is just getting started.

EPILOGUE

THE OTHER SIDE

Several thousand miles south of the Citadel, deep in the Deadlands of Temenos, a lone man sits on a cliff overlooking a dark valley. This man has deep scars on his face and long, slicked-back white hair. He wears black armor made of dragon scale. Despite his deep scars, however, he appears to be younger than middle-age, as if he had simply seen far too much in his life.

"Master Borealis, sir, our scout has reported back from Erita."

The man slowly climbs to his feet and turns to face the messenger, who nervously awaits permission to speak, and looks at him in silence for a moment.

"Speak, messenger."

The messenger stutters slightly as he reports to his master. "S-sir, the scout has confirmed that Justice is on the brink of death and the experiment has been ruined."

Master Borealis surveys the man in silence as he contemplates this information. He finally says, "I was afraid this was the case. I've already heard word of the curse failing. Who is responsible?"

The messenger answers nervously, "Two young Ceraphs, master. A young Elmeri named Tamiel and a young Mitera named Darkmoon."

A grimace of disgust crosses Master Borealis's face as he turns his gaze to the valley once again. "The *Ceraphs*. Those insufferable servants of the heretic Eden. If not for their existence, none would be able to stand against us as we complete our lord's work."

His hands radiate an intense energy as he balls them into fists. The messenger nervously takes a few steps back, worried he may suffer injury from the master's rage.

After a moment, however, Master Borealis relaxes, and the energy subsides. He folds his hands behind his back as he surveys the valley. "While they are a thorn in our sides, in the end, they will make little difference. For three thousand years, I have slowly moved forward, rebuilding and spreading the progeny of our lord. No matter how long it takes, we will be the ones to emerge victorious in the end, and the Ceraphs and their *lord*"—the word drips from his mouth with distaste and sarcasm—"will be powerless to stop us."

Another man standing nearby turns and asks in a cackling voice "Well, Father, what are my orders?"

Master Borealis turns to face the man. "You did exceptionally well in Broadspring, Lucien. Alastair has still been unable to retake the town. I think is is time for you to go to Pandora and begin laying the groundwork for the next phase of the plan."

Lucien smiles broadly "The Lord's will be done, father"

Lucien and the messenger walk away, and Borealis looks down into the valley once more, surveying the product of his current great experiment.

In the box valley, sealed by a magical barrier, a massive variety of creatures are milling around, seemingly normal on the outside.

What makes these beasts special is the potent miasma flooding the valley. It fills the air with such density that it creates a visible black haze, giving the valley a dreamlike appearance.

Hundreds of thousands of dangerous beasts inhabit the valley below, slowly succumbing to the corruption, mutating, as their DNA and instincts are broken down and remolded into tools of the corruption.

There are also multiple prison camps in the valley, where humans, Elmeri, and even some Nekomata are forced to live and work in the dense fog. They are slowly losing their free will as the corruption changes them forever.

Borealis approvingly observes the fruits of his great experiment. They may not yet be able to instill the corruption when and where they choose, but they are not short of subjects to convert the old-fashioned way. While he seeks to accelerate their plans, they can make do with this for now.

He turns and walks towards the small city behind him. In its ruins, he has made his home and base, from which he carries out his plans to complete the work of the lord he serves. Thousands upon thousands of Former and Fallen agents populate this city, living and working as they follow their master's will.

His eyes drift to the sky above, where a massive fleet of black warships float in the sky. Unlike the elegant warships of Erita or the industrious warships of Alastair, these are constructed of metals of the deepest black, with elegant yet intimidating designs using sharp angles and spines to make them more intimidating.

Belial walks up the street to his mansion and retires inside. It may be many years yet before his army is ready to take Eden, but the day will come, and the corruption will roll over the world the way Belial always intended.

This fight is just getting started.

*　　　*　　　*

Continue the adventure in Volume II: Angels Fall

ETERNAL KNIGHTS OF EDEN I

A.S.GUINN

A.S.GUINN

ETERNAL KNIGHTS OF EDEN I

A.S.GUINN

A.S.GUINN